Completely Off The Mark

Will Stebbings

3P
PUBLISHING

First published in 2020 in the UK

3P Publishing
C E C, London Road
Corby
NN17 5EU

A catalogue number for this book is available from the British
Library

ISBN 978-1-911559-99-3

Cover design: Marie-Louise O'Neill

I would like to take this opportunity to once again thank Janet Veasey for proofreading my work and preventing me from printing numerous gaffes.

I must also thank my wife for patiently reading each chapter as it is written and acting as a valuable foil for my muse.

To Darren and Sharon,
Thank you for your support,
Will
W.S. Stebbing
4/7/20

Prologue

(2016)

For the very last time, Mark Barker placed his old briefcase by the hall table where he lay down his car keys and let out a sigh.

'Is that you, Mark?' his wife called from the kitchen.

'Nah,' he replied in an exaggerated Norfolk accent. 'Tha's the milkman. I jus' called round for the usual.'

'Well, you'll have to be quick,' Helen said as she approached from the kitchen, drying her hands on a towel. 'My husband could be home soon ... oh, Mark! It's you!' She feigned surprise.

'Aah!' he said. 'Caught you! I thought as much. So it is the milkman!'

'Oh, well. You're at work all day. You know what it's like when you spend so much time on your own. At sixty-three, you have to find your pleasure when you can.

'Who lives at number sixty-three?' Mark demanded in mock anger.

'The milkman, of course.'

'Huh! I wouldn't mind,' he added, 'but we haven't had our milk delivered for years.'

'He's still good for a special offer,' she replied.

This was very similar to a conversation that had taken place a couple of years earlier and it pleased Mark that the two of them could still enjoy a bit of harmless fun. It was Mark's sense of humour which was one of the things that had helped Helen decide on marrying him all those years ago.

'Anyway, why are you home so early?' she asked.

'My manager had a meeting coming up and he needed to conduct the termination process with me first. That includes taking back my security pass which I needed to get off site, so he had to let me out early. I was pleased about that. I didn't have any work to do and I was just twiddling my thumbs ... as I've been doing for over a week now. I was just glad to get away.'

'*Termination process* sounds a bit sinister,' Helen said.

'So is an *exit interview* like the one I had yesterday with a young girl from HR,' Mark responded. 'She had a list of questions that she had to ask. One was "*Why am I leaving?*"

"Er ... I'm sixty-seven years old" I replied.

"*Have you been the victim of bullying?*" was another question she asked. I felt like making something up just to see her re-action. "*Have you ever been sexually harassed in the workplace?*" she asked. Just for fun, I hesitated to answer, I wondered what would happen if I'd said "yes."

"Do you know, I think there are more people working in HR than in the rest of the company put together. We never needed HR in the sixties or seventies ... even the eighties ... so why do we need them now? But it's not just our company; it's everywhere you go. The world has gone mad."

Mark had reached the retiring age of sixty-five when he was right in the middle of a big project and his manager had asked him to stay on. Now he was regretting it. The project had been beset with problems outside of his control and had been shelved twice. This was another sign to Mark that modern business was not fit for purpose. There had been far too many people involved; too many useless meetings and too many managers looking after their own interests. The first time the project was shelved, it had been claimed that they had gone over budget, but then the people working on it just sat around doing nothing for several months while funds were found from other budgets. They were still being paid, so why weren't they allowed to continue instead of wasting time and money?

Mark was glad to be out of it. It was all so different when he first started work in the sixties. He couldn't recall ever attending a meeting in those days, except for one to start up the Works football team.

He had been doing a lot of reminiscing lately. And when he thought of those early jobs and the people with whom he worked, he inevitably remembered the young ladies and the effect they had on him. The very first of these was Karen who rejected his advances with disdain. This was his very first experience of a broken heart – a condition that returned several times over the next few years. In fact, it seemed to Mark that in those early years after leaving school, he moved from one failed romance to another in very quick succession. He did eventually manage to lose his virginity, but he was soon on the shelf again.

He had a quick count back and decided that between 1965 and 1971, he fell in love no fewer than six times. Some of these affairs were more successful than others, but all ended in disappointment. And he never seemed to learn from his mistakes. But things had worked out well for him and he had now been happily married for over forty years.

'I thought we might go out for a meal to celebrate my retirement,' he said. 'I fancy an Indian – a chicken Tarka sounds nice.'

'I've never heard of that,' Helen replied.

'Well, it's a bit like chicken tikka ... but it's a little otter.'

2

Chapter One
(Autumn 1971)
I Just Don't Know What to Do With Myself

Mark Barker was feeling fed up.

'I'm fed up,' he said to Mary, his young colleague.

'I'm fed up as well,' she replied.

'I bet I'm more fed up than you,' Mark said.

'No, I don't think so,' she said. 'How fed up are you?'

'Very fed up!'

'Well, I'm very fed up with bells on!' she claimed.

'What have you got to be fed up about?' asked Mark.

'This boring job, for a start,' she replied. 'All I do is punch stuff into that damned silly machine ... and drink this terrible coffee.' She added the last statement as that was what she was doing at that precise moment while sitting at the desk opposite instead of in the adjoining punch room. Drinks were not permitted in the punch room.

Mary's job title was Punch Girl. In 1971, you would be hard pressed to find a Punch Boy, just as there were very few female computer programmers like Mark, although there had been one young girl on his programming course the previous year.

There were two other members of the Computer Room team. James McDougall was the manager, who also did some programming and then there was Sally, who operated the computer. Sally and Mary covered for each other occasionally, but Sally was about to move on to a new position. She had become fed up as well. At that moment, she was being lectured to by James inside the computer room itself. This room was enclosed by two glass partitions, a brick wall and another outside wall with a large picture window, which, for reasons of confidentially, had its vertical blinds permanently drawn. Entry to the room was by a solid wooden door set into one of the glass partitions and it had to be kept closed at all times to maintain the environment in which the NCR500 was located. With the printer and its carriage control constantly shuddering backwards and forwards, it was a very noisy area. The central processor, with all its flashing lights, gave off a lot of heat, so the room had to be air-conditioned and was, therefore, a popular place for the small team during the warm months of summer.

But now, it was autumn and Sally was not really paying attention to what James was telling her. He was in the throes of launching the final application for the machine. This was the Nominal Ledger and he was passing on the operating instructions, but as Sally would be leaving soon, she couldn't see the point. James had kept this last program to himself and as Mark had finished writing all his applications, he was now just there for program maintenance – hence the reason he was fed up, because this meant he had nothing to do unless something went wrong with one of the programs, which it seldom did.

And that was how he replied when Mary asked him why he was also fed up.

'I thought becoming a computer programmer meant I'd made my mark in the world. You know ... a bit like becoming a scientist. At first, I felt proud when I told people that's what I did. Not everyone can be a programmer. I had to pass an aptitude test.'

'I know,' said Mary. 'You got maximum marks – better than old Grumpy Drawers in there. He only scored nine out of eleven.'

'Exactly! I bet none of our directors or senior managers could pass the test ... and here I am twiddling my thumbs; doing nothing more than waiting for something to go wrong, so that I can fix it ... except that old Grumpy Drawers would probably interfere, because that's what he does. At least you've still got some regular punching to do. What am I supposed to do with my time?'

This wasn't the only reason for Mark's grumpiness. Only a year earlier, he was on top of the world; having started a new prestigious job, with a lovely new girlfriend and driving the car he'd always wanted.

'What's happening about your car?' Mary asked.

Mark sighed. 'Nothing at the moment. I don't know what to do about it. I daren't drive it. I am allowed to drive it to an MOT station for a re-test, but there seems no point. It needs so much work. It would cost almost as much as a brand new car – and I can't afford to get it done. It's in such a bad condition that no one will take it in part-exchange. I think it's destined for the scrap man, but I still owe money on it, so strictly speaking, it belongs to the finance company.

When Mark had bought his Wolseley 1500, some people warned him that this model was prone to rust, but he was adamant that this was the car he wanted. Nothing prepared him for how quickly it started to disintegrate. At first, some small bubbles appeared in his front wings and then they developed into holes. He duly patched them up with filler, but soon after, the filler started falling out as the rust took hold. Then the rot spread to the inside of the wings. He could see the front wheels from inside the engine compartment. He knew that wasn't right, but it all seemed like unsightly cosmetic damage to Mark's untrained eye.

4

However, when he took the vehicle for its annual MOT, he was told that the chassis and door sills were in a very dangerous condition.

A cousin told him about a self-employed welder, who operated out of a council estate garage. The welder charged Mark five pounds to do some work, but when he returned the car for a re-test, the MOT operator told him it was still not sufficient. 'Look at this cross-member,' he had said while poking it with a screwdriver and making it even worse. He then handed Mark another failure docket.

Now, just like the old days before he passed his driving test, he was back to scrounging lifts from colleagues and feeling fed up.

'Why don't you tell me one of your jokes?' Mary asked.

'Nah ... I don't feel like telling jokes. You'll only laugh at me.'

'I don't usually,' she replied with one of her wicked grins. 'Go on tell us one before Grumpy Drawers comes out.'

'Which one do you want to hear?' Mark asked.

'I don't know ... preferably one I haven't heard before.'

Mark pondered for a while, and then said 'Donald Duck went for a haircut. He asked the hairdresser for a condom. The barber asked if he should put it on his bill.'

Mary laughed and said, 'That's rude!'

Mark liked Mary, but not in a loving way. For one thing, she was very slightly built. Mark preferred a fuller figure. And for another thing, she had a boyfriend. Boy, did she have a boyfriend. She was forever singing his praises ... to the point where it could easily grate on one's nerves. Her Donald was wonderful and the best boyfriend a girl could have. One day, when she'd been droning on about her wonderful Donald, Mark said 'I bet your Donald's farts don't smell!'

'Do you know,' she replied, 'I don't believe he does fart.'

It was too much for Mark. 'Does he even shit?'

'Well, I've never seen him,' she replied in all seriousness. Mary was a good sport and didn't mind a little rough language, as long as it wasn't too crude.

Sally also had a boyfriend, so when the two girls got together, all they seemed to talk about was their boyfriends. And that was another reason why Mark was fed up. Because, at that period in his life, he didn't have a girlfriend. He had recently split up with Melody and he missed her. It wasn't that he was heartbroken about their break-up, but he had become used to having a regular girlfriend. He'd been dating her for about a year, which was the longest he'd ever dated anyone. He hadn't always enjoyed the best of luck with girls, but Melody had been near to being perfect – except that he didn't love her - and she didn't love him. There was always a strong mutual attraction between them, but never true love. Perhaps it was that he still harboured feelings for Jenny – the lady who had taken his virginity a few years earlier, only to leave him heartbroken some months later when she resurrected an old affair with a married man. Mark had always felt more comfortable in Jenny's company than with anyone else, and, in truth, his conversations with Melody were often hard work.

Nevertheless, it was a very convenient relationship for both of them. She had been renting a small country cottage and Mark had been able to enjoy the occasional overnight stay with all the benefits, but now she was gone. Her mother had been taken ill and so Melody had terminated her rental agreement and returned to live with her parents near Towcester so that she could help nurse her mother and keep house for her father. Mark had said 'Towcester? I could pop up there sometime,' but Melody wasn't in the mood for levity at that time and she didn't always follow Mark's little jokes – another area where Jenny excelled.

He'd already had one long distance affair with Sandy from Peterborough and that hadn't worked out too well. Towcester was the other side of Northampton and that was even further away than Peterborough. She didn't try too hard to persuade him, but now, there were times when he wouldn't mind 'popping up' one weekend, but with his transport problems, he had to forget that idea.

So he was, once again, celibate ... and totally fed up. For the time being, he didn't know what to do about it.

That evening, he couldn't find anything worth watching on television. Most other families could now watch any one of three channels since the introduction of BBC2, provided you had a television set with 625 lines and a UHF aerial, but the Barker household still had an old set and just the two black and white channels. Usually when this situation occurred, Mark would take himself off into the front room to play some records, but he felt in need of company, so he decided upon a walk to the Bricklayer's Arms just under a mile away. It was the pub that he and his old friend Dougie Davies used to frequent before Dougie married and became a responsible parent, so he wasn't expecting to find his friend there, but it was worth a try. Perhaps, more importantly, Dougie's father Tim might be there. Tim was a motor mechanic and it was he who told him about the Wolseley 1500 when Mark was looking for one.

Tim was there, but he was busy playing dominoes with some of the regulars, so Mark bided his time and ordered a half-pint from the Landlord's wife. 'Is Mike not here, tonight?' he asked of her.

'No, he's gone to a licence victuallers meeting,' she replied. 'That means he'll come home after midnight, half-cut and smelling of cigars. It's a good job we're not too busy.'

Mike used to work at Gresham's, where Mark and Dougie were employed, but he left to indulge his long-held ambition to own a pub. Mark was disappointed to miss Mike as he was always good for some cheerful banter.

Just as Mark's glass was getting embarrassingly low, Tim came up to the bar to replenish his own. 'Can I get you a drink, Tim?' Mark asked.

'No, you're all right. I'm getting a round in for this lot,' Tim replied pointing to his fellow players. 'Let me get you one.'

'No, it's all right, thanks. I shall be off in a moment. You know that car I bought a couple of years ago? It's rusting away.'

'I did warn you. That's a common fault with them.'

'Well, it's failed its MOT. The sills and the chassis need a lot of repair work – and the wings are hanging off both sides. Have you got any suggestions?'

'Yeah. Get rid of it. If it's that bad, it will carry on getting worse even if you can repair it. Do you want me to have a look at it?'

'Is there anything you could do?' Mark asked.

'Not if it needs a lot of welding work. That's a job for a specialist.'

'In that case, I won't waste your time,' Mark responded. 'Do you know anyone who would take it in part-exchange?'

'Not off-hand,' replied Tim, 'but if a dealer wants to sell you a car badly enough, someone will take in. Don't expect very much, though. What are the mechanics like?'

'Still very good ... and that's the annoying thing. It's got a lovely engine. I always get thirty-five to the gallon – and it will cruise all day without complaint.'

'That might help if it's good for spares,' Tim said. 'I'd better get these drinks back to my pals. Let me know if there's anything I can do.'

Mark finished his last mouthful of beer and trudged off home. He'd always had a propensity for self-pity, but he thought, by now, he had grown out of it, but 'everything in his favour was against him.' That was an old expression that a former colleague had taught him during earlier periods of self-pity. The darkness closed in on him as he kicked his way through the autumn leaves in his path.

His mood didn't lighten when he entered his home to find his father in front of the television with his feet in a bowl of soapy water. It brought back a memory of the one time when he had brought Melody to his home. On that one occasion, she had offered to do the driving so that

Mark could for once enjoy a drink without worrying about being breathalysed. Up until the point when they entered Mark's house, it had been one of the most enjoyable evenings of their relationship. His brother had always said he would never bring friends or girls back to their house because he was ashamed of it. Mark didn't wholly agree with that. Of course, it wasn't a palace but it was part of who he was even if he had always determined to do better when he got married and bought a place of his own, but seeing his father with his feet in a bowl did thoroughly embarrass him.

There was no hot running water in their house so personal hygiene was achieved by having a strip wash in the kitchen and feet were bathed in a bowl of water, and usually carried out with discretion, but sometimes, when Frank Barker had been working on his feet all day, he liked to soak them..

The evening in question had started out with Melody picking up Mark from the top of his road in her little Wolseley Hornet. It was mid-summer and would be some hours before the sun went down. He suggested a drive out to Great Massingham - one of Mark's favourite villages. They started with a leisurely stroll around the two large village ponds, watching the water birds. Mark wanted to show off his wild-life knowledge and identified the mallards, coots and moorhens. 'What's that one? Melody asked.

'That's a goose,' he replied.

'I know that – but what sort of goose?'

Mark's knowledge of birds was mostly gained from collecting the picture cards that came with packets of Brooke Bond Tea, and he couldn't recall any geese, so he was stumped. 'Er... a wild goose.'

'Oh,' said Melody with a huge dollop of sarcasm. 'I would never have known that without your help.'

He then wanted to take a photograph with his girlfriend standing in front of the largest pond with the church tower just behind her to give a sense of scale and perspective. When he got the slides back a couple of weeks later, he was dismayed to find that the tower was growing out of her head. He hadn't allowed for the fact that his viewfinder didn't accurately represent what was on film.

Following the walk and the photo-shoot, they found the fish and chip shop and availed themselves of the owner's wares. They ate them sitting in her little mini. After that, they needed a drink, so went to the village pub named *The Rose and Crown* for an enjoyable drink to round off a perfect evening. This was why a chap like Mark wanted to go out with a girl like Melody.

When she dropped him off at his house, he felt he had to offer her a coffee – and that was when they entered to find Frank Barker soaking his feet, smoking a woodbine and drinking a bottle of brown ale.

And now that memory made him feel fed up all over again.

Chapter Two

What'cha Gonna Do About It
("Wotcha")

It was a dank dewy Sunday morning as Mark set off on his bike to *The Cock Inn* to meet up with the rest of his football team. The team always met there for an away game, which that week was against the *Bull Inn* in Gledhill. The team manager divided the players into four separate cars and Mark found himself directed towards Kenny Stacey, of whom he knew little except that he was a half back who liked to venture into the opposition's half to score whenever he could and he always dressed smartly even to go to a football match.

Normally, Mark would have travelled with Dougie, but Dougie often missed a Sunday League game due to home and family commitments. Mark, being a goalkeeper would never get away with that. His team would find a replacement and he would struggle to regain his place. It meant that he had to play every week regardless of illness or injury. His teammates nicknamed him 'Mr Reliable' because of this. It had been Dougie who had recommended that the two friends switched to playing for *The Cock Inn*, stating that he always liked *The Old Cock Inn* and then went 'Phworr!' to make sure everyone understood his double meaning.

Being the taller of the three players who had been directed to Kenny's car, Mark sat in the front and, once they got moving, remarked how quiet and comfortable the vehicle was. 'What is it?' he asked, realising that he had just sat in it without looking.

'It's a Wolseley Six,' Kenny replied. 'It's an up-market version of the Austin 1800 with the bigger engine.'

'A bit pricey, I should think,' Mark said fishing for some personal information.

'Yeah, but I don't pay for it. It's a demonstration model. I get a different car every few weeks. Do you want to buy it?'

'Out of my price range,' Mark replied, 'although I am looking to replace my old car. Mine's a Wolseley, too. It's a 1500.'

'Come and see me some time. I work at Burton's on London Road.' Burton's was a car dealer.

'I would do,' said Mark, 'but I still owe three months on my HP payments.'

Kenny wasn't going to be put off. 'I'm sure we can do a deal where you can pay off the balance. Who's your finance with?'

'West Norfolk Finance Company.'

'What you do,' said Kenny, with one hand on the steering wheel and the other waving around, 'is get a loan from your bank, which is for a higher amount than what you need for your new vehicle, so that you have enough to pay off what you owe, then come and see me and I'll do you a good deal. It's usually Geraldine who you would see at West Norfolk. Mention my name. She'll probably waive the early settlement fee.'

Mark remembered Geraldine, although he knew her as Miss Tombleson. She was a very stern well-built lady, probably in her early forties, although Mark was no judge of such things. He had to visit her twice when there was a problem with the first two standing orders – and she didn't strike Mark as the sort who would waive anything. 'Are you sure about that? She struck me as quite a ferocious lady.'

'Nah! She's all right if you know how to handle her. When I was trying to negotiate a good deal on behalf of one of my customers, I had to go and sweet-talk her ... actually, I had to give her a good shagging. After that, she was like putty in my hands. To be perfectly honest, she actually shagged me ... the most violent shagging I'd ever received, but I've had no problems with her since then.' The two men in the back seat were laughing. They were familiar with some of Kenny's antics with women.

Mark wondered if Kenny was telling the truth. He couldn't imagine anyone in their right mind tackling Miss Tombleson, but then, he could picture her getting violent. 'I do remember that she had very large hands,' he said.

'Oh, yes,' said Kenny. She is a very powerful lady. She was engaged to one chap ... but she broke it off!' There were more chuckles from the back seat. 'I don't know what it was, but she had some kind of hold on you ... it may have been a full nelson!'

Dave from the back seat said, 'Is that the one that bent over for you ... and you said "What's this?" And she said, "I thought we could open a bottle of beer before we start." They were all laughing now, and Mark was now convinced Kenny was just telling tall stories.

'Seriously though,' Kenny continued, 'you'll get a better interest rate if you use a bank rather than a finance company – and the car will be yours from day one. Come and see what we've got on the forecourt. Do you have any ideas what you want?'

'I quite like the look of the Fiat 124 Sports.'

Kenny sucked in his breath. 'You don't see too many of them – and to be honest, I think you should steer clear of 'em. They have lots of known faults and you can't get the spares ... plus ... they're prone to rust.'

That last remark made up Mark's mind straight away. 'Did you want something sporty, then?'

'No, not really. I just liked the shape – not the standard 124; just the Sports version.'

'Come up and see me sometime,' Kenny said paraphrasing Mae West, just as they neared Gledhill and Mark decided he might do that.

That afternoon, he took his push-bike out to London Road and found the garage, but it was closed. Most of the second-hand cars were in a locked compound to the rear of the showroom and therefore out of sight. Lots of the bigger garages closed on a Sunday, which struck him as strange because that was when most customers would be free to look at cars. He abandoned his search for the time being.

He went home and did some sums. He was currently paying fifteen pounds a month for his rusting vehicle. He figured he could probably afford to increase his repayments to twenty pounds. Therefore, a loan to be repaid over two years could provide him with around four hundred pounds allowing for interest and paying off his outstanding loan. He didn't really want to be as much in debt, but he had little choice. At this rate, he would never be in a position to get married and buy a house, but since he didn't have a girlfriend, that didn't matter at that time. After all, he told himself, he needed a car to get a girlfriend.

He was starting to have more self-confidence in his ability to attract a girl. He now wore spectacles that were a little more fashionable and he no longer believed that wearing glasses was such a big handicap as it used to be. In fact, Melody had told him that she found him to be very handsome and considered he had a kind, intelligent face. Of course, not all girls were looking for a kind, intelligent chap for a boyfriend, but some did – and that was the kind of girl that Mark wanted anyway, especially if she had a pair of shapely legs,

So, he was now feeling a little more optimistic about tackling his lack of transport and his lack of a girlfriend. That just left his boring job to address, but he had an idea.

When he went into work the next day, he asked his manager if he could have a quiet word with him.

'I'm going to be busy for a while,' James replied. 'I'll catch up with you later,' and disappeared out of the office without even asking Mark what it was about.

Mary observed this and said 'You're not thinking of leaving, are you? I couldn't stand to be left here alone with him.'

'We'll see how I can get on when I do speak to him,' Mark replied enigmatically.

It was almost ninety minutes before James re-appeared. He was accompanied by a striking blonde who was wearing high heels. 'This is Mark,' James said waving his hand towards Mark who looked up with some surprise. 'He's written several of our programs.'

'Wotcha,' said the young lady with a broad smile.

Mark didn't reply straight away. He hadn't been told who the young lady was. He looked from her to James and back again a couple of times, waiting for an introduction.

Eventually, it came. 'This is Dolly. She will be joining us next month – as Sally's replacement.

'Ah,' said Mark. 'Hello.' He stood up and held out his hand. Dolly offered hers and Mark held it, but she let him grip it without actually returning a handshake. He was pleased with himself for not saying 'Hello Dolly.' He was sure she would get fed up with that. He quickly let go of her cold hand, feeling his usual measure of embarrassment at meeting a stranger of any gender, especially as he had to steel himself from gazing down to her impressive bosom which was peeking out of her blouse. He could tell immediately that she was going to cause a lot of interest with the other males in the building, but somehow, he didn't find himself attracted to her, even though she seemed very friendly and likely to be good fun. For him, she was wearing too much eye make-up and rouge, which didn't suit her pale complexion. He also thought it was a mistake for her to wear a vivid red jacket and matching skirt for someone of her skin tone.

James moved on to Mary, who had been busy punching data in the adjoining room but had stopped when she had heard voices. 'This is Mary who does the punching and helps operate the machine sometimes.'

'Wotcha,' said Dolly again.

'Wotcha,' replied Mary with her friendly grin. 'Welcome to the madhouse.'

'Oh, thanks,' replied Dolly with a chuckle. 'That sounds re-assuring, I'm sure.'

While they were exchanging pleasantries, Mark had a better look at Dolly from behind. Her high heels brought her up to James' height, but he was a little shorter than Mark. She had an awkward gait typical of someone who was unable to wear high heels with any degree of elegance. He often wondered why girls wore such shoes if they couldn't walk properly in them. Now, Ellie on reception could manage them and never looked uncomfortable, but then Ellie was an elegant lady. Dolly was not. She was aiming for a glamorous appearance, but then speaking with a broad Norfolk accent. It didn't work in Mark's eyes, but he knew that wouldn't deter some of the men in the other offices.

Nevertheless, he told himself to keep an open mind about her. He remembered his first encounter with Karen and how he had taken an instant dislike to her only to fall for her once he got to know her better.

James took Dolly into the computer room and closed the door behind him to preserve the air-conditioned environment. Mary and Mark could hear the raised voices above the noise of the computer and its peripherals as James introduced Sally. Mary knew they wouldn't be able to hear her over the noise from inside.

'Well!' she said. 'What do you make of that? You can put your eyes back in your sockets, now.'

'Not my type,' replied Mark, 'but she'll brighten the place up.'

'She'll certainly do that. James is all over her. Look at the silly twit. He's in his element, now.' James was demonstrating all aspects of the computer – the paper tape reader, the cumbersome printer, the magnetic card reader and then telling Dolly what all the flashing lights meant on the CPU. Sally looked as bored as usual and after a while, she excused herself to visit the ladies.

'He never talked to me like that,' she said as she closed the door behind her.

Did you want him to?' asked Mark.

'No, not really. I'm just glad he's found a replacement so that I can move on upstairs.'

James continued to demonstrate the computer to Dolly for a further forty-five minutes. Whether Dolly appreciated this attention remained to be seen, but he often took over the operating of the machine from Sally. His colleagues often said he was like a big kid with a toy. Sally declined to re-enter the room until James finally re-appeared and escorted his new member of staff off the premises, by which time it was almost lunchtime. Mark decided to take an early break and ventured down the road to the local branch of the Midland Bank to enquire about a loan. This was a small branch set up to serve the needs of the Industrial Estate.

Someone was just leaving the bank and Mark stepped aside to let him pass.

'Mark Barker?' the man said screwing up his eyes as though unsure of himself.

Mark looked at the man for a few seconds trying to imagine him without the silly little goatee beard. 'Jarvis? Derek Jarvis! It was the beard that fooled me. You didn't have a beard at school.'

Mark didn't have happy memories of Jarvis. He was forever getting Mark into trouble and even snitched on him once, resulting in a detention from Mr Beresford and subsequently a punishment from a prefect when Mark was caught trying to take retribution. Mark left school feeling frustrated that he had never given Jarvis the beating he deserved. But now, they were both adults and he had to put such feelings of revenge behind him.

'Do you work around here?' Mark asked.

'Yes, I work at Fuller Components 'round the corner.'

'Doing what?'

'I'm a Credit Controller.'

'So, you chase up bills and money owed to your company, do you?' Mark had a rough idea of what Greshams' Credit Controller did and assumed Fuller Components had the same function.

'Yeah,' replied Jarvis, 'and a few other things connected with Accounts. What about you? What are you doing?'

'I'm a Computer Programmer at Greshams.'

'Cool,' Jarvis responded. 'You were always good at Maths, if I remember right.'

'Yeah ... well, it's not so much about Maths – more a question of analysing a problem and using careful logic. Not everyone can do it.' Mark felt the need to impress his old school mate.

Jarvis nodded as though in appreciation. There was then an awkward silence as both men wondered what to say next.

'So, you bank here, do you?' Mark asked for the sake of something to say.

'No, I don't. We needed some petty cash, so I volunteered to stretch my legs.'

There was only one bank on the estate and several companies used it as a convenience for such matters even if they banked elsewhere. Mark knew that Jarvis had stayed on at school to take 'A' levels, but here he was running errands, so Mark felt justified in leaving after his 'O' levels. 'Anyway, I'd better get this money back to my colleague. It's good to see you looking so well. Perhaps we'll see each other again.'

'Yeah, take care, Derek.' It seemed strange to be having an adult conversation with Jarvis, but as he walked away, Mark noticed his old nemesis was wearing pink flares. Was that significant? Or was this how the latest fashions were going? Mark was always behind with fashion, but pink flares? Not that Mark could really pass judgement. He was wearing a lilac coloured shirt with a matching paisley patterned tie.

15

He remembered that it was Jarvis who brought some pictures of nude ladies to school and got them both into trouble because of it. He decided it didn't matter anyway. He remembered what Dougie had said when homosexuality was decriminalised, 'I don't have any objections as long as they don't make it compulsory.'

Mark entered the bank. There were just two hatches and only one of them was open with two people ahead of him in the queue. As he waited, his mind went back to those days at Parkside Grammar. They weren't always happy times. Jarvis had been one of those who had made fun of his patched-up trousers and that still rankled. Since then, he'd had very little contact with any of the boys from his year. He'd encountered a few on the football field and some in the local bars on a Saturday night, but none to really talk to apart from Dougie who was from the year above. So much had changed since those days and he now felt like a different person. He was sure that he had changed physically as well, just as Jarvis had done. But one thing had not changed. He was still living in the same house with his parents; in a home that had no hot running water and very little in the way of modern conveniences.

As well as Dougie, his friend Ray had married and was now living in Dersingham. They had become good friends when Ray had joined him in the Work Study department, but Ray had since then also started a new career – in his case at another company elsewhere in town so Mark didn't see as much of him as he used to – and having no transport did not help the situation. As much as he would like to move on to better things, he didn't think he was ready for marriage yet, so much responsibility. In any case, he couldn't afford it. His friends seem to manage their finances so much better than he. Perhaps if he didn't spend so much on records, he might be able to put some money aside – and he could do with some better fortune with cars.

Eventually, it was Mark's turn to be served. When he asked about a bank loan, he was told he would have to go to the main branch in town, but the teller was helpful enough to telephone for an appointment. Of course, it had to be during banking hours, so Mark had to settle for an afternoon appointment on the Thursday of that week. He was owed some holiday so he decided that he would take the day off.

After lunch, Mark once again asked James if he could discuss something with him. He knew that Mary was listening so just to keep her guessing, he took his chair over to James' desk and lowered his voice.

'Would you say that our computer is under-used?' he asked.

16

James agreed. 'But we've loaded everything we were asked,' he said. 'What did you have in mind?'

Mark remembered his time in the payroll office when members of the Costing team would borrow the timesheets in order to extract the labour costs for each of the contracts. He told James about this and said that he thought that computerising this process would save a lot of work and ensure greater accuracy of the data.

'I'll speak to Mr Capstick about it,' James replied. Arthur Capstick was the Cost Accountant. He discouraged his staff from using his first name, but Mark didn't think he was that senior enough in the organisation that he should oblige him and always called him Arthur, even though he knew it annoyed him. Many people called him Mr Dipstick, but only behind his back.

'I've got nothing to do at the moment,' Mark said. 'Why don't I go and have a word. I've had a little bit of experience with Costing.'

'I think he should be approached by another manager in the first instance,' James said. 'Leave it with me.'

Mark nodded in agreement. Old Slapstick could be very funny about such things, so mark went back to doing nothing – and James didn't seem to be in any hurry to respond to his suggestion. After a few minutes, Mark took out a pad from a desk drawer together with his old flowchart template. When he got a notion in his head, he wouldn't let it go. He felt that he knew enough about costing to at least make a start on the new program and at least it would keep him occupied.

As soon as James had disappeared to take a comfort break, Mary was pummelling Mark for information. 'What did you speak to old Grumpy Drawers about?' she asked.

'I just told him that I needed to take a day off on Thursday,' he replied.

'Are you going for an interview?' she asked.

'In a manner of speaking ... yes.'

Chapter Three

(Who's) That Lady

'James, have you spoken to old Slapstick, yet?' Mark asked. Mr Capstick had several nicknames – *Dipstick* and *Chopstick* were just two more.

'Not yet,' replied James, without adding anything. Mark felt like asking him why not, but he restrained himself. Instead, he carried on with his flowcharts. Even if *Old Slapstick* wasn't interested in Mark's proposed program, at least at that moment, he had something to keep him occupied.

Before joining the department, Mark had always found James to be a very affable gentleman and he had once described James as one of the nicest people you could want to meet. This opinion was gained mostly in social environments, both men having participated in the inter-departmental darts competitions and had enjoyed some of the events organised at the company Social Club, such as a cribbage and dominoes evening. But now that they were working together, Mark saw a different, more serious side to his manager, which he put down to the extra responsibility of managing the small department and he now struggled to find any redeeming facets to his character.

At least when it came to actual programming and problem solving, James did respect Mark's knowledge and capability, whereas Mary was always treated as a menial – and she naturally resented it. On several occasions James had seen fit to chastise her for minor grievances such as talking while working and chewing a toffee in the computer room. Everyone knew the importance of not taking food and drink into that area, but she felt that telling her off for chewing was over the top and had the temerity to tell him so, resulting in her being banned from the computer room for a period of time until it suited him for her to return. There was now a 'bit of an atmosphere' in the room. Mark hoped that Dolly's arrival would change that for the better.

He plodded on with the skeleton of his new program, but he was struggling as he wasn't really familiar with labour costing even though he had spent a few months in that department as a junior costing clerk. In truth, while there, he had achieved little beyond becoming proficient at filing and fetching coffee. That was where he had first met Karen, whom he had soon come to worship. Thinking about that time brought back many memories, such as his futile attempts to date her, his attempts to impress her with his sense of humour and his attempts to eye up her legs whenever he thought she wasn't looking. That was when he first discovered that he was a 'leg and bum' man.

At one time, he had been concerned that preferring the sight of a shapely bottom over a pair of breasts was something of a perversion, but he soon learnt that this not the case. He was only seventeen years old at the time and still had a lot to learn. He now knew that it was his youth and lack of experience that had meant his efforts to woo Karen were doomed to fail. If he met her now at twenty-three years of age, he might have more success, except that she was now married and he hadn't seen for many years. In his current situation, he could do with meeting someone like her.

Later that day, he heard someone enter the office. At that moment, he was concentrating on drawing a straight line to connect some of the symbols on his flowchart, so he didn't look up immediately, but he was aware that someone was looking at him as they walked past and towards Mary's punch room. When he did look up, it was to see the back of a young girl who was handing Mary a batch of clock-cards to be punched. He didn't recognise her from the rear – and he was quite good at recognising the females in the building, especially from behind. She must be new to the company, but something about her demeanour left him feeling underwhelmed.

Mary thanked her and the young girl turned to go back. Mark was again aware of her looking at him and this time, he did look up, but neither of them spoke and both looked away immediately. However, that quick glance registered a picture of an unattractive troubled girl. She was very pale and had a drawn appearance as though she had been deprived of sleep for several days. Her hair was thin and lifeless, and she walked with her shoulders hunched as though she bore the troubles of the world. She was also painfully thin. The word 'emaciated' came to mind. Her clothes were ill-fitting with no semblance of colour co-ordination. And yet, her eyes were dark and searching. She was soon out of sight and Mark turned to Mary. 'Who's that?' he asked.

'Tha's the new girl in Payroll. 'er name's Polly.'

'Not Polly!' said Mark. 'We've got Dolly joining us soon – and now there's Polly. You know there's a Molly in the Canteen, don't you?'

'Golly!' said Mary.

James joined in. 'There's a chap named Wally in the Drawing Office,' he said.

'Does he have a brolly?' Mark asked.

'He likes an iced lolly,' Mary said, which probably wasn't true, but she was encouraged by hearing James enjoying some light relief for a change.

'How jolly!' Mark said, then after a few moments having failed to find any more rhymes, he added 'She didn't look well.'

'She's an anorexic,' Mary said.

Mark had heard of the condition but knew little about it. This was the first person whom he had met who suffered from it. He didn't feel any sympathy towards her. He felt her condition was self-inflicted. He assumed that she just wanted to be as thin as possible and that seemed to be a foolish attitude, particularly as he didn't find waif-like skinny models to be attractive.

Normally, when a new girl joined the firm, he would be fishing for more information, such as whether she had a boyfriend and where she lived, but he put her to the back of his mind. She really wasn't what he was looking for.

And so, it was back to his flowchart.

'So, Mr Barker. You want to take out a loan, do you?' the Assistant Bank Manager asked in his crisp upper-class accent. 'What do you want it for?'

'I need to replace my car,' Mark replied submissively.

'And how much do you want to borrow?'

'I was looking at four hundred pounds. I've based that on what I think I can afford.'

'All right. Let's have a look at your account. I see you already have a standing order. What's that for?'

Mark was half expecting to have to answer a lot of questions, so he was prepared for it. 'That's my existing vehicle – it's fifteen pounds twenty-five pence a month. It was fifteen pounds and five shillings when it started before decimalisation. I need to pay it off before I get my new car, so I've allowed for that in the amount I want to borrow.'

'Do you have any other debts outstanding?'

'Just two things. I pay five bob a month for a suit from Fosters and a pound a month to my sister's catalogue for a record player.'

'What do you do for a living?' Mr Wainwright stared unnervingly at Mark as he asked the questions as though looking for signs of deceit.

'I'm a computer programmer.' Mark always liked to announce that.

'Oh ... a clever chap, then?'

'No, not really. It's more about analysing a problem and thinking logically.'

'Yes, as I said – a clever chap. Did you go to Cambridge?'

'Yes. I took my girlfriend. We had a lovely day out.'

The man smiled. 'No ... of course, I meant did you study at Cambridge?'

'No. My parents couldn't afford to send me to university.'

'Which school did you attend?'

'I went to the local grammar – Parkside.'

'Really!' Mr Wainwright said, suddenly showing a little more interest. 'I went there; probably a few years before you. What year were you in?'

'I started in 1960,' Mark replied. 'What about you?'

'51 to 58.'

'What House were you in?' Mark asked, realising that he was now asking the questions.

'Granville,' was the reply.

'So, you were a boarder?'

'Yes, were you?'

'No, I live locally. I was in Nelson house.'

'Fancy that,' said Mr Wainwright. If he was anything like the boarders in Mark's day, he would have looked down on any of the day boys. 'I wonder if we shared any of the masters. Was old Mortensen still teaching Geography?'

'Not in my time. We did have a new Geography master joined the same time as me, so perhaps he left just before then.'

The Bank Manager was trying to think of other masters who might have still been there. 'What about Joe King?'

'Oh, yes. He was Deputy Head – always joking about his name and the fictitious names of his relatives ... May King, Ray King, Lee King, and so on.'

'Yes, a chap in our form asked him if he had an adopted Spanish son called Juan. He took it in good spirit if I remember. There was an old chap – Maths, I think - been there forever ...'

'Tommy Thompson?' Mark suggested.

'That's him. Was he still there? He must have been about ninety. Then there was Mr Charles who liked to watch the boys in the shower.'

'Yes, he was still there ... and still indulging his little *interest*.'

'Shouldn't be allowed. I wouldn't let my children go to that school if I thought he was still doing that.'

'Well, I don't think he did anything other than looking,' said Mark. 'There were worse things than that going on.'

'Did you ever get the cane?' Mr Wainwright asked. 'I did ... several times. God, it hurt!'

'No,' replied Mark. 'I came close once or twice, but I had a few detentions.'

'Well, who didn't? Anyway, we'd better concentrate on the matter in hand. I don't see any problem with granting you an advance. I just need you fill in this form and add your signature.'

Mark wondered if the connection with the school had made the decision a little easier, but then banks make money out of loans so why shouldn't he get his money. It was interesting to observe how Mr Wainwright had changed from being so prim and proper to someone willing to share memories about receiving the cane ... and *Juan*? Who would have thought a Bank Manager would come out with that?

With that all sorted, Mark decided to use the rest of the afternoon to visit Burtons, the car dealer. Kenny was just placing a sticker in an Austin Maxi as Mark leaned his bike against a wall. 'Hey Shagger!' Kenny called. 'Have you come to buy one of my amazing cars?'

'That depends what you've got,' Mark replied.

'What about this wonderful Maxi ... great for carrying all your mates with their football kit in the boot. It's got a fifth door in the back ... a bit like an estate, but it drives like a saloon.'

'Too much money,' Mark said, noticing the price in the windscreen.

'I've got a lovely little Triumph Herald round the back ... not much good for shagging, though.'

Was that all he ever thought about? Mark thought. 'Too small,' he replied, remembering riding in one as a passenger once and finding his knees crunched up against his chest and his head touching the roof lining.

'So, a mini's out of the question, then?'

Mark had actually found Dougie's old mini surprisingly roomy, but he recalled his friend's problems when the sub-frame broke. He didn't need that sort of aggravation.

'Just a little bigger,' Mark said, '... and at the right price!'

'And what would that be?' Kenny asked.

'That depends what you're going to offer me on trade-in.'

'We don't take bikes,' Kenny joked. 'Did you say you have a Wolseley 1500?'

'Yeah ... 1964 model.'

'Got an MOT?'

'Not at the moment.' Mark didn't want to tell Kenny how bad it was. It was up to him to find out for himself.

'Well, bring it in and I'll give you a price. Meanwhile, have a look around and see what takes your fancy.'

Mark did that, but there was nothing in his price range that he liked the look of, and he told Kenny that just as he was ready to leave.

'How about an 1100?' Kenny asked. 'I've got a little pearler coming in tomorrow. One lady owner – only four years old; very low mileage – all the benefits of the transverse engine and front-wheel drive.'

Just like the mini, thought Mark. 'What's the bodywork like?' asked Mark.

'Like new. She had it factory-undersealed.'

That did it for Mark; a car that wouldn't rust – at least not for a good few years. 'How much?' he asked.

'Um ... I'm not sure at the moment ... but I'm sure we can do a deal. Bring your Wolseley in and I'll sort something out.'

'All right. Are you working Saturday morning?'

'Yeah, I'll be here till lunchtime.'

The next day, it was back to the same old boring routine in the office and Mark couldn't concentrate on work. All he wanted to do was go and see the 1100 at the weekend.

Mary waited until the two of them were alone. 'How was your day off?'

Mark knew she was still under the impression that he had gone for an interview and he felt like teasing her. 'Very rewarding,' he replied enigmatically.

'Did you have an interview?' she asked.

'Umm ... in a way, yeah ... probably more like a meeting, really.'

'Where was it?' Mary wasn't going to let this go without more answers.

'It was at a bank. The manager went to my old Grammar School. We had a good ol' chat about some of the masters.'

'So, you're in with a good chance, then?'

'Oh, I got it,' Mark replied. 'Four hundred pounds.'

'That's not very much,' she said. 'I get more than that.'

'Yeah, but I bet you wouldn't lend it to me, though. This chap has.'

Mary frowned ... then the penny dropped. 'You went for a bank loan! You've been leading me on.'

'I wouldn't dream of leading you on. What would your Donald say if I led you on?'

'He'd probably tell you to get a girlfriend!' Mary expressed her annoyance by teasing Mark in return.

'I'll have you know, I had a date at the weekend.'

'Really?' she asked, always interested to know about other people's love life.

'Yeah. We had a box left over from Christmas.'

Just then, James returned to his desk and Mary thought it best that she got on with her punching before she got another telling off.

**

It was Saturday morning. Mark was up and about early. Before he could look at the 1100, he thought he ought to visit the finance company to pay off the outstanding HP on his old car. Then he would know how much money he had left and the 1500 would be his to dispose of as he pleased.

Miss Tombleson was busy attending to another client, so while Mark waited his turn, he took the opportunity to appraise her in the fresh knowledge of what Kenny had said about her. There was no way that she could be described as pretty; and Mark wouldn't want to call her ugly. No, he thought. She was pretty ugly and had to stop himself laughing at his little private joke. She was certainly a big lady and if she had shagged Kenny, he would certainly have had the bruises to show for it.

'Next!' she said in a deep commanding voice.

'I want to pay off the remainder of my HP,' he said tentatively while handing over some paperwork.

She grabbed it with her thick stubby fingers and scanned it, before extracting his details from a filing cabinet. All the time, she worked in silence and Mark felt intimidated. 'Thirty point five pounds outstanding – and two pounds early termination fee,' she announced. Some people had taken decimalisation literally. He was expecting to owe three months payments, but he'd obviously miscalculated – it was only two. He was better off than he had first thought.

'Kenny Stacey told me that if I mention his name, you might waive the termination fee.' He watched her to see if Kenny's name elicited any sort of response. There was a flicker of recognition, then a sneer.

'Are you going to take out another agreement with us, then?' she asked gruffly.

'No, I will be paying for my next car with cash.' He decided not to mention the bank loan. It might upset her – and he wouldn't want to do that.

'There'll be a two-pound termination fee!' she announced.

He felt that he wanted to ask why he had to pay extra. If anything, he should be paying less in interest, but he thought it unlikely that she would relent. He took out his cheque book.

'I've got a stamp,' she announced. Mark was puzzled. Why would he need a postage stamp? Then he saw she had a rubber stamp ready to use for the payee's name. She also stamped his counterfoil and very nearly stamped his hand instead.

'You can tell Kenny Stacey that I don't like salesmen. The only good salesman is a dead one!'

Mark was pleased to remove himself from her company and return to his car. He was fifteen pounds better off than he expected and felt that he had a lot of money burning a hole in his pocket. He was sorely tempted to go into town and buy himself a new LP. He'd heard a few tracks off Marvin Gaye's *What's Going On* album and he hadn't bought any records for two weeks. He was getting withdrawal symptoms. He needed a fix of soul music. Reluctantly, he decided that his priority was to sort out his transport, especially as that morning, he was driving his car illegally.

As he pulled into Burtons, he could see the 1100 in pride of place at the front of the forecourt. He parked his old Wolseley to take a closer look. His face dropped when he saw the price in the windscreen – four hundred and fifty pounds! It was way too much. He quickly worked out that Kenny would have to offer him about eighty pounds on his old wreck and he thought that highly unlikely.

A different salesman came out of the showroom and approached Mark. 'Good morning, sir - a lovely morning for the time of year.' He was much younger than Kenny and was obviously trying very hard to look the consummate salesman. He wore a beige suit with wide lapels and flared trousers; not as wide as the fashion during the later seventies, but still wider than anything that Mark possessed. It was obvious that the suit was off the peg as the bottom of his trousers finished two inches above his ankles.

'A nice motor ... front wheel-drive ... hydrolastic suspension ... very popular vehicle. Is this the sort of thing sir is looking for?' he asked.

It didn't take much to make Mark feel despondent and he didn't like being called *sir*, but he replied 'Yes, but I think I need something a little cheaper' and started to walk away, but he wanted Kenny to keep an eye out for something else, so he turned and asked 'Is Kenny around?'

'He's busy with another client at the moment, sir. Are you sure you wouldn't like a test drive?'

Mark considered that for a moment. He might not be able to afford this particular 1100, but there were a lot of them around, so he'd like to know if this was the right model for him, so he agreed.

Ten minutes later, he returned the car to the forecourt. The young salesman said, 'This car suits you and your driving style.'

Mark knew that he probably said that or something similar to every customer, but in this case, he was right.

He had enjoyed the way he could throw the car into a roundabout and accelerate smoothly out the other side. He didn't know if that was due to the hydrolastic suspension or the front-wheel drive, but he enjoyed driving the car. It had a smaller engine than his Wolseley, but it actually felt faster.

That may have been down to the fact that it sat lower on the road, but he did want this car.

'How much will you offer me for my Wolseley?' he asked.

The salesman walked around Mark's vehicle and tugged at the flapping front wing making it even worse that it was. Then he pulled off a piece of rusty doorsill. 'I'm afraid we can't take this, sir. It's not the sort of vehicle that we would sell on. You could advertise it privately, but I don't think you will get much for it.'

Mark was so disgusted, that he stomped off towards his car without even replying. Just then, Kenny appeared, saying goodbye to his other customer. He spotted Mark getting into his car. 'Mark! Are you leaving? Have you struck a deal with my young colleague?'

'No, I haven't!' and with that he slammed his door, probably causing more pieces to fall off.'

'Wait a minute, Mark. I recognise this car,' Kenny said. Mark could just about make out what he was saying through the closed door, so he wound down his window. 'I sold it to you about two years ago. I thought I recognised you from somewhere. I'm not too brilliant at faces, but I always remember a car. It's a '64 model, but it didn't have the 'B' suffix for some reason'

'I bought it from Mann Egerton's,' Mark said, trying to remember the salesman who sold it, but at the time, he had been more interested in the car than the person selling it – and he'd only known Kenny since joining his new football team that season.

'Yes, I used to work there ... but it didn't look like this when I sold it to you. What have you been doing with it?'

'Nothing special, but it does get left out in the road at night.'

Kenny carried on looking at it, then added 'If I remember right, the chap who had it before you lived on the coast – probably exposed to a lot of sea spray and salt in the air. Never buy a car from someone who lives on the coast.'

'I told him we couldn't take it,' said Kenny's young colleague, but Kenny ignored him.

'So, you've had a drive of the 1100. Does it interest you?'

'Yes,' replied Mark. 'It's just what I want, but I can't afford it without a good trade-in.'

Kenny pondered a minute, then said 'Come into the office. We'll see what we can do.'

The other salesman followed them, but Kenny told him that he'd deal with it. 'It's my sale,' the younger one said.

'It didn't look like it to me. I think the customer was about to leave. Go and make some tea – there's a good chap. Would you like a cup, Mark?'

Mark took a good deal of pleasure out of watching him slope off to make the tea.

As they sat down in his office (which was really just a desk and three chairs in the showroom), Kenny said 'He's right, of course, that we wouldn't normally take your car, but I feel I owe you one. I would never had sold it to you if I'd known it would end up like that, so I'm going to try to make it right for you. Now, did you get your bank loan?'

Mark's rage had by now subsided somewhat and he sat back in the chair. 'Yes, but I've already spent some of it paying off my old HP. By the way, I have a message for you from Miss Tombleson.'

'Have you?'

Mark was going to test his reaction to see if there was any possibility of an old liaison between the two. 'Yes, she says she misses you very much and can't wait to see you again.'

'Really?' The look said it all. There was no way that there had been anything between them.

'No ... what she actually said was that she didn't like salesmen.' He didn't finish the whole message.

'Yeah ... that sounds more like old Geraldine – always playing hard to get. Now, how much money have you got left from your loan to spend on this new car?'

When it came to salesmen, Mark was of the same school of thought as Geraldine. He disliked all the salesmen at his own employers and, generally, car salesmen were even further down the evolutionary scale, but he liked Kenny and felt he had to trust him to find a deal, so he answered honestly. 'About three hundred and fifty pounds.' (Well, fairly honestly!).

'Ouch!' said Kenny. 'We're way short. Is there any way you can lay your hands on a little more?'

Mark was feeling guilty about the deceit of about twenty pounds and he really didn't want to miss out on this car.

'I get paid next week ... and now I won't have to pay this month's HP ... and the first bank loan repayment won't be until the end of the month. So I could possibly stretch to another twenty ... or possibly even thirty – except, of course, I still have to tax the new car.'

Kenny jotted some figures down on a piece of paper.

'Now the price in the window of four hundred and fifty pounds is the *on the road* price. Now, that includes six months' road tax, a full year's MOT, a full service and a six months' warranty. So you'll need the MOT – we can't change that, but I know the previous owner had the car serviced just two months ago – because we did it. So there's a saving we could make ... and if you could take it without the warranty – and to be honest, I'm confident you won't hit any problems ...'

He carried on scribbling and scratching his head.

'We're still a little short. Let me speak to my manager. I have an idea'

He disappeared leaving Mark to swig his tea.

Kenny's manager did have an office and the conversation was muffled, but Mark thought he heard the words *commission, wreck* and *waive*.

When he returned, Kenny said

'Right! We'll take the Wolseley off your hands if you can find three eighty and the road tax – no service and no warranty ... although if you hit any problem in the first week, come and see me – and a full MOT for twelve months. Can you live with that?'

Of course, he could and Kenny raised all the paperwork.

'When can I pick it up?' Mark asked, eager to get mobile again.

'We need to do the MOT, so you could have it by Tuesday.'

Mark thought about the logistics of getting his old car in during the week when he had to work. 'Any chance that I could come in one evening'

'We close at five each night,' Kenny replied.

Mark was disappointed. There was no way that he could manage that. He would have to wait until the following weekend. 'I'll make it next Saturday morning, if that's all right.'

'I won't be here, that day, but someone will sort you out. I've got a few days off - taking my girlfriend to Wales. I'm going to Bangor.'

'I hope she lets you,' Mark replied, with a grin.

'Very good. This is just like a game of football. I set them up and someone else finishes them off.'

Chapter Four

Seven Days Is Too Long

That same afternoon, Mark found Dougie waiting in his Mark II Cortina in the car park of the Bricklayers Arms. They were supposed to have met inside the pub, but his morning errands had made Mark a little late. 'Sorry Dougie,' he said. 'It's all been a bit of a rush this morning.'

'I was starting to get a little concerned. We'd be in trouble without our star goalkeeper.'

'Your only goalkeeper,' Mark said. Dougie always talked up Mark's prowess since it was he who had introduced him to Northfleet United. That afternoon's match was an away game. It was Mark's turn to drive them, but that was not possible until he picked up his 1100.

'So, how's it all going?' Dougie asked.

'Oh, I'm super ... really great.'

'Whoa! Old Markie's on a promise. Have you got yourself another bird, then?' Dougie asked.

'No, I haven't got another bird, but I have sorted myself a new set of wheels.'

'Got yourself a crumpet catcher? What is it? A Ford Capri?' Dougie asked.

'No, just a nice 1100.' Mark went on to describe his morning's work at Burtons. 'Kenny has revived my opinion of mankind. He really went out of his way to sort out a deal.'

'He's a car salesman. They always sort out a deal,' said Dougie. 'Otherwise, they don't get paid. They're paid on commission.'

'I have a feeling that he waived his commission on this one,' Mark said. 'If he did, he's a top chap.'

'I doubt it,' said Dougie. 'I always take my old man when I need a new car. He usually manages to find a minor fault; then negotiates some discount. You should have asked him to go with you.'

'Maybe,' said Mark, 'but I still feel Kenny did all right by me. I've a feeling that he won't be playing tomorrow. He's taking his girlfriend for a break in North Wales.'

'Is he taking her up the Great Orme?' Dougie asked.

Mark knew he was being facetious 'That's a bit rude! What's the Great Orme?'

'It's a big headland near Llandudno. I saw it on a holiday programme on telly. I think it might have been Judith Charmless – or it might have been Katy Boyle. I like her. Anyway, whoever it was went up to the top on a tram. It looked very nice. I'd like to take Katy Boyle up the Great Orme. She's Italian, you know.'

'What, Katy Boyle?'

'Yeah, Katy Boyle.'

'I didn't know that. I like Sophia Loren,' said Mark. 'Did you see her in that film with Peter Sellers ... wearing suspenders. I'm going to have to find a girlfriend like Sophia Loren.'

'Or Gina Dodger- a-lollipop!' said Dougie.

'Yeah, I'd settle for her as well; Or Claudia Carbonara.'

Dougie smacked his lips. 'You're making me hungry now.'

'I thought I'd be making you randy,' said Mark.

'No, I've put that all behind me now. I'm a happ ... I'm a married man.' It was Dougie's favourite joke.

***

After the football on Saturday afternoon and Sunday morning, life really seemed to drag. The office environment on Monday and Tuesday became ever more oppressive. Mark wished that he could have taken a day off to pick up his new vehicle, but he only had one day left of his annual allocation and he wanted to preserve that in case he needed to go for an interview somewhere. Saturday morning seemed an age away and without decent transport, he had nowhere to go.

During Tuesday morning, Polly once again walked past with the clock cards and Mark looked up to see the same waif-like creature wearing the same clothes as the previous week – and exchanging the same embarrassed look in return.

The office surrounding the computer room did not receive many visitors and he took to taking regular walks around the office building just to pass some time and to see if there were any interesting new ladies. He dearly wanted to go into the typing pool, but he had no reason to do so, but always sauntered past whenever he could in case the lovely Stella appeared. She was the Typing Pool Supervisor and although Stella was in a steady relationship with a well-built rugby player, Mark still went weak at the knees whenever he saw her. He knew she was way out of his league, but he still liked looking. She was blonde and built of Amazonian proportions. She was reputed to be a champion swimmer and he promised himself that he would one day find out where and when she did her swimming. Strangely, he hadn't entertained these thoughts while he had been in his relationship with Melody, but now he was sorely in need of female company. Mary and Sally didn't count. Mark wasn't alone in his admiration for Stella. He'd even heard a few women saying how gorgeous she was.

He also occasionally ventured into the factory – not on the shop floor where he was once a regular visitor in his role as a Work Study Officer and would now be banned for safety reasons, but along the perimeter corridor to the works canteen where he would sometimes drop in for a bread roll or a bar of chocolate. But these little excursions could never last very long, and he was soon back at his desk slowly counting the hours away.

Eventually, Friday came around and he was then only one day away from getting rid of his lump of rusting metal from outside his parents' house. While James was away from his desk, Mark was joined by the two girls, taking an unofficial coffee break.

'I can't wait till I get away from this place,' Sally said.

'Yeah – then it's *Hello Dolly*!' said Mark.

'Are you gonna ask 'er out?' Mary asked.

'No. I've told you she's not my type.'

'What is your type?' she asked.

Mark never knew how to answer that question. If he had been talking to Dougie or Kenny, he could have mentioned his preference for a woman's physical assets, but that didn't seem appropriate when talking to two young girls. 'Intelligence ... good sense of humour ...'

'That lets us out, then' said Sally.

'How about a big pair of bazookas?' asked Mary, obviously intimating Dolly's personal qualifications.

'More than a handful's a waste,' Mark replied.

'Well she's got some waste all right,' said Sally.

'Are you looking for a new girlfriend, Mark?' Mary asked.

'Only if the right girl comes along,' Mark lied. He was a little fussy, but she didn't have to be the 'right' one – just yet.

'I know someone who said she'll go out with you,' Mary said.

Mark suspected some kind of wind-up, but he couldn't resist finding out who might have expressed such an interest. After all, despite his improved level of self-confidence since those dark days when he first left school, he still didn't consider himself to be the greatest catch in the building.

'Polly!' was the reply.

'Polly?' said Mark. 'The anorexic? I've never spoken to her. I've only ever seen her twice. How do you know?'

'She told me in the ladies.'

'What brought this up? Were you talking about me?' Mark asked.

'That's ladies' business.'

'Yeah, well I suppose it would be ladies' business in the ladies' toilets,' he said. 'No, I'm afraid I'm not interested.' He couldn't imagine any reason why he might want to date her, which, if she fancied him, was a great pity. She was obviously desperate. No, he'd just have to keep looking.

That evening, he fussed about with his old car – clearing all his personal belongings from the boot and the glove compartment. He also dug out his logbook, and, in case it might be needed, the receipt for his final payment to the finance company to prove the car was his to trade. Mr Pettit appeared from the house across the road. Mark had never liked his neighbour and disliked his wife even more. They had crossed swords many times when he was much younger and his football had strayed into their precious garden. She always refused to return it, so he often crept in to fetch it himself, incurring her wrath.

'Evening, Mark,' Mr Pettit said cheerfully.

Mark mumbled a response that could have been taken as 'hello' or 'sod off.'

'I hope you don't mind me mentioning it, Mark, but I see your road tax has run out. I wouldn't want you to get into trouble. You know it's illegal to drive your car on the road without taxing it.'

'Yes, I did know,' Mark replied. He wasn't sure if Mr Pettit was trying to be neighbourly, but after years of rancour with him and his wife, Mark didn't want to be neighbourly and gathered up his belongings and left. This had been one of the friendlier conversations between the two. Often, Mr Pettit would ask Mark to move his car to give him more room to manoeuvre his own into or out of his drive. As Mark made a point of not obstructing Mr Pettit's drive, he almost always declined the request., usually with a caustic remark such as 'If you can't manage that, you shouldn't be driving,' a barbed inference to the fact that the old man had never needed to pass a driving test, as he had been driving before the test was made compulsory – and his driving skills were known by all the neighbours as being totally woeful.

That night, Mark struggled to sleep. His mind kept turning over all the things that could possibly go wrong with his vehicle transaction. When he did eventually find sleep, he dreamt that Colin, the young salesman standing in for Kenny, had still refused to take the Wolseley.

Mark demanded to speak to Kenny and Colin directed him to Wells (often confused with Wales!) so Mark drove over to Wells-Next-The-Sea to find Kenny, but somehow contrived to drive his car into the harbour. Kenny appeared to remind him that the sea air was not good for cars. Mark watched as his beloved Wolseley dissolved in the saltwater – then woke with a start, a chattering magpie outside his window making him think it was screeching seagulls.

In fact, the vehicle transaction went very smoothly. Colin didn't seem to be very happy about it, but he carried out the task efficiently. Kenny had left instructions to add a couple of gallons of three-star petrol, which he didn't have to do as it wasn't part of the agreement. Nevertheless, Mark wanted to check on his petrol consumption. The best way to do this was to fill up; so, on the way home, he stopped at his favourite petrol station. 'Fill her up with three-star, please,' he asked the attendant who was wearing greasy overalls. In one week's time, he would fill it again and work out the fuel used against the mileage travelled. His Wolseley had regularly managed thirty five to the gallon, so with a smaller engine, he would expect his new car to perform much better.

Before decimalisation, he would regularly ask for a pound's worth each week as petrol at that time was six and eight pence a gallon, meaning he would get exactly three gallons, but since that event, the price had started creeping up.

'Shall I check your oil, sir?' the attendant asked.

'No, it's all right, thank you.' Mark was going to check it himself when he got home. He would keep an eye on it over the first few weeks to see if his motor was using oil.

When he reached home, his mother was keen to have a look at his new motor as she had been missing her lifts to the Bingo. His father showed no interest. He'd never owned a car and Mark always felt he was a little envious of his son.

Mark really wanted to take his car for a nice long drive that afternoon, but he had a football match and it was a home fixture so he wouldn't be travelling very far. However, his journey did take him down the road where Blodwyn lived. He hadn't seen her for a while, which was strange as he often had to drive down her road to the football pitch. He had vowed to himself that he would never ask her out again after the way she had used him on a pretend date which was just a ruse to get him to provide a lift so that she could meet her old boyfriend. But Mark often thought about her. Maybe she had changed. After all, she still had the most amazing pair of legs that he had ever encountered, and he was currently without a girlfriend. He really would love to have a couple of dates with her. But he didn't see her that day and when the football was over, it was too dark for a drive anywhere other than back home, even though, that year, British Summer Time was maintained throughout the year.

With another match on Sunday morning, he would have to wait until Sunday afternoon ... except that it rained all day and he had to content himself watching an old black and white film with the rest of the family.

Chapter Five

Try It Baby

When Mark had first joined Greshams in 1965, the office building had only just been completed. The company were newly relocated to Sanford as part of the London Overspill initiative that saw several towns in Norfolk benefit from government investment to attract companies to relocate from the capital. Since that time, there had been many changes within the firm. At first, almost eighty percent of the office workers were Londoners. Since that time, many of these had either moved on to other employers or drifted back home having struggled with the different pace of life in West Norfolk. Now there were as many local employees as Londoners. The change in the factory was even more pronounced. Much of this was down to periods of expansion when it had been easier to attract local labour. There had also been times when it had been necessary to lay off workers. This was typical of any employer in the building industry, which was always the first to be affected by boom and bust economics.

Morale always suffered during the downturns and the situation was now at an all-time low. The new owners of the company had brought in a lot of their own staff to oversee a programme of change. A whole new board was now in charge causing much resentment to the staff, especially as the majority of the new board were seen as young and inexperienced and didn't like taking advice from seasoned employees. Staff turnover was at an unparalleled high. Mark's friend and ex-colleague from his time in the Work Study department had moved on. Ray had recently married and moved into a bungalow in Dersingham, meaning Mark didn't see him as often as he would wish.

Ray had often told Mark to call in whenever he wanted, but Mark preferred a more formal invitation. Not being on the telephone at home made this awkward and he was therefore yet to take up the offer. His lack of transport had deterred a visit even more, but now he decided it was time to do something about it, but he had to wait until he was back at work on Monday.

Company policy forbade the use of the firm's telephones to make personal calls. There was a public call box just outside the canteen, but it was often too noisy in that area, so Mark would often persuade Ellie to

35

let him have an outside line when no one was looking, but he had to wait until James was out of the office because Mark was sure he would prohibit any personal calls.

Eventually, late on Monday afternoon, the opportunity arose, and Mark was able to make arrangements to visit Ray the next Saturday evening. Until his new girlfriend entered his life, he felt it was important to have something to look forward to, but still the week dragged. To make matters worse, James had finally spoken to old Dipstick, but it had been decided that he alone would be able to discuss the requirements for the new program, and he would be the only person in a position to draw up the flowchart, so all Mark's efforts to date would be wasted. At least it had been agreed that Mark would write the actual coding. Mark was even more fed up than before.

In contrast, Sally was very cheerful. Friday would be her last day as a computer operator and to celebrate, she had invited several people to join her for a lunchtime drink at The White Harte in the nearby village of Fulton.

The leaving celebration was a very subdued affair. Because Sally wasn't actually leaving the company, only seven people had turned up and James had been one of them. Having a manager in their midst quelled any chance of riotous behaviour and when James announced it was time to leave, no one protested too loudly, including the two who left with him. Mark said, 'We'll join you soon ... just as soon as we've finished our drinks.' That left Mark with Mary, Sally and the lovely Ellie, all of whom were relying on Mark for a lift back to the office.

'Make sure you're back by two o'clock,' James said as he exited. They all nodded.

'Thank God he's gone,' Mary said, once he had left. 'Perhaps we can enjoy ourselves now. Mark, tell us a joke. Come on. Cheer us up!'

Mark was a little stumped. He usually had a good supply, but Mary was always pestering him for a joke, and he was struggling for any she hadn't already heard.

'I've got one,' he eventually announced, 'but it's very rude. I can't tell that in mixed company.'

'Of course, you can,' said Ellie. 'We all know the facts of life.'

'No, it's too rude ... it has a very rude word – and it doesn't work without that word.' Mark knew they would eventually prise it out of him, but he wanted to pretend he was telling it reluctantly.

'We've heard all the rude words before,' said Ellie. 'We promise we won't be embarrassed. Does the word begin with the letter 'C?'

'No ... although I do know one with that letter.'

'I've probably heard it,' said Ellie. 'My husband is always returning with rude jokes when he's been out with his mates.'

'This one involves a Country and Western singer,' Mark said.

'Oh, I have heard it,' she said. 'Does it involve a chap who's hard of hearing?'

'Yes ... and he thinks he comes from Preston.' Mark was a little surprised that the elegant Ellie would have knowledge of such a rude story.

'Yes, that's the one.' She said. 'What's the other one, then? Come on, you've got us all intrigued now.'

'All right,' said Mark, 'but I did warn you.' He took a sip of his drink before starting his tale. 'Mickey Mouse is in the divorce court. The judge says *"I'm sorry Mr Mouse. I don't believe that your wife having buck teeth is sufficient grounds for divorce."*

Mickey said *"I didn't say she has buck teeth. I said she's effing Goofy."*

They all laughed, but then, just for devilment, Ellie asked 'So what does the *eff* stand for?'

'F-f-f for Christ's sake,' said Mark and they continued laughing, but then it was time to leave and they crawled back into the office just before two o'clock. Going down the pub during their lunch break had just made the afternoon drag even more.

Mark still hadn't taken his new car for a nice long run, so as the sun was shining on Saturday morning, he went for a drive to one of his favourite spots which was Great Massingham. While wandering round the largest pond, he couldn't help remembering his time with Melody. How he wished she was still around to share moments like this.

'A lovely spot, isn't it?' a voice said. He turned to see that a young lady had silently approached him. She was dressed in a grey trench coat that almost covered her sandals and she had long dark hair that hung down past her shoulders and was tied in ringlets. Apart from her hair, she had made very little effort with her appearance and she was far from the dream he might have conjured if he was looking to be swept up by a beautiful stranger.

'Er, yes. It's very nice,' he replied.

'Do you live 'round here?' she asked.

'No, I live in Sanford. Do you?'

'Yes, we have a little commune just down the road. There are eight of us plus six children.' Mark had heard of these hippy communes and she looked the part, but surely, they were normally to be found in California – or at least in somewhere like Somerset or The Isle of Wight – not draughty West Norfolk. He was standing downwind of her and a strange smell hit his nostrils. It was not a smell he was familiar with. They were joined by another hippy who put his arms around her shoulders.

'Hi, man,' he said

'Really,' thought Mark. 'Hi, man? Did people actually say that?'

Mark just replied 'Hello.'

'Have you been chatting up my Jasmine?' the Hippy asked.

'No, I was just admiring the view,' Mark replied defensively. Was this chap looking for trouble?

'It's all right if you were. We share and share alike in our group. Do you fancy some weed?'

Was that the smell that he had detected?

'No, it's all right thank you ... I don't indulge.' Mark was thinking it was time to leave.

'Man, you should. It will set you up for the day. Have you ever tried it?'

'No, I don't want to.'

'You should try it,' the hippy said.

'Yes,' said Jasmine. 'Do try it. Then we can go back to the commune and do some acid.'

Mark decided it was time to leave. 'I've got a football match this afternoon. I need to get going.' It was just his luck that when a young female was throwing herself at him, it was someone who was totally promiscuous and likely to be out of her tree on drugs. This was not what he was looking for in a girlfriend – or, to be precise, someone else's girlfriend.

***

It was Mark's first visit to Ray's new bungalow and he was made very welcome, with the offer of a cup of coffee gratefully received.

'So how is the old place?' Ray asked referring, of course, to Greshams, while Valerie meanwhile boiled a kettle.

'Not good,' Mark replied and listed several of the people who had left recently. 'My cousin George is one of them. You know things aren't good when an accountant leaves. I think he could see the writing on the wall. Our old Work Study department doesn't exist like it used to. All that's left are two Bonus Clerks. There's a new Works Director been brought in. He doesn't seem much older than you and me. He's set a ceiling on bonus earnings so that no one can earn more than eight pounds a week; non-skilled or semi-skilled can only earn six pounds – and women, just four. He maintained that production was dropping despite people

38

earning higher and higher bonuses ... and he was right. I remember someone telling me that most incentive schemes fail after a few years as people learn all sorts of short cuts and fiddles ... and quality often drops.'

'I'm surprised the unions accepted the change,' Ray said.

'I suspect that they were told that if they didn't like the decision, the bonus scheme would be dropped altogether – and then their members wouldn't even get the eight pounds a week.'

Mark then went on to describe what was happening in his own new department and mentioned the lunchtime drink and how Ellie had known the Country and Western joke.

'I don't think I know that one,' Ray said.

'Yes, you do,' said Mark. 'You're the one who told me! You know ... a chap from Preston.'

'Oh, that one!' said Ray. 'Gosh, I'm surprised that Ellie would know that – talk about still waters, hey?'

'What was it?' asked Valerie, who by now had rejoined them.

'We can't tell you,' said Mark. 'It's too rude.'

'Oh, if it's rude, I don't want to hear it.' Valerie was a regular church goer and Mark was right in his judgement. He'd once told her a much milder joke and she had been offended. 'Have some of my cake, Mark ... go on. Try it.'

Chapter Six

Am I the Same Girl?

By the end of the year, Mark's love life was still non-existent. He had yet to enjoy the company of a girlfriend at any Christmas. Although he had been dating Melody the year before, she had decided to spend the time with her parents in Towcester.

As he had suspected, Dolly had not turned out to be the answer to his dreams. In one way, that had been ironic, because Mark liked curvy girls and Dolly certainly had curves. They just weren't presented the way he liked them. For one thing, she saw herself as a voluptuous blonde, like Diana Dors or Jayne Mansfield, but she didn't walk like either of those two icons. There was no sensuous wiggle; more an awkward stumbling gait as he often found with women who hadn't managed the art of walking in high heels which she persisted in wearing at all times. She liked to accentuate her bosom whenever she could, but to Mark, there seemed more 'wobble' than 'bounce' and, in any case, it was wasted on him because he was a confirmed 'leg and bum' man. And her legs were nothing special

On the few occasions when she wasn't wearing too much make-up, her complexion was revealed as more blotchy than rosy and Mark had never seen the point in painting one's eyelids blue.

But, of course, none of this mattered, because, like Mary and Sally, Dolly had a wonderful boyfriend. 'My Mate Lenny,' as she always called him, could never have had smelly farts, because they would have had to have emanated from the orifice from which the sun permanently shone.

Mark did have to admit that she was always cheerful. Every morning, she would enter the office with a cheery 'Wotcha' to anyone in the vicinity and she did give Mark and Mary something to talk about whenever the two of them were alone. Mark always found it easier to talk to Mary than Dolly. The latter was often laughing, but to Mark's dismay, not at his little quips. He'd often been told that people didn't always know when he was joking, but Dolly had taken her puzzlement to a new art form. He'd lost count of the number of times he had said 'I'm joking, Dolly' or 'Oh, never mind.'

One of their first conversations began with Mark saying. 'I notice you always say "Wotcha" instead of "Hello." Is that's because you don't want people to reply, "Hello Dolly!"'

'What d'ya mean?' she replied.

'Well ... you know ... like the song.'

'What song?'

'*Hello Dolly.*'

'Why would they do that?'

'Well .... they might think that was amusing.' Was she just being thick or was she just playing him along? 'Hasn't anybody ever done that ... and then sang the line?'

'No ... I don't quite follow you.'

'So why do you always say "Wotcha" instead of "Hello?"'

'I don't know – it's what I've always said. I don't understand what you're saying.'

'Never mind ... it doesn't matter.'

Ray had once told Mark that if you argue with an idiot, the chances are that you will end up being mistaken for the idiot – except that Dolly wasn't an idiot. She was actually quite bright. She was just on a different wavelength to him and he found communication with her very difficult.

Because food and drink were not allowed in the computer room, Dolly would have a short break drinking vending machine coffee at the spare desk opposite Mark, whilst listening out in case the computer should come to a halt. She had quickly learned how to deal with most situations when this happened, but sometimes she would have to call on the expert assistance of Mark or James.

During her breaks, she would often try and engage Mark in friendly conversation. On one such occasion, she asked 'Do you have a girlfriend, Mark?'

'No, I'm all right – but thanks for the offer.'

'I wasn't offering,' she responded indignantly.

'Oh? Okay ... never mind.' Mark never looked up during this conversation and he had employed his usual deadpan voice.

'Did you really think I was offering to be your girlfriend?'

'It was a joke, Dolly. But if you did want to be my girlfriend, I'm sure we could come to some financial settlement.'

'Mark Barker!' she exclaimed.

'I'll accept a cheque.'

Then she realised that he was joking. 'Oh, very funny, I'm sure. Do you often get girls to pay for your services?'

'That's confidential between me and them.'

'I think you live in your own little dream world, Mark,' she replied, finishing the last mouthful of her coffee and returning to her glass bowl.

Mary had been listening to this conversation from her little punch room and after Dolly had disappeared from hearing, she said 'Why do you lead her on like that? You know she takes everything literally.'

'It's just my way of coping with this boring job,' he replied.

And the job was still boring. His work on the new program was not going well. James' flowchart was full of holes. It would have been so much easier if Mark had talked to Mr Chopstick as he had a better understanding of the labour costing requirements, as well as the payroll itself. The program was written according to James' specification, but Mr Slapstick constantly found fault as it was tested.

So, he was feeling fed up again, both with his job and his love life. He was going to have to do something about it. He couldn't afford to sit around and wallow in self-pity. This was not the first time that he had built up his hopes that a brand-new job was going to turn his life around. His optimism at becoming a Trainee Surveyor had been dashed as he turned into a glorified filing clerk and dogsbody. Work Study should have been a glorious opportunity, but it had been ruined by personality clashes – and now, his aspirations to be a Computer Programmer had been crushed in little more than a year.

He had scoured the *Situations Vacant* columns in *The Sanford Echo* as well as *The Lynn News & Advertiser* and *The Eastern Daily Press*, but there was nothing to match his experience. He had no formal qualifications for Work Study nor Surveying and his programming experience was restricted to the NCR500 language, which was not popular, at least not in his vicinity. A visit to the Employment Exchange had proved fruitless. His one remaining hope was within his current employer who at least knew that he had a good track record of learning new skills, but that would probably mean returning to a Trainee status – and a reduction in pay.

As for his love life, he realised that he still didn't have the confidence to approach a stranger and chat her up as people like Dougie and Kenny might have done. Even if he was able to do that, he didn't feel that he wanted to go out with someone who could be picked up so easily. So how was he to find the right girl? He was too old to join a youth club and he wasn't the least bit interested in attending ballroom dancing classes.

He'd seen an advertisement in the local paper for a marriage bureau, but in his eyes, that was just for people who had nothing going for them and were desperate. No, he wasn't desperate ... yet!

During the early part of 1972, the country was beset with industrial action, including a minors' strike that resulted in several power cuts. When the weather turned particularly cold during February, Mark and his colleagues sometimes found themselves sitting in the dark in their overcoats and wearing gloves, waiting for power to be restored. In the Computer Room, priority had to be given to ensuring the weekly payroll was produced and all other applications were delayed. This meant that the testing of Mr Lipstick's labour costing was shelved. He was not at all happy about this and therefore decided that the project should not proceed; especially as implementing it would have involved many changes to his department's existing processes. He was also concerned that nothing had been planned for his materials costing. Mark suddenly found himself with no meaningful work again. This couldn't go on and with the company making cuts to save money, he feared for his job, for what little it was worth. His only consolation was that, he knew he would be needed to cover whenever James was absent or on holiday.

He decided that he couldn't wait around doing nothing, wondering if the axe would fall. When that week's newspapers revealed no suitable vacancies, he took another trip to the Employment Exchange. After scanning all the vacancies, he was about to leave when one of the assistants approached him. 'Can't find anything of interest?' the man asked.

'No,' Mark replied shaking his head.

'Can I ask what sort of thing you're looking for?'

'I don't really know. I'm currently working as a Computer Programmer, but I think I need to tackle something different.'

'Would it help to talk to one of our Careers Advisors? They're often good at assessing someone's strengths and pointing them towards a new career.'

Mark remembered the Careers Advisors at his old school. They were Civil Servants and suggested he should follow the same profession, which, after an interview in London, had resulted in him being rejected, but now he was desperate. 'Can't do any harm,' he said begrudgingly.

'Let me see if I can fix an appointment for you.'

A few days later, Mark found himself meeting a middle-aged man, who started by filling in a questionnaire on Mark's behalf. He then proceeded to make a few suggestions which were all totally unsuitable and Mark was starting to feel quite despondent.

'Why don't you like your current job?' the man asked.

'Well, I did to start,' Mark replied, 'but I soon started to run out of work. My predecessor had already done a lot of the work ... and ... for another thing, I think we bought the wrong machine. It's not a real computer ... not like an IBM or an ICL. I couldn't program one of them as they use different languages.'

'Can't you learn one of those languages?' the man asked.

'No one's going to take me on and train me,' Mark replied with his usual degree of pessimism.

'Couldn't you go to night school to learn? I wouldn't have thought that there are that many programmers around, so if you had the skills, it would make you more employable. You'd probably have to move to a bigger company, like a bank or insurance company but that has big advantages.'

'I'll consider it,' said Mark, but he wasn't too sure. He'd always hated his time at school and the idea of further study didn't appeal.

But he did consider it and discussed it with his friend Ray who had recently started night school. Ray was studying for an HND in Business Studies, so Mark consulted him on the possibility of joining him at the local Technical College. Ray got hold on the prospectus for the next term and Mark found a course on COBOL. Unfortunately, the evenings didn't coincide with Ray's, but Mark decided to enrol anyway. There were two months before the next course started. He knew that COBOL was more of a mainstream language and would increase his chances of a different job. And who knows? He might meet some girls.

As for that, he had another idea. His first success at dating a girl had been as a result of joining a small Badminton Club. That was where he had met Jenny who went on to break his heart. There was no way that he would return to that club in Hunstanton, but he had heard of one in Sanford. They met twice a week at Fenfield School.

So, one Tuesday night, he went along, feeling a little apprehensive. He had tried to persuade Ray to join him, but his friend had recently taken up golf and was pouring all his efforts and money into that activity.

After wandering around the school, he eventually found the sports hall. A few people were milling around, some of whom were busy putting up the nets, whilst others were chatting among themselves. Mark went up to one such group of three men and said 'Excuse me. I'm interested in joining the club.'

They looked at him blankly, but none responded immediately. Eventually, one of them said 'You probably need to speak to John. He's not here at the moment,' and then turned to his friends to continue their conversation.

Mark felt awkward. When he had joined the Hunstanton group, everyone, without exception, was pleased to see a new member, but here no one seemed the least bit interested in him – and he couldn't see any nice girls.

One stern looking woman, having finished putting up a net approached him. 'Can I help you at all?' she asked.

Mark felt like he was trespassing. 'I'm interested in joining the club,' he repeated.

The woman looked at his old-fashioned wooden racquet and bluntly said 'We haven't got any vacancies at the moment.'

There were four courts in the hall, so surely, they could easily accommodate one more member, but he felt as though he was not the kind of person they wanted in their precious club.

Just then a cheerful middle-aged man sporting a greying beard entered the hall. 'Hello,' he said. 'Have we got a new face?'

'Evening, John,' said the stern lady. 'I was just telling this gentleman that we don't have any vacancies at the moment.'

'That's very true,' said John who was obviously the person referred to earlier, 'but we'll always take a good player and we do need some new blood. Where have you been playing?'

'I played at Hunstanton. It was a few years ago,' Mark replied '... I might be a little rusty.'

'Well why don't you have a game and then we'll see. You look like a fit young man. Get your kit on and we'll sort out a game or two for you. The first night is free. After that we charge a visitor's fee of fifty pence. You can get changed just around the corner in the Boys' Changing Room.'

Mark was soon ready, and John arranged a mixed doubles for him. As the four players warmed up, Mark was painfully aware that he was totally outclassed. At the Hunstanton club, it had taken just a few visits before he was able to hold his own and by the time he left, he was probably the best player there.

After a few minutes, everyone was ready to play a game. His partner, who was probably in her mid-thirties, introduced herself as Jessie and asked him if he preferred playing mixed or doubles. This confused him. He thought he was playing mixed doubles. He certainly wasn't expecting her to leave him to play singles, so, with a puzzled look, he replied 'Mixed doubles.'

'No, I meant shall we play sides or front and back?'

'Um ... I don't mind. You chose.'

It was a disaster. He thought he might impress everyone with his powerful smash, but after a mixture of shots that hit the net or went long or wide, those that were in the court were returned with ease. When it was his turn to serve, his efforts were smashed back at him by the opposing man and the woman alike and he and Jessie lost fifteen four.

'I'm sorry,' he said to Jessie. 'I'm a little rusty.' But it was clear that he wasn't just rusty. He was incompetent.

It was a good forty-five minutes before his second game. Again, it was left to John to arrange this and John did an honourable thing in partnering him. It was plain that no one else wanted to play with him – and he wasn't enjoying it one iota. There was only one girl who might have been dating age, but when she wasn't playing, she spent the evening with a tall athletic Adonis who was beating everyone in sight.

After Mark's second game, which he lost just as badly, he sloped off to the changing rooms without saying goodnight to anyone.

A week later, Mark needed to visit the Works canteen to buy a bread roll. His mother normally gave him a packed lunch, but that day, she was short of bread, so he had to sort out his own lunch.

The office staff had strict instructions to avoid the factory workers' tea break, unless they felt brave enough to face the wrath of the Canteen Manageress.

So, Mark waited until he knew for certain that they would be finished. When he arrived, there was already a small queue ahead of him. One of these people was a young girl whom he didn't recognise from behind. Perhaps a new girl had escaped his radar, but he liked what he saw. She was quite shapely.

He recognised the man at the front of the queue as Daniel Peterson, the Metal Shop Charge Hand who had always been very helpful to Mark during his time in Work Study and Daniel, in return, had always expressed his appreciation of Mark's good efforts to introduce the incentive scheme in his area. Mark guessed that Daniel had probably used the tea break to set up one of the machines for a female operative, something he knew, frequently happened.

As Daniel turned, he saw the young lady in front of Mark. 'Hello Polly. You're looking lovely, today.'

'Polly? Looking lovely?' thought Mark. Was this the same Polly? She didn't look like Polly from behind. He heard a mumbled response. Then Daniel saw Mark. 'Hello, Mark. How's it all going?'

'Fine, thanks. You didn't say I look lovely.'

'I don't know how the girls keep their hands off you,' Derek said with a broad grin.

'Neither do I ... but they do,' he said with a shrug of his shoulders. Polly had turned and caught Mark's eye. She did look lovely. Could this really be the same girl who had walked past his desk and generated such apathy from him? She'd obviously recovered from her anorexia. Was that the right word, *recovered*? Does one recover from that? Anyway, she certainly wasn't starving herself anymore.

After she had been served and was walking by him, he made a point of giving her a smile – at least he thought it was a smile. He had often practised his smile in front of the mirror and was never sure of it. A couple of missing molars didn't help his cause. She returned his smile, but it was brief. She was obviously a shy person. Perhaps his smile was more of a leer?

He was kicking himself for not seizing the opportunity earlier. This was the girl who had expressed an interest in dating him – and he had spurned the chance. All these months of feeling sorry for himself and he could have been enjoying her company. He hoped it wasn't too late. Didn't girls like to be swept off their feet, not made to wait until the man had made up his mind? He needed to move swiftly, but how and when?

Chapter Seven

If I Could Turn Back the Hands of Time

As soon as he got home that evening, Mark dug out his father's ancient copy of the *Family Health Encyclopaedia* to look up Anorexia. There it was between *Anodyne* and *Anosmia*. *Anorexia Nervosa* was its full name. *'.. a nervous disorder of hysterical nature, chiefly occurring in adolescent girls ...'* Mark paused before reading further. *'... of hysterical nature?'* Did that mean that Polly was likely to become hysterical? He wasn't sure about dating someone like that. He continued reading. *'... loss of appetite ... loss of weight ... desire to remain young and not take responsibility for being an adult.'*

When he had last seen her, she gave every impression of looking very healthy and bright. He could only assume this illness was behind her and he decided that he did desperately want to see more of her. All he had to do now was find a way to approach her. That might be awkward. He didn't want to ask her out in front of anyone else and she shared an office with Penny, the Payroll Supervisor. Some employees were inclined to wander around the building exchanging gossip, but Polly didn't appear to be one of them and Penny seldom left the confines of her office. He couldn't phone because Penny was bound to answer the phone and she would have surely recognised his voice as he had worked with her for a few years.

Why was dating always so complicated? He was sure that Kenny didn't suffer these quandaries. He would have been straight in. But then, Mark didn't want to be like Kenny, who talked about women as though they were there for his pleasure alone.

A week went by with no opportunity presenting itself, and then another week. This was getting silly. Polly had already told Mary that she would go out with him, so all he had to do was ask her. He had managed to say 'hello' to her when she brought the clock cards in for punching and she had returned a very demure 'hello' in return. On the second such occurrence, he almost followed her out of the office to accost her in the corridor, but his courage failed him as it so often had.

Mary came in to work one morning and announced that she and her wonderful Donald were now engaged to be married. To celebrate, she invited Mark and Dolly to join her for a lunchtime drink that coming Friday. Friday was the traditional time for such celebrations. Ray had always called it Poets' day (Piss Off Early Tomorrow's Saturday).

'Are you inviting James?' Mark asked.

'No. I want to enjoy myself,' she said.

'He'll be a bit put out if he knows we're all going out and you haven't asked him.'

'I don't care. He's told me off once too many times,' Mary replied.

'Who else are you inviting?' Mark asked, hoping that Polly would join them.

'Not too many,' she replied. 'A couple from Costing; Ellie, of course; you and Dolly.'

'Anyone from Payroll?' Mark asked, not wanting to mention Polly specifically.

'I hadn't thought of them,' she replied. 'I might do.'

Mark didn't want to press the point and make his interest too obvious, but when they reached the pub on Friday, he was pleased to see Polly join them soon after his own arrival. There were eight people altogether and it was a much more jovial atmosphere than the last time Mark had attended a lunchtime celebration, but there was only one other male in the group. That was a young fellow by the name of Billy, who was drinking apple juice and contributing very little to the banter, which was dominated by the girls and included a lot of talk about clothes and shopping. Ellie said she thought Sanford was rubbish for shopping and preferred to visit King's Lynn or Norwich. Polly said she'd never been to Lynn, so Mark made a note of that fact.

After a while, Mary turned to Mark and asked for one of his jokes – but not a rude one! Mark had no intention of telling a rude one in front of Polly; at least not until he got to know her better.

'A man 'phoned Directory Enquiries and asked for the number for Interpol. The operator told him she didn't have one, but she gave the number of the local police station, suggesting that they could help. When he got through to the police station, he asked *"Do you have a number for Interpol?"* The man replied *"No, but I can give you a number for Scotland Yard. They should be able to help you."* So, he dialled the Scotland Yard number. *"Do you have a number for Interpol?"* he asked. The man replied *"Yes, it's ...."* and he gave him the number. Finally, he got through to Interpol.

"Is that Interpol?" he asked. *"Yes, how can I help you?"*

"I want to order some flowers for my Mother's birthday."

The joke was well received, and the laughter was dominated as usual by Dolly. Mark looked across to Polly to see that she wasn't actually laughing, but she was smiling, and he heard her say 'I like that one.' He decided that was some kind of success – and it was pleasingly unusual for Dolly to understand one of his jokes.

49

Throughout the session, he couldn't resist occasionally glancing over towards the new object of his affections. She really was lovely. He loved her shyness and her soft voice. Mark was developing one of his infatuations – and that usually led to disappointment. Would this one be any different?

Later that day, Mark encountered Polly at the coffee machine. His luck was at last changing. Immediately, his heart started beating faster. This was his opportunity. Could he do it?

'Hello,' he said as she bent over to retrieve her hot liquid, carefully balancing a second cup in a cardboard box.

'Oh, hello,' she replied.

'Did you enjoy yourself this lunchtime?'

'Yes. Did you?' she asked in return.

'Yeah ... great. It's just a shame that we had to come back to work. Er ... you were saying that you've never been to Lynn. I sometimes go over on a Saturday morning. Do you fancy joining me?'

'I can't tomorrow. I've already made plans.'

Of course, she had. It was very short notice, but he hadn't mentioned a day. 'How about next Saturday, then?'

'Um ... can I let you know?'

'Yes, of course you can.'

'I'd better get these coffees back before I spill them,' she said. 'I'll see you next week sometime.'

Well, at least she hadn't said 'no.' All he could do now was wait for her answer. It was a pity she hadn't lingered a little longer for a chat.

But that night, he couldn't sleep. He realised that he had made a big mistake. What would happen if she was busy the following week? Would he have to wait another week? In any case, taking someone shopping was not the best date he could have chosen. For one thing, he was due an away match that week so he would have to rush back from King's Lynn, leaving little time for them to spend together. She would probably want to spend the morning in clothes shops and there would be little time to get to know each other better. He should have just asked her out for a drink or take her to the pictures. He'd messed up again. He decided that when he did see her, whatever her answer to his invitation, he would ask her to go for a drink. He then tossed and turned, considering how he would word his request.

By three o'clock, he still couldn't sleep and decided to get up and read a magazine to take his mind off things. By three thirty, he was feeling cold and went back to bed, but was still not feeling sleepy and he continued to think about Polly and of the things he could have been doing with her if only he had approached her earlier.

This wasn't the first time that he had suffered from insomnia and he often tried little tricks to address the problem. Instead of thinking about his love life, he decided to name places in Norfolk that began with each letter of the alphabet. This was similar to a game he used to play with his brother when they were younger and still slept together. He got off to a good start – Aylsham, Brancaster, Cley, Downham Market, East Dereham, Fakenham, Great Yarmouth. Wait a minute. That meant he couldn't use Yarmouth for 'Y', so he switched to Gorleston. Then there was Happisburgh, Ingoldisthorpe ... and 'J' ... what began with 'J?' He couldn't think of anything. After an exhaustive mental trawl through place names, he decided that he would come back to that. He wouldn't be defeated. Next was the letter 'K.' Well, it had to be King's Lynn, but that just reminded him of his quandary with Polly.

After a weekend that dragged on, relieved only by one football match, he arrived at work early on Monday morning, hoping to receive a quick and positive response from Polly. It didn't happen; but then he knew that Monday was always a busy time in the Payroll Office, and he hoped that Tuesday would bring him the relief he needed. Recently, due to his shortage of work, he had become accustomed to leaving work promptly, at five o'clock, but this time, he waited a number of minutes longer, just in case. He eventually trudged off to the car park. There, he found young Billy from Costing, standing by Mark's car.

'I'd like a word with you,' Billy said, trying to sound aggressive, but failing miserably.

'What's up, mate?' Mark replied.

'I hear you asked my girlfriend out.'

'Your girlfriend? Who's that?' Mark was getting a feeling of *déjà vu*. He remembered when he had first tried to date Blodwyn, her boyfriend had phoned him and threatened him, but as he thought Blodwyn was estranged from her Gareth, he had no compunction about trying to date her. He didn't know that Polly – and it must be Polly that Billy was talking about – was dating anyone, else he wouldn't have dreamed of asking her out.

'I mean Polly, of course!'

'Sorry mate. I didn't know she had a boyfriend. Still ... no harm done, eh?'

'Just so you know,' Billy said.

'Yeah, all right, mate. Don't lose sleep over it.'

Mark was pretty sure he could have handled Billy in a fight, but violence was not going to achieve anything. It would have been so much better for all concerned if Polly had told him that she was dating Billy, but Mark decided that perhaps she did still want to go out with him and didn't know the best way of settling the matter. If that was so, all he had to do was bide his time. If only he could turn the clock back and ask her out earlier before Billy came on the scene.

The next day, Polly walked past Mark with the clock cards. He looked up and said 'Hello, Polly' and she returned the greeting with a shy smile but appearing to be no more embarrassed than usual. She did look lovely and events had not cooled his interest. She was wearing fashionable flared trousers that seemed sculpted around the tops of her thighs showing their shape in all their glory and accentuating her rounded hips. He wondered how easy it was for her to don such clothes. His own flares, which he only wore occasionally, were pretty uncomfortable around the crotch area and he certainly wouldn't wear them to sit around the office. They were designed for standing not sitting, but he had no objection to Polly looking fashionable.

Although Mark was no longer playing football for Greshams' Sunday League team, he was happy to attend their end-of-season dance at the clubhouse. Ray had wanted to go because Terry Betts, the King's Lynn Speedway star had agreed to formally open the new extension to the building. Ray was a big fan of speedway and went to Saddlebow Road as often as he could, but less so since his marriage. Mark had agreed to meet Ray and his wife at the clubhouse. He didn't like going to dances without a partner and by travelling separately, he could leave early if he got fed up with being on his own. There was always the off chance that he might meet up with a young unattached young lady of the opposite sex, but he knew this was very unlikely. This wasn't the type of event which single ladies attended.

He arrived before Ray and ordered a drink which he sipped at the bar while he had a good look around the half empty hall.

'Polly's not here, Mark,' said a voice. It was young Billy who was drinking ale from a pint glass, smoking a cigarette and hugging the bar. He was wearing a smart fawn coloured suit with a thin check pattern. The suit had wide lapels partially hiding a cream shirt with pictures of windmills dotted around, all set off with a wide brown tie. Mark often wore a suit and tie for a Saturday night out, but on this occasion, he was wearing flared denims and a tank top.

'Oh,' said Mark. 'Are you on your own?' Billy had caught him by surprise, and he didn't know what else to say.

'At the moment, yeah,' Billy replied.

'Why aren't you with Polly?'

'She'll be with her new boyfriend,' Billy said.

'You didn't last long,' Mark said, not bothering to spare Billy's feelings.

'No ... but I got what I wanted.'

Mark didn't like the sound of that but didn't want to probe any further. 'Who's the new boyfriend, then?' he asked.

'Some chap from her village.'

'Which village is that?'

'Wenford.'

Mark often played football against the Wenford village team. They were a hard-tackling team who played agricultural football. The village was surrounded by agricultural land, so it followed really. There was a story that they had a supporter, an elderly lady, who stood on the touchline and sometimes used a brolly to trip any dangerous looking wingers. Mark had never seen this happen, but he believed the story to be true.

He wondered if he had ever played against this new boyfriend. In any case, it looked like he had lost out yet again and wondered if the new chap would last as long as the last, but what could he do about it? Somehow, he needed to get to know Polly better and that wasn't going to be easy. Ideally, he needed to move in the same social circles. There was just one problem with that – Mark didn't have much of a social circle.

Ray and his wife turned up after the grand opening ceremony. In fact, the extension had been open for several weeks, but a formal opening was still required.

"You've missed the opening,' Mark told them when he last espied them.

'Damn,' said Ray.

'But the guest of honour is still here,' Mark said, pointing out a gentleman talking to the Social Secretary.

'I'm going to get his signature on this programme,' Ray said.

'When you get back, I've got something to tell you,' Mark said and turned to talk to Valerie. 'He's not going to be happy,' he said to her.

'Why, what have you done?' she asked.

'You'll see in a minute,' he replied and watched as Ray obtained his signature.

Ray looked angry when he returned to the pair. 'Who the Hell is Peter Padgett?' he asked, waving his Speedway programme in front of them. 'I just thought Terry looked different without his leathers.

'That's what I wanted to tell you,' said Mark. 'Terry Betts couldn't make it, so at the last minute they asked Peter to do the honours.'

'But who is he?'

'He's the captain of Sanford Football Club. You've got quite a unique signature there.' Mark was loving this.

'If he's a footballer, why did he sign my Speedway Programme?'

'Well, you asked him to. He didn't have to, did he? I think it's very nice of him' and he and Valerie laughed at her husband.

Ray did eventually see the funny side. He wasn't the kind to stay angry for long and the three enjoyed the rest of the evening, but with Mark no further on with his love life and feeling even more mystified about the enigmatic Polly.

Chapter Eight

When Love Slips Away

'No, I don't get it,' said Dolly. 'Is the funny bit because Elvis keeps falling in the swimming pool?'

'No,' said Mary who had understood Mark's joke. 'The funny bit is when he says to his wife *"I can't help falling in ... love."* There's a comma between *falling in* and *love*.

'No, I still don't get it.'

Mark said 'It's the title of one of his biggest hits – *Can't Help Falling in Love* – without a comma! Haven't you heard it?'

'No, I don't like Elvis Presley.'

'I'm wasted here,' Mark responded. 'I try to bring some sunshine into your lives and it just goes over your head.' He hated it when he had to explain a joke. It took all the pleasure out of it.

'I liked it,' said Mary.

'Thank you, Mary. So, what sort of music do you listen to?' he asked Dolly, who was just taking a short break while James was busy sorting out a problem on the computer.

'I like Bob Dylan,' she replied.

'Really ...' said Mark, '... even though you can't understand a word he says? What does it mean when he sings ... *the aunts are my friends?*' Mark sang the last phrase in a nasally drawl as his impression of the singer.

'It's ... *the answer, my friends,*' she said.

'If you say so,' he replied, 'but it could be anything. Then there's that other song of his - *Hey Mr Tangerine Man*. What's that about?'

'It's *Tambourine Man,*' she said indignantly. 'You can hear it clearly when The Byrds sing it.' Mark knew that, of course, but he wanted a little fun at Dolly's expense.

Just then, James called her name from the computer room and she returned to her work. James would not have heard their conversation because of the noise inside the computer room, but he disapproved of idle gossip, even though he would join in when it suited him.

'You're horrible to her,' Mary said from her adjacent room. 'And you can talk about lyrics. You're into this soul music stuff. I was listening to *In the Midnight Hour* the other night, and he sings about his *love comes tumbling down*. What's that mean? How can love come tumbling down?'

'You can blame the BBC for that,' he said. 'They had to change the words, or the record was going to get banned. It was originally *That's when my pants come tumbling down,* which was felt to be too rude for BBC listeners, so the writers changed it.'

'You're making it up,' she said – and she was right of course.

'Oh, God,' said Mark. 'She shouldn't be bending over the printer in those hot pants. You can see what she's had for breakfast.' He'd never understood that phrase, but he liked using it.

'Oh, my word,' said Mary. 'It's not a pretty sight, is it? Mind you, I thought you might have liked hot pants. Most men do.'

'You can call me old-fashioned, but I don't think they have any place in an office environment,' he said. Dolly's hot pants were bright red and formed part of a trouser suit – with shorts instead of trousers! It was the latest fashion. Mark had seen several women's fashions come and go since leaving school. The most popular of these was the mini skirt, which hadn't completely died out even in 1972. Then came the maxi-skirt, which he considered to be a terrible idea. Not only could a bloke not see her legs, but in wet weather, a woman's skirt could easily soak up a few inches of moisture from wet pavements. Fortunately, from the point of view of a 'leg and bum' man, the fashion hadn't lasted very long – probably to the relief of road sweepers, whose jobs may have been in jeopardy. The maxi-skirt was followed by the midi, which was neither one thing nor the other and was even less successful.

Around the start of the seventies, women and men began wearing flared trousers and Mark wondered if these were to be succeeded by these hot pants. To be successful, they had to be worn by a woman with the right legs – and that didn't include Dolly; perhaps not even Polly, since she was rather too shapely in the rear, although Mark quite fancied the idea of judging the real thing for himself, because he was, by now, totally besotted with Polly, to the extent that he had lost interest in trying to date anyone else.

He took another little look at Dolly's hot pants, just to make sure he didn't agree with them.

For over a year, Ray had become very serious about the game of golf. Mark thought he was being very amusing when he asked Ray what position he played, but serious golfers don't appreciate fun being made of their interest.

With the football season over, Ray persuaded Mark to try a game. He started by taking him down to a local playing field to give him lessons in how to hit the ball. By the end of the session, Mark felt ready to try the real thing, so they agreed to meet one Saturday morning at the car park outside Fakenham Golf Club. This was a municipal course, so there was no need to worry about membership. Ray had applied to join the King's

Lynn club, but there was a very long waiting list, so in the meantime, he was honing his talents at Fakenham.

For a beginner like Mark, this course had the advantage that it was only nine holes long. One disadvantage was that it crossed the racecourse, making several areas 'out of bounds.'

Ray had his own clubs and trolley, but Mark needed to hire his. He decided that he would save money by not hiring the trolley, a decision he came to regret by the time he was halfway round the course.

It was a warm day and after he had averaged eight shots per hole, he was starting to get bad tempered and wanted to hurl the damn clubs into the rough and drive home. To make it worse, Ray made it look so easy and managed a couple of 'pars.' Mark thought he was going to match him when he placed one tee shot on the green of a par three hole, but he then took four more shots to hole out. By the end of the morning, he decided that golf was not his sport and he left Ray to play a second round of nine on his own.

Tennis was Mark's summer sport, but that was proving problematic. The group of people from the office who normally played with him on a Friday evening were thinning out. His cousin George had left the company; his old friend Gary had married Jean and they were both busy building their own house as part of a self-build group from within Greshams; as was Dave Taylor, one of the other tennis stalwarts from previous years. That just left John Woodston, an unreliable Contracts Manager, and Wanda, who refused to hit the ball unless it was within her reach. They needed some fresh blood and at least one more female. Mark decided he would tackle Polly about joining them, even if it meant bringing her latest boyfriend, whoever he was.

He now understood that she didn't leave her office that often, but he was learning when those few occasions were. She wasn't one to look for the usual office gossip, so she tended to venture out for one of three reasons – one to visit the ladies. That was no good to Mark unless he was to meet her on the way. Secondly, she seemed to take turns at fetching coffee with her colleague, Penny; probably twice a day at most and not to any defined pattern like some employees, since he had never seen her at the same time twice. However, she did visit the canteen regularly and because of the factory workers fixed break, this was usually just after that break.

So, one Friday morning, he decided that he fancied a bar of chocolate to supplement his packed lunch. Sure enough, he saw her heading in that direction about twenty yards ahead of him. 'Hello Polly,' he called just as she was about to enter the factory building. She turned and waved but carried on her way. 'Wait for me,' he called, but she had already entered the building. He ran after her and caught her along the corridor. 'How are you?' he asked trying not to sound out of breath, which he was, not so much from the effort of catching her, but more from the fact that his heart was beating faster and he was feeling a little apprehensive as he always did when he wanted to ask a girl out.

'I'm fine,' she replied in that lovely quiet manner that appealed so much to him. 'How about you?' she asked.

'A lot better for seeing you, thank you.' He hoped that didn't sound too cheesy, but it was a line he often used when he wanted to harmlessly flirt with any of the married women in the office. One of the workers from the factory floor called out to her. Mark felt a pang of jealousy, but then realised that if she was responsible for the Works payroll, she would come into contact with many of them. By now, they'd both entered the canteen and he'd lost his first chance.

He was pleased to see Polly order two bread rolls and an iced bun; a clear indication that her anorexia was well and truly behind her. When she had finished paying for her food, he said 'Hang on a minute. I'll walk back with you.' He quickly ordered his chocolate and opened the canteen door for her.

'Do you play tennis?' he asked. He really wanted to ask her out properly, but he didn't know how her love life was situated. He certainly didn't want another boyfriend trying to warn him off.

'No, I'm useless at all sports. Where do you play?'

'We go down the council courts after work on a Friday evening, but we're short of players these days. Last week, there was only John Woodston and Wanda. We need some fresh blood.'

'And Wanda's leaving, isn't she?' said Polly.

'Is she? She hasn't said anything to me,' Mark replied. Wanda wasn't the greatest loss in the world, but now they were down to just two – and John was unreliable.

'Are you coming to the carnival, tomorrow?' she asked.

'I wasn't sure whether to or not. Are you going?' He wondered if she wanted him to go and meet her there.

'Yes, I'm taking part. I'm dressing up as Lady Guinevere. My dad's company have a float. Their theme is King Arthur and his Knights, but there are very few ladies at his place, so he asked me.'

'In that case, of course I'll go. When does it start?'

'The parade leaves the marketplace at eleven o'clock, then goes down the High Street, down London Road, past the station and onto the rec., where there will be roundabouts and various stalls. It should be good. I hope you'll come.'

They were back in the office block and Polly didn't wait for his response, but he knew that he would be there.

During the afternoon, Mark took a turn at fetching coffees from the vending machine on the first floor. He would have preferred a cup of tea, but the tea out of the machine bore very little resemblance to real tea and very few people drank it. The coffee itself was much improved from the earlier vending machine that he had first encountered in 1965, but still barely drinkable. As he pressed a button for James' black coffee, he was joined at the machine by young Billy, who commented on Mark's ingenious tray. It was a piece of plywood with four circular holes where he was inserting the cups. A shaped handle made the whole thing resemble a large table tennis bat with holes in it. 'Yes, James made it. He used to be a joiner before he took a job in the office. Saves a lot of spills,' and he pointed to the various stains on the carpet around the machine.

'Perhaps I'll ask him to make me one,' Billy said. Mark always thought Billy was a little too cocky for his age. He didn't seem that way when he first joined the company. Maybe that's the effect dating Polly had had on him. 'I hear Polly's no longer going out with that chap from Wenford,' he added. 'If you're still interested ...'

Of course, Mark was still interested – and didn't she encourage him to go to the carnival? He thought that his chance had slipped away, but now he had another opportunity.

He was so pleased with himself that he wasn't looking where he was going and almost tripped up going down the stairs. How embarrassing would that have been to spill a tray of drinks down the stairs?

At his desk, Dolly joined him and Mary for an unofficial tea break.

'I've got a joke for you for a change,' she said. 'My mate Lenny told me he's suffering from Ambrosia ... he forgot that he doesn't like rice pudding.' No one actually laughed.

'Come on,' she said. 'You always expect me to laugh at your jokes. I think that's quite funny!'

'It is very funny,' said Mark. 'In fact, I'm going to make a note of it to tell my mate next time I see him' and Mark wrote something on a piece of paper.

'So why aren't you laughing?' she demanded.

'I'm laughing inside,' he replied, 'but I've hurt my chuckle muscle and so I'm holding back for fear of straining it.'

'There's no such thing,' she said.

'There is. I heard Ken Dodd talking about it. You have to exercise it regularly or you do yourself an injury if you get out of practice. Mary thought the joke was funny, didn't you, Mary?'

'Do you know, I thought it was the best joke I've heard for ages,' she said. 'It was hilarious.'

'You're all making fun of me,' Dolly said and went back to the computer room in a huff.

'Rice pudding reminds me of those horrible school dinners,' Mary said.

Mark responded. 'Yeah, we used to get a small blob of jam in the middle to make it more palatable, but semolina was even worse. What is that? It might have been better if we were given two blobs of jam, but no, it had to be a single blob. I hated school.'

But he didn't want to dwell on unhappy memories. He was going to get a date with Polly at long last.

It was a glorious day for the carnival. He decided that he wouldn't watch the start in town. If he did, he would then have to follow it through town, taking him further and further away from his parked car. In any case, Polly would be busy with the rest of King Arthur's entourage so he wouldn't get a chance to speak to her. He parked his car near to the rec. and wandered around the stalls and the fairground. That was when he saw Blodwyn. It had been a few years since he'd last seen her. He often thought about her and the odd fantasy sometimes helped him get to sleep at night.

She was wearing a tight blue sweater and flares. He thought that she had put on a little weight since he'd last seen her and she looked like her thighs were about to burst her trousers. He remembered that some unkind people had given her the nickname of 'Old Thunder-thighs,' which he'd always thought was very unfair, although she only had herself to blame for wearing skimpy mini-skirts and now, perhaps tight flares were a mistake as well, but he still enjoyed looking at the shape of her impressive buttocks. At another time, he might be tempted to approach her and try his luck, but now he only had thoughts for Polly. In any case, Blodwyn was arm in arm with another man. Looking at her now, Mark still had regrets that he'd been unsuccessful with her.

As he wandered around the stalls, he thought about which one might give him the best chance of winning a cuddly toy for his new love. He'd never been successful at anything involving shooting, but perhaps knocking some cans down would best suit his talents. Then he'd ask her to accompany him to the pictures – or just go for a drink so they could get to know each other better. Where were those floats? They should have been there by now. He was beginning to wonder if perhaps he should have seen them start off in town. What if she hadn't turned up for whatever reason? The old doubts returned. He felt something had gone wrong.

But then, the first floats did appear. The theme for the carnival was medieval history and the lead display was a group of crusaders with fake armour and tall shields with red crosses on them. Someone had gone to a lot of trouble. Further down, Polly was seated on a 'throne' next to King Arthur and her float was surrounded by a motley collection of 'knights.' The effect would have been more impressive had the farm cart not been drawn by a noisy tractor. Polly was wearing a conical headdress which had a scarf hanging down over her shoulders. She was wearing a long green dress of many layers that left no part of her body exposed. How authentic it was, he didn't know. After all, the tales of King Arthur were only myths handed down since who knows when. Nevertheless, he could imagine knights of old seeking her favour – as he intended to do as soon as she came down off that cart. He resisted the urge to join the crowds around the floats and stood back a little way.

It seemed an age before all the floats arrived and were parked up. No one seemed to know what to do once everyone was assembled, but eventually, people starting to disembark their craft and mingle with friends. Polly and King Arthur were among the last to dismount and after a few more minutes, he could see Polly looking around the crowd. She looked in his direction and then waved. He waved back and gathering up her skirts, she headed towards him. It was really happening. She had sought him out from among all these people, He was in ecstasy. He'd finally got the timing right.

With her flowing dress, she couldn't walk very fast over the field and Mark headed towards her, pushing his way past a small group until she was in speaking distance. 'Hello Polly,' he said.

'Oh ... hello,' she said in surprise as she sped past him into the arms of her latest boyfriend, a man with long flowing blonde hair. A cheesecloth shirt opened wide to show off a medallion that said all Mark needed to know. He turned to see them walking off arm in arm as his heart dropped down into his shoes. He closed his eyes and swore beneath his breath. After the way she had brushed past him, he knew he had never really been in with a chance. She wanted someone who looked like this new man and Mark could never live up to that image.

He suddenly wanted to get away and headed for his car. He'd spent the morning cleaning it especially to impress Polly, but it had all been a waste of effort. He drove off towards his home, but at a crossroads, he suddenly decided to head towards the town centre. He had told his mother that he might not be home for tea, so he didn't want to return so quickly.

Whenever he felt down in the dumps, he would treat himself to a new record. It didn't always cheer him up, but the right song could give him another reason to wallow in pathos.

At the record store, he found they had a sale on, and he bought a copy of *When Love Slips Away* by Dee Dee Warwick. He'd never heard it, but the title sounded apt and Dee Dee could always be relied upon. When he got home, he would play it alongside another record of hers – *Another Lonely Saturday.*

Chapter Nine

Hot Pants

Mark was very pleased with his new purchase. The record was a few years old, so had probably already been deleted from the catalogues, which was why it would have been in a sale. Although the title *When Love Slips Away* mirrored his recent experience, it was a nice little toe tapper with a soulful message, whereas *Another Lonely Saturday* was more mournful and was actually a flipside. But he decided he didn't want another lonely Saturday, so after tea and having played his new record a second time, he headed out to Dersingham to see if Ray and Valerie were at home. He hadn't arranged anything with them, but Ray had often said 'pop in whenever you want' – so he did.

Even if they weren't at home, at least he'd taken himself out of the house for a while and the journey gave him time to think about his next move. He would forget all about Polly and direct his thoughts elsewhere. If she had ever really wanted to go out with him, she surely wouldn't have switched between three different boyfriends in as many months.

He did have a little idea. It involved peppermint creams.

Mark's friends were at home, but they were just on their way out for a trip up the coast road to Hunstanton and he was asked to join them.

After a very pleasant stroll along the promenade and a bag of chips near the pleasure beach, they headed back to a nice little pub in Snettisham where they sat in the beer garden, enjoying the last of a warm summer evening.

Mark told them about Dolly's rice pudding joke which failed to have them rolling around in laughter, but it did prompt Ray to tell a few new jokes that he had heard at work and suddenly the world didn't seem so bad to Mark. But he did have to find a girlfriend. It had been almost a year since he had last had sex and was worried that he might get out of practice. Not only that, but he would soon be twenty-four years old and life was passing him by. Most of his contemporaries were now married and he didn't even have a girl.

On his way to work on Monday morning, he called in at his favourite sweet shop. He had developed a taste for peppermint creams one day after James had offered him one to take away the taste of the awful coffee. The sweet shop in question also sold newspapers, magazines, cigarettes and tobacco. But the biggest appeal to Mark was the young lady who worked there.

She had long blonde hair that must have taken a lot of brushing in the morning. It reached halfway down her back. She was a little on the short side and wore spectacles that had very large lenses so that they didn't obscure her piercing blue eyes, but they did partially cover her beautiful rosy cheeks. Some might have described her as a little overweight, but to Mark's point of view, she had a delightful figure – built for comfort not speed as someone had once said to him. Her waist was not particularly small, but because she had wide hips and an enticingly shaped bosom, she came close enough to an hour-glass shape to be pleasant to look at. And just to complete the picture, she wore a mini-skirt – not too short, since her thighs were above average size, but short enough for Mark to tell that they were very shapely.

So far, he had visited the shop just three times and the only words he had spoken to her were to order his sweets. He figured that she was unlikely to go out with a stranger who had just turned up at her workplace. He would have to visit regularly and let her gradually become familiar with his face. Before entering the shop this time, he had already decided to break the ice by exchanging pleasantries about the weather, but unfortunately, he was served by another more mature lady, so he left disappointed.

He could have ordered enough sweets to last him the week, but by asking for just a half-pound, he could return in a few days. On the other hand, if he had asked for a quarter pound, she might think him a cheapskate and that wouldn't do.

He knew she didn't wear a ring, and as pretty as she was, her size and the fact that she wore spectacles might deter other suitors, so he felt he had a reasonable chance with her. He would return in a day or so.

Dolly was wearing her hot pants again. Mark always found this distracting, especially when she bent over the console in the computer room. During the morning, James told Dolly that he wanted to test an amendment to a sort program, so he asked her to take a break. She fetched some drinks and sat at the desk opposite Mark and read a magazine.

After a while, she stood up to pull down her pants which had risen up. At that precise moment, Mark looked up from his work and found himself staring at her crotch area. He quickly averted his gaze, but he was painfully aware that Dolly had seen him looking. He hadn't meant to. It was almost a reflex action. He looked across to see that she had sat down again but was still staring at him. He needed to quickly say something amusing to avert his embarrassment, but nothing came. He went back to his work, but he could still feel her eyes bearing down on him.

After a few more painful minutes of this, James called her back. She didn't move immediately, but eventually, she stood up and moved to the door of the machine room, all the time still staring. Suddenly, Mark thought of a witty response and looked up ... but no, the moment had gone, and he once again found himself returning Dolly's gaze. She was making him feel like some kind of dirty old man. It was her fault. She shouldn't wear such clothes.

As she disappeared from view, he closed his eyes in exasperation, then walked over to Mary's punch room and told her what had just happened. 'I wouldn't worry about it,' she said. 'She should expect people to look at her if she wears pants like that.'

'I know, but you should have seen the look she gave me. I had a great line if only I had said it straight away. I should have said "Oh ... airing your views again, Dolly" If I'd have said that at the time, we could have just laughed it off.'

'Don't worry about it,' said Mary, smiling at his witticism. 'Anyway, I've got a bit of gossip for you. My lovely Donald has a mate who went to a dance at Wenford a couple of weeks ago and he said that Polly had gotten drunk and was taking on all comers in the back of a van.'

'What do you mean ... fighting?'

'No, silly ... letting them ... you know ... have a turn at her. Apparently, she's always like that when she's had a few drinks.'

'I don't believe it,' said Mark. 'Polly's such a quiet young thing. She wouldn't she?' He then remembered Billy's statement that he'd got what he wanted out the relationship – and she had just had three boyfriends in quick succession.

'It's common knowledge in her village,' Mary added. 'Her brother knows all about it, but he feels powerless to do anything.'

'Well, in her defence,' said Mark. 'I know one drink and I'm anybody's ... trouble is, no one wants me.'

Mark now felt a huge sense of relief that he hadn't ended up dating her. He remembered the time that he had been going out with Maggie and she phoned him to warn him that she may have contracted a dose of the clap. It was a false alarm, but that was the point when he had ceased the relationship and never wanted to date another girl who had multiple partners. Maggie seemed positively innocent compared with what Mary had just described of Polly. Did that mean she was a nymphomaniac? Or was it just a drink problem? Either way, he was better off out of it.

In any case, he now had another target for his amorous needs, and he couldn't wait for his next visit to the sweet shop.

The next day, he was sorely tempted to drop into the sweet shop again but decided that he mustn't make his campaign too obvious to the young lady. However, he would try again on Wednesday.

Later, when Polly walked past his desk with the clock cards for punching, he looked up to receive a polite smile. He watched her as she spoke to Mary. Could this sweet young thing really have allowed so many men to thrust their attentions on her in the back of a van? He tried to imagine the scene and it left him feeling dejected. He decided it didn't matter. The way she had swept past him on her way to her new boyfriend on Saturday had convinced him that she wasn't interested in Mark. It wouldn't serve any purpose to maintain an interest, not when there was another who might appreciate him.

Nevertheless, he would still be polite to her. As she turned from Mary, he asked 'Did you have a good time at the carnival?'

'It was all right,' Polly replied, 'but it wasn't a lot of fun up on that cart with everyone staring at me. I couldn't go anywhere until we reached the park, but the fair was good fun. How about you?'

'Not my sort of thing if I'm honest. I didn't stay long. I needed to get a couple of things in town.' He wasn't going to tell her that he only went to see her and went off in a sulk.

During the afternoon, James disappeared for a while. When he returned, he told Mark that Mr Tollet wanted to see him. This was the Company Secretary who had joined when Mark's cousin George had left. He was James' boss and had previously worked at the head office of the new owners and so far, Mark had never spoken to him.

'Me?' said Mark. 'Why does he want to see me?'

'He'll tell you himself,' James replied.

Mark was worried. He could think of only one reason why James' boss would want to speak to him.

'Now?'

'Yes, he's expecting you right away.'

Mr Tollet's door was closed as it usually was. Mark gathered himself before a nervous knock and gently opened the door. 'You wanted to see me?' he said apprehensively.

'Yes ... come in. Take a seat. I'm sorry we've never had a chance to talk before.'

Mr Tollet was a tall austere looking gentleman. He had dark hair and a permanent five o'clock shadow and dark sideburns. Mark imagined him playing the role of Mr Rochester in *Jane Eyre*.

The Secretary didn't waste time on niceties. He came straight to the point. 'I understand you are not fully occupied in your work.'

'Well,' Mark replied, going on the defensive, 'sometimes more than others.' He was going to be made redundant; he knew it. He'd heard of so many other employees at Greshams who had faced a similar meeting and he also knew that business was not improving. 'But I am required to cover when James is on holiday. No one else can provide that cover.' He was scrabbling to justify his existence, but he knew he had a weak case. His predecessor was still on the premises, so at a pinch, he could provide cover. In a way, Mark almost welcomed an end to his misery.

'We can't afford to pay employees to sit around just in case they're required.' Mark could see what Mr Tollet was going to say next. It all seemed so unfair. 'So, I've come up with two possible solutions.'

'One of which is to make me redundant,' thought Mark. So, what was the other one?

'We could transfer you to head office ... still as a programmer,' said Mr Tollet, but he didn't sound too positive about this idea.

Mark replied 'But I understand they have a Century computer. That doesn't use the same language.'

'Well, you can be trained. I understand you have an aptitude for programming.'

'And that would mean moving to Oxfordshire,' Mark said.

'Yes, that's true. Where do you live?' Mr Tollet asked.

'New Street.'

'No, I mean do you own your own place?'

'Um ... no, I live with my mum and dad – my parents.' Why did he add the last words? Mr Tollet knew that 'mum and dad' meant parents. He was not feeling comfortable about this meeting. It looked like he could go and work in Oxfordshire - or be made redundant. Neither option appealed.

'But there is another option,' said Mr Tollet. He steepled his hands before proceeding and Mark braced himself for the bad news.

'I understand you worked in the Work Study department for a couple of years. Did you ever do any O&M studies?'

That was not what Mark expected to hear and was taken aback. 'Er ... no, not really. There was originally the intention to do more in that way once the incentive scheme was established, but it never really happened. As a department we did a few studies to improve productivity, but we had mixed success ... and as I say, the incentive scheme took precedence.'

'Well, to put you in the picture, we are seconding Tom Winbush-Smythe from head office to look at the various procedures at Greshams. He'll be analysing the flow of various documents and trying to streamline a number of processes that haven't been touched for many years. It's time that Greshams were brought into the seventies. Tom is going to need some help with all that and you've been at the company a number of years, so your company knowledge and your proven analytical skills will be invaluable to him. Of course, if you prefer the programming option, I can look into that for you, but performing O&M work will mean you stay at Sanford.'

Mark was dumfounded. This had all come completely out of the blue and was something he had never considered as a career option. If nothing else, it might buy him some time until he had completed his COBOL course.

'Right then,' Mark replied. 'When will all this start?'

'If you're interested, I'll let Tom know. He will be paying a visit on Thursday. You can meet him then and the two of you can take it from there. For now, you will continue to report to James and keep your current desk.'

Mark wanted to ask about money but decided that should wait for another time.

'So, what exactly is O&M?' Mary asked. She had pummelled Mark as soon as he returned from his meeting with Mr Tollet.

'Organisation and Methods,' interjected James.

'Yeah, but what does that mean?' she asked again, still looking at Mark.

'Well ...' said Mark, wondering how best to make it sound impressive '... in a way, it's a bit like Work Study, but it covers the whole gamut of management and control of the whole organisation, right from the lowliest punch operator, to the top programmer. Work Study is concerned with the methodology and efficiency of a process, including aspects such as ergonomics, productivity and work measurement and is most usually associated with manual tasks. But it will not just cover the operative, it will also ensure machinery and even space is optimised.

'O&M is all that and more. It encompasses administrative issues, such as the flow of documentation through an organisation.'

'So, what will you be doing?' she asked.

'I have absolutely no idea,' he said with a grin.

'Is it the same as time and motion?' asked Dolly who was still acting a little frostily towards Mark.

'Time and motion is only a small part of it,' he replied.

'Cause I imagine you'd be quite good at studying people,' she said.

Mark didn't reply.

The next morning, he called into the sweet shop on his way to work. Once again, to his chagrin, the young lady was not serving. She was busy stacking some newly delivered cigarettes. Mark was second in the queue behind an elderly gentleman who was paying his paper bill and querying the amount thus holding up proceedings. After a while, a small queue built up behind Mark and he wondered about abandoning his visit until the next day.

The lady who was serving, called to the young girl. 'Janine! Can you help serve? There's a bit of a queue forming.'

Mark couldn't believe his luck. She was going to serve him. And now he knew her name.

'What can I get you?' she asked.

'I'd like a half pound of mint creams, please,' he replied, trying to think of what to say to engage her in conversation. He didn't want to mention the weather as it was a horrible day and he didn't want to say anything of a negative nature.

'The Clarnico or the loose?' she asked.

'Oh, the loose, please.' Buying the loose ones meant better value for money.

She reached up to the second shelf to retrieve the jar and Mark was able to admire her calves. He always thought you could tell a lot from a girl's calves. If they were skinny, the chances were that the girl would be skinny too. If they were fat, she was likely to be overweight, but Janine's were perfect – not too fat and not too skinny – and a delightful hint of muscle to give a little shape.

As she poured the sweets onto the scales, he said 'I like my mint creams. The coffee out of our machine at work isn't very nice, so I always have a mint to take away the taste. I get through quite a lot.'

She smiled politely, but didn't reply, except to ask for payment. Mark proffered a pound note. He thought that might impress her more than a load of loose change.

His visit to the shop had set him up for the day to come.

Later in the day, when they were alone, Mary asked him 'What do you really think about this new job?'

Mark sighed. 'I don't know. It doesn't sound like a lot of fun, but I can't go on like this. Much more of this and I'm going to wind up an idiot – and Dolly's the idiot I'm going to wind up!'

'Have you looked around for other jobs? 'Mary asked.

'I've seen a job in a Space Hopper shop. Can you picture me as a bouncer?'

Chapter Ten

Sweet Love

That evening when he arrived home, Mark was excited to see that the new television had been delivered. The family had been discussing what they could do about the old set which had been unreliable for some time. Mark's sister had been in possession of a colour set for several months and he and the rest of his family often conjured up an excuse to visit. On Mark's first such visit, he had been blown away by the wonders of a wildlife documentary about the Camargue in the South of France.

More and more people were switching to colour. One of his aunts had started renting a new colour set and had been boasting about it to his mother at the Bingo. Mrs Barker enquired at Radio Rentals and came back with a figure that was achievable if the family all chipped in with a monthly contribution. At first, Mark was reluctant to agree, feeling that this was what he was already paying his housekeeping money for, but when he saw which programmes, he had been missing on BBC2, he decided to agree. A new aerial was required to receive the UHF signal and he was compelled to contribute to that as well, placing a huge stress on his finances.

His mother gave him a quick demonstration of the features of the new set. Like any television set of the day, it took a little while to warm up, but once this had happened, there was a knob on the front that could be pushed to set it to a 'standby' mode similar to today's appliances, but without a remote control. By pulling the knob out, the picture and sound were available almost instantly.

He grabbed a copy of the Radio Times to see what delights were in store for that evening and immediately switched on to get the last few overs of the first Test between England and Australia. He didn't usually bother to watch the cricket in black and white, but this was suddenly much more interesting. Normally, the programmes on BBC2 didn't start until 7.35, and then it was only the *Open University* followed by a lengthy news programme, but at nine o'clock, it was *Pot Black* – in glorious colour! Meanwhile, *Mission Impossible* would be appearing on BBC1, soon after *Nationwide*. Even mundane programmes such as *Nationwide* seemed more exciting in colour and the enhanced picture quality made watching so much more enjoyable. Over the next few weeks, Mark and his family spent more time than usual in front of their new 'friend.' No one was interested in watching old black and white films anymore.

It was still summer, so he would have to wait several weeks before he could watch any football. Viewers in Sanford and much of West Norfolk were unable to watch *Match of the Week* from Anglia TV. Instead, programs were transmitted from Yorkshire Television, which meant Mark's family could not witness the local teams such as Norwich City, Ipswich Town and Colchester United. Yorkshire TV' s equivalent programme included such as Leeds United, Bradford City, Huddersfield Town and the Sheffield clubs.

On Thursday, Mark was introduced to Mr Winbush-Smythe. Despite his double-barrelled name, the O&M expert did not have an upper-class accent like most of the other employees seconded from head office. In fact, he had a gentle West Country burr not totally dissimilar to a Norfolk accent. He was much older than Mark had expected, again in contrast to the other gentlemen from head office. His rotund shape sported a fine head of white hair on top of a jovial red face. He was introduced as Mr Winbush-Smythe with no mention of his Christian name. Mark wondered if that meant that was how he was meant to address him, just as no one addressed Mr Tollet by his first name.

The Company Secretary explained that Mr Winbush-Smythe would only visit for a few days each month and would therefore not have his own office; at least not until one became available. Mark wondered if that meant someone else was due to be made redundant; a frequent occurrence in the current climate at Greshams.

Mr Winbush-Smythe talked about doing some critical path analysis work on several processes, at which point, Mr Tollet lost interest and told them both to take themselves off to Mark's office. Mark wondered if he was expected to be expert on critical path analyses. He'd heard the term, but that was it and as soon as he and the O&M man got together, it was plain that he had been expected to know a lot more about the subject.

Realising this, Mr Winbush-Smythe set Mark to reading up about it in an O&M manual that he produced from an ageing briefcase.

Mark's mentor seemed to have other work to pursue while Mark was left with his studies. He was already thinking ahead to when he started his COBOL course at college during September. O&M did not fill him with any enthusiasm as a career.

Mr Winbush-Smythe seemed easily distracted whenever Dolly moved about the office, despite no longer wearing her hot pants. Dolly tended to have an effect on men of a certain age, but Mark was content to pursue less flashy young ladies like Janine. He decided that he would visit the sweet shop the next morning to further his acquaintance. He was already working on what he might say to her – provided, of course, that she was the one to serve him.

Mr Winbush-Smythe occupied the spare desk that was used by Dolly and Mary when they had their coffee breaks, so they resorted to sitting close to Mark's desk. The atmosphere in the office became very subdued due to the presence of the newcomer. Anyone from head office had this affect. Employees always felt they were being spied upon.

When, after a few hours, he disappeared for a meeting, the girls opened up at last. 'What's that you're reading?' Dolly asked Mark, at last back on speaking terms with him.

'It's an O&M manual. I'm meant to be learning all about critical path analysis.'

'There's one down our road,' said Mary. 'That needs to be analysed. Someone's going to hurt themselves one day, but the council don't do nothin' about it.'

'You're talking about the footpath down your road?' Mark asked.

'Yeah.'

'And it's critical, is it?'

'I think so.'

'Okay,' Mark said. 'I'll make a note for Mr Winbush-Smythe. I'm sure he'll look into it.'

'We've got one down our road,' said Dolly, joining in the levity. 'There's a loose manhole cover.'

'That definitely needs looking into,' Mark said, and they all had a chuckle as though to let off steam after the earlier subdued atmosphere.

'He's a bit of a dirty ol' man,' said Dolly. 'He keeps staring at my boobies.'

Mark wanted to say that he wasn't too surprised as she always wore provocative clothing. Instead, he said 'I think he has a shared interest in your guitar playing.'

'I don't play the guitar,' she replied with a puzzled look on her face.

'Oh,' said Mark. 'Perhaps I've got the wrong end of the stick. He told me that he wanted to twang your G string. I thought you only got G strings on a guitar.' In truth, Mark didn't know exactly what a G string was, but he knew it was something to do with women's underwear.

The next day, Mark was able to visit the sweet shop again and implement his plan to further his acquaintance with the lovely Janine. Of course, it would all go wrong if she didn't serve him, but he was in luck. As usual, he ordered his half pound of mints.

'That will be loose?' she asked rhetorically as she reached for the sweet jar from the shelf. He must have made some impression on her because she had remembered his preference. He was feeling very pleased with himself.

'Looks like a fine day,' he said. 'I hope it stays that way. I want to play tennis after work this evening. Do you play?'

'No, I can't play tennis,' she replied.

That was not the answer he had hoped for. He could have pressed her for a reason, but that might have sounded too pushy. Instead, he asked 'Do you play any sports?'

'Yes, I play Hockey.'

'Who do you play for?' he asked.

'The High School Old Girls,' she said, pouring the sweets onto the scales.

'Oh, the HOGS,' he said, remembering the affectionate term Melody had used for her team. 'My ex-girlfriend played for them – name of Melody Morris?'

'No, I don't know her. I only joined last season.'

Yes, she probably last played for them the season before.' He handed over another one-pound note, pleased to have said 'ex-girlfriend,' but it didn't produce any sort of response. What did he expect? She was hardly likely to say how pleased she was that he was available.

'Have a good game,' she said as she handed him his change.

As he headed for work, Mark felt pleased at his progress. He was now just about ready to take the plunge and ask her out. He just hoped his courage wouldn't fail as it had done so many times in the past.

He now had a surfeit of mint creams, so was very liberal with offering them to his colleagues.

'You like your mint creams, don't you?' Mary said. 'Where do you get them from?'

'There's a little sweet shop on the Downham Road,' Mark replied.

'My next-door neighbour works there,' said James who often liked to interrupt a conversation. He had to because no one bothered to engage him in idle chatter.

Mark looked across to him with sudden interest. 'Is that the young girl or the older lady?' he asked.

'The young one – Janine; a very nice young girl.'

'Yes, she's very friendly,' said Mark.

'Oh, hello!' said Mary. 'It's like that, is it?'

'I just said she's very friendly,' Mark said, defensively.

'Well, he's wasting his time, there,' said James. 'She's going off to University soon. And she's engaged.' He seemed very pleased with himself for having just crushed Mark's dreams.

'James!' said Mary. 'You might have broken it to him more gently. Look at his poor little face.'

'Haven't you got any work to do,' Mark demanded, trying his best to hide his feelings.

'Don't take it out on me,' she said. 'I was trying to sound sympathetic,' which was true, of course, but Mark didn't want sympathy. He wanted a girlfriend.

As the day progressed, Mark decided that perhaps James was mistaken – or even if he was right, couples do break up from time to time. He wouldn't give up just yet. Instead of concentrating on his reading of the O&M manual, he found himself considering his next move with Janine. He didn't want to let another possible girlfriend slip through his fingers.

That evening, he relieved his anxiety about his love life by enjoying the novelty of his family's new colour television. His parents usually went out on a Friday, so he had free rein to watch whatever he wished.

This included the end of the second day's play in the Test Match. England had already bowled out Australia for 146 and were in the process of taking a good first innings lead, despite the presence of Dennis Lillee in the attack.

Later on, he was able to enjoy the international version of *It's a Knockout* from Spa in Belgium, and later, there was *Dave Allen at Large*.

During the weekend, he hardly moved from the chair in front of the box. Ray had already told him that over the weekend, he and his wife were involved with various family activities so there was no point in Mark visiting Dersingham.

It was Tuesday before Mark next called in at the sweet shop. He had a few ideas about what to say to Janine should she serve him, which she did.

'Mint creams?' she asked, recognising him.

'No, I think I'll have some *Victory Vs* for a change,' he replied. 'Just a quarter, I think.' *Victory Vs* were stronger that the mint creams and he would break each one in half, meaning he would get much better value for money.

'I understand you live next door to my manager ...' he said. '... James McDougall.'

'Oh, yes. I know Mr McDougall. He's your boss, is he?'

'Yes. He tells me that you're off to University soon. Which one?' Mark noticed that the other lady was watching them. He hoped that she didn't mind him conversing with her assistant.

'I'm going to Durham – just a couple of months away now,' Janine said. 'I'm a little nervous.'

'And you're engaged to be married. That could be a strain.'

'Yes, but I'll come home regularly. Les and I talked about it and agreed it will have to be a long engagement.'

'Well, I wish you both well,' Mark lied, handing over the correct change for his sweets and popping one in his mouth.

She thanked him and he left with a heavy heart. It didn't look promising. He would just have to look elsewhere for his affection. What made it worse was that she looked particularly attractive that morning.

During the day, Ray telephoned to ask Mark if he wanted to meet up for a drink that evening. Valerie, who couldn't yet drive, needed a lift into town to visit her mother who was holding a *Tupperware* party and Ray didn't fancy listening to 'women talk' all evening. At the same time, Mark was pleased to get out for a while. There was always the hope that he might run into an unattached young lady which he could never do sat in front of the television: except that the pair agreed to meet at 'The Bricklayers Arms' where there was always a good chance of a game of dominoes but was not a place that unattached ladies frequented.

Mark was keen to tell Ray all about his new television, even though Ray had owned a colour set since he had married. 'Did you watch the Test Match?' Mark asked.

'No, I don't care for cricket. It's too slow for me,' Ray said, seeing an opportunity for a joke. 'A friend and I have been following the snail racing competition in Congham.'

'And cricket's too slow?'

'Don't knock snail racing. It's the world championship, you know ... in little old Norfolk. One competitor removed the shell off of his snail, thinking it could move quicker without a shell on its back ... but it didn't work. It just made it a bit sluggish!'

Mark groaned. 'Is that the best you can come up with? A bit sluggish? I bet you and your mate laughed at that for ages.'

'We did actually,' Ray replied. 'I'll let you borrow that one. You can tell your girls at work all about that. How's the girl with the hot pants?'

Mark had mentioned Dolly's hot pants before and now Ray always asked after her, but Mark had no intention of talking about the incident when he was caught staring at her crotch area. It still embarrassed him whenever he thought about it. However, he did talk about Polly and the incident where men were queuing up for her.

'So, you didn't fancy joining the queue?' Ray asked.

'Would you?' Mark asked. 'I mean knowing several others had been there just before. It's such a shame. She seems such a nice girl and I really did fancy her.'

'So, now it's Polly gone!' Ray said.

'Thank you, Ray. If I had joined the queue, it would be Polyfilla! Anyway, how is work?'

'It's very good, thank you. Our Work Study department is completely different to the one at Greshams. The incentive scheme is well established and needs little work, which means we're able to do a lot more actual Work Study.'

Mark was pleased that Ray had fallen on his feet and envied him that. Ray's new employer manufactured valves for high end stereo systems and televisions. He said he was glad to be out of the building industry which was always prone to economic fluctuations. He maintained that the world would always need valves.

The next day, Mary saw Mark eating his *Victory Vs*. 'So, you've abandoned her in favour of another sweet shop, have you?' she asked.

'What?'

You've switched to *Victory Vs* instead of your favourite mint creams.'

'I don't know what you're on about,' he said. 'I just felt like a change – and I did get these from my usual shop.'

'Sorry,' she responded. 'I thought you only went there to see your little girlfriend. You still haven't got a girlfriend, have you?'

'No. I'm not in a hurry. I'm just a bit fussy, that's all.' That was partly true. He was getting to the age when he wouldn't mind settling down, but it had to be the right girl. However, after being without a love interest for almost a year, he probably would lower his standards, but if he didn't actually meet anyone, it didn't matter what his standards were. In a few more months, he would have the opportunity to test his preferences.

Chapter Eleven

Two Lovers

At last it was September and Mark was able to start his COBOL course at the local Technical College. His O&M work had dragged on without ever having achieved anything. Mr Winbush-Smythe had instructed him on how to record the flow of several internal documents without ever explaining the purpose of his actions.

However, it did give him the opportunity to spend time in other parts of the building, starting with the Buying Office. He was familiar with each of the buyers, thanks to his occasional participation in the inter-departmental darts matches. The Head Buyer, one Barney Briggs, was a cheerful soul who had always reminded Mark of a spiv from an Ealing Comedy. He was always well dressed, sported a pencil moustache and invariably wore a waistcoat under his smart grey suit. He had moved up from London in 1965 when the rest of the company had relocated as part of the government's London overspill policy.

'Now, my ol' son ... what do you wanna know?' he said when Mark first arrived. Mark was tempted to ask if he had any petrol coupons but decided that Barney might take offence and he needed his full co-operation for the task ahead. Instead, he asked a few general queries about the process of raising a Purchase Order; the trigger for raising one and how the document flowed through the business after that; how delivery notes and invoices were married up against the original requirement and so on.

Barney was naturally talkative and was unable to confine himself to the questions in hand. He was glad to explain everything that happened in his domain, including how his 'merry men' had a remit to negotiate the best deal with each of their suppliers. This wasn't just a matter of obtaining the best price, but also entailed securing a long-term business arrangement for the foreseeable future. He proudly boasted that none of the buyers had to worry about their drink requirements at Christmas time. He also told Mark that his department had a 'slush fund' for a reciprocal arrangement where that might also benefit the business. Mark knew that the building industry had long indulged in such dubious transactions which bordered on corruption but was nevertheless necessary to compete with competitors who were all playing the same game.

None of this was particularly relevant to the matter in hand, but Mark didn't mind and as the conversation digressed in many directions, the rest of the staff joined in.

There were four buyers in total (all male) and one female secretary. She was the delightful Susie, a diminutive married lady who was not especially glamorous, but that didn't stop Mark from harbouring feelings that he shouldn't, because she was married. She constantly reminded her colleagues of that fact because, in their eyes, flirting with her was part of the daily routine.

Charlie Sands was the youngest of the buyers and the worst culprit. Mark heard him ask Susie 'You know … if you were just to pay me a nice complement, I'll be happy to give you one.'

Mark said 'Ignore him, Susie. He's like one of those dogs that chases cars. If the car stops, he doesn't know what to do about it.'

Susie giggled infectiously.

Mark, too, liked to flirt with her from time to time, knowing full well that it was a harmless pursuit enjoyed by both parties. He often saw her at the drinks machine, and he tried to amuse her whenever possible, because she had the most delightful laugh he had ever heard. She didn't conform to his usual taste in women, being not much taller than five feet and probably weighing a little over six stone, but she was full of vitality and he always enjoyed her very feminine company.

Ted was the oldest of the buyers and he greeted Mark with his usual question. 'Is Dolly wearing her hot pants today?'

'No, not today, Ted, but she is wearing those kinky boots,' Mark replied.

'You're a lucky bugger, working with her,' Ted said.

'How can you say that, when you work up here with Susie? You can swap places if you like.'

'Yes, please,' said Susie, not from any great love for Mark, but because Ted had a reputation as a dirty old man. He wasn't satisfied with a bit of harmless flirting. He often made lewd suggestions to various members of the female population at Greshams and Susie had to withstand more than her fair share.

Mark was wary of the fine line between humorously intentioned flirting and something more sinister. He was also very careful of the recipients of his attentions, especially those who did not have a keen sense of humour.

'You wouldn't catch me wearing hot pants,' added Susie.

'You shouldn't knock it,' said Ted.

'No,' said Mark, 'I'm afraid that Dolly does have to put up with her knockers.'

'Tits like coconuts!' said Charlie.

'Charlie!' said Susie. 'There's no need for that!'

'What? Blue tits and great tits like coconuts. Everyone knows that. I often hang them out in my garden.'

'Tits like melons, I'd have said,' responded Ted and everyone thought that he had gone too far so Barney said it was time for everyone to get on with their work so that he could concentrate on helping Mark with his enquiries.

That morning spent in the Buying Office was the most interesting time Mark had enjoyed while doing his boring O&M work, but now he was sitting in a lecture room in the college, as the lecturer introduced himself as Dave. Mark could never imagine any of his old masters at school using their first names to pupils.

There were seven students in total, two of whom were female, much to Mark's delight. The person seated at his right was a tall slim dark-haired lady who introduced herself, when asked by the lecturer, as Claire. The other lady was sitting in front of Mark and to his left, so Mark couldn't see her face, but she had much fairer hair and from behind seemed to have a much squatter build. She said her name was Margaret and did so with a heavy local accent in contrast to Claire's more neutral tone.

Dave pointed out that the course was a six-week introduction to the subject and at the end, attendees would benefit by continuing their learning on the job if at all possible, otherwise a more advanced course would be required. Mark knew that the first option was not open to him at that time, so before deciding about the latter, he would see how he progressed.

He recalled the three-week intensive course he had attended when he first became an NCR500 programmer and soon realised that COBOL was a completely different language. It looked, at first, like it would be much easier to learn. For a start, it used words that could be easily recognised, such as ADD, PRINT and COMPARE, instead of convoluted numerical codes, but then the lecturer confused him by mentioning GEORGE.

'Who on Earth was George?' Mark thought. After a while he twigged that GEORGE was the operating system for the college's ICL machine. The NCR had never needed such a thing. You just loaded the program from punched tape, but larger ICL and IBM machines used JCL, which Dave said stood for Job Control Language. To Mark's relief, Dave told them not to worry if they weren't familiar with GEORGE as he would provide the JCL when they were ready to run programs.

At the end of the lesson, Mark felt punch drunk. He wasn't sure how much of this had sunk in. As he gathered up his notes, Claire said to him 'Do you think the Refectory will still be open?'

'I've no idea,' Mark replied, especially as he wasn't sure what a refectory was. Didn't they have them in monasteries?

'I'm dying for a coffee,' Claire added. 'Shall we go and look?'

'Yeah, I'm ready for a drink after that,' he replied and followed her. She seemed to know her way around the building. He was already assessing her as a possible girl friend. She was as tall as him, but oh so thin! However, he was sure she wasn't suffering anorexia like Polly. For one thing, she didn't share Polly's earlier look of gaunt emaciation. In fact, Claire was quite attractive with a healthy glow about her ... just impossibly thin. But then, he thought that a lot of people admired those skinny models, so perhaps there was something he had been missing out on. In any case, who was he to be picky?

The refectory was closed. There was a coffee machine, but Mark lied about not having change. He didn't like coffee from a machine, and he had another plan. 'There's a pub just around the corner – *The Swan*. Do you fancy a quick drink?'

Claire looked at her watch and said 'Yes, I think I've just about got time. I am rather thirsty.'

As they walked out of the building and into the dark night, Mark started by asking her if she had any previous programming experience. He considered it best to talk about their current endeavours rather than getting too personal at first.

'No ... I've been working as an operator for the council and this seemed like a logical step upwards. Plus, I'm fed up with the shifts. My last boyfriend split up with me because he could never see me when he wanted. How about you? Why are you here tonight?'

Mark explained his situation and his reasons for taking the course, but before he could go into much detail, they were inside the pub, which was quite busy due to its proximity to the college. He bought them both a drink, but there was nowhere to sit down, and it was too noisy for easy conversation. Now he wished they had availed themselves of the coffee machine.

After struggling with the noise for a while, Claire downed her half of cider and pointed to her watch. Mark finished his drink and escorted her to the door.

'God, why do people have to raise their voices when they've had a few drinks?' she said once they were away from the noise in the bar. 'What I was trying to say was that I have a bus to catch.'

'Where do you live?' Mark asked.

'Baker Lane,' she replied. It was a little out of his way, but he didn't mind that.

'I'll give you a lift,' he said, then added '... if you like.' He realised that she didn't really know him and might not want to get in a car with a stranger.

'No, I'll be all right,' she said and started walking towards the bus stop and away from where Mark had parked his car, but then she stopped and added 'Is it out of your way?'

'Only a little,' he replied without pushing the situation. It had to be her decision. After all, he would be seeing her regularly for the next five weeks so there might be other opportunities.

'To be honest, it is a bit of a faff. There isn't a direct bus service to my area. I have to catch one bus to take me into town and then another from the bus station. If you're sure it's not out of your way.'

Mark led her to his car and opened the door for her like a gentleman. His mind was racing now. How was he to approach her for a date? He knew some girls liked to be swept off their feet, but he didn't want to rush it and frighten her off. If he dived in too quickly, she might think he had an ulterior motive for offering her a lift, but once in the car, she initiated the conversation.

'What do you like doing when you're not programming?' she asked as he drove off.

He listed some of his interests and ended up with tennis. 'Do you play?' he asked.

'No, I'm absolutely useless at all sports. Because of my height, at school, I was pushed into netball, but I could never catch the ball. I was always called *Beanpole*. I can eat as much as I like and I never put on a pound.'

'I was very thin when I was at school,' he responded. 'My aunt once said I was like a matchstick with the wood scraped off, but I'm not quite so thin these days.'

'No, you look as though you're in good shape,' she said. 'It must be all the sport you do.'

'She's paying me complements,' Mark thought. This looked promising. He had been getting ready to ask her to play tennis, as that might be interpreted as not an actual date, but that was no longer a viable option. What was his next move?

82

'Oh, and I like to go to the cinema occasionally,' he added.

'What sort of films do you like?' Claire asked.

'Er ... a good comedy ... umm ... anything with a good story.'

'Have you seen *The Godfather*?' she asked.

'No, have you?'

'Not yet, but I see it's on at *The Odeon* this week.'

She had to be suggesting something, but still Mark hesitated. He could be wrong about this, but there was only one way to find out ... and yet...

'Are you going?' he asked.

'I'm thinking about it,' she replied. 'It's got some very good reviews, so I'd like to see it sometime. Claire was wondering what she had to do to get him to force the issue.

And still he hesitated. Why couldn't he just ask her? What was the big deal? The worst that could happen was that she would say 'no,' He decided that he was going to do it ... but not just yet.

Claire now thought that either he didn't like her, or he already had a girlfriend.

He changed the subject. 'What else do you like doing?'

'I do a lot of reading. When I'm doing the evening shifts, I often sit with a book while waiting to change tapes or load fresh paper in the printer.'

By now, they had passed the top of Mark's road and time was running out. 'I'm thinking that I might like to see that film. Would you like to come with me?'

He'd done it! He'd asked her. But she wasn't answering. God, he hated being rejected.

Eventually she said 'The only night that I can make it is Saturday. Is that all right? I know you said you play football on a Saturday.'

'No, Saturday will be fine,' he answered trying to hide his sense of relief. 'I don't know what time the film starts, but I'll need time to clean up after the football. Shall I pick you up at seven o'clock?'

'Yes, you'll see where I live in a moment. It's just around this next bend ... Number 26. Don't drive down the road. It's a dead-end and not easy to turn around.'

It rained on Saturday. Mark always liked to give his car a good clean before a first date, but that was not possible on this occasion. He had a strange feeling that things were not going to turn out well that night. His doubts were magnified when his football team lost for the first time that season and he was partly responsible for two of the goals. He never liked playing in the rain. He had a constant battle to keep his spectacles clear and the ball was skidding alarmingly. No one spoke to him in the changing room afterwards.

Although the rain had ceased by the time he left for Baker Lane, his mood had not improved very much. What was really bugging him was that he was not experiencing any feelings of lust – and that was unusual for him. He desperately needed a girlfriend and Claire seemed perfectly delightful, but she didn't generate any lustful thoughts in his mind. His previous girlfriends had been a variety of shapes and sizes. Yet they had always produced carnal desires, but Claire didn't. If he had been on his way to see Blodwyn for instance, he would by now have been sensing a tightness in his underpants. He told himself that he was being too negative, and he should enjoy himself.

Sure enough, he did enjoy her company that night. The film was one of the best he'd ever seen and despite being quite long, there was still just enough time for a quick drink in a nearby bar, where they were able to get to know each other a little better. He asked to see her again, but she told him that she was working shifts the following week apart from the evening of the course when she had been able to switch with a colleague. They agreed to arrange something when they next met on the course.

As they neared Baker Lane, Claire told him to stop at the top of the road as she knew it was awkward to turn around in the cul-de-sac. He'd already discovered that fact when he had picked her up right outside her house. He'd been thinking for some time about fixing a reversing light to the rear of his 1100 and now he knew that it would be an excellent idea. Baker Lane was quite dark, the streetlights being sparsely spaced apart, so he insisted on walking her to her door.

As they walked the fifty or so yards, he reached for her hand which she surrendered willingly. He was surprised how bony it felt and he didn't enjoy the sensation. Things had been going so well that, at her gate, he felt emboldened to hold her around the hips and kiss her gently, but it wasn't the burning sensation he had been expecting. Her hips were so bony – and even her lips felt thin. He knew at that moment that he was never going to feel any physical excitement from someone so thin – but he'd just asked her for another date. He couldn't go through with it. He had to stop it before it started. Supposing he became emotionally attached, but was never able to consummate their affair? That wasn't fair on either of them.

'I'm sorry. I can't do this,' he said, realising that it sounded a little melodramatic.

'What's up?' she asked.

'I've got to be honest with you,' he said. 'I've only recently finished with my girlfriend and I'm not ready to go out with anyone else just yet. I thought I was, but as soon as I kissed you, I knew I need more time. I'm so sorry. Please don't think this is any reflection on you.' He hated telling lies, but the truth would be even more upsetting.

'It's all right,' she said, touching his shoulder. I quite understand. I went through something similar when my last boyfriend broke up with me. I thought you seemed a little ... um ... I don't know ... not committed? Is that what I mean to say? Can I ask why you broke up?'

The problem with telling lies is you have to have a good story, so he decided to use an element of truth using his breakup with Melody as a basis for his tale of woe. 'Her mother was taken ill and she moved back home to take care of her and her father. They live nearly a hundred miles away. We talked about trying to keep it going at a distance, but we thought it better to have a clean break rather than making hard work of it. I know it made sense at the time, but it hurt me more than I thought it would. I am so sorry.'

'Don't keep saying that. It's quite all right. It would have been hard work for us anyway as long as I'm still doing these shifts. You get yourself off home and I'll see you next week at the college.'

'I have enjoyed myself tonight and you're a very nice person,' he said, and he meant it, which made him feel even more guilty.

As he drove home, he felt quite wretched; not just at the way he had just treated a perfectly nice young lady, but because he was back where he started – without a girlfriend! There was always Margaret; the other lady on the course, but that was going to be awkward with Claire still around – and he still hadn't spoken to her or had a good look at her. She was probably married or engaged or a lesbian or something. He was feeling very pessimistic at that moment. Everything in his favour was against him.

Over the next few weeks, the group of students on Mark's course gradually got to know each other better and as a result, the atmosphere became much more relaxed. Mark at last managed to exchange a few words with Margaret, but it was all very formal at first. She was completely different from Claire in many ways. For one thing, she was shorter, but she made up for that in build; probably weighing a stone or two more. She had fair hair and delightful bright blue eyes, rosy cheeks and a warm smile, but she was more reserved than Claire and Mark's first conversation with her concerning the course was brief.

At the end of the second evening, Mark asked Claire if she would like a lift home, which she gratefully accepted and he was pleased to enjoy her company again. He did consider that if he ever needed a companion for another visit to the cinema, he would feel comfortable about asking her, but not on this occasion.

At the end of the third lesson, a friendly young fellow name Tom told Mark that some of the students were going down the pub for a drink. 'Are you going to *The Swan*?' Mark asked, remembering how noisy it was.

'No,' said Tom. 'There's too many students go there. We're going to *The King's Head* up the road. It's much quieter and the beer's better.'

'Yes, I'll join you. Thank you. Do you want to come, Claire?' he asked.

'No, I think I'd rather get home,' she replied. 'I'm feeling a little tired. You have a good time.'

The King's Head was further away than *The* Swan, so he decided to take his car. It wasn't too far to walk, but he noticed Margaret joining the group, so he wanted to be prepared in case she wanted a lift.

There were only four in the group including Mark, so he was pleased to find himself sitting next to Margaret. She was more reserved than the others adding little to the stilted conversation, so Mark tried to engage her in conversation.

'Why do you find yourself on this course?' he asked, realising as he spoke that his sentence was rather clumsy.

'I'm looking for my next career move,' she replied. 'I'm currently working as a typist and I think I can do better. The Careers Advisory chap at the Labour Exchange suggested I could move into secretarial work or possibly programming. So, at the moment, I'm doing this on a Thursday and a Secretarial Course on Mondays and Wednesdays ... to see which suits me best. What about you?'

Mark repeated his story which Tom had already heard before – then added 'I wonder if you visited the Labour Exchange just after me and that's where he got his idea from.'

'Possibly,' she replied and then went quiet.

There was a lull in the conversation from the group as a whole. Mark never liked a lull, so he took the initiative. 'Anyone here play tennis?'

There were shakes of the head and a mumbled 'no' from one person.

'I used to play a bit at school,' Margaret said. 'Why do you ask?'

'I play with some colleagues from the office. We go after work on a Friday, but we've lost a few people and we could do with one or two more players to make it worthwhile. Are you interested?'

'Well, I am very busy with all this course work, but I'd like to get back into tennis. I think I could spare an hour on a Friday. Where do you play?'

Mark gave her all the details, trying his best not to sound too excited. He missed out the bit about the possibility of no one else turning up.

The following evening, he left work excitedly on the dot of five o'clock and made his way through the rush-hour traffic to the tennis court. As he had thought, no one else was joining them that evening. He saw this as a mixed blessing. It meant that if Margaret turned up, he would have her to himself, but on the other hand, a game of doubles would have been more enjoyable given that, being a man, he would expect to easily dominate the game.

She wasn't there, but it was still early. He went to the small hut that served as both a changing room and the park attendant's shelter, but it was locked, and the attendant was nowhere in sight. Mark had already changed at work as he half expected this. It was late in the season and the group of colleagues hadn't turned up for two weeks.

Margaret had told him that she would make her own way there but hadn't mentioned how. He assumed she had her own transport. He kept looking out anxiously for her car, but none came. He was about to give up when a bright red Triumph Spitfire parked on the road at the edge of the park. It was her.

'Sorry, if I'm late,' she said as she walked swiftly towards him, already wearing a knee length tennis skirt. 'I had to finish a letter for one of the managers – and then I thought I'd better change before I left. I wasn't sure if there were facilities here.'

'There are,' he said, pointing to the hut, 'but it's locked. I'm sorry, but no one else has turned up.'

'It's just as well,' she said. 'I'm a little rusty. I don't want to make a fool of myself. I hope you're not too good.'

It was already starting to get dark and the courts were surrounded by trees, so Mark didn't think they would be able to play for long.

She turned out to be a reasonable player, albeit, as she had told him, a little rusty. Even so, he soon realised that he could beat her easily if he really wanted to, but he wanted her to enjoy herself, so he took it easy on her and she steadily improved. At least she wasn't like Wanda who wouldn't run for anything. Margaret was quite prepared to try for every ball and had a very competent forehand, but it was soon too dark to continue.

'I really enjoyed that,' she said. 'Do I owe you any money?'

'No, there's no one here to collect it,' he replied. 'You're a good player.'

'I think you took it easy on me,' she said.

'At first, perhaps, but you had me running around a few times. I've built up a thirst. Do you fancy going for a quick drink?'

'No, I'm not dressed for going into bars, but thank you for the game. Can we do it again sometime?'

This was going well, but Mark was disappointed not to buy her a drink. 'I don't think it's going to be light enough after work next week,' he replied reluctantly.

'What about a Saturday afternoon?' she asked.

'I play football on Saturdays, but maybe a Sunday afternoon.'

'What about this weekend?' She was keen.

'I will need to 'phone the council to book a court and they won't be open over the weekend. Let me set it up for the following Sunday and I'll confirm it with you next Thursday ... unless you'd like to go out for a drink one evening?'

No, I'm too busy with my course work, but I am keen to play tennis.'

'Okay,' Mark said. He was getting mixed signals here, but a few games of tennis might change that. 'Do you play any other sport?' he asked, wanting to chat a bit longer while he had the chance.

'I did at school, but my main interest was always riding ... hence these thighs.' She slapped her thigh and Mark could tell it sounded very solid.

For a moment, he stood there with his mouth open, not knowing how to respond. 'Lucky old horse' would not have been appropriate.

'Do you have a horse?' he asked eventually

'Not anymore. For my twenty-first birthday, my father said I could either have a new horse - or a car. In the end, I decided the horse would not have been suitable for visiting my friends in the country. There's always my next birthday.'

'Do you live in the countryside, then?' Mark asked.

'Yes, I live on Willow Farm – at the end of Field Drive.'

'Oh, yes. I know it,' Mark said. He remembered it as a very large farm with lots of land.

'Anyway,' said Margaret, 'I'd better be off. Thanks again for the game, I really enjoyed it.'

'So, did I,' Mark replied and they both walked off in different directions.

In the space of a few weeks, He had been out with two different girls, although he realised that one quick game of tennis didn't qualify as a date. Even so, he felt his luck changing.

Chapter Twelve

I Want You

'You know who he's talking about, don't you, Ray?'

Ray looked at his wife in bewilderment.

'It's the girl Stephens. I went to school with her. Her father owns Willow Farm. I'm sorry to say, Mark, that you have no chance with her.'

Mark looked hurt. 'Why?' he asked.

'No disrespect to you, but you don't move in the same circles as her family. You're not exactly from the hunting and shooting fraternity, are you?'

'I once won a goldfish in the rifle range at the King's Lynn Mart,' he replied, trying to lighten his mood. 'Anyway, it's Margaret I'm trying to date – not her family.'

'I'm sorry to hurt your feelings. But she won't go out with you.'

'She wants to play tennis with me. I don't see why I shouldn't get a date with her.'

Valerie hadn't finished. 'When her grandfather decided to retire, her father and his brother took over the business. Her uncle built another farmhouse next to the main building and the two brothers share the responsibility of the farm, but there was also a sister and she ended up marrying another farmer from out Little Snoring way – or it might have been Great Snoring; somewhere out that way. Margaret will be expected to follow suit and she will be mixing with the young farmers. It will be expected of her. You won't get a look in. Even if she wanted to go out with you, her family wouldn't let her. I know what they're like. They own loads of land around here, don't they, Ray?'

'Yes, they do,' he replied, but he was sympathetic to Mark. He couldn't see why Mark stood no chance at all.

'For one thing, you'd never fit in with her circle of friends,' Valerie added.

'She might enjoy meeting my small circle of friends,' Mark said.

'Well, I suppose zero is a small circle,' said Ray.

Mark decided to change the subject. He didn't want to hear any more. He was quite capable of a little pessimism without the help of others. He saw Valerie's words as a challenge. He would win Margaret over. After all, he wasn't asking for her hand in marriage. A few months with her as a girlfriend would suffice; just enough to make up for the long, long months without a girlfriend.

The next day, he found himself in Kenny Stacey's latest motor on the way to an away match.

'You work at Greshams, don't you, Mark?' Kenny asked.

'Yes, I do. I joined in 1965.'

'So, you will know Polly, then?'

'Yes, I know Polly. What about her?'

'She was at *The Jenyns Arms* last week, surrounded by young men. They seemed to chase her everywhere she went – like bees round a honey pot.'

'Or dogs round a bitch,' said Mark, thinking this was a more appropriate analogy, though less complimentary. 'Was she drinking?'

'No, she seemed to be drinking orange juice or something similar. She had a friend with her who was just as attractive, if not more so, but the boys all wanted Polly.'

'I'm afraid, 'said Mark, 'that she has a bit of a reputation has young Polly. When she has a drink or two, her inhibitions desert her. It's such a shame.'

'Have you had a go?' Kenny asked in his usual forthright manner.

'No – I was a little tempted once, as she is a very nice girl, but ... er ... not once I'd heard about her ... er ... little problem. The last thing I want is to catch a dose of the clap. I've never been to *The Jennings Arms*.' He had misheard the name of the establishment. 'What's it like?' He didn't like talking about Polly like this, so he wanted to change the subject.

'It's the place to go around here – at least during the week. At the weekend, it's *The Kit Kat* in Hunstanton, but *The Jenyns* mid-week. They play all the latest dance records, but it's mostly for young people. It makes me feel a bit too old really, but it's a good place to meet young girls. How's your love life, Mark?'

'Looking up – nothing regular, but I've been out with two different girls in just a few weeks. That's good for me.'

'Well done,' said Kenny, but there was a big hint of sarcasm in his voice. For him that would have been a lean period.

Mark wondered if Margaret would enjoy a visit to *The Jennings Arms*. She was the centre of all his thoughts now and Polly was no longer his concern.

At the next COBOL lesson, Dave issued the results of everyone's first attempt at writing a program. Each person had been asked to store a small number of monetary amounts, print them in a column and provide a grand total on a new page.

Mark's effort was reasonably successful, but his layout could have been neater. Claire's attempt was spot on and made her squeal with joy, in contrast to Margaret, whose effort was disastrous.

'That does it,' she said. 'It will be a secretarial career for me.'

Mark tried to console her, saying there was probably a very simple explanation, but she was adamant. At that moment, it occurred to him that she was a strong-minded individual who was not prone to changing her mind easily. He had the good grace to say 'Well done' to Claire, even though he was more concerned with Margaret. He guessed that she would now abandon the course and he might not see her again.

As soon as the lesson was over, he approached her to confirm that he had booked a tennis court for the coming Sunday afternoon. He just hoped that the weather would stay kind, for he might never have another chance to worm his way into her affections. He also asked if she was joining the other men down the pub, which she was, so he had another chance to talk to her. He had already decided that he would impress her with his blistering sense of humour, because up until that point, the opportunity hadn't arisen. He was a little anxious about this, because sometimes, when he tried too hard to be funny, he failed miserably, and this was one occasion when he dearly wanted to succeed.

There were five in the group heading for the pub, but Claire again declined the invitation.

Mark soon saw a chance for his first witticism. 'My mother made a rhubarb pie on Sunday. It was one inch thick and fifteen inches long.'

'Do you still live with your mother?' asked Tom before anyone could burst into hysterical laughter. There then followed a discussion on the merits of living with one's parents or setting up independently. Mark felt aggrieved at this change of topic and retired into his shell for a while. The same joke had worked when Ray had told him the previous week.

A little later, he tried again. 'I've been training for a marathon, you know,'

'Really?' said Margaret, suddenly showing a little more interest.

'Yes,' replied Mark, 'it's going well. I managed a *Mars Bar* last week.'

Everyone groaned. He tried a few more jokes, but for some reason, this group did not seem ready for his brand of humour and he decided to give up.

The next topic of conversation was music and much to his dismay, everyone else was talking about pop music. As each group and singer was mentioned, Mark felt ever less inclined to join in with the discussion, until Margaret decided to ask him whom he liked. He mentioned a few names which resulted in no response from anyone else. That was until he named the Temptations.

'Oh, I know them,' said Margaret. 'They're one of those Tamla Motown groups, aren't, they?' When Mark confirmed that, she added 'I like The Supremes ... and Diana Ross. I think she's gorgeous. I'd love to have a figure like hers.'

'You're joking,' said Mark. 'She's as skinny as a rake. She's like a matchstick with the wood scraped off. You've got a far better figure than her.'

Margaret snorted. 'Have you seen these shoulders? I got these working on a farm – humping bales of hay during my teenage years.'

Mark did not think her shoulders looked particularly unusual and given half a chance, he would have loved to have joined her humping some hay. He desperately wanted to assure her that she had a great figure but realised that this wasn't the time and place to force the issue. In any case, he couldn't think of the right thing to say, because, at that time, his mind was in turmoil. One thing was certain ... this was the woman he wanted. He wanted to explore those shoulders and those thighs that she had slapped after the game of tennis. She was a million miles from the *Miss Beanpole* that he had unceremoniously rejected a few weeks earlier. With Margaret, he would certainly rise to the occasion given the right opportunity.

Perhaps, after the tennis on Sunday, he might try again to date her. The disadvantage of playing on a Sunday afternoon was that all the pubs would be closed and there was nowhere to go to round off the afternoon.

He was relieved that he had not incurred any injury during either of his two weekend football matches. He parked his car in the same place that Margaret had used the previous week. His thinking being that at least he would be able to walk her to her car after the tennis. She was already there ahead of him. He decided that this was a good sign. In his mind, she was keen to see him again.

'I hope I didn't keep you waiting too long,' he said, knowing that he was a little early himself.

'No, I've only just got here,' she said.

Mark wanted to tell her how lovely she looked, but that would have presumed that this was a date and a Sunday afternoon game of tennis barely qualified. In any case, she obviously hadn't made any special effort to make herself presentable. He just liked what he saw.

The game proceeded and although it was still a little one-sided, she had improved now that she was less 'rusty', and he found himself enjoying the game. Halfway through the afternoon, they were interrupted by the arrival of the park attendant who wanted to collect the fee. Mark broke off to pay him and was told that the nets would be taken down the next day meaning there could be no more tennis until the following spring. That was definitely not what he wanted to hear.

Meanwhile, two young girls, who had been watching from outside the fence were talking to Margaret. He heard one ask, 'Is that your boyfriend?'

'No, he's not my boyfriend.'

'Do you like him?'

'He's all right,' Margaret replied, not realising that Mark could hear.

What did 'all right' mean? Was that a good thing – or was he just 'all right?'

At the end of the game, Margaret told him how much she had enjoyed playing. That made it all the more painful to tell her what the attendant had said.

'I'm afraid we won't be able to play again until the spring. The old boy just told me that they take the nets down tomorrow.'

'Oh no,' she said. 'I was just getting into it again. Is there anywhere else we can play?'

'I don't know of anywhere else,' he replied. 'If there is, the chances are that they will be closing for the season as well. What a shame I didn't meet you earlier in the year. Do you play squash? I know where we could get a game of that.'

'No, I tried it once and didn't enjoy it. I kept wanting to play tennis shots. I hope you'll bear me in mind when you start playing again next year.'

'Of course,' he replied. 'I hope I'll see you before then, though. Are you giving up on the COBOL course?'

'Yes ... it's not working for me. I have no difficulty in learning all the symbols for shorthand, but I'm struggling with programming. I think I've been taking on too much at the same time. Anyway, I quite like the idea of being someone's personal secretary. I see myself looking after a managing director somewhere; being privy to all the workings of a company and working in a directors' suite away from the other staff who just want to gossip all day.'

By now, they had reached the cars and Mark still hadn't asked her for a proper date. 'Can I see you again?' he blurted out.

'Yes, of course ... if you can organise some tennis.'

'No, I mean ... er ... can I take you for a drink or something sometime?'

'No, I don't think so, but I'd still like to play tennis with you. I enjoyed that.'

It looked like Valerie had been right about this. Margaret was happy to use him for a game of tennis, but nothing beyond that. And yet, he wanted her so much. He couldn't just give up. If only he could get a proper date with her, he would surely win her over with his wit and his charm. His boring old 1100 wasn't helping his cause when she had a sleek sports car.

'I like your Spitfire,' he said just to avoid saying goodbye.

'Yes,' she said. 'I'm very pleased with it. It's probably too small for someone of your build, but I like it.'

He watched as she slid into the driver's seat, revealing an inch or two of substantial thigh, unaware of the effect that it had on Mark. 'Goodbye, then,' she added as she fired up the engine and disappeared down the road with a squeal of the tyres.

'God, I want you,' he muttered to himself.

Mark had once again fallen deeply in lust.

Chapter Thirteen

My Whole World is Falling Down

During Tuesday morning, James returned from a meeting and said, 'Mark will you go and talk to Mr Tollet?'

Mark was pleased to get away from his desk and his boring work. During the last few months, he had often visited the Company Secretary to discuss his progress with his O&M work. Tom Winbush-Smythe was spending less time in Sanford than he originally intended and so Mr Tollet had taken the role of monitoring Mark's progress even though he didn't really know much about O&M.

'Come in, Mark. Take a seat.' He cleared his throat and said 'I'm afraid this isn't working out as we'd hoped. We're not going to proceed with the O&M work any further. What we've seen so far isn't going to produce significant savings or benefit to the company, so we're going to have to let you go.' He paused for a moment to let the news sink in.

'You'll be paid a month's money in lieu of notice and you'll get the statutory redundancy pay, which is all detailed in this document. Your last day will be this Friday, but you'll be paid to the end of this month as well as the money in lieu. Feel free to take off any time you need for job hunting or interviews. I'm very sorry about this, but I'm sure you realise that we can't continue to pay for someone who's not productive.' Mark felt unable to speak, so Mr Tollet continued.

'I know this is going to come as a bit of a shock, but we have no choice, I'm afraid. You've been a loyal servant to this company in a variety of roles and we have tried to make an opening for you, but it hasn't worked out.'

The news shouldn't have been a surprise, but it had caught Mark unawares. In a way, it was a relief, but now for the first time in his working life, he was on the dole.

'Do you have any questions, Mark?'

Mark sighed. 'No, I don't think so ... not at the moment anyway.'

'Well, come and see me if you do have any ... and, of course, if anyone asks us for a reference, we will be happy to oblige.'

Mark sloped off to his desk. 'Well, tha's a bugger,' he said as he entered his office.

'Are you all right?' asked James.

'No,' Mark said replied bluntly. He knew that James would be fully aware of the reason for his visit to Mr Tollet. 'I think I'll go and pay a visit to the Labour Exchange if you don't mind.' It didn't matter whether James minded or not; Mark was going, and he didn't want to explain anything to his two female companions. James would do that in his absence.

His visit to the Labour Exchange proved to be fruitless. If he was to make use of his COBOL training, he would have to find an employer who used a computer. That would probably mean a fairly large employer, like a bank or insurance company. One employer he knew of was the local council and he knew someone who worked for them – Claire. He decided to ask her when he next saw her at the college. Meanwhile, as he was in town, he purchased a copy of the *Lynn News & Advertiser* and that day's edition of the *Eastern Daily Press*. He'd already looked for jobs in the latest edition of the *Sanford Echo*. The next edition was not due until Friday.

He had been hoping that Margaret might have a change of heart about the COBOL course: or even a change of heart about seeing him again, but when Thursday evening came around, she was nowhere to be seen. He wasn't very keen on joining the drinkers at the end of the lecture, so he asked Claire if she wanted a lift home.

'Aren't you going down the pub with the rest?' she asked.

'No, I want to talk to you about something,' he replied.

'Oh, that's sounds intriguing,' she said.

'I'll tell you about it in the car.'

As they walked towards the car park, Claire asked 'Is it because Margaret's not here that you're not going to the pub?'

'Certainly not! I told you I wanted to talk to you about something.'

'All right, but you do like her, don't you? I can tell by your body language when you talk to her. I've been reading about body language. For instance, if you cross your arms or legs, it means you're shutting someone out.'

'Whereas,' Mark said with a grin, 'if you open your arms and legs out wide, you're welcoming someone. I don't think you need to read a book to work that out.'

'Go on, you can make fun of it, if you like, but I think there's something in it. Am I right about Margaret?'

'I'm not sure,' he lied. 'I enjoyed a game of tennis with her, but I still keep thinking about my old girlfriend.' That was the problem with telling lies – you have to keep it up once you've started.

As he started his car and prepared to drive out of the car park, he told her about losing his job and asked if she knew of any programming vacancies at the council.

'There is one coming up and I'm going to apply. You've probably got a better chance of getting it than me because you've already got programming experience.'

'No, I'm not going to get in your way. You need to get away from working those shifts. No, I won't do that to you. In any case, you've probably got a better chance than me because they already know you. Councils like to promote from within, don't they?'

'Possibly,' she replied, 'but you're going to be out of work. So, you must apply.'

'No, I hope you get the job, I really do. You deserve it.'

'You're a real gentleman, Mark,' Claire added.

'A gentleman is someone who takes the weight on his elbows,' Mark said, then wondering if he should be making such jokes to someone like Claire.

'Do you know the definition of a lady?' she asked.

'Er ...'

'It's someone who only swears when it slips out!'

Mark laughed but was surprised to hear this from Claire and said so.

'Oh, you'd be surprised what I hear working with the other operators. I hear a lot worse than that.'

'We only have one operator' said Mark 'and I can't imagine her saying that – doing it, yeah. I can imagine her swearing when it slips out. Anyway, if you hear of any other opportunities, can you let me know?'

'Well, if I get the job, there will be a shift operator's job going.'

'No thanks.'

Mark's leaving 'do' that Friday lunchtime was a great success and he was on sparkling form. Most of his guests were female, but he regretted one absentee. He had been unable to invite Stella, the gorgeous Amazonian Typing Pool Supervisor as he rarely came in contact with her and he didn't want to enter the Typing Pool itself because there were five other typists, whom he barely knew. He didn't want to invite all of them nor appear to snub them by not doing so. He would dearly have loved to sit and chat to Stella, but by way of compensation, the delightful little Susie was there.

She and Barney Briggs were the last to arrive and as she entered the bar, he ordered her to sit beside him. 'Come here and tell me how much you're going to miss me,' he said.

'Oh, Mark! There aren't words that could describe how we all feel to see you go. Have you got anything lined up yet?'

'I've got a couple of strong possibilities,' he replied. 'The first is as a life-guard. They sit there doing absolutely nothing for ninety-nine per cent of the time. Then when they are called into action, they're suddenly a hero and all the girls flock around him. There's only one problem ... I'm not a very good swimmer.'

Susie was already giggling. 'What's the other one?' she asked.

'I wondered about being a dustbin collector. They only seem to work on Mondays.'

'They work on Wednesdays, where I live,' said Dolly.

'Thursdays for me,' said Mary.

'Damn!' said Mark. I'll have to think again.' Susie's infectious laugh always inspired him to witticism. This was all in stark contrast to his unsuccessful effort with the COBOL group when he wanted to impress Margaret with his wit. On that occasion, he had barely raised a titter.

'Do you know how to make a pretty girl curious?' he asked Susie.

'No,' she replied.

'I'll tell you later,' he said, but launched into his next jest before she could react. 'This morning, there was an accident down our road. This chap overturned his car when he collided with the tree - right outside where Mr and Mrs Smith live, and they share a drive with Mr and Mrs Ball. He was trapped inside, but he was very lucky ... he was dragged out by the Smiths!'

Mary was the first to laugh. 'I don't get it,' said Dolly – always the last.

Mary did the explaining.' He could have been dragged out by Mr and Mrs Ball ... but he wasn't. He was dragged out by the Smiths.'

'No ... am I being thick?' Dolly said.

'Nah,' they all said and left her to puzzle it out in her own time.

'Mind you,' said Mark. 'I came close to having an accident last year. I had to pull out suddenly to avoid a child. After that, my girlfriend made me wear a condom.'

That wasn't too far from the truth as Melody had always insisted, he wore protection – something he regretted at the time as he felt it robbed both of them of some of the sensation. But, now, having not had sex for well over a year, he would gladly accede to the requirement. Although he felt he would have to double-check the 'use by' date on the packet that he carried with him wherever he went.

'Here's one for you, Dolly,' he said. 'What's the definition of a lady?'

'How would I know?' she replied in her cheerful chuckling voice.

'Someone who only swears when it slips out.' Everyone laughed at that one, including Dolly whose laugh at times resembled a snorting pig and he felt grateful to Claire for her joke.

'Has that ever happened to you, Dolly?' Mark asked, trying to milk the moment.

'I don't think so,' she replied. 'I've got a joke. What's brown and sticky?'

'A stick!' said Billy and received a hard stare from Dolly and little response from the audience. Even Susie stopped giggling. Billy had ruined Dolly's moment.

Mark was particularly annoyed – not just for spoiling the joke for Dolly, which he considered was always bad form, but also because Billy hadn't been invited. Polly had brought him along and the two of them sat side by side, snuggling up to each other occasionally.

Mark wondered what sort of relationship they had. First, they had dated each other, then they had split up and Polly had had other boyfriends since then, and now they seemed to be an item again.

'Okay, Billy,' Mark said. 'You tell us a joke.'

Billy thought for a moment and said, 'What wears glasses and comes in a yellow bag?'

There was no reply. Mark knew the answer, but thought the joke was in bad taste for mixed company.

'John Lennon,' Billy said. Everyone seemed to agree with Mark's view and the atmosphere suffered for a few moments until Barney broke the spell.

'What are you going to do, Mark? Are you looking for another programmer's role?'

'Well, I've been studying COBOL ... at evening classes at the Tech.' He had been keeping this quiet from colleagues. Only Mary knew about it.

'What's that? It's a metal, isn't it?' asked Barney.

'No, that's cobalt. COBOL is a programming language. I think it stands for ... er ... Common Business ... something ... Language. It's the one that most decent size companies use. We use NCR500 on our little machine, but it's not really a proper computer.'

'Oh, thank you,' said Mary and Dolly, almost together.

'Well, it's not, I'm afraid. It's a glorified accounting machine. That doesn't mean it's easy to program and operate. In fact, it's not. The bigger machines like IBM and ICL are much more flexible, but, of course, they cost more. That's why Greshams went for our little Mickey Mouse machine.'

'I never realised,' said Barney. 'I assumed if you write a program, it could run on any computer. How many of these languages are there?'

'Oh, lots,' said Mark. 'It depends what you want your program to do. Scientists and mathematicians might use PASCAL. There are others called ALGOL, FORTRAN and ASSEMBLER, but they tend to be more specialised. COBOL is the most popular and can be used on different machines.' Mark wanted to show off in front of his mainly female audience.

'So, you're looking for a job as a COBOL programmer?' Barney asked before Mark could bore them all with more terminology.

'Yes,' Mark replied, but he was a little distracted by the antics of Polly and Billy who were obviously uninterested in this talk of computers and were billing and cooing to the disgust of Penny who had the misfortune to be seated next to them. Polly was wearing her flares and as she crossed her legs, the luxurious swell of her upper thigh momentarily stopped Mark in his tracks. 'Anyway,' he said, returning to the real world,' that's enough about boring old programming. Let's change the subject.'

'What memories are you taking away from your time at Greshams, Mark?' It was Penny, who had been his first regular colleague when he worked in the Payroll department.

'Let's think,' he said. 'Well, there was the time I had a sensible conversation with Dolly. That was quite memorable.'

'When was that?' Dolly asked. 'I don't remember that.'

Mark ignored the question, as the incident hadn't actually happened.

'Then there was the time when James was nice to Mary.'

'I certainly don't remember that,' Mary said. They had all been relieved that James had not joined them for a drink. Mary had told Mark that she might not appear if James had come, such was the animosity she felt for her manager.

'Anyway, Penny,' Mark said, 'I hear your department has a new name.'

'Not as far as I know,' she replied.

'Yeah, I heard Mr Tollet use the new name. Is it the Payroll Management Team? I think that's what he called it. Mind you, he used the initials. He told me he had to visit the PMT office.'

Again, Dolly was the last to grasp the joke, although Polly and Billy didn't look as though they were interested. Mark wondered what Margaret would look like if she were to wear the same sort of flares that Polly was wearing. Thinking about it, they wouldn't suit her. Polly's legs were longer, and she had well rounded hips. He didn't feel flares would suit Margaret's stocky build. He had to stop thinking about her.

Penny hadn't laughed at his last joke. Perhaps it had been too close to the truth, because Mark had occasionally found her to be moody and hadn't missed that side of her personality. Susie, on the other hand, was still laughing and he had never known her to be moody. Her laughter always stimulated Mark's funny muscles and he continued to revel in being the centre of attraction. It was an enjoyable time and would leave him with pleasant memories.

After the euphoria of his lunchtime celebrations, Mark came down to Earth with an almighty bump. He would probably never see any of these people again and he was now out of work. Depression soon set in. His life suddenly seemed so empty and unsure.

His mother was not very sympathetic. 'You'd better get out and find another job. I will still need my housekeeping money from you,' she said.

That night, he couldn't sleep. He could still hear Susie's delightful laughter. He was puzzled as to why he lusted after Margaret's stocky little figure, or Polly's shapely hips, but at the same time, had been captivated by little Susie. They were all completely different personalities and shapes, but each stirred something in him. Margaret had recently been the subject of his night-time fantasies in a way that Susie would never do. And yet, if Susie was single and available to him, he knew that a date with her would inevitably end up in passionate lovemaking. But she was happily married so it didn't matter. Margaret, however, was single and he hadn't given up on her.

He imagined what it would be like to actually date her. Given enough time for his witty personality to shine through, he would soon be seducing her and exploring her wonderful body. Of course, he had no first-hand knowledge of her physique, but his imagination soon had him picturing its delights. After a short period of exploration and foreplay, she was soon ready to receive him, but then turned him over so that she could ride him just like she rode her horse. If those legs could control a half ton horse, she had no problem controlling a mere man. It was only a matter of time before he had satisfied the matter in hand. Soon he was lost in sleep and for a few hours, his worries disappeared.

Chapter Fourteen

Ain't That a Shame

When Mark returned from his Sunday morning football, he was surprised to see his mother conversing with her next-door neighbour. Sunday mornings were normally reserved for preparing each family's Sunday lunch, but both ladies must have slipped out for a few minutes – probably due to some very urgent gossip.

'I'm sorry to hear about your redundancy,' Mrs Nichols said.

Mark was already in a bad mood. His team had lost again and hearing his neighbour addressing him so angered him even more, but he just mumbled a polite 'Thank you,' and went indoors. When his mother followed him, he tore into her. 'Why did you have to tell her about me losing my job?'

'I thought she might know somewhere where you could get a job.'

'And did she?'

'No, she didn't, but she said she'd let me know if she heard anything. Why are you so angry about it?'

'Because I don't want every Tom, Dick and Harry knowing I'm on the dole – that's why!' Mark felt that there were two types of people on the dole – people like himself who had lost a job through no fault of their own, and those who preferred not to bother and were happy to pocket the dole money for doing nothing. He did not want to be mistaken for the latter. His sister and brother had never taken the dole and he was the first to bring shame on their family.

Except that when Monday came around, he found that he wasn't on the dole. Or at least, he wasn't entitled to any dole money as he had been paid a month's money in lieu of notice. He duly 'signed on' in order to keep his National Insurance stamps up to date, but he was told he would not receive any money for several weeks. He had hoped that the redundancy money and the pay in lieu would enable him to maintain a bank balance for once in his life, but if he was unable to obtain a job in this timeframe, such plans would come to nothing.

Having scrutinised all the jobs on offer at the Labour Exchange and finding nothing of interest, he decided to drive over to King's Lynn; his idea was that their Labour Exchange might display some different positions. Lynn, being a larger town, might also present a better chance of employers advertising computer vacancies. This proved to be a wasted journey, except that he now had some money burning a hole in his pocket and so he wandered around town with a view to visiting the record stores.

Lynn had changed dramatically since his childhood – and not for the better in his opinion. New Conduit Street and Broad Street were barely recognisable. Along both streets and others in town, someone had decided to pull down rows of interesting old buildings and replace them with bland shops made of glass, concrete and brick. A little use of the local carrstone or flint would have enhanced the appearance, but the architects could not see that.

Elsewhere in town, whole rows of terraced houses had been pulled down and replaced with modern properties, Highgate being a prime example. Buildings around Purfleet and the corner of Queens Street had been replaced with blocks of flats. Further out, farmland had been given up to large housing estates or industrial complexes. Lynn, like Sanford, had been a prime location for the London overspill in the sixties and now it continued to expand, swallowing fertile farmland, year by year.

One of Mark's favourite shops, Wheelers, had relocated from the corner of Tower Street to one of the modern shops built just off Baxter's Plain. Somehow, the shop, by moving into a more spacious property, had lost some of its atmosphere and in the record racks he found nothing to his taste.

He moved on to a store that he had never noticed before. It was called *The Soul Bowl*. Situated at the eastern end of Norfolk Street, it seemed to sell nothing but soul records. Mark was suddenly in vinyl heaven. Why hadn't he found this shop before? Almost all the discs were American releases with the centres missing, just like the ex-juke box records he had once purchased from a pub. Fortunately, he already owned a few adaptors to click into these. He wanted to buy everything in sight, but he had to discipline himself and selected a few that he didn't believe had ever been issued in the UK.

He was a big fan of Curtis Mayfield, so he felt obliged to buy a couple on the *Windy C* label because they had Curtis' name in the credits. As he went to pay for his selections, Mark noticed another rack containing what were described as *soul packs*. There were two sizes. You could buy 100 records for ten pounds or ten for one pound. The proprietor guaranteed that if there were any duplicates, Mark could exchange them. He considered that ten pounds was too extravagant in his current circumstances, so he took two of the smaller packs. They were all taped up, so it was impossible to tell what he was buying until he got them home. He considered that if there were only one or two good records in each pack, it would be worthwhile. His only concern was that he might already own some of them and then it would be money wasted. He hated waste.

He raced home to play them. He was not disappointed. There were a few artists with whom he was already familiar, such as The Spinners on the *Motown* label and Edwin Starr on the *Gordy* label, but there were also little gems that he had never heard of, such as a sweet soul group called The Persians on the *GWP* label. For an hour or so, he was contented, but it didn't last.

The next few days were a trying time. He was not used to feeling so useless. There were no suitable jobs in any of the newspapers nor the two Labour Exchanges. What was even more depressing was that he couldn't see any prospects of the situation improving since his work experience didn't lend itself to anything. His time as a Trainee Surveyor had not equipped him for pursuing that as a career and if he was honest with himself, his Work Study experience didn't look good on paper. If he pursued that as a career, he would be up against candidates who belong to the Institute of Work Study Engineers.

He might have sought a role in a Payroll office, but he considered that to be a backward step unless he found a Payroll Manager's position, but he had no management experience. His only hope appeared to be in programming, but he was sure he wouldn't find another local employer with an NCR500 machine and he had no work experience with COBOL.

Depression set in, relieved only by his new records. His mother nagged him to visit the Labour Exchange every day, which he did, but each trip proved fruitless and deepened his despair. The only thing he could look forward to was the final COBOL lesson on Thursday evening.

At the start of the final lecture, each of the students was presented with a set of punch cards that contained their final test programs. Claire was used to seeing punch cards in her position as an operator, but the others studied theirs with great interest. Each card represented a line of coding with the relevant holes punched through and the coding printed on the top of the card. It was a nice memento and they were also allowed to take away the remains of any unused coding pads.

At the end of the lesson, there was general agreement that everyone should congregate down the pub for a farewell celebration. Mark quickly decided that he didn't want to go and made to leave, but Claire stopped him to ask if he was joining them.

'No, I don't think I'll bother.'

Claire looked disappointed. 'I thought, as it's the last night, I might, but ...' she left the sentence unfinished.

'Well, have a nice time,' Mark said, but then realised something. 'Will you be able to get home afterwards?'

'I'd probably miss my bus if I go. I'll see if anyone else is going in my direction.'

'No, I'll go if you're going. I can give you a lift home.' Mark realised that it might take him out of his depression if he socialised with people.

'No,' said Claire. 'I'll be all right. You needn't come if you don't want to.'

'No ... it is our last lesson. We should celebrate. Just one thing, though ... don't say anything to anyone about me being out of work. I don't want everyone to know.'

'Why not for Heaven's sake?' she asked. 'It's nothing to be ashamed of. Lots of people get made redundant. It's not your fault.'

'But not everyone sees it that way.'

Most people would have shared Claire's view and would not have judged him harshly, but Mark still felt that being on the dole was not something to boast about.

The atmosphere in the pub was much more jovial than on his previous visits. By now, the group had known each other for six weeks and people were surer of each other. Claire insisted on buying Mark a drink. He protested saying that he could still pay his way, but she said it was to thank him for all the lifts over the past few weeks, so he accepted graciously.

One of the students, a man about Mark's age named Sammy, was obviously from Liverpool and his accent raised several comments. Mark said, 'There are lots of very good groups come out of Liverpool.'

'Tha's very true, Mark. They do.'

Sammy was expecting a discussion on the merits of some of the famed Liverpudlian acts, but Mark added 'Yeah, they go there once and then they can't wait to get away again.'

Claire joined in the conversation. 'I've got a cousin who's in a local band. They're doing ever so well. They're already taking bookings for 1975.'

'That's very good,' said Mark recognising Claire's joke. 'That's nearly twenty quid!'

'Are you two a double act?' asked Tom after the laughter had subsided.

'I think we could be,' replied Claire not minding that Mark had finished her joke for her. It worked better that way. He was more concerned that her reply might have had a double meaning and realised that he had to be careful not to mislead her.

106

Tom said 'I'm taking part in this year's Sanford Players' pantomime. I hope you'll all come. Last year, my character was Wishy Washy ... and that was one of the better reviews.'

This time, the group gathered together were more amenable to some of Mark's jokes and he was able to repeat some of those he had used at his office farewell, there being a brand-new audience. He was once again in good form and realised that it was probably Margaret's presence that had stifled him previously. This wasn't the first time that he had found trying too hard to be funny didn't work. He noted that Claire had not been tempted to tell her 'definition of a lady' joke.

On the way home, Mark said 'I enjoyed that. I'm glad you persuaded me to go. I've been a right miserable so and so these last few weeks.'

'I'm pleased you came,' she said '...and not just for the lift, by the way.' Again, he was concerned that she might be reading more into their relationship than he would want ... and yet, he did like her a lot and always enjoyed her company. He also realised that this could be the last time he would see her and that saddened him. When he first left school and sought a girlfriend, it never occurred to him to seek someone with whom to have sex. He just wanted a girlfriend, a female companion. But once he tasted the pleasures of the flesh, his needs changed. Claire would have been ideal had he met her six or seven years earlier.

'What will you do with your Thursday evenings now that the course has finished?' he asked.

'Oh, I don't know. It depends on whether I'm working a late shift or not,' she replied.

'Have you ever been to *The Jennings Arms* at Denver?' he asked.

'No. I've never heard of it. Is that somewhere special?'

'Well, I've been told that it's the place for people to go mid-week,' he answered.

'So, it's a pub, is it?' she asked.

'Do you know, I'm not sure. I imagine it's a pub with a club attached. I know they play a lot of music and a lot of young people go there. It's probably like one of these discos, I would think.'

'So, you haven't been?' she asked.

'No. All my mates are happily married, and I don't get to go to places like that with any of them. And I don't think it's the kind of place that I would want to visit on my own.' He realised that he'd already taken this conversation in one direction only. He was going to have to ask her.

'Would you fancy keeping me company one time – as friends as it were? You know ... a kind of Teutonic relationship.'

'You mean platonic, don't you?' she suggested.

'No, I was thinking you could wear a spiked helmet and jack boots.'

She laughed and said 'All right. If it's the place everyone goes to, I will have to see what it's like. Were you thinking of a Thursday, then?'

'Er ... yeah. I suppose so. Is next week all right?'

'Yes, I'm on earlies next week.'

'Right, shall I pick you up at ... er ... seven thirty? I don't really know what time people get there, but if you're on earlies, you probably won't want to be home too late.'

Claire was very pleased at the invitation, despite the 'platonic' implications. She figured that given time, Mark would recover from his broken heart and move on.

Mark was more concerned that he might develop an infatuation for her. This would have to be a 'one-off' date.

Chapter Fifteen

Disco Lady

Friday morning saw a more optimistic Mark Barker rise from his bed. His evening spent with Claire and the other students had re-invigorated him. He was now twenty-four years old, out of work and with no girlfriend, but he felt this was the day when everything changed. After a bowl of cereals, his mother appeared to spoil him with a boiled egg and toast, accompanied by a cup of tea. The gesture was soured when she announced that the eggs 'needed eating.'

As soon as he had finished his breakfast, he sat down with the local paper to scour the *Situations Vacant* column. There was nothing suited to his talents, but he was not to be downhearted. He still had Friday's edition of *The Lynn News & Advertiser* to look at. He would fetch that when he went into town to visit the Labour Exchange. He turned to the sports pages to see if there was a write-up for either of his two weekend football matches. There was nothing about Northfleet's Saturday match, but there was one for his Sunday League game. As usual, the writer was more concerned with the goal scorers, but it did just say 'Keeper Barker was unable to get his hand to either of the fierce shots.' That was true, but the article didn't mention the two saves he had made and the comment that said 'unable to get his hand' didn't make it clear that the two goals were not his fault. At least it didn't blame him for the defeat.

His trip to the Labour Exchange proved as fruitless as all his previous visits. He was thankful that the building was a little away from the main shopping area, meaning that he would not be spotted there by any of his acquaintances – or so he thought. The disadvantage of the building being away from the shops was that if he was spotted in the vicinity, it was a fair guess where he had been. The person to spot him was none other than his old school 'chum,' Derek Jarvis.

'Hello, Mark,' he said. 'Fancy seeing you again.'

'Hello Derek,' Mark replied, still wanting to call him 'Jarvis' as he had always done at school. His mind was thinking of ways to explain his presence near the Labour Exchange, but Jarvis solved the issue.

'Are you out of work, as well?' The fact that Jarvis had said 'as well,' meant that he too was now out of work and was in the same situation. Consequently, Mark did not feel the need to hide his shame.

'Yes, I've been made redundant. It was my own fault really. I've finished writing all our programs and they're so well written that I'm not required to maintain them.' A little embellishment of the truth made him feel better about his being out of work and a little of the schoolboy 'one-upmanship' had returned. 'What about you?'

'Yeah, well ... our business hasn't been doing too well. There are three of us in my department, but the other two have families, so it had to be me. I can't blame them. I'm actually still there 'till the end of this month, working my notice.'

'Oh,' said Mark. 'I received a month's money in lieu of notice, so I've got a bit of time to make the right choice.' Not that there was any choice at that time, but Jarvis didn't need to know that.

'Are you married?' Jarvis asked.

'No ... there are far too many pretty young girls trying to get their hands on me, so I'm not in a hurry. What about you?'

'Same, really,' replied Jarvis. 'I'm not sure that I'm the marrying type. You know, it's funny ... we went to the same primary school; the same grammar school; ended up in the same form all the way through school; worked on the same industrial estate; and now end up out of work at the same time. That's an awful lot of coincidences, don't you think? We'll have to go for a drink together sometime.'

'Yeah, perhaps we'll end up working for the same company next. I hope you have better luck at the Labour Exchange than I have.' This was Mark's way of closing the conversation. At school, he had always despised Jarvis and even though they were both now more mature, Mark still liked to hold a good grudge. The thought of socialising with his old nemesis did not appeal. Neither did working at the same establishment.

Back at home, the *Lynn News & Advertiser* did not reveal anything of interest. He wondered if there was any point in paying a visit to the Lynn Labour Exchange. He decided not. Surely someone with a programmer's vacancy would prefer to place an advertisement in the newspaper.

Just as he was about to discard the *Lynn News*, a thought struck him. Didn't he see a vacancy for an Accounts Clerk? That might suit Jarvis who wouldn't necessarily bother to look in that newspaper. Still, that was his problem. Mark wasn't there to look out for Jarvis. On the other hand, if the shoe was on the other foot, would his old sparring partner think of Mark? He decided that after lunch, he would try to contact him again. It would be his good deed for the day.

Later, as he walked down to the phone box, he had another thought. Which employer did he know that might have a computer - other than the Council, of course? As Margaret had considered programming as a career, wasn't it likely that her firm had one? It was a possibility. But he couldn't call Margaret. She would think he was using it as an excuse to contact her – and, he didn't want her to know that he was out of work. Nevertheless, if they did have a vacancy, he would get the chance to see more of her. He had to think about this.

First, he rang Jarvis, who expressed his thanks and promised Mark a pint if he was successful in getting the Accounts position in Lynn. Mark told him that wasn't necessary – and he meant it.

Then he found the telephone number of Margaret's employer; still a little unsure of how to word his enquiry. Some companies had a Personnel Officer who administered job vacancies, but Greshams didn't. They left it to the individual manager, except in the Factory, where the Works Manager did all the recruiting. Mark didn't know about Sanfreeze – Margaret's company. Had it been Greshams he was 'phoning, Ellie would know what to do, so perhaps Sanfreeze had their own lady in the know. He went for it.

A receptionist answered the 'phone. 'Oh, hello,' he said. 'I was wondering if I could speak to someone about any vacancies you might have there.'

'What sort of work are you looking for?' asked the polite lady.

'Well, I'm a programmer, so preferably something along those lines,' he replied.

'I don't know of anything like that, but I expect Mr Valentine would know. He's the Chief Accountant. I'll put you through to his secretary. She'll be able to help you. Hold on.'

'Thank you,' said Mark and waited a minute, getting ready to repeat his question. 'Hello. Mr Valentine's secretary' said a voice.

'I was wond....' Mark stopped abruptly. It was Margaret. He put the 'phone down quickly and started panting. He hadn't expected to hear her voice. As far as he knew, she worked as a typist. She must have been successful in attaining a secretary's position. But how could that be? She still had several more weeks of her course. He just hoped she hadn't recognised his voice. He had hardly uttered anything, had he? On the other hand, Margaret might be curious and ask the Receptionist what the call was about and then been told it was someone who was a programmer. Margaret would surely guess that it was him. It was too late now. He'd already slammed the 'phone down. He felt distraught.

The failed 'phone call was enough to send him back into the doldrums – at least until Thursday when the thought of a night out gave him something to look forward to.

Mark picked up Claire as arranged and they headed off towards *The Jenyns Arms*, not sure exactly where it was, but he knew it was somewhere near the Denver Sluice, which he had found on his road atlas. Although this appeared to be in the middle of nowhere, there seemed to be several vehicles heading in the same direction, so he assumed that they were on their way to the same establishment and followed them.

As he pulled into the large car park, he realised that the name of the pub was *The Jenyns Arms*; a simple mistake to have made as it was an unusual spelling.

This was his first venture into a night club and it was with a certain amount of trepidation that he entered, although he tried not to show it to Claire who was looking as lovely as ever in a long blue skirt and pale lemon jumper under a green suede coat.

He had heard of night clubs in London charging exorbitant sums for cheap champagne, but he needn't have worried; the drinks were reasonably priced as they had to be to attract such a young audience. The music was loud, and the light subdued as they looked around unsuccessfully for somewhere to sit. Instead, they stood and watched the dancers, trying hard to talk above the noise of both the music and the voices.

Mark spotted Kenny Stacey on the far side of the dance floor and received a wave which he returned. Kenny was with a willowy blonde. That was predictable Mark thought to himself. He also recognised quite a few men from various football teams that he had played against, most of them in groups of men. On the dance floor, young girls swayed around their handbags. Most of these ladies were wearing flares, but a few wore short skirts. There were also some hot pants on show and in due deference to Claire, Mark ensured that his eyes did not linger on any individual. The men were wearing a selection of flares and jeans, with the occasional jacket, mostly with wide lapels. Cheesecloth shirts like his own were also in abundance.

He continued to look around to see if there was anyone else, he might recognise, particularly anyone who looked like Margaret. She was always on his mind. He also thought that this was just the sort of place where he might see Blodwyn or possibly one of his other love interests from the past. But the only other person he recognised was Polly, who was dancing with a friend. She was attracting the interest of a group of young men who were hugging the edge of the dance floor. That was no surprise because she looked gorgeous in a tight-fitting blue-green dress. Could this really be the same girl that he had snubbed when she was suffering from anorexia? He was struggling to keep his eyes off her and Claire noticed this.

'Is that someone you know?' she asked.

'Pardon?' he replied.

112

'Do you know her,' she said, raising her voice.

'Oh, yeah. That's Polly. She works at Greshams.'

'She's pretty.'

At that moment, Polly saw him and waved. He waved back but remembered that she had fooled him once before. Nevertheless, when the record finished, she made her way over towards him. This time, he looked around to see to whom else she might be waving. He couldn't see any obvious candidates and then she was upon him.

It was soon obvious that she had consumed a fair amount of alcohol. 'Hello Mark,' she said. 'Have you come to wish me a happy birthday?'

'Happy birthday, Polly,' he replied, conscious of Claire staring at them both. 'Can I ask how old you are?'

'I'm twenty today.'

Just then, the opening bars of *Backstabbers* sounded.

'Oh, I love this,' she said. 'Come and dance with me, Mark.'

'I'm with someone, Polly. This is Claire.'

'Claire won't mind, will you Claire? It's my birthday.'

But Mark didn't think it right. 'No, I'm sure there are plenty of other people you can dance with.'

'No, I want to dance with you. I miss you. Come on!'

Claire said, 'Go on Mark. I'll be all right. I'll hold your drink. Go on.'

At that point, Polly moved to grab him, but stumbled and Mark held out a hand to steady her. His hand found the small of her back. It was deeply indented, and it felt good. He wanted to follow the indentation down, but instead found her wonderful firmly rounded hips and helped her onto the floor.

It was an up-tempo tune and he readied to do some disco dancing, but Polly wanted to hold him as though it were a smooth waltz. In truth, she needed him to support her, so he obliged and held her close. It felt so good. He'd heard that some animals gave off pheromones to attract a mate and he wondered if that what was Polly did, because he'd never felt so enamoured before. As they stood there, barely moving from the spot, he was aware of a stirring in his pants, but his tight flared trousers were doing a good job of containing his erection.

'Where's Billy, tonight?' he asked, but the reply was mumbled, and he didn't feel inclined to pursue the matter.

She leaned her head on his shoulder and asked, 'Are you taking me home tonight?'

Taking her home meant only one thing in his eyes and as much as he wanted to, he knew he couldn't For one thing, he knew that it was the drink talking. For another, he knew that he could not abandon Claire. Even so, it was hard when he repeated that he was with someone.

At the end of the dance, he escorted back towards her friend. 'I think she needs a coffee or something,' he told the friend.

'She's all right. It's her birthday. She's enjoying herself.'

He thought that Polly deserved a better friend than this and with reluctance he returned to find Claire. He gratefully retrieved his drink and took a large swig, aware that his erection was still being contained by his tight trousers and hoped that it didn't show.

'Do you want to dance?' he asked of her.

'In a little while,' she replied. 'Let's finish our drinks first.' That made sense as there was nowhere to leave them while they danced. Conversation was minimal as it involved a degree of shouting which made it hard work. A little later, Jackie Wilson's *I Get the Sweetest Feeling* started playing.

'Are you ready to dance now?' he asked.

'Yes, all right,' and the two of them deposited their empty glasses on someone else's table. Mark only liked dancing to records that he enjoyed and had tried to ignore all the other pop-oriented tracks.

Claire had a natural rhythm and moved nicely in time to the beat. Mark tried to mimic some of her moves, and he was soon building up a sweat. He was pleased not to be dancing too close because he was sure that Polly's scent was still on him bringing back enjoyable memories. When a T-Rex song started, he used the excuse that he had spotted a free table and led Claire towards it.

'I think they're doing food in a basket over at that bar,' he said. 'Do you fancy anything?'

'I'll share some chips with you,' she replied. 'Let me pay?'

'Of course not,' he said and walked off to the food bar before she could protest further.

When he returned with scampi and chips, she was nowhere to be seen, but she had left her suede coat on their chairs together with his jacket to ensure they didn't lose their seats. He assumed that she had visited the ladies, but she returned with a repeat order of their two drinks.

'Thank you,' he said as she sat down again. 'I hope you like scampi. I've never tried it before.'

'Oh, I love scampi,' she replied and the two of them tucked into an enjoyable snack, washed down by their drinks.

'Do you want to dance again?' he asked when a slower number played.

'Yes, all right,' she replied.

As they danced, Mark held her close, but again, he found her bony physique caused him anguish. This was a woman with whom he could easily fall in love, but with whom he would probably struggle to make love. He felt no physical desire for her, yet in so many other ways, she was perfect for him. He decided that he mustn't see her again or he might end up in love and frustrated – and so might she.

'What time do you want to be home?' he asked, trying to break any magical spell that might exist between them.

'I'd better not be too late and if I'm honest, it's a bit too noisy in here for my liking.'

And so, at the end of the record, they picked up their coat and jacket and made their way towards the exit. On the way out, Mark glanced across to see Polly and her friend dancing with a couple of long-haired youths who looked barely old enough to be out in such an establishment. He had no doubt about the outcome of Polly's evening. It could so easily have been his lucky night and after so many months without sex, that was bitterly frustrating, but he'd long decided that Polly was not the woman for him, as lovely and enticing as she was.

As Mark drove them home, he asked 'What do you think of the *Jenyns*?'

'It's fine if you want to dance, listen to the music or have a drink, but no good if you want to have a conversation.'

'No, it's not a place for a romantic evening, but you can understand why so many young people want to go there. There's plenty of atmosphere.'

'So, will you be going again?' she asked.

'I doubt it,' he replied, 'but I'm glad to have tried it ... and I thank you for coming with me. I would never go somewhere like that on my own.'

'Me neither,' she said. After a pause, she said 'That Polly seems to like you a lot. Don't you like her?'

'She's a very nice girl, but ... er ... a bit young for me. She's only twenty ... and she acts it.'

'How old are you?' she asked.

'I'm twenty-four.'

'That's not a huge gap. She's very pretty.'

Mark didn't want to tell tales about Polly's sexual habits, so he just added 'Not for me.'

'You're still thinking about your last girlfriend, aren't you?'

He sighed. He was going to have to tell more lies. 'I'd rather not talk about it, if you don't mind.'

'All right,' she said. 'It's just that I don't like to see you unhappy.'

'I think that once I get a new job, I'll be able to throw all my energies into making that a success. I won't have time to feel sorry for myself. There's bound to be something of interest in tomorrow's paper.'

'I think they're going to advertise our programmer's vacancy very soon. Why don't you put in for that?' she suggested.

'Because I want you to get it,' he said and this time, he was telling the truth. 'Anyway, you've done a lot better on the course than me.'

'Ah, that's because I cheated,' she said. 'One of our programmers at work often stays behind in the evening to test his programmes and I help him. In return, he has talked me through some of his work. I think you learn a lot from mistakes – even other peoples'.'

'Yes,' said Mark. 'Anyone can make a mistake, as the Dalek said climbing down from the dustbin.'

'Do you think Daleks have a sex life?' Claire asked. 'They've all got masculine voices.'

'I think they're probably hermaphrodites,' he replied.

The conversation continued at a similar philosophical level until they reached the end of Claire's road.

'Are you coming in for a nightcap?' she asked.

Mark hesitated. Could this develop into something that he should avoid? Yet, he might not see her again and he didn't want to say goodbye in a dark car.

'Yes, thank you. I am a little thirsty,' he replied.

Claire's mother was still up watching the television which she turned off as soon as they arrived.

'Mum, this is my friend Mark.'

Her mother was much shorter and dumpier than Claire and she greeted Mark with a warm smile. 'Come and sit down in front of the fire, Mark,' she said. 'I'll put the kettle on. You'll have a bite to eat, I'm sure.'

'Thank you, but we did have some chips at the club,' Mark replied.

'Well, I know Claire will always find room for more. She never stops eating.'

'I'll sort it out, mum. You sit and entertain Mark.'

'I bet I know what you're thinking,' said her mother to Mark as Claire disappeared to the kitchen. 'Am I really her mother when I'm short and fat? Well, I can assure you that I am. She takes after her father. He's in bed at the moment – always retires early – has to be up to start his shift in the morning. No, our Claire has always been on the lean side, but she eats like a horse and never puts on a pound. They're all like that on my Walter's side of the family. Would you like a sherry while Claire's making the coffee?'

Mark declined. The news about Claire never putting on a pound confirmed his worst fears. He had been wondering if it were possible to fatten her up a little, so she didn't feel so bony.

A few minutes later, Claire re-appeared with a tray of coffees and four rounds of cheese-on-toast. 'Here are, Tuck in, Mark.'

He loved cheese-on-toast but offered some to Claire's mother first. 'Oh no, thanks. I have to watch what I eat before going to bed,' she said and continued to dominate the conversation, mostly talking about Claire's ability to eat without gaining weight.

'Mum ... Mark doesn't want to hear about my eating habits.'

'I used to be very thin, you know,' he said. 'I was barely eleven stone when I left school at seventeen. Now I'm about thirteen and I'm not eating any different. It's just natural growth.'

'You've probably put on muscle,' said her mother.

'Well, you wouldn't mistake me for Charles Atlas, but you'd be hard pressed to find any fat on me.'

'Perhaps Claire should put on some muscle.'

'No thanks,' said Claire. 'I don't want to look like one of those Russian shot putters.'

'I think some of them are men,' said Mark. 'And the East German women are all on drugs. They're not real women.'

'They're probably hermaphrodites,' said Claire.

'Or Daleks,' added Mark.

'I haven't a clue what you two are on about,' said Claire's mother.

'Don't worry about it, mum. It's just a conversation we had earlier.'

'Just keep your dustbin well out of sight,' added Mark and the two of them laughed out loud.

'Shh ... you'll wake your dad!'

Claire had finished her two rounds of toast, while Mark was making hard work of his second, but he wasn't going to let a woman out-eat him and kept going.

'I'll be off to bed,' said Claire's mother. 'Don't be too long, Claire. You have to be up early.'

'Oh, yes,' said Mark, swallowing his last mouthful. 'I forgot you're on an early shift. I'd better be off' and he finished his coffee. 'Thank you both for your hospitality.'

'I'll see you to the door,' Claire said.

At the door, he said 'Thank you ever so much for coming with me tonight. It's been very enjoyable.'

'I've enjoyed it as well,' she replied. 'You need to keep going out to enjoy yourself and keep feeling positive about your future. I'd like to know how you get on with finding a job. Will you keep in touch?'

'Of course. Give me a call when you know about your job.'

'You'd better give me your number, then,' she said.

'We're not on the 'phone at home. You can call me at work ... oh, no, you can't, can you? I'll call you sometime.' He thought this unlikely, but it sounded like the right thing to say.

He gave her a peck on the cheek and made off to his car.

'You'll have to do a three-point turn, she said after him. 'There's nowhere to turn.' But because he still hadn't fitted a reversing light, he had to take it carefully and ended up doing a five-point turn.

As he drove home, he contemplated driving back to Denver to see if Polly was still available, but he had an urgent need to visit his outdoor privy instead.

Chapter Sixteen

The Turning Point

Mark parked his car outside of *The Auto Centre* where he knew they sold almost everything connected with automobiles. Before leaving home that Friday morning, he had read up about fitting a reversing light, so he knew which parts he would need to buy. He had first bought a copy of *The AA Book of the Car* when he needed to know how to apply filler to his old Wolseley and now the lavishly illustrated volume was going to prove its use again.

Inside the store were dozens of racks containing everything from fluffy steering wheel covers to brake pads. Before picking up the items that he needed, he wandered around and considered possible future purchases such as a centre console containing a handy cubby hole for cloths and sweets; a set of sheepskin seat covers and a clear panel that could be adhered to his rear window to prevent condensation. This was a time before heated rear windows might be a standard fitting in a family saloon. He eyed a front spotlight and considered that if his reversing light was effective, he might move on to something like that. Then he saw a selection of stripes for fixing to the side of a vehicle. There were two basic types – those that were affixed like a transfer and those that acted as a stencil for painting. He quite fancied a discreet white stripe to set off his car, but he would decide which type to choose another time. His priority that day was to get a reversing light.

He selected a reasonably priced unit, along with a length of suitable wire, a box of connectors and a switch to fix to his dashboard. When he came to pay for the items, the shop assistant asked, 'Is the switch for the light?'

'Yes,' said Mark thinking it was a stupid question.

'You can't use that. It will be illegal unless you also fit a warning light. It's the law. If you fit a reversing light, there must be a warning light to indicate when it's switched on – unless you fit a switch to the gearbox. That's a bit of a specialist job. We do sell switches with a built-in warning light. Shall I show you a selection?'

Mark chose one where the toggle switch itself lit up. He thought that looked cool.

Having already studied the local newspaper, he had decided not to visit the Labour Exchange that morning. Instead, he would go home and make a start on his lamp, but the traffic was heavy, and it proved difficult to turn right out of the car park. After a few frustrating minutes, he turned left towards town. After all, he needed to pick up the Lynn newspaper, so he might as well go into town to ensure there were no vacancies at the Exchange.

It was as well that he had made this decision. There was one card that caught his attention. It read –

Are you looking to change career?
Are you ambitious and keen to maximise your earning potential?
Do you have a clean driving licence?
Then we want to hear from you.
Full training will be provided.
Call us now on 0603 123145 to arrange an interview.

There was no information about the role, but he was certainly looking for a career change. He could see that it was a Norwich number. Was Norwich too far away to commute? Possibly, but there appeared to be travelling involved so one would expect assistance with travelling expenses. The one drawback for him was that he would need to pay for a distance 'phone call, which meant pummelling a phone-box with silver. Perhaps, he could persuade one of the clerks to make the call for him.

A polite young lady, who was manning the desk, was only too happy to oblige him and duly dialled the number. She reported that the person she needed to speak to in Norwich was unavailable that morning, but his assistant told her that he was conducting interviews on Monday afternoon if Mark would like to attend.

Mark wanted to know more about the position, but the man's assistant was unable to provide details, so he said 'yes' and the young lady took down details of the time and place, which was two o'clock at The Post House on the Ipswich Road and he was to ask for Mr Palmer. Mark had a street map of Norwich in his Road Atlas, so it was all agreed. Holding an interview in an hotel seemed a little strange, but he wondered if this employer was in the process of moving to Norwich and their own premises were not yet available. At least he had an interview.

When he returned to his car and looked at his street map, he found that the Ipswich Road was quite long so he would have to get there in good time to find it, but a large hotel should be easy enough to find.

When he announced the news of his interview to his mother, she suggested that the job sounded like a door-to-door shoe salesman and then reminded him that it was the end of the month and his housekeeping money was due. 'I'm not earning any money! How am I supposed to pay you what I don't have?'

'You seem to find the money to buy records and go out drinking,' she replied. 'I've still got to provide food and electricity for you. I want my money this week.'

Of course, Mark still had his redundancy money untouched, but he knew that his mother really wanted the money to go to Bingo so he would hold out as long as he could.

That afternoon, he got stuck into the task of fitting his reversing light. Mark had never been very good with manual tasks. At school, he was glad to have switched from woodwork to Latin after only one year. But he had clear instructions in his *Book of the Car,* and he followed them carefully, so that, by tea-time, he had a functioning light and illuminated switch. It had been a frustrating exercise as he lacked the correct tools and wires kept coming loose from their connections. It also didn't look very elegant. The toggle switch was not very secure, and he was unable to point the lamp in the direction that he really wanted. The wires were also a bit of a mess. In places, they were safely secured under the rubber mats, but in others, they were exposed and in danger of being damaged or pulled from their connections, but it worked, and he eagerly awaited the chance to try it out on a dark road.

The following evening, he drove over to Dersingham where Ray and Valerie welcomed him. Ray spent his evenings during the week studying for his HNC, so he was always pleased for a distraction at the weekend. Mark immediately told them all about his forthcoming interview.

'It sounds like an encyclopaedia salesman to me,' said Ray. 'I'm sure I've seen adverts like that before. Mind you, they normally announce what it is that they're selling, so who knows?'

There followed a conversation about how Mark might prepare himself for the interview, which they all agreed was awkward if he didn't know what the job entailed, and it only made him anxious.

Valerie said 'I hope you don't mind me saying this, Mark, but ...'

He knew that whenever someone started a sentence in this way, they were going to have a go at him.

'... if someone doesn't know you like we do, you can come across as being a bit pessimistic and negative. You need to go into this with a positive mind and look like you want the job.'

'But I don't know if I do want the job until I know what it is.'

'That's what I'm saying,' she said. 'You mustn't go into it thinking that way.'

'But it is the way I think. Suppose they want me to work in an abattoir ... or the sewage works?'

'You can still go through the motions,' said Ray, ever keen to spot the opportunity for a jest.

'I might get the wrong end of the stick,' added Mark, dipping into his collection of sewage farm jokes.

'See, that's what I mean,' said Valerie. 'I'm not being funny, but ....'

That was another start to a sentence that led to something unpleasant.

'... you are inclined to try to be funny all the time – and not everyone shares your sense of humour. Take it seriously – and above all else, go into the interview being positive.'

'Hang on,' said Mark, 'aren't you the one who told me I had no chance with Margaret? What's all this about being positive when you put the mockers on that?'

'That was different,' she replied. 'I knew she would never go out with you – and I was right.'

'I haven't given up yet,' he said. 'You might still be surprised – and I still don't know if I want this job.'

'Never mind,' said Valerie with a sigh. 'At least you can use the opportunity to do some shopping in Norwich.' That set some thoughts into Mark's mind and it did relieve some of the anxiety. If nothing else, it would be useful practice for any future interviews.

It wasn't long before Ray was steering the conversation onto some of his latest jokes. 'I wanted some porridge this morning, so I opened a tin of evaporated milk. Blow me! The tin was empty.'

'Don't tell me,' said Mark. 'It had evaporated! The clue is in the name.'

'Oh, you two!' said Valerie. 'You're like Morecambe and Wise!'

'I say, I say, I say,' said Mark. 'My dog's got no nose.'

'Oh Gawd,' said Valerie who was a churchgoer and didn't normally utter blasphemous remarks.

'Your dog's got no nose,' said Ray. 'How does he smell?'

'Well, he doesn't, does he?' replied Mark. 'As I said, he's got no nose.'

'I'm making some coffee,' said Valerie.

***

On Sunday morning, Kenny accosted Mark in the football changing rooms, eager to talk about their respective visits to *The Jenyns Arms*. 'I saw you getting in close with young Polly. She looked like she wanted to eat you.'

'Yeah, well, I was with someone else.'

'I noticed ... nice looking lady.'

'Yes, she is.' Mark felt Kenny was fishing about Claire, but he wanted to ask about Polly. 'Did you see who Polly went home with? Was it one of those long-haired lads she was with when I left?'

'I think she went home with Denny Gorman,' Kenny replied.

'Should I know him?' Mark asked.

'He plays football. You've probably played against him ... he's from Tilney or Terrington, I think ... one of those village teams from the Fens. You might have seen him Thursday night ... tall lad with an afro ... wearing a Ben Sherman and Levis. Are you jealous?'

'No, it's just that I worked with her ... and I like to know the latest gossip.' That wasn't the whole story. Mark did have a bit of a soft spot for her and that dance had definitely roused something in him, but it wasn't jealousy – it was lust.

Despite the fact that Norwich was Norfolk's County Town, Mark had only ever visited it a few times. The last time had been with Melody when most of the trip was taken up with a look at the magnificent cathedral with its tall spire - the second highest in the country. On that day, he had spotted a second-hand record shop, but had disregarded it so that Melody would not have to stand around while he searched for a bargain. Now he decided that he would make the most of his day out and allow sufficient time to find the shop again.

He also saw it as an opportunity to exchange his Green Shield stamps for an item from their catalogue. When garages first started offering the stamps, he had resisted as he could obtain his petrol cheaper elsewhere, but gradually, as many petrol stations started offering double, then quadruple stamps, he succumbed. He now had three books completed and this would be an opportunity to exchange them for a gift. There were no stores nearer for him to do so.

He set out on his journey in good time and made the Green Shield store his first visit. He had decided upon a Nottingham lace tablecloth which he would give to his mother for a Christmas present. Finding the record shop proved a little more difficult but he eventually succeeded only to find there was no segregation of the musical genres and so he ended up wading through dozens of racks to find something of interest. When he did find something to his taste, it was too expensive and so he abandoned his search in that particular store, determined to seek out another record shop elsewhere in the city.

He wandered down some of the little alleyways that led off from the main thoroughfares, but time was running away with him and he decided that his priority was to eat, drink and find Ipswich Road. A small cafe satisfied his first need in the way of a delicious bacon roll. A strong cup of tea fulfilled the second need, but left a bitter taste in his mouth, which was mollified by a bar of chocolate and he felt ready to face the worst.

It was still a little early for his interview, but there wasn't sufficient time to look for any more record shops. In any case, he felt a little self-conscious in his best suit, so he made his way back to his car and headed towards what he thought was the start of Ipswich Road.

This involved following the inner ring road and looking out for road signs directing him towards Ipswich. He figured that any hotel that catered for visitors to Norwich would be as near as possible to the city centre, so he started his search at the top of Ipswich Road. After crossing the busy outer ring road and heading further away from the city centre, he started to worry that he'd missed it. He was about to turn around when he spotted it on the other side of the road.

He was still a little early, so he sat in the car park for a while, but soon got fed up with that. He donned his tie and went inside. There was always the chance that his interviewer was available to meet him at an earlier time.

Mark had only ever stayed in one hotel in his life. That had been a much grander affair when he had attended his programming course in London. The Post House was still big enough and smart enough to make him feel a little anxious as he entered. He approached the reception desk where a smartly dressed lady smiled at him. He realised that his best suit made him look like a possible guest but one without luggage. 'Can I help you, sir?'

'Yes, I have an appointment with Mr Palmer.'

'Is he a guest of the hotel?' she asked.

'I don't know. I've come for an interview.'

'We don't appear to have a Mr ...'

'That will be me,' said a voice behind Mark. It was owned by a smartly dressed man, not very much older than Mark. He was just finishing a cup of tea and replaced the cup on its saucer as he stood up and gestured to Mark to join him.

'Sorry, I'm a little early,' said Mark. 'Please finish your tea.'

'No, it's fine, thank you. I'm glad you're early. Sit down.' He moved a newspaper from a chair and extended his hand to Mark. 'I'm James Palmer. Here's my card. Sit down. Now you're ... let me see ...' he shuffled some papers and opened a smart leather-bound file containing a foolscap writing pad.

'I'm Mr Barker,' Mark replied, trying to read the business card. The name of Mr Palmer's company was Pratt & Walker and they were based in Hadleigh, Suffolk. Their business just said, 'Windows and Home Improvements.'

'Ah yes, we spoke on the 'phone, didn't we?'

'Um, no, you weren't available when we called.'

'Really? Oh well, never mind. Tell me why you want this job.'

Mark remembered Valerie's advice about saying something positive. 'Well, your advert said you were interested in anyone who was ambitious and was looking for a change of career.' That must have sounded positive.

'What selling have you done before?' Mr Palmer asked.

So, it was selling. 'I once sold a stamp album to an old school mate.' He just couldn't resist a little humour, despite Valerie's warning that not everyone understood his jokes.

'Did you strike a good bargain?' The interviewer was treating this as a sensible response to his question.

'I got thirty bob. I didn't want to collect stamps anymore and the other bloke had just started, so we were both happy. I went out and bought a new LP, so I was pleased with the outcome.'

'Right ... so you've never sold anything professionally, is that right?'

'That's right ... but I'm here to sell myself to you today.' Valerie would be proud of that statement.

'Go on, then!'

'Well ... I'm honest, hard-working and reliable. I have a sense of humour and I always have a positive outlook on life.' Some of that was true.

Mr Palmer seemed pleased with that response and asked, 'What work are you doing at the moment?'

'Well, I've been working as a computer programmer, but I'm not sure it's what I want to do for the rest of my life. It involves working in isolation and concentrating for long periods without interaction with others. My previous position was in a Work Study department – with the same company. Can you tell me more about the job you're advertising?'

'Yes, of course. My company is Pratt & Walker. We're based in Hadleigh and we mainly produce aluminium windows. We've had considerable success in Suffolk and Essex and now we're looking to expand into Norfolk and Cambridgeshire. We manufacture the windows in Hadleigh and that is where our head office is, but we are considering opening a small office base somewhere in Norfolk. Watton is one place we're looking at.

'As a result of this expansion, we are looking for salesmen to cover the new areas. Obviously, we would prefer someone with a good track record of selling, but we are prepared to give full training to anyone of the right calibre. The job is commission based. I trust that won't be a problem to you?'

'So, the more I sell, the more I earn.' It was an obvious statement to make, but Mark was weighing up the implication of this in terms of actual remuneration.

'Exactly!'

'And what would be someone's typical take-home pay?'

'It varies a lot. Some of our salesmen take home over a thousand pounds a month.'

'Presumably, there is some kind of basic salary to cover lean months?'

'No, there's no salary at all. If you don't sell, you don't earn.'

Mark had been prepared to consider the job if he was accepted, but he wasn't sure if he was salesman material – and with no salary, it was highly likely that he would end up penniless. He would be better off on the dole.

'No, I don't think it's for me,' he said.

Mr Palmer didn't move or say anything. It was an old salesman's trick. The first to speak had lost the battle, but Mark wasn't interested in playing games. He had wasted his time.

He stood up and said 'What a pity your advert didn't explain what the job was all about. We could have both saved ourselves a lot of bother.' He didn't bother to shake hands – he just walked out the door and tore off his tie.

He sat in his car for a few moments and fumed. He had wasted a day and a lot of petrol. He hadn't even bought a record or two. He contemplated going back into the city, but that would mean driving home in the rush hour. He still had a long journey home and it would be getting dark by the time he reached Sanford now that the clocks had gone back. So much for positive thinking.

Had he been a little rash? After all, he was out of work so what did he have to lose by giving it a try? It was probably the fact that he had been lured all the way to Norwich on false pretences that had caused him to walk out. It made him feel stupid. He felt useless. He had no job and no girlfriend – and he couldn't see that changing in the near future. Perhaps he should apply for the programmer's job at the Council. It would mean going back on his word to Claire. What sort of a person would do that? Someone without a job, that was who.

He didn't know it, but he was about to reach a turning point in his life.

Chapter Seventeen

Happiness is Just Around the Bend

'You'd better find yourself a job today. I'm sick of you hanging around this house all day using our electricity, food and heating. There are loads of jobs in today's paper. Get off your lazy arse and find one.' This was Mark's mother's way of motivating him to find a job.

'Do you think I want to sit around in this cold smelly dump all day? I can't conjure up a bleeding job if there aren't any.' He had risen from his bed at nine-thirty. The bedroom was so cold that he preferred to remain under the eiderdown. If he hadn't been bursting for a pee, he would probably still be there.

He was anxious to find the job page in the local newspaper, but out of some strange sense of not tempting fate, he left the jobs page until last.

On page five, he was stopped in his tracks by a photograph of Blodwyn in a wedding dress. She had married someone called Chas Simmons, a tall good-looking lad who played rugby for West Sanford. She once told Mark that she liked rugby players. He felt a little disappointed to see her married. Now he would never experience those wonderful thighs at close quarters. It was another chapter in his life now closed. She wasn't the first of his earlier love interests to tie the knot. Karen, his first real infatuation, was long married. Debbie Pope was now Debbie Masters. He wondered about all the others, most of whom he hadn't seen in years. It really was time he was settled down, but that prospect looked a long way off. Instead of living in wedded bliss, he was still stuck at home arguing with his mother and feeling totally useless.

Perhaps today would be the day when it all turned around, but he continued reading the rest of the newspaper. There was little else of interest, so he braced himself to look at the jobs page. He had already told himself that if the programming job with the council was advertised, he would apply. After all, Claire had given him her blessing even if it meant going back on his word.

And there, in the middle of the second column, in a large display box. He saw the wording -

Junior COBOL programmer required.

But it wasn't the one with the council. It was with a company called Greyfriars. He'd never heard of them, but the address in the advertisement was in town. He knew of the Greyfriars Tower in King's Lynn, where there was also a Blackfriars Road and he seemed to remember an area called Whitefriars. Then of course, there were lots of fish fryers. He sniggered at his own little private joke. He'd never heard of any Greyfriars in Sanford, but he knew where Ransome Road was. The stated salary was £1200 to £1500 p.a. depending upon experience. The advert also said that knowledge of OS would be an advantage, but not essential. Did that mean that Greyfriars had something to do with the Ordnance Survey? He liked reading maps. Applicants were to write, detailing their experience and current availability.

He immediately set to work on drafting his application. Then he had a thought. The advertisement used the word *Junior*. He hoped that didn't mean an office junior. He'd had enough of that, but then he realised the salary range quoted could not apply to an office junior. Anyway, who was he to be fussy? If he was to obtain a job as a COBOL programmer, of course he would have to be a *junior* programmer at first.

He decided not to mention his experience of COBOL – or rather his lack of experience. Nor did he think he should talk about OS, in case it had nothing to do with map reading. He was quite capable of looking silly without taking any unnecessary risks. Instead, he highlighted the work he had done as a programmer. The first step was to obtain an interview. If he got that far, he could dazzle his potential employer with his astounding personality - and his love of maps.

He wondered how he should answer the question of his current availability. They would eventually find out that he was out of work, but he didn't want to advertise the fact too early. Instead he answered that he was available at short notice, which was certainly true.

He re-wrote the letter in his best handwriting, determined to give the best possible first impression. Then he took his letter to the main post office in town to ensure the speediest delivery. In the meantime, his family informed him that Greyfriars were a builders' merchants with branches throughout East Anglia and beyond. That rang a bell, because he seemed to remember a delivery vehicle at Greshams that had their name on it; probably delivering timber.

On the Wednesday of the following week, he received a reply asking him to attend an interview. He'd tackled the first hurdle.

A week later, he had a new job. He had been interviewed by two people. Adam Chandler was the Programming Manager. He was the one to ask most of the questions and although at first, he seemed like a round-faced jovial person, it was soon clear to Mark that he was the more astute of the two interviewers. The other man was Geoffrey Gardiner; slightly older than Adam and introduced as Adam's boss. He was the Systems Manager. He was tall and smartly dressed and he made careful notes of all of Mark's answers.

It didn't take the two managers long to suss out that Mark's only experience of COBOL was on an introductory course, but they both seemed impressed when Mark explained the various applications that he had already programmed.

'So, what was the operating system of this NCR500?' Adam asked. 'I take it that it wasn't OS?' So now Mark knew that OS was an operating system.

'No - strictly speaking, it didn't have one,' Mark replied. 'That is to say, that you operated it from a console to load up a program on paper tape and the program took over.'

'But how did the program know where to store the program and the data?' Again, it was Adam asking the question.

'That's all built into the program.' Mark couldn't understand why this was so difficult to understand.

'So, the program wasn't held in a program library?'

'Well, the program tapes were stored in a locked cupboard.' Mark had never heard of a program library.

'And was the data stored on disk or magnetic tape?'

'It is stored on magnetic ledger cards,' Mark replied. He realised that he was using a mixture of past and present tense. 'We didn't have any magnetic tapes – just paper tapes. We didn't have any disks either. The CPU is divided into four planes, each of which stores one hundred cells and each cell is twelve characters long. A cell can contain a program instruction or data. If it's an instruction, it will also contain the address of the next command. The programming language is unique to the NCR500 and is nothing like COBOL.'

'And you managed to run all these applications on that small amount of space?'

'We had to.'

'Presumably,' Geoffrey asked, at last joining in the questioning,' You could only run one program at a time?'

'Oh, yes. Mondays and Tuesdays had to be reserved for running the weekly payrolls.'

Both interviewers were amazed that Mark had managed to run these applications on such an archaic machine and that counted in his favour, as did his previous roles within the company.

They then allowed Mark to ask them some questions and he found out about the company and the kind of work that they ran on their IBM computer. He felt pleased at his questioning. He wanted to give the impression that it was just as important for Greyfriars to impress him as it was the other way around.

At the end of the interview, the two gentlemen asked Mark to wait in reception while they had a discussion. The attractive receptionist engaged him in polite conversation and made him feel at ease. He wondered if she was unattached. If he got the job, he would make it his business to find out.

After a few minutes, he was summoned back into the interview room.

Geoffrey spoke first. 'We've now seen all the applicants and it seems that most of them are in a similar position to yourself in that they've attended a course, but you are the only one with actual programming experience. So, we'd like to offer you the position on a salary of twelve hundred pounds per annum.' That was at the bottom of the salary range quoted in the newspaper. Mark wanted to negotiate. He remembered when he had started at Greshams, he had been stuck on a low salary for quite a while and he didn't want a repeat of that. On the other hand, he realised that his lack of COBOL experience didn't put him in a very good position to negotiate.

'I was hoping for a little more.' This produced no reaction. 'How often are your pay reviews?' he asked.

'Every year in April,' Geoffrey replied. He seemed to be doing all the talking now. 'But you wouldn't be eligible in the first year. Instead, we would you put you on six months' probation and review the situation at the end of that period. If you've done well, you would expect a rise.'

'When can I start?' Mark asked.

'As soon as you like,' Geoffrey replied.

'Tomorrow?'

'Well, no ... I have to send you a letter offering you the job. That has to come from our Managing director. Then we have to receive your acceptance in writing, but I'm glad to see you're keen.'

They shook hands and Mark walked to his car with a childish spring in his step. He wanted to tell everyone and celebrate, but everyone apart from his mother would be at work. He could phone Claire. He promised her that he'd let her know if he got a job, but then he thought that she might have been one of the other candidates and it wasn't his job to tell her she had been unsuccessful. He would have to wait a few days.

Ransome Road was just of Lynn Road, so he headed off towards King's Lynn. He would celebrate by buying a record or two from The Soul Bowl record shop.

He arrived home with two new soul-packs and greeted his mother with his good news before blasting out her ears with his new purchases. 'When do you start?' she asked above the music.

'When I've received a formal job offer and replied,' he said.

'So, it's not definite, yet?'

'Yes, they just have to get the Managing Director to sign the offer.'

'Well don't celebrate until you've got the job,' she said.

That dampened his mood. It was highly unlikely that they would change their minds at that point, but she was right in a way. Because of this, he didn't tell anyone else about his good news, even though he was bursting to tell the world.

Feeling frustrated with life, he tried to busy himself by listening to his records or watching *Pebble Mill at One* on TV and the afternoon repeat of *Mastermind*. In the evenings, he watched such programmes as *Mission Impossible* and *Softly, Softly: Task Force*.

Each day, he waited anxiously for a letter in the post. It eventually arrived on the Friday of the week of his interview. His understanding was that once a job offer had been made, his new employer could not withdraw it. He'd done it. Before sending off his reply, he checked the Sanford newspaper to see if there were any other jobs that he might consider; not that he wanted any other at that time, but he was in the habit of checking each week.

What he did find in the newspaper, however, was that *Lady Sings the Blues* was on at the local cinema. He wanted to see that film and considered calling Claire to invite her to join him. It was just an excuse to see if she had any job news. If she had applied for the position at Greyfriars and hadn't heard anything, he would keep quiet about his good fortune for now. He would call her at work in the afternoon, but during the morning, he had one of his brainwaves.

The film he wanted to see starred Diana Ross – and who was a big fan of that lady? Margaret, of course. Should he risk another rejection? What did he have to lose – apart from his dignity, that is? Yes, he would do it. But as the time drew near, he kept putting it off.

The 'phone box was near to the post box and so he headed down the road with his acceptance letter in his hand. All kind of thoughts were now entering his overactive mind – how best to start the conversation; reasons why she would refuse him; whether she might be too busy to talk to him. Just to make matters worse, he had forgotten her surname.

131

Could he just ask for Margaret – the typist who may now be a secretary? No, it wouldn't do.

He remembered what Kenny had once told him about getting a good result when selling a car. 'Don't give the punter an opportunity to say 'no.' Once they start saying 'no,' it becomes easier to keep saying 'no.' Then there was something about 'open' and 'closed' questions. What was it? Instead of asking 'Is this the car for you?' one should ask 'What sort of car are you looking for?'

If Mark wanted a positive outcome to his quest, he had to prepare his questioning very carefully. He decided to sleep on it.

The next morning, he thought he was ready for the task in hand. 'Is Margaret there?' he asked when a man answered the phone with the announcement 'Willow Farm.'

'Who wants her?' That sounded like a very protective father – or just someone who seldom answers the 'phone.

'It's Mark,' he replied in an apologetic tone. He was already on the defensive.

'Hang on – Margaret! It's a chap for you!' her father shouted without shielding the mouthpiece.

After a minute, during which time, Mark's ears returned to near normal, a breathless Margaret said 'Hello?'

'Hello, Margaret. It's Mark.' His heart was racing, but he tried to sound calm.

'Who?' This was not helping his confidence.

'Mark Barker – from the course ... we played tennis together.'

'Oh, yes. Hello Mark, how are you?'

That was better. 'I'm very well, thank you – and you?'

'Yes – fine, thank you. Have you got a game of tennis arranged for us?'

'Er ... no. I'm afraid not. I noticed that Diana Ross is on at the Odeon next week ... *Lady Sings the Blues*. I know you're a big fan of hers.'

'Oh, yes. I've been waiting to see that. Is it on now?'

'No, it starts on Monday. I'd quite like to see it. It's got some very good reviews.'

And then he paused to see what she said next.

'Yes,' she said. 'I'd quite like to see it.'

'I could take you if you like,' he said. This was the big moment.

'The thing is,' she said, 'I'm very busy with this course.'

'But you used to be free on Thursdays when we had the COBOL course.'

'That's true. I could make Thursday. Shall I meet you there?'

Mark couldn't believe his ears. She was actually agreeing to meet him, but that sounded risky. She might not actually turn up.

'There's no point in taking two cars,' he said. 'I'll pick you up at your house – at seven fifteen?'

'Do you know where I live?' she asked.

'Yes, it's *Willow Farm* – down Field Drive. I'll see you on Thursday. 'Bye for now.'

'All right, then,' she said. 'Goodbye.' He put the 'phone down before she could change her mind, hoping that didn't sound too abrupt.

This was the happiest Mark had felt for some time and he couldn't wait to tell everyone about his two pieces of good news. He decided that in the evening, he would drive over to see Ray and Valerie. He particularly wanted to tell Valerie that she had been wrong about him not getting a date with Margaret, but Thursday seemed a long way off and he knew there was plenty of time for it to all go wrong.

He would have liked to have told his old mate Dougie about his job news, but Dougie no longer played football for either of his old teams. Now that he had a second child, he felt the need to spend more time at home, helping his wife to look after their two children as well as working on home related tasks. He had told Mark that he had always wanted three children, but now that he had two, he wanted one. He didn't mean it, of course. He loved both of them, but Mark couldn't see himself ever giving up his football at such a young age. Nevertheless, he envied his old chum his domestic situation.

That evening, as he pulled up outside Ray's house, he noticed a strange vehicle parked outside and he wondered if they already had company. Ray was not on the 'phone, so Mark nearly always turned up unannounced.

He knocked on the door and was greeted by Ray. 'Mark ... come on in. Valerie's parents are here, but I'm sure that there's room for all of us.'

'Er ... no. I won't intrude if you already have visitors. I'll see you another time.' The last thing, Mark wanted was to have to be on his best behaviour in front of strangers. He knew that Valerie was a dedicated churchgoer, so he imagined that her parents would find his and Ray's humour a little on the racy side. They would both have to refrain from upsetting them. Mark had been looking forward to a good laugh. Ray always had some new jokes, but he wasn't going to be telling them that evening. 'I just wanted to let you know that I've got a job at last.'

'That's great. Come in and tell us about it.'

'No, you've got company. Can you also tell Valerie that I've got a date with Margaret? I'm sure she'll be pleased to hear that.'

'Well done on both counts,' said Ray. 'Are you sure you won't come in? I see you've got your suit on.'

'Yeah, I thought we might go down the pub to celebrate, but perhaps another time. Enjoy your evening.'

'Yeah, give me a call at work during the week and we'll arrange something. What's this job, anyway?'

'It's a programmer's job at Greyfriars – the builders' merchants in town. I'll tell you all about it next time. 'Bye for now.'

He was determined that he wasn't going to join Ray's visitors, although he suspected that Ray would welcome the diversion from his in-laws. At least he had been able to tell someone about his good news. He had been bursting to tell someone.

Chapter Eighteen

It's You That I Need

Margaret was already waiting for Mark at the end of her road. He was a little early himself. Did this mean she was keen to see him ... or did she want to avoid her family seeing her date turn up in an old Austin 1100? At least she had appeared which quelled his fears of the last few days.

'I hope you haven't been waiting too long?' he asked. 'It's quite cold out there.'

'No, I've only just arrived. When you live on a farm, you don't worry about a little cold weather. I didn't want you to have to drive down that dark road. There are ditches on both sides of the road and there are two different farms at the bottom. I just thought it would be easier if I waited at the top.'

'Well, it's nice to see you again,' he said, although he couldn't actually see her as it was dark.

'Did you 'phone me at work, a couple of weeks ago?' she asked.

He might have known that she would have guessed that it was him who 'phoned. He could have lied and tried to bluff it out, but if he was going to win her heart and form a long-term relationship, a little honesty was important. 'Well, I didn't actually 'phone *you*. I 'phoned your company and you answered the 'phone. I recognised your voice and figured you might think I was pestering you ... and without thinking, I just put the 'phone down.'

'Why were you 'phoning my company?'

'I was after a job. I figured as you had been on the COBOL course, your company might have a computer. I wanted a programmer's job and I couldn't think of anyone else who might have a machine. I know big companies like banks and insurance companies have them, but they're mostly based in big cities like London or Edinburgh where the head offices would be. I hope I didn't cause you any ... I don't know ... um ... you know.' Mark was floundering.

'We don't have a computer,' she said. 'I went on the course because that idiot at the Labour Exchange suggested it.'

'Well, as it happens, I've got another job now. I'm starting at Greyfriars next week as a programmer.'

'Well done,' she said, and she sounded as though she meant it. 'I've also got a new job. I'm now the directors' secretary.'

'Have you finished your secretarial course, then?'

'No, I'm still doing it. There are only a couple more weeks to go. The woman who was previously doing the secretary's job has left to have a baby. They could have sacked her, but they want her to come back later, so I was given the role on a temporary basis. I'm hoping that if I can do a good job, they won't want her back. It's going well so far. Even if she does come back, it's very good experience and they may even split the role. I think I've fallen on my feet.'

'Good for you,' Mark said. 'Companies will always want secretaries. We've both fallen on our feet. It's a new start for both of us.' He was hoping it was a start that they would share together, but it was still early days.

Then the conversation hit a little lull. Mark was desperately trying to think of something else to say and he was struggling. As usual, he resorted to a joke.

'Did you know that thirty per cent of people work in nationalised industries ... and the rest just watch them or drink coffee.'

Silence.

After a minute, Margaret twigged. 'Oh, you mean thirty per cent of people who work in a nationalised industry. Oh, very good.' But she wasn't laughing.

He decided to give up on jokes for the time being but stayed quiet for a little. Eventually, he asked 'Do you like Billie Holiday?' He assumed that she knew whom the film was about.

'I don't really know her stuff. What about you?'

'Same as you, really,' he replied. 'She was before my time. I know one or two of her songs, but by other people. I've got a version of *Don't Explain* by Lou Rawls on an LP.'

'I don't know Lou Rawls. Is he a blues singer?' she asked.

'No, he's a soul singer – but a little jazzy. He's got a great voice.' Mark had gotten onto his favourite subject and the conversation was now flowing a little freer, but by now they were at the cinema. He hoped they might continue the topic later.

As they entered the auditorium, a Bugs Bunny cartoon was showing, and the lights were down. An usherette showed them to a couple of seats in the middle and they sat down with Margaret to Mark's right. She removed her coat and laid it on her lap. He was wondering if at some point he might feel bold enough to put his arm around her shoulder to see how tossing bales of hay had influenced her build, but he wasn't sure if this would be too forward on a first real date. He also remembered once when he had taken Melody to the pictures and after doing just that, his arm had gone to sleep after ten minutes. After which, his hand had dropped to her knee and he was able to feel her shapely legs. That was another thing that wasn't going to happen with Margaret – at least not that evening, but he had strong ambitions for the near future. Her previous mention of her thighs riding a horse had piqued his interest.

After another cartoon, the lights went up for an intermission, allowing time for the audience to purchase ice creams or drinks from the young lady who had made her way down to the front of the auditorium. A small queue soon formed to take advantage of her wares.

'Would you like an ice cream?' he asked.

'No, thank you,' Margaret replied. 'It hasn't been long since I've eaten. We always have a big meal in the evening and I probably shouldn't have had that extra portion of apple pie. We're all big eaters in our family, but don't let me stop you if you want one.'

'No, I'm fine, thank you.' He had enjoyed looking into her piercing blue eyes. She didn't look as though she had made any great effort with make-up, but he didn't think she needed to. She had a firm chin and the rosy healthy cheeks of someone brought up on a farm. Before the evening was through, he would try to kiss her soft inviting lips.

He had considered wearing his best suit to create a good impression but had decided that wouldn't have been appropriate for a cinema. He was wearing a smart sports jacket and his best flares, which after a while, he found uncomfortable. They weren't designed for sitting down. He had liberally splashed himself with Mennen after-shave and took every opportunity to sit closer to her to give her a tantalising waft. Looking at her made him feel he wanted to hold her and explore her charms, even though he knew that was unlikely to happen that evening. Then he was struck with an idea, one that might present him with the opportunity to hold her closely – a dance!

'Have you ever been to *The Jenyns Arms*?' he asked.

'Yes,' she replied '... and I never want to go again. It seems to me that some men like to go there just to have a fight. It's a bit much when you can't go out for a drink and a dance with friends without some load of idiots brawling in front of you. I hope you never go out looking for a fight, Mark.'

'No, I haven't been involved in a fight since leaving school. There's been a bit of pushing and shoving on a football pitch, but nothing serious. If someone shoves you, you shove them back – otherwise they keep doing it and you're seen as a wimp. I've only been to *The Jenyns* once and I didn't see any sign of fighting.'

'Well, I did – and I won't go there again.'

'Do you like dancing?' he asked. It was plain that he wouldn't get his smooch dance with her at that venue, but perhaps somewhere else?

'I'm not that fussed,' she replied.

Mark realised that she had just answered two questions negatively and he remembered what Kenny had said about 'punters' getting into the habit of saying 'no.' He had to ask her something that would elicit a more positive outcome. He tried what Kenny would call an 'open' question.

'How long have you been working at Sanfreeze?' he asked.

'Just over three years. I joined straight from school.' He calculated that this would indicate that she had stayed on for 'A' levels.

'Did you go to the High School?'

'Yes, of course.' she replied.

'In your nice little green uniform?' he said. It was a stupid thing to say, but he's always found the uniform to be quite attractive and very feminine.

She asked. 'Did you go to the Grammar School?'

'Yeah, I was a Grammarshite,' he replied.

'I've never heard them called that before,' she said.

'It's what the kids from Fenfield School called us. I was always proud to be a Grammarshite.'

'It doesn't sound very nice, though, does it?' she said.

'At school, we used to write on slates,' he added.

'Really? Surely not?'

'Yeah, but when the rain washed away the chalk we had to come down off the roof.'

Margaret showed no sign of being amused. 'Anyway, as I said, I went straight to Sanfreeze from school. It was the only job I could find – despite having 'A' levels. All the jobs around were aimed at men. You can understand why these women's libbers are up in arms. Fortunately, my dad had dealings with Sanfreeze, and he pulled a few strings. He's been providing farm produce to them for years. I'd already done some typing at home. We have a typewriter because my mother does the books for the farm business and she taught me to touch-type, which helped secure the job.'

Just then, the lights dimmed, and the ice-cream lady returned up the aisle.

While the advertisements were being screened, Mark tried to take in what she had just said. He had a little sympathy for Margaret's situation with jobs, but he wasn't sure about this women's lib. In his view, if a woman wanted to pursue a career instead of settling down to raise a family, that was fine, but if everyone did it, it would upset the natural order of things. Men were the breadwinners and women raised the children and looked after the home. It was what his mother had done and what his elder sister was now doing.

Anyway, he was getting a little ahead of himself. He had yet to secure a second date with Margaret, so there was little point in thinking about their future together.

Of course, Margaret hadn't said that she was a women's libber, but Mark had a habit of jumping to conclusions. Moreover, he was a little concerned that although there had been a reasonable amount of conversation, he had yet to enjoy any kind of sexual chemistry between them – lust, on his part, yes, but nothing more than polite conversation from her. He needed this to work. He needed her. He had been too long without a girlfriend and Margaret seemed ideal to fill that need.

At the end of the film, everyone stood up to leave, but it seemed to be taking forever for their row to move. Mark was never the most patient person around, and he couldn't understand why everyone seemed to be dawdling to get out.

By the time the rest of their row had reached the aisle, they were at the back of the queue to leave the auditorium. Margaret was in front of him and was ready to join the end of the queue, when Mark gently held her by the shoulders and led her towards the fire exit.

As she had previously indicated, her shoulders felt solid but not exceptionally so. 'This way,' he said and led her down a dimly lit passageway where a security door faced them. He pushed the horizontal bar that opened the door and suddenly, they were in the car park. The door was normally kept shut to prevent people entering without paying, but no one stopped them. He had done this before.

The cold night air hit them. He said 'I'm ready for a drink. Do you want to walk down to *The Golden Fleece* or shall we drive out to somewhere more salubrious?'

'I don't mind a little walk,' she said. 'We've been sat down for quite a while.'

The Golden Fleece was about a hundred yards away and Mark was regretting not bringing a coat, but Margaret looked snug in hers. He had carefully not asked if she *wanted* to go for a drink and his ploy had worked. To him, this was now a crucial part of the evening when he would seek to further their relationship, by first dazzling her with his wit and repartee and then sealing it with another date, but as they walked along, he was struggling to think of something to say – and his teeth were starting to chatter. 'Cor, winter drawers on,' was all he could manage.

'Didn't you bring a coat?' she asked.

'Er ... no, I didn't think I would need it.'

'Never mind, we'll soon be in the warm,' she said and didn't seem to mind a brisk walk.

He contemplated reaching for her hand but decided that their relationship hadn't reached that stage yet.

Inside, they were greeted by Kenny Stacey, who was standing at the bar with a new girlfriend. 'Mark! How's it going ol' mate? Great save on Sunday.'

'Thank you,' Mark replied modestly, wondering which particular save Kenny meant.

'Mark's our goalie,' he said to his girlfriend. 'We call him *The Cat.*'

'Why's that? She asked.

'Because he's always asleep!'

'Thanks, Kenny,' Mark said.

'No, seriously, it's because he's agile and has lightning reactions. We're just off to *The Jenyns*, Mark. Are you coming?'

'No, we've just been to the pictures and having a quick drink. Margaret doesn't like *The Jenyns*. There's too much fighting going on.'

'Well, that can be a problem when young lads can't take their drink,' Kenny replied, 'There was a nasty bundle last week', he added.

'Yeah, I'm sorry about that,' said Mark, ever looking for a little whimsy.

'Nah, not you, Markey Boy. I put you down as a lover not a fighter. Is that right, Margaret?'

Margaret didn't really want a part of this conversation, but she responded. 'Well, I've never seen him fight, so I wouldn't know.'

Mark thought that was a clever response. She hadn't admitted to any loving, but she hadn't denied it either.

Kenny looked at her for a second as though recognising something. 'Triumph Spitfire,' he said. 'I never forget a car and a customer. You came with your father to pick it up.'

'That's right,' she said. 'I love my Spitfire.'

'Yes, I never forget a car,' said Kenny. 'Right, we'd better be on our way. It can be murder trying to park at *The Jenyns*. See you both again.'

After buying their drinks, Mark found them a seat near the window. This was now a crucial time for him to make his move. Ideally, he had to turn into a dazzling raconteur. He remembered watching Peter Ustinov on television with Michael Parkinson. Ustinov was the epitome of a raconteur. He'd been to lots of places; done a lot of things and met a lot of interesting people – much like Mark except for those last three things.

Mark didn't know any interesting people; had hardly ventured outside of Norfolk and done nothing of any great interest.

'What did you think of the film?' he asked to get the ball rolling.

'I enjoyed it ... a bit sad in places, but she's a good actress. What about you?' She'd already batted the conversation back in his direction: now to say something interesting.

'Yes, I enjoyed it.' Now what?

'I think the film is based on a book that she wrote herself,' he said. 'You would think that would make it accurate, but I read somewhere that she married three times. That wasn't mentioned in the film – and if they can't be bothered to get that right, it makes you wonder how much else is true. She was certainly on drugs for most of her life and she may well have seen scenes like the lynching. America is a terrible country.' He knew he was rambling.

He continued. 'Do you know that in their petrol stations – or gas stations, as they call them – black people aren't allowed to drink from the same drinking fountain as a white man? All the theatres are segregated so you will never see white people sitting down to enjoy an act with black people – unless there's a barrier between them. I think it's gradually getting better, but I think it's a dreadful place.

'Of course, I get a lot of this in some of the records I buy. I've got a lot of sympathy for the Civil Rights movement, but I'm not sure I want to hear it when I sit down in my living room to play a record.'

He stopped talking for a few seconds. This wasn't being a raconteur. This was having a bit of a rant and she wasn't responding in any way. He decided to change the subject.

'How big is your farm?'

'Oh, gosh ... I don't know,' she said, taken aback by the change in subject. 'We own all the land around Field Drive – and some more over near North Walton.'

'I've got a couple of acres,' he said.

'Have you?' she said with surprise.

'Yeah, it's these tight flares.' He couldn't help himself form switching to a little humour, but she didn't laugh.

'You like cracking your little jokes, don't you?' she said.

'Yeah, well, life's too serious to be taken short ... no, hang on, that's not right, is it? You don't seem to laugh very much?'

'I do. I like a good laugh. I don't always laugh out loud, but I like a good comedy on television.'

'Like what?'

'I love Dick Emery; *The Two Ronnies* and, of course, *Dad's Army*, My father was in the Home Guard, you know.'

'Was he really?' Mark asked. 'Does he think it was really like that?'

'Yes, he said it was at first, but as the war rolled on, they became much more sophisticated. They learned to lay booby traps and dig tunnels. They were preparing to set up a resistance movement in case we were ever conquered. Dad was in a reserved occupation, but he wanted to do his bit.'

By now, they had both finished their drinks. 'Do you want another?' he asked.

'No, I think I ought to be going. We've got the monthly Board Meeting tomorrow and I have to be there in good time to sort out the Agenda and The Minutes – and the coffee. I'm still trying to make myself indispensable.'

'I'm sure you will,' he said, helping her with her coat.

Had he done enough to secure a second date? There was only one way to find out and as they walked back to his car, he asked 'Can I see you again?'

'Oh, well, I'm still keen to play tennis,' she replied, dodging the issue.

'No, I mean a proper date,' he said, fearing the worst.

'I'd rather not at the moment,' she said. 'I'm sure you can find someone else to go out with.'

'But I don't want anyone else. I want to go out with you.'

'I'm sorry. I'd rather not,' she replied, and they continued in silence. After that, he decided that he couldn't be bothered to talk to her. He realised that it probably looked like he was sulking, but there was no longer any point in trying to get to know her better.

In the car, they were halfway home before Margaret broke the silence.

'Do you start your new job on Monday?' she asked.

'Yes ... time for a new start,' he replied. 'A new challenge, new opportunities; new surroundings; new people ...' He was thinking there might be new girls, as well.

And then they were at the top of her road.

'Don't drive down our road,' she said. 'It might be awkward to turn around and there's ditches both sides of the road.'

'But it's dark,' he said.

'It's all right. I've walked down here enough times. I'll be all right.'

'I'll keep my headlights on until I see you reach your front door,' he said.

'There's no need,' she said. 'Thanks for taking me. Goodnight.'

And she was gone. Mark did leave his lights on as he had suggested.

As he drove home, he decided that despite his initial feelings of great disappointment, it really wasn't the end of the world. In truth, he hadn't enjoyed the evening as much as he had hoped. There was no great chemistry between the two of them and he realised that, as usual, his desire to date Margaret had been driven much more by lust than anything else. If he could have combined Claire's personality with Margaret's figure, he might have achieved his real desire, but that was silly make believe. People weren't like that.

His search for a soul mate would continue.

Chapter Nineteen

Starting All Over Again

On Monday morning, Mark set out with a feeling of trepidation. It had been several weeks since he had last worked for a living and even longer since he had faced a busy working environment. He wondered if, during this period of inactivity, he had lost the ability to cope with a full day's work. He decided to put such thoughts to the back of his mind and instead remembered the friendly and attractive receptionist at Greyfriars. She was young enough to be single, but that didn't mean she was unattached. In any case, there were bound to be other young ladies ready to pounce on him as soon as they discovered his eligibility.

But as he entered the reception area, he could see a different lady manning the reception desk. This one was a little older, although not unattractive.

'I'm here to see Adam Chandler,' Mark said.

'Oh,' said the receptionist, searching for a piece of paper. 'Please bear with me. This is my first day. I'm just a temp. Now let's see ... ah, yes ... here we are ... Adam Chandler.'

Seeing someone else facing a daunting new start made him feel a little more relaxed.

'Sorry,' she said. 'What was your name?'

'Mark Barker,' he replied, 'but everyone calls me ... Mark!'

She looked at him for a moment as though he were some kind of idiot before realising that he was trying to lighten the mood. 'Oh, yes,' she said with a smile.

'It's my first day, as well,' he said.

'Really? What's your new job?' She had a very friendly smile and he felt as though he would like to stand there talking a while longer instead of having to face an unknown future.

'I'm a programmer,' he replied, 'and Adam Chandler is the Programming Manager.'

'I think my friend works as a programmer,' she said, looking thoughtful for a minute and then she remembered her job. 'Just a minute.' She found Adam's number and dialled it. 'Hello, Mr Chandler? You have a visitor in reception ... a Mr Mark ...'

'Barker,' Mark reminded her.

'Barker,' she added. 'All right.'

'He'll be right out,' she said. 'I'm Maisie, by the way. I'm only here for a week while the other lady is on holiday.'

Mark had never met a Maisie before and despite her being probably in her thirties, he took an immediate liking to her, but he noticed that she wore a wedding ring. He sometimes fantasised about an older woman, ever since one of his previous girlfriends, Sandy, had an attractive and unattached mother. Before he could engage Maisie in further conversation, Adam Chandler appeared.

'Mr Barker,' he said, thrusting a hand in his direction.

Mark wondered if Adam had forgotten Mark's Christian name, but he just replied, 'Hello Adam.'

'Follow me,' Adam said. 'We might have to leave you to your own devices today. We're in the middle of an implementation and it's not going too well.' Adam was leading Mark up a flight of stairs while talking. Mark was not happy to be left 'to his own devices.' He'd had enough of twiddling his thumbs during his last year at Greshams and dearly wanted to be kept occupied.

Before they reached the top of the stairs, they were passed by a young man, obviously in a hurry. 'Excuse me, gents. I'm a little late. Good morning, Adam.'

'Good morning, Mr Freeman,' Adam said. He had again omitted the young man's Christian name.

Mark's new office was at the end of the corridor next to the first-floor fire escape. As he was ushered in, he could see that it was an open plan office; hardly conducive to concentration when writing programs, he thought to himself.

The nearest desk was occupied by a long-haired man whom Mark assessed as in his early thirties. He was studying a coding sheet and a deck of punch cards.

'Can I disturb you, Mr Sherman?' Adam asked.

'If you must,' the man replied.

'This is our new member – Mark Barker. Mark, this is Gervaise Sherman. He's our senior programmer.'

'Hello,' said Mark, but Gervaise just waved a hand in acknowledgement. Mark was not impressed with this; nor was he impressed with Gervaise's appearance. The elder man was wearing sandals with black socks, denim jeans and a scruffy tee-shirt. And he badly needed a shave.

'How did it go over the weekend, G?' Adam asked.

'It still crashed,' Gervaise answered. 'Bloody amateurs!'

'What time did you leave?' Adam asked again.

'Just after two o'clock. I might have sorted it if I'd been allowed to continue, but that idiot of an operator wouldn't let me. I offered to close the machine down myself and lock up, but he said I wasn't allowed to. Now I have to wait until this evening to try again.'

'He's only doing what he's been instructed to do. He's only allowed to stay if it's a production problem or it has been authorised beforehand.

'Anyway, I'll catch up with you later. Gervaise is also our Systems Programmer,' Adam added as they moved on to the next desk. 'He was heavily involved with the setting up of the machine, working with the IBM engineers and a couple of other colleagues.' Mark had no idea what a Systems Programmer did, but he was now more interested in the next desk along as it was occupied by a young lady.

'Ms Barton,' Adam said. 'Can I introduce you to Mark Barker who is our new COBOL programmer? Mark this is Chris Barton. She's our other Senior Programmer. She mainly writes and maintains our Assembler routines.'

'Hello, Mark,' she said. 'Welcome to Greyfriars. Where have you come from?'

'Er ... just over there,' he replied, pointing to Gervaise's desk. He couldn't resist trying to stamp his claim as the office joker. It was his natural reaction when he was feeling a little anxious, and, in truth, he felt a little overawed by this reasonably attractive lady who obviously had superior knowledge about programming.

'Oh, Gawd,' she replied, 'not another joker! I'm only kidding. You need a sense of humour to work here. I meant, of course, where have you been working?' Mark was struggling to place her accent. There were hints of a Londoner, but nothing like the Londoners with whom he worked at Greshams.

'I was at Greshams – on the industrial estate.'

'Do they have an ICL machine?' she asked. She would be aware of all the local IBM users.

'No, it's an NCR500,' he replied, hoping she would enquire more so that he could at least impress her with some knowledge that she wouldn't have.

'Was that using COBOL?' she asked.

'No, the NCR has its own unique programming language – nothing like COBOL. It's all weird numbers and hieroglyphics; not much good for anything except an NCR500 machine. 'Is Assembler easy to pick up?'

'Um ... not really. COBOL is much easier.'

Mark tried to see if there was any sign of a ring on her finger. He couldn't see one. Adam had referred to her as 'Ms.' Did that have any significance? He wanted to talk to her a little longer, but Adam moved him on to the next desk which was unoccupied.

'Is Lance not in?' he asked of Chris.

'No, we haven't seen or heard from him, yet. But he had that tour this weekend, so don't be too surprised. You know what he's like.'

'Ah, yes,' said Adam and turned back to Mark. 'Lance plays rugby and his team went on a tour this weekend, which usually involves a little imbibing.'

Mark knew nothing about Rugby, but he asked, 'Is he a flanker, then?'

'You could say that,' Chris replied with a nice smile, 'but I've no idea what position he plays.'

'Now then, Ms Barton,' Adam said. 'We mustn't cast aspersions on our colleagues, must we?'

'No, 'she said. 'We'll leave that to Gervaise, shall we? He's the one who had to sort out his work this weekend.'

Mark took one last look at Chris before he followed Adam down the office to the next desk. She wasn't particularly glamorous, but there was something about her that appealed to him. She was wearing what looked like a man's shirt which concealed her shape. She also wore some shapeless dark green slacks. If she wore make-up, he couldn't detect it, but she had a smooth slightly tanned complexion. Above all, she had a friendly disposition and a pleasant smile. He was still struggling to place her accent. It might have been Australian, but not a typically broad accent. Can you have an upper-class Australian accent?

At the next desk, sat the fellow who had overtaken them on the stairs. 'Tom, can I introduce you to Mark who is joining our band of merry men.' This time, no surnames were used at all. 'Tom joined us two years ago as a junior programmer like yourself and is now a fully fledged COBOL programmer. How's that report program coming, Tom?'

'Nearly there,' Tom replied with a nod of the head. 'Do you drink coffee, Mark?' he asked.

'Er, yes ... yes, I do,' Mark answered thinking it was a bit early to be offered a drink already.

'Good! Would you like to join our little coffee club? It's fifty pence a week and you can have as many cups as you want. It's only powdered milk, I'm afraid. We tried bottles of milk, but it used to go off too quickly.'

'I'm sure you can sort that out later,' Adam said. 'I would like you to mentor Mark during his first few months. I'm sure I can rely on you, Tom.'

'Sure,' said Tom with a cheerful smile. Mark didn't easily warm to strangers, unless they were female, but he felt confident of a good relationship with Tom.

'That just leaves one person in our team,' said Adam, moving Mark down to the last desk in that section of the office. 'This is Rose. She's our other junior programmer. Rose, this is Mark.'

They exchanged greetings. Rose was a petite round-shouldered lady, perhaps in her mid- to late twenties. She looked like someone on the point of bursting into tears.

'Everything all right, Rose?' Adam asked.

'Well, I suppose so,' she mumbled, in direct contrast to the cheery response from Tom a minute earlier.

'That's the ticket, Rose,' Adam replied, obviously not wanting to prolong the conversation. 'I'll just take you into the Systems area,' he said to Mark. The open plan office was almost split in two by two metal cupboards placed on each side of the room offering a demarcation barrier which the two men now crossed.

'This is where the Systems Analysts work, although there only seems to be one of them here at the moment. I'll just introduce you to him. Mike, this is Mark who is joining us today as a programmer.'

Mike had a very firm handshake which he held for longer than what Mark considered necessary. 'Welcome, Mark. I've heard all about you.'

'Have you?' said Mark with surprise. 'Why's that?'

'Geoff tells me that you worked at Greshams. We're trying to sell them a stock control system.'

'Oh, I didn't know that. You know they have their own machine, don't you? Nobody there ever talked about computerising their stock.'

'No, I don't think it will come to anything, but if it does, you might be able to help us with some inside information.'

Mark just nodded. He wasn't too sure what a Systems Analyst actually did, but then he knew he had a lot to learn. He also didn't understand why Greyfriars should be trying to sell a stock control system, He thought they were a builders' merchant, but decided he would raise some of these questions at a later time, especially as Adam seemed to be in a hurry to move on.

'Right then, Mark' he said as they returned to the programming half of the office. 'This will be your desk.' He pointed to an empty desk close to Rose. Mark thought it would have made more sense to be closer to his mentor, but there seemed to be a hierarchical placement of the desks, with the two junior programmers together.

'As I said, we're a little busy at the moment, so for now I'd like you to familiarise yourself with our standards' and he went to a cupboard to pick up a lever-arch file labelled *Systems Standards*. 'Have a read of that ... and if you need any stationery, it's all in that cupboard. I'll catch up with you later.'

Mark's heart sank. Everyone else in the room was too busy to speak to him and he wanted to ask so many questions. He opened the file he had been given. Greshams had never felt the need to issue a set of *standards* whatever that meant, but he realised that this was a much more professional computer environment and with so much to learn this was perhaps a good place to start.

He looked at the *Contents* page, some of which made sense; some of which didn't. There were headings such as *File Naming Standards, File Space Allocation, Job Naming Conventions, Programming Standards* and *Program Testing Facilities.* He spent half an hour scanning the file before embarking on a concentrated effort to read all of the contents. Before proceeding, he sat back to gaze around the room, hoping one of his new colleagues might want to engage him in conversation, but they all seem to be concentrating on their work and the room was unnaturally quiet. His eyes fell upon the stationery cupboard and he decided to go and investigate its contents.

There, among the conventional stationery items such as pens, rubber bands and paper clips he found some coding pads similar to those used on his COBOL course; boxes of punch cards of various colours and some *Print Layout Charts*. He had never felt the need to use the latter in his previous role, but he could envisage their usefulness. He helped himself to a lined foolscap pad and a pen, thinking he might make some notes as he went back to the *Standards* file.

After a further half hour, Tom suddenly stood up and said 'I'm ready for a coffee. Who wants one?'

'Yes, please' said Chris.

'Yes, please,' added Mark.

'What about you, Rose?'

She sighed. 'I would really like something a little stronger.'

'You can have an extra dollop of coffee. I'll just go and fill the kettle,' Tom added and disappeared for a few minutes. When he returned, he said 'How do you like it, Mark?'

'White with one sugar, please. I've only got a pound note, but you can keep that for two weeks, if you like.'

'Do you think you're gonna last that long?' Tom asked. 'The last person who worked here left after one week as a gibbering wreck.'

'Don't take any notice of him, Mark,' Rose said.

'It's all right, Rose. I left my last job as a gibbering wreck so he might be right. And if I win the pools this week, I will be leaving, so you can keep the change.'

'We have one strict rule with our coffee club,' Tom said. 'There's a dry spoon for the coffee and milk – and you're not allowed to stir your coffee with it. I always get a large tin of coffee from the Cash and Carry. It's much cheaper that way. You'll need to provide your own mug. I'll use a visitors' mug for now. Chris has her coffee black with one sugar; Rose has hers black, no sugar and I have white with two sugars.'

'What about Gervaise?' Mark asked.

'He's not in our scheme. He brings his own revolting green juice thing. He's a vegetarian and some kind of hippy.'

'I'm not a hippy!' Gervaise called, 'and you'd be better off not eating and drinking the rubbish you put in your mouth.'

'And he lives in a commune,' Tom added for mischief.

'It's not a commune!' Gervaise announced forcefully.

'Well, he lives with two women and another bloke ... and they've got five kids between them, so you decide.'

Gervaise didn't add anything else. Mark could tell that Tom liked to wind him up, so maybe life wouldn't be so dull in this office after all. His understanding was that hippies were usually quite laid back – so Gervaise certainly wasn't a hippy.

While Tom poured out the drinks, Mark asked 'What's this report program you're working on?'

'It's for the Delilah project,' Tom replied.

'What's that?'

'The customer is Sampson's Components. They manufacture electrical components. Delilah was the code name we gave the project before the contract was signed – as in Samson and Delilah. We sold them a stock control system, which is due to go live in the new year, so there's a bit of pressure to complete everything.'

'I don't understand why we're selling people a stock control system,' said Mark.

'Well, when we developed ours, it had to cater for all the different branches, so it was designed and written to cope with their different requirements. Different branches tend to sell different products and at different times of the year – and that flexibility in the program meant it could be tailored for other users, so we started marketing it. This will be our fifth outside customer ... sorry ... we have to call them clients for some reason.'

'So, your report program has to be written specifically for Sampson's?'

'That's right ... but it is based on the original Greyfriars report.'

Mark turned to Rose 'And what are you working on?'

Rose pulled a face. 'I've got to write the JCL. Are you any good at OS, Mark?'

'Er ... no. I've only worked with GEORGE. Even then, we had someone else to provide the JCL.'

Rose pulled another face and took her coffee back to her desk. Mark wasn't taken with her. She had a dowdy appearance and a dowdy disposition. He was disappointed that Chris hadn't joined their conversation, but she remained working at her desk as Tom delivered her drink. Mark found her to be the more attractive of the two ladies and would have liked her to have shown some interest in him.

Just as they all returned back to work, another man entered the room. He was tall and slim and wearing a suit, but with his top button undone and his tie loose, he looked rather unkempt. 'Is the kettle hot?' he demanded. 'I'm dying for a coffee.' Mark guessed this might be Lance, the other COBOL programmer, although he always imagined rugby players as being particularly well-built, but this chap was tall and skinny.

'Good afternoon, Lance. It's good of you to grace us with your presence.' Tom obviously liked a bit of sarcasm. 'Did you win?'

'Won one, lost one,' came the gruff response as Lance stirred his coffee.

'That's the dry spoon!' Tom said.

'Give it a rest, Tom,' said Lance.

'We don't have these rules for nothing,' Tom said. 'I hope you're going to wash and dry that spoon so that others can use it. And when are you going to bring your own mug?'

'Sod off, will you. I've got work to do.' At that point, Gervaise summoned him.

'Come here, Lance. I think I've sorted out your cock-up.' Mark couldn't hear the rest of the conversation, so he never learned the cause of the 'cock-up.' He returned to his *Standards*. It remained quiet in the office for the next few hours apart from the occasional need for someone to visit the toilet facilities and he continued to learn some important information, which only made him feel more frustrated that he couldn't do some actual work.

Just after noon, Tom called over 'What are your plans for lunch, Mark?'

'I've brought a packed lunch ... and then I thought I'd have a little stroll outside while the weather's reasonable.'

'Yes, it is quite mild for the time of year. Mind if I join you?'

'Of course not. I might ask you a few questions about work if you don't mind.'

'No, that will be fine,' said Tom.' Do you want to join us Rose?'

'No, it's too cold for me,' she replied.

Mark noticed that Tom hadn't asked any of the other team members, but he considered that would give him a better chance to probe for some personal information – for example, was Chris married or attached to anyone.

The first question Mark asked was 'Does Rose ever do any programming?'

'Yeah, she has done. Her problem is that she doesn't seem able to concentrate for very long. She's got a lot of personal problems, you see. She's just been through a messy divorce ... spent a lot of time – and money – with solicitors. I used to try and give her some support, but it was hard work. My advice to you is not to get too close to her. She can drag you down.' Mark had already decided that for himself.

'What sort of programming has she done?' he asked.

'Just a few tweaks here and there' Tom replied. 'I often get her to check some of my work.'

'Chris seems very nice,' Mark said, hoping he might find out more about her.

'Yes, she is ... and very helpful.'

'What sort of work does she do?'

'Almost exclusively Assembler work; most of the main applications for the business, such as accounts and payroll, are written in Assembler. The main core of the Stock Control system is Assembler and we write the front-end and report type routines to tack onto it.'

'And does that apply to Gervaise as well?'

'He's heavily involved in the Stock Control. It's really his little baby. He helped design it along with Mike.'

'I see,' said Mark. He didn't want to just dive in and ask the question he really wanted to.

'What about Lance? What does he do?'

'He plays rugby. He drinks. He rushes his work ... and he annoys me!'

'Yeah, I gathered that,' said Mark, 'but what is he supposed to be working on?'

'He's been writing the front end for Delilah ... it's meant to validate all the data before it's passed into the stock control system, but every time they test it, the program dumps.'

Mark didn't really want to show his ignorance, but he had to learn. 'Dumps? What does that mean?'

'It crashes. It ABENDS. When that happens, the program prints out a dump of what's in the mainframe at that time, and then someone like Gervaise or Chris has to read the dump to find the cause. Gervaise reads a dump like some people read a magazine. It's usually a 'data exception' which means the program doesn't like the data that Lance's program is allowing through.'

'I see,' said Mark. He hoped none of his programs ever caused a dump. It sounded serious.

'Do you play rugby?' Tom asked.

'God, no! The only thing I know about rugby, is that it's a game played by men with funny shaped balls.'

'Well, I've never been close enough to any to check that,' said Tom with a grin.

'And where does Adam fit into all this?' Mark asked.

'He just manages the team. He doesn't get his hands dirty. He's ambitious. His plan is that this team becomes some kind of *Team of Excellence* and he'll get all the glory. There is talk that they're going to establish a new company called something like *Greyfriars Data Services* or *Greyfriars Computing*. I overheard Mike talking about GDS, so I assumed that would be *Greyfriars Data Services*. Then they'll get some salespeople in - and who knows?'

Mark had run out of work-related questions and they were now heading back towards their office building. 'How about you? Are you married?'

'Me? Oh, yes. Well and truly. Happily married with three children – one of each! I like being married. My parents have been married for forty years and my father gave me some advice ... marriage is all about compromise ... if you argue, never go to bed on an argument, he would say; then he'd add that he seldom went to bed at night! What about you? Are you married?'

'No, I'm between girlfriends. I'm hoping there might some gorgeous young girl at Greyfriars who will tempt me.'

'Don't build your hopes up too much. Mind you, we don't get to mix very much with the main office staff. They're not allowed into our room – and we have little cause to visit them, so I don't know everyone. There are the punch girls, of course – and the typing pool, but, as I say, I don't know much about them.'

'What about Chris? Is she attached?' Mark had finally asked the question that had been burning him.

'Ah ... well, you see ... she bats for the other side.'

Mark had never heard that expression outside of cricket. 'I don't follow you,' he said.

'She is in a relationship ... with a divorcee named Maisie.'

'Not the temp on reception?'

'Is that Maisie?' Tom asked. 'I didn't know her name. She only started today. I don't suppose there's that many people around named Maisie. Perhaps Chris put her up for the job. Judy, the usual receptionist, is on holiday.'

They passed through reception and received a smile from Maisie. As they walked up the stairs back to their office, Mark asked 'Judy is the pretty little dark-haired girl I saw when I came for my interview, was she?'

'That sounds like her,' Tom replied.

'And is she married?'

'Oh, yes.'

Mark's heart sank. That was three possible young ladies out of the picture in one fell swoop. He'd just have to find a reason to visit the punch room or the typing pool.

Chapter Twenty

Just One Look

Over the next few months, Mark gradually established himself as a member of the programming team, although he was hardly indispensible. Tom adequately fulfilled his role as Mark's mentor, introducing him to the delights of OS JCL and all the necessary working procedures, as well as slowly improving Mark's programming skills.

Although the two men did not socialise outside of work, they soon became office friends and often teamed up to make fun of both Lance and Gervaise, but Mark never went too far with Gervaise as he knew he might need to call on his expertise at some time. However, he soon came to share Tom's dislike for Lance who seemed to perform his duties to never more than an acceptable standard.

Lance also continued to abuse the rules for the coffee club to add to his other annoying little habits such as breaking wind with childish glee and depositing cigarette ash wherever he went. Nobody liked to visit the toilets soon after him as he smoked in the cubicles and left other annoying traces of his visits.

Mark still harboured an interest in Chris. She was the first lesbian whom he had knowingly met and he wondered if this was a "condition" that could be rectified by the love of a good man, but she never seemed to show anything other than a professional interest in Mark, who wasn't sure how he should behave with her. Was flirting with a lesbian permissible?

He had discovered that she had been brought up in Australia by English parents who had returned to the U.K. after an aborted attempt at emigration, hence her unusual accent. Tom told Mark about the day she had returned from her lunch break with some 'arse cream.'

'Is that a treatment for piles?' Mark asked.

'No, it's for eating ... arse cream ... Wall's arse cream!'

'Oh, you probably won't want that on your piles!'

Rose continued to be a less than engaging presence. Her conversation consisted only of work and her personal problems. She sighed a lot and frequently complained of feeling depressed. Mark had experienced his own low moments after struggling with his infatuation with Karen and his split with Jenny, so he knew that what Rose probably needed was plenty of distraction, but Tom's warning of not allowing Rose to 'drag him down' persuaded him to avoid getting involved. As he did not find her attractive, he did not struggle with that policy, although he often felt he would have been a better person if he had been more charitable towards her.

The office banter was never as enjoyable as that which he enjoyed when he worked with his old friend Ray, nor even with Mary and Dolly, but Mark still tried, hoping Tom could act as his foil just as Ray used to do. He tried an old joke.

'She chased me in a well-known farm-yard vehicle' he said to Tom.

'What? Who did?'

'No, Tom. You're supposed to say *a tractor.*'

'Why's that?'

'I'm trying to tell a joke. Let's try again. She chased me in a well-known farm-yard vehicle.'

'Was it a tractor,' Tom said.

Mark let out a sigh. 'Just say *a tractor.* Try one more time. She chased me in a well-known farm-yard vehicle.'

'A tractor?'

'I s'pose I musta done,' Mark said emphasising his Norfolk accent.

Everyone groaned, but Mark would try again another time. He was determined to raise the level of banter.

He was beginning to feel that he might end up as a bachelor for the rest of his life. He knew there were girls at Greyfriars, because he sometimes caught a glimpse of them entering and leaving the building, but their paths never seemed to cross. Because the programming team dealt with potentially confidential data, colleagues were dissuaded from visiting their office, and Mark never had a need to call on other parts of the building, except a visit early on in his career at Greyfriars to present his P45 and National Insurance card to the Chief Accountant.

Then everything changed. It was early one morning just before spring and he was entering the office building. He was aware of footsteps behind him, so he made to open the door for his colleague whoever that might be. And there she was. She gave him a lovely smile and said, 'Thank you,' but he never responded. He just stared and she preceded him into reception.

Writers talk of falling in love at first sight as though it happens all the time. Mark wasn't sure that it was love, but he was certainly smitten at first sight – and it wasn't mere lust as was usually the case with him. There was just something about her that screamed 'Notice me!' She had thick raven coloured hair and a vivacious smile through inviting red lips. She wore a thick black coat with fur trimmings and glided through reception with all the grace of a swan – a black swan. Then she was gone through the double doors that led to the ground floor offices.

'Good morning, Mister Barker,' Judy said from behind the reception desk. She always insisted on calling him *Mister*, even though he had told her his first name several times. She did it for everyone, but it wasn't like the mock respect Adam used when citing people's title instead of a Christian name.

'Er, morning, Judy,' he replied just remembering his manners.

He was halfway up the stairs when he turned back. 'Judy ... I'm sure I recognise that lady who just walked past.' He hadn't really, but he wanted to know more about her. 'But I can't quite remember from where. What's her name?'

'Oh, Helen? That's Helen Bradfield. She's nice, isn't she?'

'Helen Bradfield,' he repeated as though he was trying to recall her from his past. 'The name rings a bell. Where does she work?'

'I think she works for Mister Stannard ... the Personnel Manager.'

'I see. Thank you.' Mark was immediately trying to conjure up reasons to go to Personnel, but he couldn't think of anything.

From that one brief meeting, Helen was now his purpose in life. When he took an interest in a young lady, the pursuit took over his very being, to the exclusion of all other matters and of all other potential love interests – and Helen was to be no exception. But first, he had to find out if she was unattached.

Programming usually requires high levels of concentration and for the rest of that morning, Mark's attention wandered frequently back to that one brief meeting at the front door. By lunchtime, he had achieved very little workwise. As most of his colleagues left the office for their break, he found himself alone with Tom, who was complaining about Lance's work. 'You know what they say? If it ain't broke, break it ... that's his motto. One of these days, I'm going to forget that I'm a nice chap and report him to Adam.'

Mark sympathised with Tom about their colleague but had other things on his mind.

'Tom, do you know Helen Bradfield?' he asked.

'Um ... is that the dark-haired lady in Personnel?'

'Yes,' Mark replied.

'Hello,' said Tom, 'do I detect a love interest, here? No, I don't really know her. She's nice, isn't she?'

'Well, I've only seen her once,' said Mark, 'but ... yeah, she looks nice. So, you don't know if she's attached?'

'No,' Tom replied. 'I don't know, but I'd be very surprised if she hasn't been snatched up.'

Just then, Chris returned to the office and Mark expected that to be the end of the conversation. He didn't want Chris to know of his interest, but Tom said 'You should ask Chris. She's bound to have talked to her in the Ladies. That's what girls do.'

'Who are we talking about?' Chris asked.

'It doesn't matter, Chris,' Mark said, but Tom insisted.

'I think Mark's taken a fancy to Helen Bradfield. Do you know if she's single?'

Chris smiled knowingly at Mark. 'She's nice, isn't she? She is single. She recently split up with one chap. She told me he was getting a bit too serious and decided to end it before it was too late. She doesn't strike me as someone who wants anyone too clingy.'

Mark thought that sounded like a warning so decided not to pursue the matter, even though he had more questions he would have liked to have asked.

He returned to his desk to consume his cream crackers and cheese. It seems that if he ever should get the opportunity to approach Helen, he must avoid giving the impression of being too 'clingy.' She sounded like a strong-minded lady, so she probably preferred strong-minded men. He was sure that he could be strong-minded – just not always with women!

Later, that same afternoon, Adam started summoning each of Mark's colleagues to his office. Gervaise was the first and he left reluctantly. He didn't like having his work disturbed.

'This is it,' said Tom.

'This is what?' asked Mark.

'Brown envelope day.'

Mark was none the wiser. 'What's that?' he asked.

'It's when we get a brown envelope telling us about this year's annual review,' Tom replied.

'Oh,' said Mark. 'I won't get one. I have to wait until my six months' probation is up.'

One by one, each of the programmers was called and in order of seniority. The reaction of each was markedly different. Gervaise seemed to show no reaction and didn't respond to enquiries from his colleagues who were eager to know if the rises were generous or not. Chris seemed very pleased with her rise but wouldn't expand. Lance was angry, but no one wanted to ask him how much he had received, if, indeed, he had even received anything. Tom was quite excited, and Rose was close to tears, but then, she often was.

Mark was surprised to hear that Adam wanted to see him.

'Hello, Mister Barker,' he said as Mark entered his office. 'Take a seat. How are things?'

'Quite good, I think,' Mark replied.

'Is the job what you expected?' Adam asked.

'Er ... I don't know what I expected. It's different to my last role.'

'In what way?'

'Well, for one thing, I used to be involved in the whole process of writing a program; from talking to the user and finding out their requirements, to writing a specification and designing the program; all the way through to testing it, performing parallel runs and implementation, working with the user. I also designed forms and wrote user documentation. All I'm doing here is writing the program to someone else's design and with a little bit of testing. There's no interaction with the users at all. It's a very isolated role – not that I'm complaining, but it is different to what I'm used to.'

Adam had just watched Mark all this time without showing any reaction. 'Yes, I can see that it is different, but that's how we operate here.' He didn't look like he was prepared to address that issue, instead, he continued with the main purpose of the meeting.

'Now, as you know, when you joined, you were put on six months' probation. This was to make sure that if things didn't work out your employment could be terminated at any time during that period. You were not classed as a permanent employee, making it easy for us to release you if necessary, It's something we do with all new employees and it's usually just a formality.' All the time, Adam was speaking in his most solemn tone.

'Well, after due consideration, we have decided that because of your performance to date, we are going to terminate that probationary period a little early.'

Mark's heart sank. He thought he had been doing quite well. He felt he had contributed more to the business than Rose who still appeared to have a job – unless that was why she was close to tears.

Adam's solemn expression suddenly lightened, and he said 'So from now on, you will be classed as a permanent employee. We're pleased with the way you apply yourself. You have a one hundred per cent attendance record and you're always willing to come back in the evening to do some testing. Accordingly, there is an increase in your salary as detailed in this letter' and he handed Mark one of the notorious brown envelopes.

Mark tore it open and ignoring the preamble quickly found the section detailing his new salary. He was now to be earning £1,350 per annum. He had hoped for a little more and said so to Adam.

'I thought you'd be pleased,' said Adam, looking affronted by Mark's reaction. 'We took a chance on you when we employed you as you'd had no COBOL experience and you've still got a little way to go.'

'I'm likely to be looking to buy a house this year,' Mark lied, 'and the Building Society will only lend me two and a half times my salary. That's not going to help me get a mortgage. When will I get another rise?'

'The reviews are once a year ... in April of each year,' Adam replied. 'In the salary range for your position, only a really exceptional person could expect to receive the maximum – and I have to say that you haven't reached a level where we could call you *exceptional.*'

'Am I still classed as a *Junior* Programmer?' Mark asked.

'Yes ... you would expect to stay at that for at least two years.'

'I was a full programmer at my previous job – and now I have to go backwards for at least two years.'

'But sometimes you have to go backwards to go forward.'

Mark could see that he wasn't going to change anything. 'I know where there is another COBOL job going – and it's not a *Junior* role,' he said. 'I may have to consider that.'

Adam wasn't going to succumb to threats, but he added 'Sometimes in September, a small sum of money is made available to use to address anomalies, such as someone getting a mid-term promotion, so there might be something we can do then, but I can't promise. Meanwhile, you have to do what you consider best.'

Mark sloped out of Adam's office as though he really was considering another position, but he was actually quite pleased to receive a rise and end his probation. He often felt he had been badly treated at Greshams having fallen foul of Government pay restrictions that shouldn't have affected him and he was forever trying to catch up for lost rises, so he wanted to show that he wasn't going to just roll over each time a pay review was in the air. That stand was to pay off because he did receive a small raise in September.

***

Back in his office, Tom was the first to quiz Mark about his meeting. 'Did you get a raise?' he asked.

'A little,' Mark replied, 'but more to the point, I'm now classed as a permanent employee.'

'Does that mean I don't have to be your Probation Officer anymore?' Tom asked.

'That wasn't discussed,' Mark responded, 'but I'm still classed as a lowly Junior Programmer, so I doubt it.'

'I'm glad you think I'm lowly, too,' said Rose.

'And I was a lowly Junior Programmer not too long ago,' said Tom. 'So, don't demean us, if you don't mind.'

'I'm sorry. I didn't mean to offend anyone, but I've never liked being called a *junior* anything,' said Mark. 'I spent a couple of years as an office junior and I hated every minute of it. I was just a dogsbody doing nothing but fetching coffee and filing.'

'Well, being a Junior Programmer is not being a dogsbody,' said Tom. 'Now if you wouldn't mind, it's your turn to make some coffee ... and perhaps you could file that program listing.' Mark realised that this was just a little joke and returned to his desk, although it was his turn to make the coffee.

It was usually quiet in the programming office as each person concentrated on their work, but every now and then, there would be few minutes of office banter like this, but now, everyone continued with their work. Mark wasn't going to just jump up and make the coffee. He would leave it a few minutes just to prove that he wasn't at anyone's beck and call. Instead, he opened his envelope to study the wording of the letter. It congratulated him on completing his probationary period and detailed his entitlement to sick pay and annual leave. It also told him that he was now entitled to join the company pension scheme if he wished, but he wasn't automatically enrolled. He had to write to the Personnel Manager who had written the letter – except that there was a different signature against his name, It was Helen's signature; at least he thought it looked like her signature against the letters "pp" and Mister Stannard's printed name

He stared at the signature for a minute or so. He'd only met her for the first time that morning and the sight of her writing had set his pulse racing. That was just silly. Anyone would think that she had written to him personally, but she had managed such an effect on him with that one smile – just one look, as Doris Troy had sung in that wonderful song that The Hollies had managed to mangle.

As he left the office that evening, he loitered around the car park for a few minutes in the hope of catching another glimpse of Helen. He had no idea if she owned a car, but it was worth a shot, although he wasn't sure what he would do if he actually saw her. He then spent a little longer sitting in his car pretending to fiddle with something, but eventually he

161

gave up and made his way home, looking out for her at the first bus stop on his route.

That night, he came up with a bright idea that might help him meet her.

In fact, he came up with two ideas.

Chapter Twenty-One

Park Avenue

As he rode the bus to work the following morning, his first bright idea didn't seem as promising as it had the night before, but he proceeded with it anyway.

He had surmised that as he could never remember seeing Helen in the office car park, it followed that she didn't have a car, or at least, didn't drive it to work, so she had to have some other means of commuting. There were several possibilities, one of which was the bus. He preferred the convenience of driving himself to work, but using the bus was no great hardship.

He had chosen a window seat to the left so that he could watch other passengers joining along the route. As he had no idea where Helen lived, he could not be sure if she travelled from this direction, but he had purchased a ticket to take him all the way to the bus station which meant only a short walk back to his office.

As he disembarked at the end of his journey, he casually wandered from one end of the bus station to the other before heading in the right direction for his office. There was still no sign of her, which in itself was not conclusive proof that she didn't bus to work, but he had reduced the odds.

That left just a few other methods of commuting. Rail travel was not one of these as the railway line to Sanford had been closed and dismantled as part of the Beeching cuts, much to the displeasure of many local people who had relied on the trains.

Taxis were an inconvenient and expensive form of transport in Sanford, and he couldn't envisage Helen cycling to work with that thick coat and still leaving her lustrous hair and make-up intact. So, she either lived within walking distance or she obtained a lift with someone else, which could be a colleague, a neighbour, a friend or helpful family member. So, he wasn't really any the wiser, which was why his first cunning idea hadn't been as clever as it had seemed the night before. He would have to rely on his other idea. This might involve a little help from one or more unsuspecting colleagues.

He waited until there was one of those little 'banter' moments during the morning's work. At the break for morning coffee, it was Tom who got proceedings off with one of his witticisms. 'Did you know that there

163

are three teams in the English Football League who have rude words in their names? Do you know what they are?'

Mark was first with a response. 'You're probably referring to Arsenal as one,' he said.

'Yes – one point to Mark,' Tom said. 'Now, who else?'

They were all stumped, so Tom told them the second. 'Scunthorpe United, of course.' This needed no further elaboration, but no one could think of a third.

'Do you all give up? It's bloody Leeds United!'

'I don't understand that,' said Chris and neither did Rose, so Mark had to explain it. Leeds at that time was one of the most successful teams in the league, but if you didn't actually support them, you probably despised them. They were successful because of their professional attitude to the game. When they played at home, they usually played very attractive football, but in away fixtures they were more concerned about not losing and preventing the opposition from playing. They were a team made up of mostly international players from around the British Isles melded with some talented local Yorkshire men. Tom was obviously not a fan and his joke had fallen a little flat, so Mark used the ensuing awkwardness to change the subject and implement the first phase of his other brilliant idea.

'Anyone here play tennis?' he asked. 'I'm thinking of starting up a little group to play one evening after work.

'I love a game of tennis,' said Tom. 'Count me in.'

That was a good start, but no one else responded.

'What about you, Chris?' Mark asked. 'Australians are supposed to be good at tennis.'

'No, I play a lot of squash which uses more of a wrist action. The last time I tried tennis, I nearly broke my wrist trying to play the same shots. Maisie plays. I'm sure she'd like a game. I'll ask her ... assuming you don't mind her joining you?'

'No, she'd be very welcome,' said Mark. 'Anyone else?' Rose shook her head. 'What about you, Lance?' Mark didn't really want him joining them, but he had to ask.

'No, tennis is for poofs,' he said.

Mark wasn't going to accept that insult without a comeback. 'Says the chap who plays a sport where they like to shove their heads up in each other's arses to form a scrum. I've heard you're a flanker. Did I hear right?'

'I heard he's a total flanker,' said Chris who liked to join in whenever anyone was attacking Lance.

'Right,' said Mark wanting to get back to his original brilliant idea, 'We don't really want to play with just three people.' He explained how they had organised their tennis at Greshams and that he'd like to do something similar at Greyfriars, so he announced that he would place an advertisement on the office notice board and would let everyone know the outcome. His idea was that perhaps Helen would join them, but he kept that to himself. If possible, he would avoid Fridays which had always been the preferred night at Greshams. Anyone going on holiday or having a weekend away would drop out and frequently mess up the numbers.

During the next few days, he received two 'phone calls from interested parties. The first was from someone named Clive who worked in Accounts. Mark didn't know anything about him, but that didn't matter.

The second was from Ginny who worked as a Data Controller. Mark knew all the Data Controllers as part of his job required him to hand over any production programs for them to administer once they went live. She was a very pleasant young lady, although inclined to be a little scatter-brained at times, so wasn't trusted to deal with any external clients. She asked if she could bring her boyfriend to the tennis, to which Mark wholeheartedly agreed. So that now made six players. That, in itself was very satisfying, but there was no call from Helen. He was tempted to ring her but decided against it. He had been hoping that their first meeting had left her feeling smitten at first sight like him, but for some strange reason this had not been the case.

***

A few weeks later, their first game took place. Mark had been looking forward to seeing Maisie again. He guessed that she was at least five years older than him, but that had never prevented him from finding a woman attractive and the fact that she was a lesbian didn't stop him fancying her. He often wondered about how a lesbian relationship worked. In a conventional heterosexual partnership, one person was substantially more masculine than the other, so he wondered if that was the case with Chris and Maisie.

Chris always wore trousers at work and usually wore what looked like a baggy man's shirt that concealed her shape. Her hair never looked like it had been to a woman's hairdresser's, but his one memory of Maisie was that of a very attractive feminine lady – and she had been married at one time so didn't that signify that she liked men? He would never seek

165

to break up their relationship, but if it ever did fail, who knows? However, that wasn't his motive for wanting to see her again. He just liked attractive women.

In any case, the lesbian relationship was all rumour and conjecture. Just because two people lived together doesn't mean they're having an affair.

Although homosexuality between men had been decriminalised a few years earlier, there was still a stigma about making one's sexuality public knowledge. This was starting to change more in America, particularly in places like Los Angeles and New York where the term 'gay' was now in common parlance.

When Mark had recently listened to *Twistin' the Night Away* by Sam Cooke, he noticed that Sam had sung about a place 'Where the people are so gay.' Of course, the singer was using an alternative word for 'happy,' unless Sam Cooke was way ahead of his time. A few years after the song's original release, it sounded wrong, but it had to rhyme with *New York Way*.

Ginny's boyfriend James seemed as scatter-brained as Ginny and the two of them made a matching pair. Neither could be described as a good player and they insisted that they wanted to play together in each game, so when it came to Ginny's turn to play singles, she asked if James could face her. As the other four players were of a higher standard, this worked out well. Maisie was good enough to not be overawed by playing with three men.

This was the first time that Mark had met Clive and he immediately resented the fact that he was tall and good looking as well as being perhaps the best player by a small margin. He also had the best kit and racquet which added to Mark's unjustified resentment.

They had booked two courts for two hours. Towards the middle of the second hour, Chris appeared and took a seat on the bench outside the mesh fence. This would be the first time that Mark had seen the two alleged lesbians together, so he was interested to see how they behaved with each other in public. Would they greet each other with a kiss or a hug? Would they walk along hand in hand?

While he was considering these things, a second lady joined Chris on the bench. Mark had only ever seen her once, but he was sure it was Helen. She looked different in her casual clothes, but it had to be her. He suddenly lost all interest in Chris and Maisie's relationship. There had to be only one explanation for Helen's arrival. Just as Chris had appeared to meet Maisie, Helen had arrived to meet someone else. It surely couldn't be Tom. He was happily married. And it obviously couldn't be

Ginny or James, nor could it be Maisie. That left only one person – Clive; bloody good-looking Clive with his smart kit and tennis racquet. It made sense. They both worked downstairs and would see each other every day, unlike Mark who was cocooned in the upstairs part of the building.

Mark decided to take out his frustration on his new enemy. It was his turn to serve and as he faced Clive, he sent down the fiercest serve he could manage. It was filled with venom. Unfortunately, it was also way too long and he was obliged to play a safe second serve which Clive despatched with ease. The next time he faced Clive, he decided to try one of his heavily sliced serves. These seldom worked and he'd earlier seen one of his attempted serves come off the edge of his racquet into the other court, hitting James near the groin area, causing James to squeal with surprise.

Tom said, 'New balls, please,' but James wasn't amused.

If this serve failed, Mark will probably look an idiot in front of Helen, but his only thought was to embarrass Clive. It was a peach and Clive nearly fell over in his failed attempt to reach it. Mark felt pleased with himself even though he and Tom still lost the set to Clive and Maisie.

Ginny and James announced that they had to leave and while all the others discussed whether to carry on a little longer, Mark overheard Chris talking to Helen. 'You should talk to Mark,' Chris said.

'Is that Mark?' Helen asked, pointing in his direction. Mark waved in acknowledgement at hearing his name. She approached the mesh fence. 'Hello, Mark,' she said. 'Would I be allowed to join your little group next week?'

He was out of breath – not from the tennis, but from the effect she had on him. 'Of course, you can,' he replied in a hoarse voice. 'The more the merrier.'

'Won't seven be an awkward number?' she asked.

'Who knows how many will turn up next week? It might be more, it might be less, but we'll cope somehow. Please come.' He wanted to say 'Please, please, please come,' but restrained himself.

She smiled as though to thank him. 'I haven't played since school, so I'm not sure if I'll be up to your standard. That's why I didn't respond to your advert. I only live across the way down Park Avenue, so I thought I'd wander along to see what it's like.'

As she spoke, he just gazed into those mesmerizing eyes that were not dimmed by the mesh fence. 'Well, as you can see, we are a mixture of talents so however you play, I'm sure you will fit in nicely.' He wanted to add 'very nicely,' but he didn't. 'We aim to start at six o'clock, but just come whenever you can,' he added.

'Thank you. I'll see you all next week,' she said and turned to walk back towards Park Avenue which was at the far end of the recreation park. Mark had never ventured down that road, but he knew of it as a middle-class area where people like doctors and lawyers were likely to live.

He was feeling thirsty and in need of a drink to celebrate this first hurdle on the path to happiness. 'Anyone ready for a drink?' he asked of the remaining group.

'We've got something on,' replied Chris.

'I haven't had any tea, yet,' said Tom. 'My wife will kill me if I don't go straight home.'

'That sounds like just you and me, then, Mark,' Clive said.

Mark didn't really want to go drinking with Clive, but he couldn't back out of it without looking extremely rude. In any case, he felt he owed him something for wrongly supposing he had stolen Helen from his grasp.

'Right you are, Clive ... just a quick one, though. I haven't had my tea, yet.'

'What do you do at Greyfriars?' Clive asked once they had sat down with their drinks.

'I'm a Programmer,' he replied. 'I work with Tom and Chris.'

'What about Jenny?' Clive asked.

'Jenny who? Oh, you mean Ginny, with a G. She's a Data Controller.'

'That's all to do with computers, right?' Clive asked. 'So, she works in the same area as you and Tom.'

'Well, not really. Data Processing is split into two departments. I'm in Systems, which includes Programmers and Systems Analysts. We do all the development work. Once all the development work is completed, we hand over to the Operations department, which includes the operators and the people who run all the production jobs. That's Data Control where Ginny works. And then there are the punch girls who prepare all the input data.'

'Ah, yes,' said Clive. 'I know about them because we send them our ledger forms for processing. So that's all punched onto tape, right?'

'No, they punch it onto floppy disks which then get transferred to magnetic tape. They actually punch the data twice. The second time is what's known as verification. If there's any variance in the two sets of punching, the punch machine flags it up and it has to be corrected.' Mark wanted to show off his knowledge of how the whole process works. He was getting ready to talk about demountable disk packs, track allocation and cylinders, but Clive was more interested in the people.

'Where does Maisie work?' he asked. Mark noticed that Clive was more interested in the women.

'She doesn't work at Greyfriars. She's with Chris – the lady who was waiting for her. Chris is another Programmer.'

'When you say, she's *with* Chris, do you mean in a relationship?'

'Well ...' Mark hesitated. He didn't want to spread unsubstantiated gossip. '... they live together, that's all I know.'

'Fancy that,' said Clive. 'She's a fine-looking woman. You can never tell, can you? What about you, Mark? Are you married?'

'No, I'm resting at the moment.'

'What do you mean – resting?'

'Well,' replied Mark, 'when actors are between roles or can't get a job, they say that they are resting. It sounds better than saying they're out of work. I'm between girls, at the moment.'

'Ah, I see, but you're looking, right?'

'I'm always looking ... just not always finding. What about you? Are you married?'

'No, but I'm with a girl. I don't know for how much longer. She's not very good in the kitchen. She's no good at cleaning. In fact, she's only good for one thing. Come to think of it, she's not really very good at that.'

Clive seemed to think that was amusing, but Mark was not very impressed with his attitude to his girlfriend. Holding such views was bad enough, but to criticise her to someone whom he'd only just met was way out of order. Mark often wondered if he would have had more success with girls if he hadn't always paid them so much respect, but that was how he was, and he wasn't going to change. He was sure that previous girlfriends like Melody and Sandy had appreciated the esteem in which he had held them.

Clive noticed the disappointed look on Mark's face and decided to change the subject. 'What was Helen talking to you about?'

'She wants to join us next week. It might mean we have to play with seven people, but if we can get an eighth person, that would be an ideal number. She seems like a very nice lady.'

'Er ... yes, but before you get too interested, you might find her a bit frigid,' said Clive.

'Why do you say that?' Mark asked before realising the tone of his voice might be giving away his feelings.

'I'm a pretty good judge of women, Mark. Just trust me on this one.'

Mark had had enough of this misogyny. He wasn't sure if Clive really was a good judge of women or not, but he'd rather find out for himself.

'I think I'd better make a move if you don't mind,' without trying to sound in any way disappointed that it was time to leave.

'Yeah, we'll have to do it all again next week,' said Clive, as he drained his glass and placed it on the table, prepared to leave it there for someone else to tidy up. Mark picked up both glasses and returned them to the bar to receive thanks from the barman.

As they returned to their cars, Mark reluctantly praised Clive's sporty looking Ford Capri.

'Yes, it's the face-lifted new shape,' Clive said, looking pleased with himself. 'This is the 1600 GT model with a twin-choke Weber carburettor; nought to sixty in about eleven seconds – faster than an MGB. There's not much room in the back, but it's got reclining seats, which have already proved useful.'

'Nice colour,' said Mark, walking around it. 'And I like the black vinyl roof.'

'It's called Daytona yellow,' Clive added. 'I think they've improved the look of the car with the changes. I like the power bulge in the bonnet. You can't beat a power bulge.'

'I might get one when I've finished paying for this,' Mark said as he unlocked his car and stepped in. 'See you next week.'

Mark had achieved his aim of potentially seeing more of Helen and he felt quietly pleased with himself as he drove home, but he wondered about Clive's comments about her being frigid. It was a word that he might have expected to be used about a husband who was no longer enjoying his conjugal rights, not a single person. He suspected that Clive had made an advance on her and been rejected. For someone like Clive that meant she was either a lesbian or frigid. Mark had found Sandy to be lacking in passion, but he always put that down to her wanting to preserve her virginity and he would never have used the word *frigid* about her. Perhaps of more concern should be that Helen had finished with her previous boyfriend because he was too clingy. Mark would have to tread the thin line between showing his interest and not showing too much. That might all be difficult unless he can see her outside of the tennis. But he had an idea. He was full of ideas, but he still didn't have a girlfriend.

Chapter Twenty-Two

Raindrops

It was raining as Mark made his way to work the next morning. He had been tempted to make a detour via the top of Park Avenue, but he was running a little late and decided that if, indeed, Helen was walking to work, he would have already missed her. Park Avenue was within easy walking distance of Ransome Road, which was connected to the park by a good footpath.

Greyfriars' employee car park was on a piece of land between the office building and the customer retail store. The rain had eased a little as he walked towards the office block where he could see Helen shaking her umbrella before entering the building. He hurried up to catch her, but she was already inside and, too late, he saw her disappearing through the doors to the ground floor office area. How that would have made his day if he had been able to speak to her, albeit for a few brief moments.

The first thing he did as he entered the programming office was to berate Tom for not joining him for a drink the night before. Tom defended himself. 'Apart from not letting my meal get spoiled, I like to see my children before they go to bed. You single people don't know about such things. It's all part of a parent's solemn duty. One of the things I had to do was to convince my son that there's nothing to be ashamed of if you wet yourself ... but he was still determined to make fun of me!'

Mark laughed but added 'I had to endure drinking alone with that Clive bloke. God, he fancies himself with the ladies!'

'I'd have swapped with you,' said Rose. 'I think he's a bit dishy.'

'I'd have thought you've had enough of such men,' said Mark, not realising how tactless that sounded and predictably, Rose went into a sulk.

'Thanks, Mark,' she said and buried her nose in her work.

'Well done, Mark,' said Chris.

'I was just making the point that he has a bad attitude towards women,' Mark said without any hint of an apology.

Chris added 'Well, I know that Maisie said she didn't like the way he looked at her ... and he kept looking across at Ginny. Sounds like a funny bloke to me.'

'But did Maisie enjoy the tennis?' Mark asked.

'Oh, yes. She hopes you're going to play every week. She's looking forward to next week.'

So was Tom, but not as much as Mark – but for a different reason.

Less than half an hour later, Tom said 'Anyone know what's happened to Lance?'

Chris replied 'Tuesday night is his rugby training night. I bet he went for a drink and had a skinful. He'll probably come wandering in when he's ready.'

Gervaise, who, as usual, had hardly spoken all morning, said 'He gets away with murder, that bloke.'

Mark said 'I agree. It's time someone did something about it. I don't think we'd miss him.'

A little later, Adam entered the office with a very serious look on his face. That wasn't too unusual, but there was something about his demeanour that made several of the programmers look up expectantly.

'I have some very sad news for you all,' he said, and everyone stopped working. 'Lance went to his rugby last night and injured himself in a tackle. He just seemed a bit dazed at first and after a few minutes carried on playing. A little later, he keeled over and they sent for an ambulance. Before he could receive treatment ... he ... died.' Adam had to collect himself before continuing. 'It seems he had broken his neck in the tackle, but no one realised. If he had stopped then and gone to the hospital, he ... he might still be with us. I know this is a big shock to you all ... and ... well, I don't think I can add anything at this time.'

'His poor wife,' said Rose, almost in tears.

'And his children,' said Tom.

Mark was thinking back to his earlier comment about how he didn't think they would miss him. They were about to find out. Mark had never experienced death in a way that might affect him. He'd lost his grandmother a few years earlier, but she was quite old and had suffered ill health, so it hadn't hit him that hard even though he had loved her in his younger days. There was a chap who worked in Gresham's factory who had been killed in a car accident, but Mark didn't know him that well, but Lance had been part of his day to day life for several months and it was strange to think that he just no longer existed. For some reason, he felt guilty that he had never liked Lance.

For the next two days, the atmosphere in the office was very subdued. There was none of the usual office banter and Mark was pleased when Friday evening came around and he could go home. The football season had almost finished for him and there was no game that weekend, so it promised nothing to relieve the gloom. On television, it was the weekend of the boat race and the FA cup semi-finals. His parents always watched the boat race, but Mark couldn't see the point of two anonymous teams slogging their way up a dirty old river. It might be of relevance if you had attended either of the two universities, or had an interest in rowing, but otherwise it seemed quite meaningless. He had heard that the winning team dip their cocks in the water at the end of the race, but that certainly wouldn't persuade him to watch.

He would stay up to watch one of the semi-finals on *Match of the Day*, but as it followed the dreaded *Eurovision Song Contest*, he would have to occupy himself for a few hours playing some records, so that afternoon, he took himself off to King's Lynn to buy a couple of *soul packs* from the Soul Bowl.

He told himself that after the next game of tennis, he might have a new girlfriend to occupy his time and it wouldn't matter what was on television. However, it might not be that easy to grasp an opportunity to speak to Helen alone, but that was where his cunning idea would come in.

Except that when Tuesday came around, it was raining again. In the office, there were a few negative murmurings during the morning, but Mark was optimistic that the rain would cease in good time. However, by the middle of the afternoon, the rain looked set for the rest of the day. Ginny called to say that she and James wanted to make alternative plans for the evening before it was too late. Tom told Mark that he was going to call his wife to tell her that he would be home earlier than planned.

Mark had no choice but to admit defeat and he called Helen to give her the bad news. She said that she was disappointed but hoped for better luck the following week. She asked Mark if she should tell Clive that it was off. Mark was pleased not to have to talk to Clive and thanked her, but then he had an idea.

'We were all wondering about re-arranging the tennis for another night this week. Are you interested?'

She hesitated, and then said 'Which night were you thinking about?'

'Erm ... not tomorrow. I've got a football match tomorrow, so it will have to be Thursday or Friday.'

'Er ... no, I don't think I can,' she said, 'but I'm definitely free next Tuesday.'

'All right, then. Let's hope it keeps fine.'

He would have to wait another whole week. It was going to be the longest week of his life. In the meantime, he would be wondering what Helen would be doing on those other nights – and whom she might be doing it with. Of course, he had lied when he said they had been talking about re-arranging the tennis, because nobody had said a word about it.

The next morning, the atmosphere in the office was still subdued, so Tom tried to lighten it. 'I went to visit a car dealer on my way home last night. I saw a nice four-year old Ford Anglia. I thought I'd get it for my wife but decided that I would miss her. She's good with the kids.'

Mark laughed, but he was the only one. Perhaps the others didn't get the joke – or perhaps they weren't in the mood for levity. It was the day of Lance's funeral and Adam was going to attend to represent the department. Mark was glad that he hadn't been asked. It was gloomy enough in the office without attending a funeral.

His greatest fear had been that it would be raining again when Tuesday came around again, but it turned out to be a fine evening for tennis. Ginny had 'phoned to say that she and James had another arrangement and would not be attending. This is what had happened with the tennis at Greshams. Other people didn't have the same level of commitment to the sport that Mark felt was necessary to make it work. He wouldn't be surprised to see this pair cry off quite frequently, but Tom and Maisie were still keen. Mark called Helen to remind her and asked her to tell Clive. Five would be an awkward number, but they would each have to take a turn at sitting out. At least Mark was able to save money by calling the council to cancel one of the courts.

He made sure he wasn't the first to sit out by arriving in good time, closely followed by Tom. As they warmed up, Maisie arrived to join them. Mark started to worry that Helen might not turn up. He knew little about her, so he didn't know how reliable she was, but he needn't have worried. As she had to walk home from work, she had taken the opportunity to change into her tennis outfit, which looked brand new. There was still no sign of Clive, but as they were now four, that was no bad thing.

Mark had previously only seen Helen in black, but in her white tennis kit, she was just as lovely. She was wearing her hair up to avoid it blowing into her eyes as she played. This revealed her long sensuous neck and he knew he was going to struggle to concentrate on his game.

As Mark had already been warming up against Tom and Maisie, Helen partnered him, saying 'Don't expect wonders. I haven't played since school.'

'You know we play for money, don't you?' he replied, hoping a little levity might dispel her fears.

She smiled and said, 'You'd better prepare yourself to lose a lot of money, then.'

174

He had longed thought of Helen as this wonderful elegant lady and her different appearance in white only reinforced that impression, but as soon as she played her first shot and missed completely, he realised that she was a flawed goddess and it only made him want her more.

As the game progressed, she missed more shots than she hit and their opposition felt no compunction about playing on her weaknesses. After Mark and Helen had lost the set six games to love, she apologised profusely, but Mark told her that she was improving, which was not a lie. Tom suggested that they swap partners, but Mark insisted that they were just getting to know each other's game and wanted another set. Tom gave Mark a knowing smile.

This time, they closed the gap to six games to two and there was much light-hearted banter. Mark played much better this time once he had decided to stop staring at Helen's shapely legs. He also relaxed a lot more as they exchanged snippets of small talk between games and he felt a real connection with her. He just hoped that she felt the same.

For the third and final set, they did swap partners, giving Maisie the opportunity to pass on her observations. 'You two are getting on well,' she whispered to Mark.

'What do you mean by that?' he asked in return.

'Tom told me that you have an interest. I think she likes you.'

'How can you tell that?' he asked, but Maisie just smiled.

At the next opportunity between games, she said 'Are you going to take her for a drink afterwards?'

'I'd like to, but that may be pushing my luck. Did you want to go? She's more likely to come if she thinks others are going.'

'All right. Chris has a squash match this evening, so I'm in no hurry to go home.'

He wasn't sure why he had asked her that, except that maybe if Helen didn't go, he might still enjoy Maisie's company, but then he realised that by doing that he would scupper his cunning scheme.

They all decided that the third set would be their last for the evening. Tom was, as ever, keen to get home to see his family and enjoy his evening meal before it spoiled. 'So, you're not going for a drink?' Maisie said. 'What about you, Helen?'

That was clever thought Mark. If Helen didn't want to go, Mark could easily duck out, too.

'I'm not really dressed for it,' Helen replied.

'I don't think any of us are,' Maisie said. 'Where do you usually go, Mark?'

'*The Three Horseshoes* is just 'round the corner – or should that be *are* just 'round the corner? That's where we usually go. I think they're used to seeing people in their tennis gear.'

'I haven't brought much money,' Helen added.

Was she trying to get out of it, or did she genuinely not want to sponge off other people?

'I'm sure I can afford a round,' said Mark.

So, the three of them said goodnight to Tom and headed off up the road towards *The Three Horseshoes*.

'Did you speak to Clive, Helen?' Mark asked as they walked along.

'Yes, he said he was coming,' she replied.

'I expect a better offer came along,' Mark said. 'It was just as well as it left us with four players.'

'Do you work with him, Helen?' Maisie asked.

'No, he's in Accounts. I work in Personnel, but I see him every day. I don't like him very much. He's always trying to get off with me - and all the other women in the building. The other week, he kept going on about wanting to show me his power bulge. '

'What's that?' asked Maisie.

'I've no idea and I didn't ask,' Helen replied.

Mark helped out. 'It's that bulge in the middle of the bonnet on his new car.'

By now, they had reached the pub and Mark ordered the first round of drinks. Both ladies asked for a half of cider.

As they sat down, he wanted to ask Helen all sorts of questions to get to know her better, but he thought that would sound rude in front of Maisie. Instead, he asked 'Are you working anywhere at the moment, Maisie?'

'Yes, I'm working at a firm of solicitors in town.'

'Oh, which one?' Helen asked with great interest.

'Hanson and Jeffries,' she replied.

'No!' exclaimed Helen. 'That's where my father works.'

'What's his name?'

'Henry Bradfield.'

'I know Mr Bradfield - a very nice man. In fact, they're all very nice people ... if a little formal. I suppose that goes with their type of business.'

The two ladies then continued talking about the various members of staff at the firm and Mark felt decidedly excluded from the discussion. He wished he hadn't asked Maisie where she worked. He wanted to join in but couldn't think of anything relevant to add, so he just admired the two ladies instead.

Eventually, they paused and Helen said 'Sorry, Mark. We're not including you in the conversation. Do you enjoy working as a programmer?'

'Yes, but it's not what I want to do forever. I think I want to get into the analysis side of Data Processing. Programming leaves you a little isolated. It leaves you working on your own too much. It's hard to interact with colleagues because they also have to concentrate ... and I never get to visit other parts of the building.'

'And, of course, you recently lost a colleague,' Helen said in a reverent tone. 'Will he be replaced?

'I don't know. No one's said anything. They probably think it's indelicate to do it straight away.'

'How many people work with you?'

'About half of them,' he said, pleased at the opportunity to use one of his old jokes.

Both ladies laughed. 'He died playing rugby, didn't he?' asked Helen.

'That's right. I've always thought it was a dangerous sport.'

'So, you don't play rugby?' she asked.

'No, I play football. I'm a goalkeeper and the goals are much too big in rugby.'

That joke didn't work so well.

'Have you always been a programmer?' Maisie asked.

'No, I've done a few things. One of the more interesting jobs I had was doing the dishes.'

Both ladies looked astonished. 'Really?' said Helen.

'Well, it was at Jodrell Bank,' he added.

'That's not true, is it,' she said smiling.

'No. Before being a programmer, I worked in Work Study, but I saw a programmer's job being advertised and so I went for it. What about you, Helen? Have you always worked in Personnel?'

And so the conversation continued, with Mark seeking every opportunity to include a witticism and trying to include both ladies in the conversation.

After a while, when all their glasses were empty, Maisie asked 'Anyone want another?'

'Not for me, thanks,' said Mark. 'One pint on an empty stomach is more than enough, but you carry on if you want. I'm just enjoying the company of two attractive ladies.'

'What a charmer!' Maisie said. 'How about you, Helen?'

'I'm all right, thank you,' she replied.

'Well, I'll get a round next time,' Maisie said as they all stood up to leave.

Mark was pleased to think there would be another time. He just wished that some of his old friends and colleagues could have seen him entertaining two attractive ladies. At one time, not too long ago, he would have been pleased to have been seen with just one pretty young girl.

They reached Maisie's Hillman Imp and it was time for Mark's cunning scheme to come into play. 'Where's your car, Mark?' Maisie asked.

'It's at the other end of the park,' he said pointing northwards. He had deliberately parked at the other side of the park so he would have to walk in the same direction as Helen. A few raindrops were falling, but most of the path would be sheltered by the trees, so they took their leave of Maisie with promises to do it all again.

'Did you enjoy the tennis?' Mark asked.

'I did, but I feel guilty about spoiling it for the rest of you. I think I'll give it a miss for now.'

Mark felt as though a knife had just pierced his heart. 'That's nonsense. You didn't spoil it. It would have been worse if we only had three players. You must keep it up. You were improving during the evening.'

'No, I don't want to play if I'm not playing well.' She seemed adamant and he remembered that he expected her to be strong willed.

Mark wasn't going to let it go that easily. 'I remember when I first started playing after leaving school. I was the worst player in the group, but I kept playing and within a few years, I was as good as any of them. You will improve if you play regularly.' It was time for another of his clever ideas.

'I've an idea,' he said. 'If you played singles a few times, it would give you chance to get your eye in. Why don't we hire a court for an hour or so later in the week? If you play singles, you will have to concentrate all the time and you'll soon improve.'

'But that won't be much fun for you,' she said.

'I'm sure I will enjoy helping you,' he said. He didn't want to sound too obvious, but he thought if she saw more of him, then she was more likely to go out with him on a date.

'Are you doing anything Friday evening?' he asked. 'Just for an hour?'

'All right,' she said after a little more thought. 'I do want to play, but if I don't improve, I won't be playing next Tuesday.'

'Right ... I'll get a court booked around the same time of night.'

As they reached the road, Helen said 'I would invite you in for a coffee, but my mother doesn't like unexpected guests. She's very house-proud.'

'I quite understand,' said Mark, thinking that in his case, he has to warn the visitors of possibly shocks – like his father bathing his feet in a bowl of soapy water! 'I'd better dash, this rain is getting heavier.'

As he headed for his car, he thought he must be in with a chance, else why would she even mention inviting him in?

Chapter Twenty-Three

Save the Last Dance for Me

Things had worked out as well as he might have expected. Maisie had played a big part in that and he must remember to thank her. He was also pleased with his own efforts. He liked a woman who laughed at his humour and Helen had proved to be a good foil for his quips. He considered that he had been in good form during the evening. Normally, in such circumstances he might have felt a little tense, but this time it had not been the case. This was, in part, due to his increasing self-confidence, but the events in the office had led him to feel that if he didn't succeed with Helen, it wouldn't be the worst disaster in the world.

Lance's death had made him realise that being without a girlfriend could never be as bad as losing a loved one. He couldn't imagine the pain that Lance's wife must be feeling. He remembered the misery he had felt when Jenny had dumped him, but does that really compare to the death of a loved one? He was determined to capture Helen's heart, but if he failed, he would survive. Fifty per cent of the world's population were female, so there would always be other possibilities, despite the long periods he had endured without a partner.

Nevertheless, he was still agonising about all the things that might go wrong before his next meeting with her. It might rain again. There might not be any courts available on that night. Either of them may fall ill and have to cancel. His car might let him down. She may just get cold feet and call it off – or worse still, she might not turn up on the night. No, Helen didn't seem like that sort of person. She would cancel in person.

And then there was the question of how he should handle the evening. He remembered when he had played tennis with Margaret, there was a certain 'awkwardness' about being at opposite ends of the court and trying a little small talk when they changed ends. It wasn't until the end of the game that they were able to talk to each other and then Margaret just wanted to go home. This time Mark wanted to make some kind of progress. He would definitely invite her for a drink, but would she go?

His fears were all unfounded. He was able to book a court at the time he wanted which was one hour later than usual. His thinking was that they only needed one hour for their game and they could both go home from work beforehand to have a bite to eat and get changed in comfort. The weather for the evening was dry if a little cloudy.

Mark had taken the opportunity to have a shave and refresh his deodorant, but it made him a few minutes late and Helen was already there before him.

'I've already paid for the court,' she said. The park attendant sometimes sat in his little hut waiting to pounce on anyone who thought they could play without paying. Other times, he turned up a little later and disappeared just as quickly. Mark didn't know if the attendant had pounced on Helen or not, but he said 'You didn't need to do that. I usually settle up.'

'No,' she said. 'I'm paying tonight. This is all for my benefit and I insist. I also booked a court for the same time next week. If you don't want to play or can't make it, we can always cancel, but as someone is already on the other court tonight, I thought I'd book it before some else does ... and if you don't want to play again, I might try to find someone else. I think you were right that playing singles a few times will help my game.'

'I'm sure I'll be happy to join you again next week,' Mark said. 'I'll pay next week.' He hoped she wasn't just using him for a game of tennis the way Margaret did, but the idea of seeing more of Helen certainly appealed to him.

As they started playing, she still made a few mistakes but as the evening progressed, she steadily improved and even took a game off him, helped by a few double faults as he tried to improve his own accuracy with his second serve which had always been a weakness.

At the end of the second set, they still had ten minutes of their allotted time available. 'Do you want to carry on?' he asked.

'Can I just practice my backhand?' she asked, and he was perfectly happy to help her in her quest to improve her game.

'You're definitely improving,' he said at the end. 'I think this was a good idea – even if I say so myself. I think you should play next Tuesday as well as Friday. The more you play, the more you'll improve.'

'But I don't want to spoil it for other people,' she said.

Mark wasn't going to let her off so lightly. 'When I spoke to Tom the next day, I told him what you had said to me and he feels the same as me. He still enjoyed the game on Tuesday.'

'What about Maisie?' she asked.

'I haven't seen her, but I'm sure she'll agree with me and Tom.'

'All right,' she replied. 'That's assuming the weather is kind to us. Can I ask? How do you know Maisie?'

'I really only know her through tennis. Why do you ask?'

'Well, at first, last week, I assumed she was your girlfriend. You seemed to be getting on so well together. You looked like a couple until you asked her where she's working. She's very nice.'

Mark realised that Helen didn't know about Chris and Maisie. 'She does seem very nice,' he said, 'but we're definitely not a couple.'

'You could do a lot worse,' Helen said. 'Is she spoken for?'

'Er ... well ... she is living with Chris,' he said, trying to be a little cagey.

'What Chris Clements in Purchasing?'

'No, Chris Barton in my department.'

'Oh ... female Chris. I see,' but she didn't want to pursue that conversation any further, much to Mark's relief. He'd left her to make her own assumptions.

'Did you want to go for a quick drink?' he asked.

'I've got a better idea,' she said. 'Why don't you come back to mine for a coffee? I feel a little self-conscious wearing my tennis gear in a pub.'

He hadn't expected that. 'Well ... yes, all right then.' He would prefer a long drink to a coffee, but this was a development in their relationship which he welcomed.

They gathered up their tennis balls from around the court. Mark was glad that he had bought some of the new yellow balls. It made it easier to distinguish them from those on the adjoining court and they played just as well as the traditional white balls.

As they headed down the path towards Park Avenue, he asked 'Do you walk to work each day?'

'Yes, it's only a short walk. I enjoy walking ... even if it's raining. I've got an umbrella. Do you like walking?'

That question surprised him. How can anyone enjoy walking? It's just a means of getting between two places if you've got no other means of transport. 'Er, well, it depends on who I'm walking with ... and where I'm walking. This is nice.' Then he added 'I like walking along the prom at Hunstanton.' He had bad memories of having to walk a lot before he bought his first car and again when he had problems with his old Wolseley, but he didn't want to say anything negative.

'You don't ever go for walks in the countryside?' she asked.

'What, you mean like rambling?'

'Yes, if you like. Last year, we went up to the Peak District as a family. We climbed up Mam Tor. It was brilliant ... wonderful views from the top – and you get a real sense of achievement.'

Mark had never heard of Mam Tor and it sounded a bit like mountain climbing which had never appealed to him. 'Sounds good,' he said. 'I've seen Monsal Head – just while driving through on business a few years ago. That was lovely. I'd like to go back there again sometime.'

This was the first time that Mark had ever ventured down Park Avenue. All the houses were detached with well manicured front gardens and most had garages. There were only two cars parked in the road itself. Helen led him through the wooden gates along a gravel drive. He looked up to see a mock-Tudor frontage and two bay windows either side of a porched entrance door.

Inside was a tiled entrance hall that led to several rooms and a substantial staircase. Mark felt overawed. He had never entered a house of this quality,

'This way,' Helen said leading him into one of the front rooms. 'I'll just let mum know I'm home. Take a seat.'

But which seat? He didn't feel right sitting on the comfortable three-piece suite in his tennis shorts, but the only upright chair looked like it might be a valuable antique, so after consideration, he sat on the settee and gazed around the room. Unlike his own front room, this one was colour co-ordinated. The chintz three-piece was a similar coral colour to the patterned wallpaper, which complemented the red curtains and the paisley patterned carpet.

In one corner was a solid looking mahogany radiogram while in the opposite corner was a glass cocktail cabinet stocked with several bottles and an assortment of fine crystal ware. In front of him was an elegant mahogany coffee table which sported a copy of *The Times* covering various magazines.

After a few minutes, Helen re-appeared carrying two bone china plates each containing a slab of sponge cake filled with butter cream and jam. 'The coffee will be ready shortly,' she said. 'I think you've earned a little treat. I do hope you like cake.'

'This looks delicious,' he said, taking one of the plates and a spork. He'd never seen a spork before and just took it for a strange shaped fork. He was glad that he had been given sponge cake rather than fruit cake, with which he usually struggled.

He perched himself on the edge of the settee to ensure that he wouldn't spill crumbs on it. Helen took one of the armchairs. 'This is amazing,' he said as he finished his first mouthful and scoped up another.

'Thank you,' she replied.

Just then, her mother walked in with a tray containing a pot of coffee and two mugs. For some reason, Mark instinctively stood up. 'Thanks mum. This is Mark.'

She placed the tray on the table and said 'How do you do, Mark. I'm very pleased to meet you,' and she held out her hand.

Not wanting to spill any crumbs, he put down his plate before offering his hand and tried to empty his mouth as quickly as he could. 'How do you do,' he said. 'This cake is delicious.'

'Yes, it has come out well.' She held his hand for a few seconds. She had quite a firm grip for a woman and Mark felt embarrassed as she held his gaze as well as his hand. She was a handsome looking lady with just the slightest hint of grey in her otherwise dark hair. He could see the resemblance and wondered if this is what Helen would look like in about twenty or more years. She held herself very erect and was aware of the effect she was having on him. He knew this was not a woman to suffer fools.

'Did you have a good game?' she asked of Mark.

'Yes, thank you. I think we both enjoyed it.' He looked to Helen as though he needed rescuing.

'Yes, we did,' said Helen. 'Mark was very gentle with me; although he made sure he didn't lose.'

'Quite right, too,' her mother said. 'I'll leave you two alone. I'm sure you don't want me hanging around.'

'Thank you for the refreshments,' said Mark as she closed the door behind her.

He'd never drunk coffee from a pot before. It was stainless steel in contrast to the chinaware beside it.

'I'll pour it in a moment, when we've finished our cake.' Helen said. 'I'm so pleased you like it. Do you take milk and sugar?'

'Yes, please.'

'One sugar?'

'Two, please,' he replied.

'Two? Do you need all that? It will spoil the taste of the coffee.'

'I always have two,' he said and then in order to justify himself. 'You have to bear in mind that I was raised on Camp coffee, which is very sweet. We've moved on from Camp now, of course.'

'Well, just for me, try it with one spoonful. You'll get the full taste of coffee that way.'

'Does your mother bake a lot?' he asked.

'Mother? No, I usually make the cakes. She cooks the main meals, though.'

'Did you make this cake?' he asked.

'Yes, of course. I thought you'd realised that. I did get an 'O' level pass in Domestic Science, you know – as well as five other subjects.'

Mark was impressed with her baking skills. 'Can I take you out tomorrow night?'

'What because I can bake a cake?' she said with a laugh.

He realised that his timing had been wrong. 'No, I've been building up to ask you. It just came out on impulse.'

'I hope that's the only thing that comes out on impulse,' she said. 'I'm afraid I've got other plans tomorrow. I promised my cousin that I would support him at his disco. He runs Sammy's Mobile Disco and I promised to round up a few friends to go and see him.' She saw the look of disappointment on Mark's face. 'Why don't you come along? As I said, I'm going with some friends, but if you could make your own way there, we could meet up. It's at the South Walton Village Hall.'

'I've got bad memories of Walton Village Hall,' he said.

'Why's that?' she asked.

'I was fresh out of school and a colleague told me that she knew someone who wanted to go out with me, so I caught the last bus there, only to find that this friend had changed her mind and hadn't turned up. I was so annoyed that I turned around and walked home – in the pouring rain.' He missed out the bit about a colleague fortuitously driving past and giving him a lift part of the way.

'How awful!' Helen said. 'A blind date that went wrong. I've had a few of those.'

'You? Had a blind date? Blind dates are for people who can't attract anyone.'

'Nonsense!' she said. 'Anyway, it won't be like that tomorrow. I'll definitely be there, but don't come if you don't fancy it.'

'Of course, I'll come. What time does it start?'

'I think it's eight o'clock. My friends and I are meeting up at seven thirty. We've all got tickets but I'm sure you can pay at the door. I don't think it costs very much.'

She then poured the coffee into the two mugs which had been placed in front of the settee and sat down beside him. Her tennis skirt rode up a little. It took all of Mark's willpower not to gaze down to her thighs, but he was all too aware of them.

She added a spoonful of sugar to each mug and stirred both. While she did this, he took a surreptitious glance at her legs. They were a delightful shape and he took a mental photograph for later.

She took the jug of cream and gently poured it over the spoon into Mark's mug allowing the cream to settle on the top of the coffee. She repeated this for her own mug.

'Now try that,' she said. 'Drink the coffee through the cream.'

He did as he was told and savoured the taste. 'Very nice,' he said.

'I saw them doing that once in the Globe in King's Lynn. They call it a Berni coffee. You must stir the sugar first or the cream won't float. Needless to say, it won't work with ordinary milk. Now drink up. I want to have a shower and get changed.'

That told him and he soon stood up to leave. He wanted to kiss her, but their relationship had not yet reached that stage, but he dearly hoped it wouldn't be too long before he could taste those delicious looking lips.

The next evening, he arrived at the South Walton Village Hall at eight fifteen. He didn't want to arrive before Helen and her companions. His one fear was that her party would include a boyfriend. There had been no mention that this was a date. Yes, she had encouraged him to attend, but was it just to swell the numbers in support of her cousin Sammy?

After paying his entrance fee, he wandered towards the 'bar' for want of a better description. It was a table covered with various bottles, particularly Babycham and several small bottles of orange juice. There were also cans of Watneys Party Seven; a canned version of Red Barrel, specifically aimed at parties. As Mark didn't like Red Barrel, he decided to steer clear of this. He knew his mate Ray would not approve. Ray liked 'real' ale, but Mark had still to discover the difference between 'real' and 'artificial' ale. Ray also liked to visit the 'Free Houses' in the vicinity, but whenever Mark had accompanied him, he found you still had to pay, so how was that free?

He would return to the 'bar' later when he was more desperate for a drink.

He looked around to find Helen. As the hall was only half full, it wasn't too hard to spot her. She was on the dancefloor with another girl and two men dancing together as a group. She spotted him and encouraged him onto the floor. He didn't really want to dance in a group, but he reluctantly joined them. She tried to introduce everyone, but the music was too loud. The record being played was by The Jackson Five, which was reasonably acceptable to his tastes. He was usually quite fussy about which records he would dance to, but he realised that if he wanted to impress Helen that night, he would have to make allowances, but when *Crazy Horses* was played next, the dance-floor emptied and he was more than happy to follow suit.

'We've got a table at the back,' Helen said as they moved further away from the speakers and indeed, it was much quieter at their table, allowing conversation of sorts.

'Louise is my old school chum,' she said, pointing to the other lady, 'and that's her boyfriend, Stan. With them is Kelly, Louise's neighbour. This is Mark, everyone.'

Mark waved to them all and wondered about Kelly. Was he just there to swell the numbers?

'What have you been doing today?' she asked.

'Oh, I washed the car,' he said honestly, but he wanted to be witty, so he added 'and I've been helping my mate with his loft extension. The people in the flat above aren't too happy about it, but there you are.'

'Very funny,' said Helen.

'That's one of Ken Dodd's,' he added, wishing to deflect the blame. 'Tom came in the other day and told us he'd got a Ford Anglia for his wife. Then he added that he will miss her.' It took a moment before anyone realised that it was another joke.

'Oh, you mean he swapped her for a car,' said Kelly, in case no one else understood it.

Mark wondered if he was 'with' Helen, but he was sitting on the opposite side of the table so it didn't seem likely.

One of the next records was *Me and Mrs Jones*. Helen said 'I like this. Shall we dance?'

Mark didn't need asking twice. He stopped her getting too close to the speakers so that they could talk, although she started the conversation. 'You made a good impression on my mother,' she said.

'Did I? What did I do?'

'You stood up when she walked in the room. She said you were a real gentleman.'

'Well, it seemed the right thing to do,' he said.

'Do you have a girlfriend?' she asked.

'Not at the moment,' he said. He almost said 'Not yet,' but decided that might be pushing his luck. 'However, I do have my eye on someone – someone special.'

'Really? Tell me more. What's she like?'

'Well, she's very pretty with dark hair; brown eyes; high cheek bones; a small dimple in one cheek only and a wonderful smile. She also has a graceful neck and a fabulous figure.'

'What about her personality?' Helen asked.

'She's vivacious; intelligent; got a good sense of humour and she's very strong-minded.'

'She sounds great. Have you asked her out, yet?'

'Yes.'

Helen looked up at him as she asked, 'And what did she say?'

'That she was busy, but I could join her with some friends.' He looked back at her to gauge her reaction.

'Maybe you should ask her out again.'

'I might do,' he replied, 'or I might just play hard to get.'

'I wouldn't do that,' she said. 'If she's strong minded like you say, she might not appreciate that kind of behaviour.'

'No, but I'm a bit wary of being rejected. After all, I'm no great catch and she's the best-looking girl here tonight.'

Helen looked around. 'Is it that girl over there? She's very pretty.'

'No, she's much too thin – like a matchstick with the wood shaved off.'

'Oh, you like a girl with a bit of meat on her, do you?'

'Not too much. My mate Kenny always says that given the choice between a girl with skinny legs and one with fat legs, he prefers something in between.' Mark wondered if that last remark was a bit too near the knuckle.

'Is Kenny your best mate?' Helen asked.

'No, he's just someone I play football with. I don't go out with him or anything. He can be a bit coarse sometimes.'

Helen didn't seem to take offence. 'So where's the gorgeous woman you fancy?'

Mark pretended to look around and then feigned surprise 'Oh, there you are.'

She leant her head on his shoulder and pulled him closer. The next song was *If You Don't Know Me by Now*. This was his sort of music and they carried on dancing. To him, they seemed to be getting closer all the time. He could feel her impressive breasts thrusting into him and he was aware of her deliciously firm thighs against his own. There was a predictable outcome on his genitalia and he wondered if she would notice.

'Are you enjoying yourself?' she asked, looking up to him again.

'Of course,' he replied.

'I can tell,' she said, but she was speaking light-heartedly.

Crocodile Rock was the next number and Mark decided he was at last thirsty and asked if she wanted a drink. They strolled over to the 'bar' together and both struggled with the options available. 'There's a pub 'round the corner,' he said. 'We could pop out there for a better selection.'

'I can hardly leave my friends, can I?' she replied.

'No, of course not,' he said. 'I think I'll make do with an orange juice.'

'Me too,' she said.

They had several dances together. The remainder were almost all up-tempo. Helen was an elegant dancer rather than an over enthusiastic mover like several of the other attendees. The last number of the evening was announced as another slow tune and much to Mark's dismay, Kelly was first to ask Helen to dance, so Mark was left sitting all alone at the table, watching them and resenting it when Kelly held her close. Mark waited until they returned and smiled as though nothing was wrong. He still hadn't managed to ask her for a proper date and he didn't really want to do it in front of the others, but as she excused herself to visit the Ladies, he caught up with her.

'Would you like to go out with me tomorrow night?' he asked.

'Um, I don't really like going out on a Sunday. Everywhere seems so dull on a Sunday. That's when I do my baking. Why don't we go for a walk in the afternoon, instead?'

'Yes, that will be nice. Where do you want to go?'

'Have you got any proper walking boots?' she asked.

'Er, no – I've got some football boots, but I don't think that would be suitable.'

'Oh, I don't know. I can just imagine you walking along with a football ... dribbling all the way. I bet you're good at dribbling.'

'Yeah, you have that effect on me.'

'Well, I think that we'd better avoid country paths.'

'We could go to the seaside,' he suggested, 'Walk along the prom at Hunstanton.'

'I think it needs to be a little nearer,' she replied. 'We won't have that much time.'

'I know,' he said. 'How about The Walks in Lynn?'

'That's where the football ground is, isn't it? It doesn't sound that interesting – unless you like football.'

'No, the football ground is at one end, but there are lots of paths through avenues of trees. I won't need boots to do that. And at the other end are some formal gardens which always look nice from the road.'

'All right,' she said. 'I'll believe you. Will you pick me up? I usually finish lunch by about two o'clock.'

And so it was arranged. He decided that this was a proper date. It had been a long time coming.

Chapter Twenty-Four

You Got Me Walking

Helen was right about Sundays. In 1973, licensing hours forced pubs to operate reduced opening hours and many people regarded the evening as bath night or hair washing night. It was a night for staying in and watching *Sunday Night at the London Palladium* on the television followed by a Sunday night play. Very few shops opened during the day and these were mostly newsagents, many of whom closed by lunchtime. So had Helen granted Mark an evening out together, it would have to have been at a near deserted pub or the cinema, which was one of the few establishments that operated as normal. Even Fish and Chip shops were closed. So a walk in the park was the best he might have hoped for.

He arrived at her house on time and was greeted by her mother who welcomed him with great enthusiasm. He wondered what he had done to merit such a welcome – other than standing up when she had entered the room earlier in the week. Perhaps Helen's previous boyfriends had not shown such manners. 'She'll be ready in a moment,' her voiced boomed. 'Just step inside.'

Mark stood just inside the hallway and he wondered if his appearance did not warrant being allowed any further. He was wearing his favourite cheesecloth shirt and some black cords, but then what did one wear for an afternoon walk? He had agonised for some time before donning these garments. He wanted to look smart but his normal evening wear would look silly strolling along The Walks. When Helen appeared, he was relieved to see that she was wearing a cotton blouse and denims.

'Should I bring my walking boots?' she asked.

'It's tarmac all the way,' Mark replied. 'I think you'd look a bit odd wearing boots down The Walks.'

'I saw you had baseball boots,' she said.

'That's because I don't have anything else other than my leather shoes.'

'And your football boots,' she added.

'I decided to leave them at home,' he said.

'So no dribbling today, then?' she said.

'We'll see. I do need to practise my ball control.'

'That's not the only thing you need to control,' Helen said with a grin.

'Whatever are you two talking about?' her mother said, guessing that it was all a load of innuendo. 'You'd better be on your way before you score an own goal.'

As Mark led Helen towards his car, he said 'Your mother seems like a good sport.'

'Mum? Oh, yes ... she can be good fun. Dad is the opposite. He does have a sense of humour, but being a solicitor, he always acts more dignified.'

'Do you have any brothers or sisters?' Mark asked.

'No,' she replied. 'I lost a younger brother at birth and mum was advised not to have any more after that. She'd been taking thalidomide, you know.'

'Gosh!' Mark said. 'But not with you, though?'

'I don't think so. I never like to ask. It's not a subject that crops up too often.'

'Was he born with limbs missing or something?'

'I think his internal organs were malformed, but I'm not entirely sure. They didn't know at the time that the drug was the cause.'

As they reached his car, he decided that this was not a subject to pursue on a nice sunny afternoon. He opened the door for her and she stepped in gracefully.

'What about you?' she asked, as they drove away. 'Do you have any brothers or sisters?'

'Yes – one of each,' he replied echoing Tom's response to a question about his children, except that Tom had three and his response had been more amusing. 'They're both older than me and both married. I'm now living with a woman.'

'You're what?' Helen exclaimed with surprise.

'The woman is my mother ... and there's my dad as well.'

'Oh, very funny,' she said with a grin. 'How long is this walk we're doing?'

'It depends how far you want to walk,' he replied. 'We could just go up and down and that would take about half an hour. Or we could go round in a circle to more or less double that. If you want to go a bit further, we could go around Greyfriars.'

'Greyfriars? Why would we want to do that?' she asked, thinking he meant one of their employer's branches.

'I'll show you when we get there,' he said. 'I think we should do that. It's not worth driving all that way for a half hour walk. Do you drive?'

'I can drive, but I don't have a car at the moment. I walk to work and I can sometimes borrow dad's car if he's not using it.'

'What car does he have?' Mark asked.

'It's a Rover,' she replied. 'It's nice to drive. I'll borrow it sometime so you can see what it's like.'

'What model is it?' he asked, thinking how wonderful it was that she was including him in her future plans.

'I don't know. It's about eighteen months old,' she replied.

'It's probably a Rover 2000 then. They are nice. I'd like to change this, but I'm still paying for it.'

'What's wrong with it?' she asked.

'Well, it doesn't exactly turn heads. But it has been reliable. I like the front-wheel drive. I quite like the look of Clive's car – complete with power bulge.'

'I'm sure you don't need a power bulge,' she said. Mark wasn't sure if she was inferring his bulge when they had been dancing, but he didn't pursue the matter.

'Did you ever find out why Clive didn't turn up last Tuesday?'

'No, I haven't spoken to him since,' she said.

Have you ever been out with him?' he asked.

'No way – he has asked me out a couple of times, but he's not my type.'

'What about Kelly?' he asked.

'Kelly – ah well ... he was one of those blind dates I referred to – one that didn't go so well. He's nice enough, but er... '

'Not your type?' Mark finished her sentence for her.

'Yeah, you could say that. Louise feels sorry for him as he can never get a girlfriend, but er... not for me.'

'So what is your type?' Marl asked.

'I don't have a *type*,' she replied laughing. 'I like someone who's honest and reliable; reasonably intelligent with a sense of humour.'

Mark thought she could be talking about him, but he probed further. 'What about physical appearance?' he asked.

'Physical appearance isn't important to me; but not too short ... someone who is reasonably fit. I'm not bothered about looks.'

That sounded even more like him.

All the way to King's Lynn, the conversation never wavered and the journey seemed to take no time at all. He parked his car beside the football stadium.

'Is this where King's Lynn play their matches?' she asked.

'That's right. It's called *The Walks* Stadium.'

'I bet you have aspirations to play there, one day,' she said.

'Actually, I have played there,' he announced. 'It was against Lynn A.'

'Is that their reserve team?' she asked.

'No, they have three teams. The first team and the Reserves normally play here, alternating as fixtures dictate. Both those teams are semi-professional, so we would never play them, but their third team is called Lynn A and they play in the local junior league at a similar level to our team. I think they usually play on a local council pitch. A couple of years ago, we played them in the Norfolk Junior Cup. That's a competition for teams right across Norfolk from Lynn to Yarmouth. There are teams from Norwich, Brandon, Thetford ... and Sanford, of course. With their first two teams not using the stadium that week, they decided that they might overawe us with this.'

'Did they?' she asked.

'They didn't, but it was strange to play on a pitch with so much space. Our usual home pitch is quite narrow so we struggled and lost by a single goal.'

'Were there a lot of people watching?' she asked.

'No ... not much more than our usual games, so it was a bit echoey.' He locked his car doors and added 'This whole area round here is called The Walks and we're going to start by walking along this path towards the town centre.'

As they set off, Mark decided to chance his arm and he reached for her hand. She let him take it and gave a little squeeze and a friendly smile. It was the first time in many months that he had held a girl's hand and he felt a warm glow pass through his body. Before the day was through, he was going to try a kiss, but in the meantime he was walking on air.

'This is a nice area,' she said. 'You must have walked along here several times.'

'No, this is the first time that I've walked this section. I've been along some of the other parts before. When I was a lad, we used to come here train spotting. That's the railway station over the other side. We would bring a football to kick around when it was quiet ... or go on the swings and roundabouts where we still had a good view of any trains coming or going.'

'You'll get on well with my father,' she said. 'He's a big train spotter. He told us that his parents wanted him to study law in Cambridge, but he said the trainspotting was better in Durham! I don't know if that's true or not, but that's what he always tells us.'

'I would have agreed with him,' Mark said. 'Durham is on the East Coast Mainline and he would have seen loads of wonderful express engines. When was this?'

'Right after the war,' she replied. 'He had to serve a couple of years in the RAF during the last part of the war, so he was a little late attending university. He took us to Bressingham last year. We weren't sure about it at first, but we did enjoy it.'

'I went last year,' Mark responded. 'We might have been there on the same day.'

'It was a Sunday when we went,' she said. 'And it was very busy.'

'We went on a Wednesday,' he said. 'They are only open on Sundays and Wednesdays. I took my mother and Uncle Len and his wife. He used to be a train driver and I'm sure I saw a tear in his eye when he looked up at *Oliver Cromwell*. He said he used to drive one just like that.'

'You must talk to my dad when you see him. Mention Nigel Gresley to him and you'll have a friend for life.'

'He is my hero, too,' said Mark. 'He died too young. You can't help wondering what else he might have designed.'

By now, they had reached the gate set into the old town wall and crossed over a waterway.

'Is this a river?' she asked.

'Yes, it's the Gaywood River. It's not very long, but it's quite interesting. It meanders around Gaywood then it's diverted under the railway and re-appears here. As it gets to the main road, it's diverted underground again and comes out at the end of The Fleet where it flows into the Ouse. I've seen an old picture of when the Millfleet was a river. You probably know that The Fleet used to be the bus station until just a few years ago.'

'Yes, I do remember,' she replied. 'How come you know so much about this area?'

'I used to go out with a girl who liked the local history and geography. She worked in a local school and used to take her children on field trips. She taught me quite a lot.'

He was thinking 'in more ways than one.'

'What else did she teach you?' Helen asked detecting that there was more to his statement.

'Not to trust women,' he replied bluntly; then regretted saying it. He had vowed to himself that he would never again bring up Jenny's name when talking to another girl.

'Well, thank you for that,' she said, equally as bluntly. 'You think men are more trustworthy?'

'No, of course not,' he replied meekly and they both went quiet for a few minutes.

194

At some point during that conversation, they had ceased to hold hands. He didn't remember that happening and didn't feel it appropriate to try again; at least not for a while.

After a few minutes, he said 'I'm sorry. You know that wasn't aimed at you.'

'I hope not! It sounds like you've been out with some bad women,' she said.

'No, not really ... just the one who destroyed my trust, but I don't wish to talk about it. It was a long while ago.'

They soon emerged from The Walks out onto the main road. 'That didn't take that long,' Helen said. 'What now?'

'We'll cross the road into that park,' he said pointing the way.

As they entered the Tower gardens, he said 'Damn! It's covered in scaffold.'

'What is it? She asked.

'It's Greyfriars Tower,' he said as they walked towards it. A large yellow sign with red lettering declared that the builder's name was 'Carter.' The base of the tower was fenced off and it was clear that some essential maintenance was being carried out above.

'This all used to be a priory,' he added.

'Presumably pulled down by Henry the Eighth,' Helen said.

'No, I think it was the owners of the Bingo Hall next door,' he said.

She didn't laugh and after consideration, he decided it wasn't very funny anyway.

'The flowers are very nice,' she said, but somehow he detected that her admiration for the glorious display should have been more enthusiastic. He felt that perhaps his comment about not trusting women had set back their relationship and he couldn't allow that to continue.

'Shall we just sit down for a while?' he suggested, pointing to a bench. 'I'm sorry if I offended you.'

'Offended me?' she said taking a seat beside him. 'You haven't offended me. What gives you that idea?'

'I shouldn't have said that I've learnt not to trust women. Perhaps I could have said that I should be wary of trusting anyone, but that certainly wasn't directed at you.'

'I didn't think it was,' she said. 'If I'd have thought that you would know about it. Now what else can you tell me about this tower?'

'Er, not a lot, really. I know there were other priories in Lynn, because there is a Blackfriars Road – and I think there may be a Whitefriars somewhere. Lynn used to be a major port in the old days – one of the biggest in the country.'

'You seem to know a lot about Lynn. Did you get this from your old girlfriend?' she asked.

'Not all of it. As well as train spotting, we used to come here to the Saturday morning pictures at The Majestic down the road. Afterwards, we would walk along Tower Street, past The Model Shop and the pet shop – I think it was called The Zoo –and then on through these gardens, playing through the arches and out the other side to the bus station. Sometimes, we would buy a packet of chips on The Millfleet. Or if it was raining, we might go into the library.'

'It's nice to have memories,' she said, 'and this is nice.' She reached for his hand and he took hers to his lips. 'Now what's next?' She asked.

'There's another park over the road,' he replied, 'then we head back into The Walks again. It's funny, though, this park seems so much smaller than I remember from my childhood.'

They left the park by a different gate and crossed over St James' Road into a larger park. As they did so, a young girl in a school uniform, rode past on her cycle. It stirred another memory from Mark's past. 'Did you go to Sanford High School?' he asked.

'Yes, I did. I managed to get a few 'O' levels. Did you go to Parkside?' she asked in return.

'Yes,' he replied. 'Did you have one of those nice green uniforms?' It was a stupid question because all the girls wore the same outfit.

'Of course,' she replied.

'I always liked that uniform,' he said. 'Every boy from Parkside would have aspirations of meeting a pretty young girl from the High School and whenever such a girl walked past in that uniform, he would perk up with great interest. Do you still have your uniform?'

'Of course not. If I did, it wouldn't fit me anymore.'

'Pity,' he said.

'Do you like girls in uniform, then?' she asked. 'I've got a French maid's uniform at home – short skirt with suspenders.'

'Really?' he said, his eyes lighting up.

'No! Why would I have such a thing? You men are such perverts.' She wasn't serious and she gave him one of her lovely smiles which filled him with such happiness. 'So you went to Parkside,' she said.

'Yes, I was a grammarshite,' he said.

'What a horrible term,' she said.

'It's what everyone called us. Haven't you heard that before?'

'No, I haven't,' she said. 'I think it's horrible.'

'Well, I was proud to be a grammarshite. I don't remember the High School having a nickname, but then I didn't mix with any of the girls there.'

'Better late than never!' she said.

'You're telling me,' he said.

'These begonias are lovely,' She had changed the subject. 'I suppose it's the council who look after this. What a shame that our council isn't so active in our little park.'

Mark didn't know which flowers were begonias and didn't want to show his ignorance so he changed the subject once more.

'Have you decided if you're playing with us on Tuesday?'

'If you're absolutely sure that no one else will mind,' she said.' I'm quite happy to leave it another week after one more game of singles.'

'I'm sure no one will mind,' he replied. 'You're probably as good as Ginny anyway – and what happens if it rains on Friday. No, I'm sure if you play twice this week, you'll carry on improving.'

'All right, then,' she said. 'Do you want me to ask Clive if he's playing?'

'You can if you want to, but frankly, I don't want to be chasing people up every week. They all know we intend to play every Tuesday, weather permitting, so they either turn up or they don't. I've achieved my aim, which was to use the tennis to meet you.'

'To meet me? Do you know, I never know when you're being serious or not.'

'Oh, I'm serious, all right,' he said. 'I've wanted to go out with you since the very first time I saw you and it's taken all this while for it to happen.'

'So what would you have done if I hadn't started playing?' she asked.

'I'd have to come up with another cunning scheme and at least I've had a few games of tennis which is better than sitting at home thinking about you. I've thought of nothing else for months.'

They had stopped walking now and she was staring at him. 'But it was only a short while ago that we actually spoke to each other. How did you know what I was like?'

'Well, I didn't, of course,' he replied, 'but that didn't stop me thinking about you. You may still have some horrible faults that might put me off, but, so far, I haven't seen any.'

'Oh, I've got my faults, don't you worry about that,' she said.

'Well, I'm sure they're not serious. You're not a member of the Nazi party or anything are you?'

'Now how did you find out about that?' she said to lighten the mood.

'I think the swastika hanging from an upstairs window was a clue,' he said.

'Oh, that!' she said. 'That's just mum airing the bed linen. You don't want to take any notice of that! Anyway, I thought you liked uniforms.'

He was trying to think of a way to repeat his joke about a Teutonic relationship, but it didn't work, so he left it.

They had walked more or less diagonally across the park and were then exiting the far corner. 'And here we are back in The Walks,' he said. 'This avenue is parallel to the first one. We could go straight down and then along the road at the bottom, but I'd rather cross over. I think you'll find it more interesting.'

As they walked past the municipal tennis courts where a few people were playing, he asked 'I know I'm going to see you again on Tuesday and Friday, but can we go out on a proper date?'

'This is a proper date,' she replied. 'I'd much rather being doing this than sitting in some smelly pub, going home smelling of beer and cigarettes. But I don't mind seeing a film if there's anything decent on.'

'There's *The Exorcist* this week,' he replied. He'd already checked in anticipation of trying for another date.

'No, I don't want to see that. I'd like to see *The Sting* if it comes to Sanford. That looks quite good, but I'm quite happy for you to come 'round and watch a bit of television together. We can have the use of the front room to ourselves. It's only a small black and white set, but that doesn't matter, does it? You'll find that I don't need a lot of entertaining. My last boyfriend used to take me out to a pub and then leave me to play darts with his mates.'

'Don't you play darts?' he asked.

'I can do, but he didn't give me chance. What's that strange looking building?' She was pointing to a hexagonal red brick building standing on a mound.

'That's the Red Mount,' he replied. 'It's a small chapel that was used by passing pilgrims who were visiting the shrine at Walsingham. There is a story that there is an underground tunnel that leads all the way to Castle Rising.'

'That can't be true,' she said. 'We're miles away from Castle Rising. No one could build a tunnel that long.'

'No, I agree,' he said. 'And it would be impossible for anyone to be able to breathe without ventilation shafts every few yards. But some people believe it. Did you know that Castle Rising was once right beside the sea? It makes you think, doesn't it? In this country, there are places where the coast is being washed away and in others the land is stretching out where there used to be sea.'

'It's an interesting old building,' she said as they came right up to it. 'Can you visit it?'

'I don't know. I've never seen it open.'

Helen decided to walk all around the building, but there was nothing around the back that was of any further interest, so they carried on walking and came up to a short length of old wall and the point where they rejoined the original avenue. 'This wall must be very old,' she said. 'What do you know about it?' she asked.

'Er ... nothing, really,' he said. 'It might be part of the original town wall, but I'm not sure.'

'You're letting me down,' she said. 'I expect you to know these things.'

As they returned along the avenue where they had started, she took Mark's hand again and said, 'I've really enjoyed this little walk and you've been very helpful in educating me about the area.'

He wanted to put his arms around her shoulders, but it was a hot day and he wasn't sure if he was too sweaty so he contented himself with holding her hand. When they passed a younger couple who were kissing and cuddling each other in a most ungainly way, he realised that he had probably made the right decision. Helen was too classy to indulge in that sort of thing in public, but that didn't stop him from wanting to find the right moment.

'Are you making another delicious cake tonight?' he asked.

'Yes, it's going to be cheesecake this time,' she replied.

'Cheesecake?' he said, a little louder than he intended. 'You mean a cake made with cheese?' He'd never heard of such a thing.

'Yes, of course. Have you never had cheesecake? You haven't lived.'

'I think I'll give that one a miss,' he said. 'I thought carrot cake was bad enough, but cheese? No thanks.'

'It's delicious. You must try it before you pass judgement. It's made with light cream cheese – not cheddar or Wensleydale or anything like that. It's all whipped up onto a biscuit base.'

'Cream crackers, I suppose.' he said. 'So it's really a savoury flan of sorts?'

'No, it's a dessert. I used digestive biscuits for the base. I promise you that you will like it – and what's more, you're going to try it.'

They were back at the car and Mark decided not to pursue the subject. With a bit of luck, he would avoid having to taste her cake made from cheese, but he had enjoyed a wonderful afternoon and didn't want anything to spoil it.

But that was all about to change.

He didn't know if he had done anything wrong. He had to admit that his concentration was not one hundred per cent on his driving. Apart having his mind on Helen, he was also struggling to hold the steering wheel which was baking hot after the car had been left in the blazing sun for over an hour, but the squeal of tyres braking and the sound of a horn soon had his attention. He looked in his rear view mirror to see a large man in a large white Ford Zephyr gesticulating wildly. Mark hadn't noticed him coming around the corner, so he assumed he must have been travelling at some speed to have warranted the fierce application of brakes.

'What's going on?' Helen asked.

'I think I've just upset one of the locals,' Mark replied.

Helen turned around to look behind. 'He doesn't look like one of the friendly natives. Whatever did you do?'

'I'm not sure,' he replied. 'I didn't see him coming, but I do know he was travelling too fast.'

'I think you should pull over and let him pass,' she said, but Mark wasn't going to admit that he felt intimidated, especially in front of a girl. He proceeded towards the level crossing sticking closely to the speed limit. The Zephyr was following far too closely for Mark's liking and he was a little concerned when he saw the level crossing closing ahead of him. The chap was obviously in a great hurry and waiting at the gates was not going to improve his mood.

Mark looked towards the station and could see that the signals showed that no train was about to leave the station. That could mean one was about to enter or that a freight train was being moved. As it happened, it was neither of those two things. It was a diesel shunter moving a single truck along the track and once it had passed through, they expected to move off quite quickly. Instead, after a long delay while points were changed, the shunter returned along a different line.

But still the gates were shut. After a further delay, during which Mark could see the irate driver behind banging his steering wheel, a railcar passed into the station at a frustratingly slow speed. At last, the operator re-appeared to open the gates to traffic. Mark made sure he was well out of the way before moving off, despite being honked from behind. As a former train spotter, Mark was familiar with these shunting delays, although, in his day, it would have been a small 0-6-0 tank engine steaming backwards and forwards.

A couple of times, the Zephyr made to overtake Mark, but there was a steady stream of traffic heading towards them and each time he had to return to Mark's tail. A warm sunny afternoon in the summer always meant these roads would be busy as people returned home from the seaside. At one time, this traffic would have been nose to tail and a delay at the level crossing would have caused the traffic to tail right back to *The New Inn* at South Wootton, but the new bypass now diverted most of the cars around Lynn.

The delay at the railway crossing meant there were only two cars queuing to cross onto Gaywood Road and many of the cars coming from the east were turning into Tennyson Avenue so Mark, trusting the signals of those motorists soon succeeded with his next manoeuvre towards Gaywood. Whereas the irate driver behind upset someone who was not turning into the road they had just left and he returned a blast on the horn with one of his own.

'He's a bit of a nutter,' Mark said. 'I'll be glad to see the back of him,' but at the Gaywood Clock where Mark wanted to turn right towards Gayton, the nutter waited behind him in the queue to turn right.

A kind motorist flashed Mark to let him cross onto Gayton Road and again, the nutter was right behind him, not waiting to be ushered across. Mark said, 'He's still there,' and pointed a finger to his temple in the universal method of indicating someone's mental health is in question.

Helen turned to have a look for herself. The nutter, having witnessed Mark's gesture and seeing her turn, pointed two fingers at her to mimic a gun. 'He looks like a psycho to me,' she said.

Mark was tempted to turn into one of the side streets to let him pass, but he feared that they may be dead-ends and he might get trapped by the psycho. He was now getting quite scared although he wasn't going to admit it to Helen. He was sweltering in the heat as he had wound up his windows soon after the incident started flaring up.

Once again, the psycho decided to overtake even though it was far from safe to do so. Mark decided to help him by slowing down, but when it was clear that the manoeuvre wasn't going to be successful because of oncoming traffic, that caused the Zephyr to brake violently and only annoyed the driver even more. He tried again and this time Mark drove at the speed limit. For a moment, he was out of sight as Mark's car did not have wing mirrors, but then Mark became aware of him from his peripheral vision. He decided not to make eye contact, but Helen looked across to see Psycho staring at them and making a throat cutting gesture.

He was past. Now Mark could quickly disappear up a side street – except that there wasn't one. They were almost at the roundabout where the bypass crossed north to south. A few cars waited at the roundabout and the Zephyr had to stop. Mark stayed a few yards back leaving him a little room to manoeuvre if necessary.

To their alarm, the psycho got out of his car and pointed at them. He was huge – and ugly with it. He went to his boot to find something.

'Oh, my God! What's he looking for?' Helen exclaimed. 'Is he looking for a weapon?'

He turned round holding a long-handled mallet and made his way towards them.

The cars ahead had moved across the roundabout and Mark put his foot down, narrowly missing the man who jumped back in surprise. Mark went straight round the roundabout and turned south along the bypass, which was not the direction they needed to get home, but Mark figured that if he drove towards Gayton, which was the quieter road, the Zephyr would soon overhaul them and possibly run them off the road. The road to the north was wider for a while and would also present opportunities for overtaking. Mark had to get away and he decided that if this man was in such a hurry to drive down Tennyson Avenue, he would not want to head in the opposite direction.

Progress down the bypass was slow due to the holiday traffic returning from the seaside and Mark kept looking in his rear-view mirror but there was no sign of the distinctive white Zephyr. Helen turned around to look as well. 'Here he comes,' she said, but then changed her mind as it was a smaller white vehicle. Mark was tempted to try and overtake a few cars, but his 1100 was not built for speedy overtaking. At least it was a common brand and didn't stand out like a big white Zephyr.

They reached the queue for the Hardwick Road roundabout and they were starting to feel that at last they had escaped Psycho. Mark turned left onto the A47 towards Swaffham. He could have turned back up the bypass to resume their original route, but he just wanted to make sure of their safety. They could cut across country after a few miles. By now, he felt safe enough to open his window and drive at a leisurely forty miles an hour. At the turning for Blackborough End and Middleton, he turned left, and once out of sight of the main road, he pulled to a safe stop and let out a huge sigh. His hands were sweaty and had been slipping on the plastic steering wheel.

'I need some fresh air,' he said, stepping out of the car and walked around in a small circle to restore the circulation in his shaking limbs.

Helen joined him. 'I'm sorry to have put you through all this,' he said.

'It wasn't your fault. You did the right thing,' she said and put her arms up to his shoulders and leant against him.

He wanted to hold her, but he knew he had been sweating and so just leant into her. 'I'll get you home in a minute,' he said.

'There's no hurry,' she replied. 'Just take a few minutes.'

'I feel I should have stood up to him,' he said.

'What and get yourself injured? I think you did exactly the right thing. There's no telling what he was going to do with that hammer.'

'I suspect he was going to damage my car,' Mark said, 'and he would have done if I hadn't driven off. I contemplated driving into him at first, but then I saw the traffic move so I thought that was a better option.'

'You did right,' she said. 'If you had driven into him, you would have gotten into a lot of trouble. This was best' and she squeezed his shoulder. 'Are you feeling better now?'

'A little, thank you. How about you? You must have been terrified.'

'Yes, I was,' she replied, 'but somehow I felt safe with you. It's just shame that the day had to end like that. I think I'll remember this day for a long time – good and bad, but mostly good.'

He kissed her gently on the lips but didn't prolong the experience. He hoped he had left her wanting more. 'Let's get you home,' he said.

The journey home was uneventful. She invited him in for a cup of tea, but he replied, 'I think I'll go home and change these trousers.' He hoped she saw the humour in that and told her he would look forward to seeing her at the tennis on Tuesday.

Chapter Twenty-Five

Could It Be I'm Falling in Love

The next morning, Mark kept looking in his rear-view mirror. He had spent a troubled night thinking about the incident the day before. At first, he had felt safe once back in his home, but he started wondering if he was likely to encounter the psycho again. Where was this man likely to live? The direction in which he was heading at the time Mark left him could indicate Sanford. Or he might have been heading for the coast; or possibly somewhere in the direction of Gayton or Fakenham. It was possible that he was not even heading for his home and was just visiting the area.

And why would anyone carry a large mallet in the boot of their car? Mark dismissed the idea that he played polo – or that he was a croquet player. A demolition expert perhaps? The more Mark thought about it, the more he convinced himself that the man carried a mallet to help him smash up the bars and shops of people who wouldn't pay their protection money. If so, Mark was in big trouble. He eventually decided that the most likely explanation for the incident was that the dangerous looking man was just in bad mood because he'd fallen out with his girlfriend or relative and was rushing home in a rage – and Mark was in the wrong place at the wrong time.

A different vehicle appeared from a side street and filled his mirror. Mark would do everything in his power to drive carefully and not upset anyone. He was relieved when he arrived at work and entered the office. He contemplated ringing Helen but he'd seen her three days in a row and didn't want to appear to be pestering her. He remembered that Chris had told him that Helen had ended her last relationship because her boyfriend had become 'too clingy.' He had to tread the thin line between showing genuine interest and annoying obsession. He would wait to see her at the tennis the next evening.

But it was Helen who 'phoned him. Because he and his colleagues had little need for business 'phone calls, the six programmers shared two extensions. Although only a Junior Programmer, he was fortunate in that the person who had occupied the desk before him was one of those privileged to have a 'phone on their desk. Gervaise had the other one.

As soon as the 'phone rang, he knew that it was Helen. He just knew it. 'Hello, Mark Barker,' he said, trying to sound professional even though he knew it was going to be her.

'Hello, it's me,' she said. He liked that. How boring it would have been if she had announced herself as 'Helen from Personnel.' He felt one of those warm glows flowing throughout his body which he felt whenever she spoke to him.

'Are you all right?' she asked.

'All the better for hearing your voice,' he replied.

'Have you got over yesterday's ordeal?' she asked.

'Seeing you is never an ordeal,' he said.

'You know what I mean,' she said.

'Yes, I'm fine, thank you,' he said,' although I do keep looking in my mirror ... when I'm driving, I mean ... not when I'm in the bathroom. Are you all right?'

'Yes, I'm all right, thank you. I've been thinking about what we can do together,' she said.' Have you got any plans for this weekend?'

'Nothing at the moment,' he replied, 'although I'm half expecting a call from Raquel Welch, but I think I can put her off.'

'Well, don't put her off on my account.'

'It's all right. You know what these Hollywood superstars are like. She can be very demanding – like wanting my full attention when I'm trying to have a game of darts with my mates. What did you have in mind?'

'Well, Sammy runs his disco most weekends. I could give him a call and find out what he's got on this weekend, if that meets with your approval. You can bring Raquel if you want.'

'Why would I want Raquel if you're going to be there?'

'Well, I can be very demanding as well,' she said.

'All the more reason to forget about blinking Raquel,' he said. 'Yes, I think I'd like that.' At least that would give him another chance to hold her as they danced.

'Right,' she said. 'I'll let you know tomorrow night. We'd better get on with some work. Are you busy?'

'Yes,' he replied. 'We're still a man short. They've advertised for a replacement, but I haven't heard if anyone's applied.'

'I haven't seen anything,' she said. Helen would probably have seen any applications as they had to go through Personnel.

Mark had read the advertisement in the local newspaper. It called for an experienced programmer. A good working knowledge of OS JCL would be an advantage. Since the quoted salary was more than he was earning and as this description applied equally to his own experience, he wondered about applying, but decided that his gesture wouldn't be appreciated.

Later that morning, Adam, the Programming Manager, paid a visit to his team. Just as he entered the room, Gervaise lifted his backside and broke wind.

'Gesundheit!' Adam said. 'That vegetarian diet of yours has a lot to answer for!' It was the nearest thing to humour that Mark had ever seen from his manager. Being their boss, some of the others laughed respectfully.

'Good morning, guys,' he added. Mark cringed. He hated the use of the word 'guys' at any time, but especially when it was intended to include ladies.

'As you know,' Adam continued, 'we've been advertising for a replacement for Lance. We've had no external applicants at all, so we've decided to promote from within.' Mark decided that this meant him. He was going to lose his 'Junior Programmer' title.

But he was mistaken. 'Steven Mickleburgh has asked to be considered – and after very careful consideration, we've decided to appoint him as a Junior Programmer starting as soon as his replacement is up to speed.'

Steven Mickleburgh was one of the Data Controllers.

'Are you serious?' Tom asked. 'The fellow is an idiot.'

'That's a bit harsh Mr Freeman,' Adam said. 'He has his faults, but he has been studying COBOL at Tech. and is very keen to better himself.'

'He's a lazy sod!' Tom added.

'He is fully aware that he has to work hard at this, because if, after his probationary period, it doesn't work out, his current position will already have been filled. I'm going to ask you, Tom, to act as his mentor. Mr Barker, here, is now perfectly capable of standing on his own two feet.'

As if to prove the point, Mark stood up and pretended to wobble a little. 'Just about,' he said with a grin.

'Thank you, Mr Barker. Your humour is always appreciated,' Adam said, although he wasn't laughing.

'Would you mind finding someone else?' Tom asked. 'I can't work with him.'

Mark knew that Tom had already had a couple of run-ins with Steven and didn't trust him to run his latest program. Tom was one of the most easy-going individuals that Mark had ever met, so Steven must have really upset him to warrant that reaction.

'No, no one else is available at the moment – and I trust you to do a good job.'

'And he's another smoker,' Tom said, even though he knew that would not change Adam's decision.

Mark had had little dealings with Steven, but he had seen him around and knew he fancied himself as one for the ladies even though he was engaged to be married. He wore his hair long in the seventies fashion with a bushy moustache. Data Controllers did not earn as much as a programmer, but that didn't stop Steven from indulging in the latest clothes styles. What Mark had observed about Steven was that he liked to address all the ladies as 'darling,' which had resulted in at least one severe chastisement that Mark knew of and that was from Chris.

While working at Greshams, Mark had often indulged in some harmless flirting. This had always been with those ladies who were in a relationship and while he had been younger, most of those ladies were happy to go along with the fun, but now that he was a little older, he had curbed this activity especially as he knew few ladies outside of his own work area. Now that he was dating Helen, he was even more unlikely to indulge in what had once been one of his favourite pastimes. Having observed Steven's attempts at flirting convinced him that he was wise to do so.

Tom was in a bad mood for the rest of the morning so Mark decided that he might try to cheer him up. After he had consumed his packed lunch, he asked Tom if he fancied a little stroll in the sun. Tom always had a joke or two, but sometimes they were not suitable for mixed company, so they might share a joke or two. And Mark wanted to tell someone how well his weekend had gone.

'Have you got the hump over Steven?' Mark asked.

'Yeah ... I'm likely to thump him if he messes me up again – and then I'd lose my job. I can't afford to do that.'

'Perhaps Adam is right and he really does want to make an effort in his new job,' Mark suggested.

'Oh, I've no doubt that he'll make an effort to start with, but a leopard doesn't change its spots,' Tom said. 'Anyway, let's talk about something else. How are you getting on with the lovely Helen? Have you had your end away with her yet?'

'If I had, I wouldn't tell you, but it's going well, thank you.'

'I love the way she does her hair,' Tom said. 'This weekend my wife put her hair in a bun. It tasted horrible!'

It took Mark a second or two for the penny to drop. 'Oh, a bun! Very funny.'

Mark told him about the disco and their delightful walk through The Walks. Then he told him about his encounter with the Zephyr driver.

'Was it one like that?' Tom asked pointing to a vehicle in Greyfriars' customer car park.

Mark's heart started thumping when he saw it. From where they were standing, they couldn't see the registration number. If the psycho was a builder, as indicated by the mallet in his boot, he might well visit a Builder's Merchant. Mark wondered about venturing into the car park for a closer look, but decided that might not be wise. As they were almost out of sight of the retail building, they heard a door open and a scruffy looking middle-aged man headed towards the Zephyr.

'Is that him?' Tom asked.

'Hardly,' Mark replied. 'He doesn't look big enough to manage a large mallet.' He didn't want to admit how relieved he was. He hoped never to see the other man again.

At the tennis on Tuesday, Helen was the last to appear. By the time she arrived, the rest had already started playing. This time, Clive had turned up meaning there were six already on court.

'As I would make an odd number, I'll give it a miss tonight,' she told Mark in between points.

'Nonsense,' he said. 'We can play with seven people. I've done it before with a different group of people.'

'No, I'm still not good enough. I'd only spoil it for everyone else.'

Mark wasn't having this. For one thing, if she left right then, he might not see her again until Friday and that was not in his plans. 'Listen, everyone,' he said. 'Who thinks Helen would spoil our game if she played tonight?'

Of course he knew no one was going to admit that. In fact, there were several calls for her to stay. 'Just wait until we've finished the next game and you can join in,' he said to her.

His plan worked well with everyone taking at least one turn at playing a conventional doubles as well as with just three people.

Mark overheard Maisie telling Helen that she was improving. 'Have you been taking lessons?' he heard her ask, but he couldn't hear Helen's mumbled reply.

After a convivial drink enjoyed by everyone except Tom who went straight home for his tea, Mark found himself walking Helen back towards her home. 'I'm glad you persuaded me to stay,' she said.

'So am I,' he said. 'I knew you'd enjoy it once you started playing again ... and I wanted the chance to find out when I can see you again.'

'Why don't you come round ours tomorrow evening?' she said. 'You can try my cheesecake. It's come out very well if I say so myself. We can watch a bit of television if there's anything on – or play a few records.'

'I think it's *Colditz* on a Wednesday,' he replied. 'Do you watch that?'

'Sometimes,' she said. 'Dad always watches it, so we can watch it with him in colour or go into the front room to watch on the black and white set.'

Mark didn't say it, but he would prefer it if they could be alone. For one thing, he still wanted to get to know her better. Usually, when he first started dating someone he would be asking lots of questions to ascertain her taste in music and films, but such had been their early encounters, that there had been barely any lulls in their conversations that warranted asking lots of personal questions. But the main reason that he wanted them to be alone is that he felt he was due a little kissing and cuddling, which they could hardly do in front of her parents.

The next evening, he arrived in Park Avenue at twenty minutes past seven. Helen had told him to get there whenever he wanted, but he was keen to see her again despite it only being one day since they had last met. Nevertheless, he had taken the time to shave and refresh his deodorant. This had to be a chance to advance their relationship a little further. Of all the girls with whom he had ever shown an interest, Helen was the one that showed the most promise for a long-term future.

He had heard all the songs and words about love at first sight, which he regarded as romantic nonsense. Even so, something had happened on that day when he first saw her and since then, his desire had grown almost day by day and no one else had ever had that effect before. He didn't kid himself that he was in love – yet.

In any case, what was love? In a song by Ben E. King, the singer sought answers from *The Hermit of Misty Mountain* and was told a lot of old nonsense about boats that sailed to Heaven on an endless river. Should he find love, he'd hear songs and see lots of stars. Well, Mark had heard songs and seen lots of stars without ever being in love: unless, what he had with Jenny was love. If so, it wasn't the once in a lifetime thing of which writers pen, because Jenny obviously didn't love him. But then, if it wasn't love, how would one explain the pain that he endured for months afterwards?

Helen greeted him with a kiss which took him a little by surprise. 'I love your after shave,' she said.

His budget didn't stretch to expensive fragrances so he had to look at reasonably priced options. He had recently switched from *Mennen* to *Yardley's Gold* having discounted *Hai Karate* despite the incessant television advertisements.

Before he could react, she said 'We're in the garden. It's such a lovely evening that we've opened the French windows.' Mark's home had

French windows, but they hadn't been opened for years and he wasn't sure they would still open.

There in the garden, sat Helen's parents drinking tea from a small coffee table that had been carried from the house. They were seated on two deck chairs. Two other upright chairs had been set out for Helen and Mark. Helen introduced Mark to her father who didn't bother to stand and just said 'Hello.'

Helen's mother was more forthcoming and after welcoming him, asked Mark if he would like a cup of tea. Despite having a dry mouth, he declined saying he had only recently consumed one. He didn't want to risk needing to later ask for the toilet. He was also aware that a cup of tea might be accompanied by a slice of Helen's weird cake made from cheese and he didn't want to offend her by refusing.

'I've spoken to Sammy,' Helen said. 'He's doing a disco on Saturday at Dersingham. Do you want to go?'

'Only if you're going,' he replied.

'Of course I'm going,' she said. 'Why do you think I mentioned it?' and he felt silly for trying to be facetious.

'Is anyone else joining us?' he asked, thinking that last time they went to Sammy's Disco, he had to share her with her friends.

'I haven't mentioned it to Louise. Do you want me to?'

'I'd rather it was just us two this time,' he said, adding '... unless you really want to ask her?'

'No, it would be easier if we make our own way there. If it's too loud or too hot, we can leave whenever we want.'

'We'll have to ask him to play our song,' Mark said in a low voice, aware that her parents were listening to every word.

'You've got your own song?' Helen's mother asked.

'I wasn't aware that we had,' Helen said.

'*Me and Mrs Jones,*' Mark said. 'It was the first record we danced to. You said you liked that one.'

'Oh, that,' she said.

'Who's that by?' her mother asked, addressing Helen.

'I don't know. Who's that by, Mark?'

'Billy Paul,' he replied.

'I've never heard of him,' Helen said. 'What else does he sing?'

Mark wasn't too sure. 'As far as I know,' he replied,' He's never had any other records released – at least not in this country, but I could be wrong. Actually, thinking about it, it's probably not an appropriate record for us. The lyrics are all about being unfaithful and committing adultery. A lot of these black soul singers sing about similar themes. One of my favourite songs is by Luther Ingram and that's all about the same subject. Then there's one by Al Green called *One Woman* and ironically, he's got two women.'

'I haven't heard of any of these people,' Helen said and his heart sank. He had hoped she would enjoy a similar taste to his own, but she was interested in what he was saying. 'Who's your favourite singer?' she asked.

'Probably Jerry Butler ... he had a small hit in this country with a song called *Moody Woman*. Actually, it was produced by the same people as the Billy Paul song – Gamble and Huff, but most of his stuff gets ignored over here. He had the original version of *Make it Easy on Yourself* before the Walker Brothers copied it and had a bigger hit. He also had the original vocal version of *Moon River.*'

'I thought that was Andy Williams,' Helen's mother said. Her father was reading a newspaper and didn't seem interested in joining the conversation.

'No, his version was later,' Mark said,' but Henry Mancini, who wrote the song, had an instrumental version 'round about the same time as Jerry's.'

'Now, I like Henry Mancini,' her mother said. 'What was that nice record he made?'

'Do you mean *The Days of Wine and Roses?*' Mark replied.

'Yes, that's the one.'

'He also did *The Pink Panther,*' Mark added.

'Did he really? You know a lot about music, Mark.'

'Well, I read a lot about it. It's better than drinking, gambling and chasing loose women.'

This killed the conversation and once again, he regretted his facetiousness. Melody had once warned him that not everyone understood his sense of humour and that he should be more wary of what he said and to whom he said it.

But Helen soon changed the subject. 'Mark's a fellow train spotter, dad,' she said.

'Was!' Mark corrected. 'I haven't done any train spotting since I hit puberty – not that the two are connected, I have to say. It was about that time when steam more or less disappeared.'

Helen's father suddenly seemed interested in participating in the conversation. 'Where did you do your spotting, Mark?'

'Well, to start with, in Lynn, but we had a few day trips to Peterborough and March.'

'Did you ever have a trip around the Whitemoor Marshalling Yard?' her father asked.

'Yes, I went with a trip organised through school.' Soon, they were both engrossed in discussions about Sir Nigel Gresley, A4 Pacifics and 9Fs and the two women felt excluded.

After a while, Helen managed to get a word in. 'What time is *Colditz?*' she asked.

'It's not on this week,' replied Mark. 'I think last week was the last episode.'

'Was there anything else you wanted to watch?' she asked.

'Nothing really,' he replied.

'In that case, let's go into the front room and listen to some records. Help me carry these two chairs back into the house.' Mark was sorry to end his conversation about steam locomotives, but was certainly ready to spend some time alone with Helen.

As they entered the front room, she said 'Well done. It's not everyone who can engage my father in conversation.'

Mark smiled and said 'I can't remember the last time I sat down and talked about the good old days of steam engines. A little longer and I'd have moved on to tractors.'

'Tractors? What do you mean?'

'I used to be a big fan of tractors, but not anymore. Now I'm an ex-tractor fan.'

She groaned. 'Did you go through all that just to crack that silly joke?' She leaned over and kissed him on the cheek.

'I've got loads more like that if I'm going to get a kiss for each one,' but he was feeling in need of more than a kiss.

Their relationship might be reaching a critical point. What if the records that she wanted to play didn't conform to his taste. What if she liked all those British pop groups with their twangy guitars and poor vocal harmonies?

'I don't buy many records,' she said. 'Most of what we have belong to my parents, but you're welcome to see if you can find something to your taste. We don't have any singles at all.'

She pointed him to a record cabinet and he knelt down to peruse the selection which was mostly show music or film scores and they were arranged haphazardly. He wondered if a Frank Sinatra LP might put Helen in a romantic mood, otherwise he was struggling to find anything that he might like. 'Is there anything you'd like?' he asked. 'Frank Sinatra, perhaps?'

'No, not my thing, I'm afraid. There's a Simon and Garfunkel LP there somewhere. Someone bought it for me. I don't mind that.'

It was almost the last album he looked at and handed it to her to play. It was *Bridge Over Trouble Water* and he had once borrowed it from Della – a work colleague for whom he had once developed feelings. There were several songs on the LP that he had always enjoyed much to his surprise.

He handed the album to her and she placed it on the turntable, and then joined him on the settee. As she did so, she snuggled up against him. When the title track started playing, he said 'This is nice.'

'Yes, it's one of my favourites on the LP,' she said.

'No, I meant this is nice us sitting here together' and he kissed her hair.

He was about to take the kissing a little further, but she asked, 'Do you collect many records?'

'Yes, I've been buying them since about 1963 when we first got a record player. Do you buy any at all?'

'I never know what to buy,' she said. 'I'll hear something on the radio that I like, but I never bother to find out what it is.'

'What sort of thing do you like?' he asked, at last getting around to the question he'd been wanting to ask.

She thought about that for a minute or so. 'It's more a question of what I don't like. I don't like loud rock music like the Rolling Stones or The Who; nor do I like Jazz or Opera. I like a little classical music, but not all of it. You'll have to play me some of your things – like this Jerry Butler. It would be nice if we both enjoyed the same music.'

He liked that reply. He just hoped she would enjoy Jerry Butler and his ilk.

He tapped his feet to *El Condor Pasa* and was contemplating the best way to attempt a full-blooded kiss when the door opened and Helen's father entered.

'I thought you might be interested in these,' he said to Mark and handed him five small books. 'They're written by Alan Bloom.'

'The chap who runs Bressingham?' Mark asked, knowing full well who he was but wanting to impress with his knowledge.

'The very same,' was the reply. 'They're all published by Jarrolds of Norwich. I find them a mine of information. There's one for each of the four regions and one for the Standards.'

Helen stood up. 'If you're going to be talking about steam engines again, I'm going to make some coffee.'

The two men exchanged further reminisces about the glory days of steam and Helen returned just as the last track on the LP was playing.

She was carrying a tray with two mugs of coffee and a single slice of cheesecake. 'You didn't want one did you, dad? You don't normally drink coffee this time of night.'

Her father took the hint. 'No, I'll leave you two in peace. There's no hurry to return the books, Mark. I'm sure you'll enjoy reading them.'

'I'm sure I will. Thank you very much.'

'I've missed that last song,' Helen said placing the tray on the small coffee table. 'I'm going to put it on again. Who is this Frank Lloyd Wright? Do you know?'

'Yes,' said Mark. 'He's an American architect.' He knew because he had asked Della the same question a few years earlier.

'That's a funny topic to write a song about,' she said. 'Still, I like the song. I've saved you one piece of cheesecake.'

'The last piece,' said Mark. 'You have it.' He was determined that he wouldn't enjoy it.'

'No, I've saved it 'specially for you. I had to fight off the rest of the family to save it and you're going to eat it.'

He looked at it as she replaced the stylus on the last track. He had to admit that the cheesecake looked enticing. On top of the creamy fondant filling was a layer of raspberry puree; but how could you mix raspberry with cheese? It sounded like a revolting combination.

She stood over him and said, 'Go on eat it.'

'You have it,' he replied. 'I'm not that hungry.' When he could see how determined she was, he added 'Perhaps we could share it.'

'If you don't eat it, I'm never going out with you again.' So he would have to eat it after all. It obviously meant a lot to her. 'Now open wide,' she said as she spooned a small slice and held it up to him. 'I'm going to treat you like a young child playing trains. 'Here comes the train towards the tunnel. Choo! Choo! Choo! There that wasn't too bad, was it?'

He moved it around in his mouth expecting a weird combination of tastes, but, to his surprise, it tasted amazing. There was no cheesiness in the flavour at all.

'That's delicious,' he said and took the spoon from her to help himself to another amazing mouthful. He was soon halfway through devouring her masterpiece.

'Do you still want to share it with me?' she asked.

'There's only one person I would share this with,' he said, '... but she's not here' and he carried on eating having received a hefty thump to the shoulder.

'That was sensational,' he said as he wiped a crumb from his mouth, 'and you're sensational. Come here.'

She sat beside him and he embraced her passionately, helping himself to the full-blooded kiss he had needed since the day he first laid eyes on her.

'You men,' she said, as they separated for air. 'A piece of cheesecake and you turn into a sex maniac.'

'I think you're an enchantress,' he said. 'There was magic in that food. You've added a love potion or something.'

'Drink your coffee,' she said. 'It's only got a little sugar in it this time. I'm going to put the other side of this record on.'

After, drinking their coffee, they embraced again and this time, Mark decided that his hands would wander a little to some of those areas that he had been longing to explore.

'Don't get too carried away,' she said. 'My parents are in the room next door.'

Chapter Twenty-Six

Hey Girl Don't Bother Me

For the rest of the summer of 1973, Mark and Helen continued to see each other regularly and they became almost inseparable. He enthusiastically introduced her to soul music and she mostly found it acceptable without ever sharing his deep passion for the genre. Occasionally, she would say that she recognised a certain number which was usually because she had heard it at one of Sammy's disco nights even though she had no idea who the artist might be. After a while, Mark realised that he had tried to bombard her with as many new records as possible when he should have been repeating some of the best so that she became more familiar with them. Once he changed his policy, she warmed to many of his favourites although seldom remembering the singer's name or the title of the records. However, she readily agreed that Jerry Butler merited Mark's appreciation as his favourite singer.

She, in turn, introduced him to the pleasure of country walking. At first, he just accepted this as an inexpensive way to spend more time with her, but gradually, he came to enjoy the peace and quiet of the open air while learning more about the flora and fauna of the English countryside. They both loved the coastal paths of the North Norfolk coast and soon became ever more familiar with the unique character of each of the small villages in that area.

He stubbornly continued to wear his old baseball boots despite Helen insisting that he must buy some proper walking footwear. To him, leather boots looked clumsy and ungainly, and he couldn't imagine them ever being comfortable enough for walking any distance – and they cost considerably more than a pair of baseball boots. This was fine as long as they were walking the gentle paths of Norfolk, but she pointed out that if they ever ventured to more rugged parts of the country, he would have to take the plunge. That sounded as though, at some future date, she would like them to go further afield together, but she already had holiday plans for a summer break with her parents. A trip to North Devon had been booked long before Mark had appeared on the scene, so he would have to wait for the pleasure of a break together. She had already used up the majority of her annual leave and only a few days remained whereas Mark was in the opposite situation. He had still never enjoyed a proper holiday and every year, he would hang on to his holiday allowance as long as possible in case he ever struck lucky with a girl, which until that point had never been his lot.

They often had conversations about where they would like to holiday in the future. If money was no object, they agreed on Norway or Switzerland. Mark said he liked the Swiss flag. When she looked puzzled, he said 'That's a big plus with me.'

Helen said she had really enjoyed her previous holiday in the English Lake District, and without either of them committing themselves to another year together, they discussed that as a possibility sometime in the future.

And he now had a sex life of sorts, but just as had been the situation with Jenny, a suitable venue was always the sticking point. Mark tried his luck during their moments alone in Helen's front room, but she constantly warned him not to get too carried away fearing a visit from one of her parents who did occasionally enter without knocking. But, sometimes, they would find themselves alone in the house and they would passionately slake their ardour. Mark often expressed a desire to take her to bed and wake up to her charms. He suggested a short break away together. Helen felt it was too early for them to consider such a move, but didn't totally dismiss the notion.

It was in the first week of August when Cheryl came into the picture. That was the week when Helen and her parents went away on holiday. On the day she left for Devon, Mark decided that he would venture into town to purchase one or two new records. Since dating Helen, he had not felt the same need to enhance his collection as he had been too busy playing his old records to her, but now he faced a whole week alone and on his first free day, he decided to enjoy his enforced freedom.

He was on his way back to the car park when he heard his name called. 'It's Mark, isn't it?' she said.

He turned to see a tall rangy looking woman with a fetching smile. She appeared to be slightly older than him and her face looked vaguely familiar, but he couldn't quite place her. She was wearing a blue, sleeveless top and tight flares, both of which perfectly sculpted her figure, which should have given him some clues, but he still couldn't work out where he had seen her before.

'I'm Cheryl – with a C-H; as in *chaste*,' she said seeing the puzzled expression. Somehow, Mark didn't think for a minute that she was *chaste*, but appreciated her self-effacing irony. She wore more make-up than he liked to see.

'Um ... er, Cheryl?' he said with a frown. He didn't want to appear foolish by not recognising her, but he obviously needed some help.

'Mr Gregory's secretary,' she said and then it dawned on him. She worked downstairs and he must have seen a glimpse of her at some time, but not enough for it to register. Had he still been unattached, he would have made it his business to seek out the ladies at his place of work.

'Of course,' he said. 'Sorry, I was struggling to place you. I don't get downstairs very often.'

'No, I don't go upstairs very often either,' she said. 'Are you enjoying your first day of freedom? Helen's on holiday, isn't she?'

'I'm just doing a little shopping,' he replied, feeling it inappropriate to say he was enjoying his freedom. 'I'm just heading back home.'

'Are you going my way?' she asked. 'I live down Fletcher Lane. I've a flat there. I had the choice to buy a car or rent a flat, so I use the buses a lot. If you're going my way, you could save me the bus fare.'

Mark knew where Fletcher Lane was. It was where he used to drop off Della on their way home from work when he worked at Greshams. It was a little out of his way and he told her so, but agreed to give her a lift anyway. He didn't want to be rude to a colleague.

As they drove off, she said 'Are you going out on the razzle, tonight?'

'No, I shall be spending a quiet night at home; catching up on some reading and playing my new records.'

'Well, that's a waste of a good opportunity, isn't it? While the cat's away, the mice should be out on the razzle.'

'I don't think anyone should describe me as a mouse,' he said. 'Are you going out on the razzle, then?'

'Only if some nice gentleman invites me,' she replied. This made Mark feel a little uneasy. 'If not, I might get a bus to Hunstanton and go to *The Kit Kat*. Do you ever go there?'

'I've never been. I've seen it from the outside, but I've never been inside.'

'You could save me a bus ride,' she said.

'No, I'll be staying at home tonight.'

'Being faithful, eh? Are you and Helen going to name the day?' she asked.

'We've only been going out together for a few months,' he said.

'Well, I know she thinks a lot of you. She's always talking about the things you do together – your little walks in the countryside and so on. I think she's pleased to have met someone who likes walking. I can see you two getting hitched.'

'I think it's a little early for anything like that. There's plenty of time.' Despite enjoying the last few months, he still wasn't sure that Helen was the one with whom he would choose to settle down with – and he certainly didn't want to discuss the matter with someone whom he hardly knew.

As they pulled into Fletcher Lane, it brought back emotive memories of his time working with his married colleague Della and the disturbing effect she had had on him. He hadn't seen her for more than two years. He didn't know if she even still lived in the area, but it didn't stop him from casting his eyes around to the building where she had lived. It turned out that Cheryl lived in the very same block of flats. Perhaps she had taken over the same flat.

'Do you want to come in for a coffee?' Cheryl asked, waking him from his reverie.

'No, thank you. I'll be home soon and I'll have a drink with my dinner.' He still referred to his midday meal as dinner and his evening meal as tea.

'I just wanted to show my appreciation for the ride. I don't bite, you know.' As she said this she curled her lip to give a suggestion that she might actually bite but he still declined the invitation.

As he drove home, he couldn't help thinking how easy it would have been to have accepted Cheryl's invitation for coffee – and whatever else was on offer. She certainly wasn't chaste. How typical it was that he had been celibate for well over a year; a year when he would have loved to had this very same opportunity, but at this time, he had more sense that to succumb to her charms.

After a few days of his so-called freedom and already missing Helen like crazy, Mark was really looking forward to his Tuesday game of tennis, albeit without her. He always changed into his tennis gear in the office toilets since there were no changing facilities at the park. As he headed for his car in the office car park, he saw Cheryl wearing a more formal outfit than on his previous encounter, but still sporting too much make-up.

'I've missed my bus,' she said. 'I wonder if you could give me a lift home. I know it's a little out of your way, but you're a gentleman, aren't you?'

'I can't tonight,' he replied, knowing full well that her bus service ran every fifteen minutes and therefore not feeling under any pressure to save her. 'I'm playing tennis and I'm already late. There'll be another bus along soon. Sorry.'

But Cheryl wasn't prepared to give in so easily. 'I've got a meal on the timer and it will spoil if I wait for the next bus. There's enough for two if you like. It's my famous chilli con carne. I like it hot. I'm sure you do, too.' Mark detected a little innuendo.

'No, thank you. I have to be down at the park right away,' he said. 'I'm the organiser and I've got the balls.'

'I'm not so sure you do have the balls,' she said as she stomped off towards the bus station.

Mark enjoyed his tennis, but felt a little deflated when no one was interested in a drink afterwards. He had nothing else to look forward to until Helen returned from holiday. It would be a long week. He had tried to call Ray, but he and Val were away on holiday as well.

Helen had promised to send him a postcard so he eagerly anticipated the post each day, but the card never arrived and he started to worry that she was enjoying herself too much to remember him.

She and her parents were due to arrive back on the following Saturday, but she warned him that it would be too late for them to meet up and that he should call at their house on the Sunday afternoon.

When Saturday came and there was still no postcard from her, he became quite despondent. Perhaps she had met someone in Devon: a handsome surfer, perhaps? He had heard of these holiday romances, but never having had a proper holiday himself, he didn't know if this was just Hollywood romanticism.

By Saturday evening, he had worked himself into one of his self-pitying moods and when he found himself alone in the house, he took to playing his most emotive soul records. During a particularly sombre Walter Jackson record entitled *Not You*, there came a knock on the door. Reluctantly he removed the stylus from the single and went to the door.

Helen looked at him a little sheepishly as though she shouldn't be there, which in the scheme of things, she shouldn't have been. 'Hello,' she said.

He returned the greeting but with no great feeling. In his mind, this was like a repeat of the time when Jenny had arranged to meet him to tell him that it was over.

'Aren't you pleased to see me?' she asked.

'Of course, I am,' he replied, but she wasn't sure that he meant it.

'Are you going to invite me in?' she asked.

'Yes, of course. Come in.' He stood back to let her in. It was the first time that she had entered his home and he was fearful at what she would see, having not anticipated visitors that evening. As he looked around, he could see that it was no worse than it usually was.

She held a postcard in her hand and said 'Here is the postcard I promised to send. I've had it for several days, but didn't know what to write. I didn't want to say anything too soppy because I didn't know who might read it. That's the problem with postcards; so in the end I've

220

decided to deliver it personally. We've only been home for a couple of hours but I couldn't wait to see you ... but now I'm not so sure this was a good move. What's the problem?'

'There's no problem,' he said, '... except in my head.' He flung his arms around her and they kissed passionately. Eventually, they parted and he said, 'I thought you'd met someone else on holiday and had come round to break it off.'

She laughed. 'That's so sweet ... and so wrong. Are we alone?'

'Yes, my father's at the pub and my mother's at the bingo. I was just playing some records. Do you want a drink?'

'Not at the moment, thank you. You can carry on listening to your music while we catch up.'

'Did you have a nice time?' he asked.

'Yes, but it didn't feel right. We did a lot of lovely walks along the coast. The Valley of The Rocks was amazing - and I saw a seal swimming in the sea – and there were lots of lovely little coves and fishing villages, but I wanted to share them all with you. I've had lots of nice holidays with my parents, but on this occasion, it didn't feel the same. It didn't help that mum and dad often hold hands when they're out walking, so I felt a little out of it. The next time I go on holiday, I want it to be just you and me.'

'Wow,' he said, 'but that could be almost a year away. Can we wait that long?'

'I've only got a few days of my holiday left, but we could have a long weekend away together – perhaps in September?'

'It will be the football season, then,' he said. 'Can we go during the week – just a couple of days away would be nice?'

'You men and your football. Can't you miss a game or two?'

'Not if I can avoid it. Being a goalkeeper means that if they get another 'keeper in and he plays well, I might not get my place back ... but if you were to insist.' That last phrase was a big statement for Mark. If push came to shove, he would miss a game or two to be with her, but if he could avoid it, so much the better.

'We'll have to see what we can do,' she said. 'Where could we go?'

'I've always fancied the Peak District, but if it's only a short break, perhaps Suffolk or the North Norfolk coast? I'll get my AA book out and see what hotels there are.'

'Yes, but not right now,' she said. 'I'm still a little travel weary. It's a long drive from Devon. I took a few turns with the driving, but that makes it even more tiring. There was so much traffic on the roads. Anyway, what have you been doing while I've been away?'

'Ah, I'm glad you asked. I was propositioned by a lady. I say *lady* but I'm not too sure about that.' He told her the full story, being careful not to omit anything.

Helen was most amused. 'And you passed up the chance for some quick nookie. I didn't think men were capable of refusing an offer like that.'

'I would never do that to you and I don't think you'd do it to me,' he replied.

'You know she's on the pill, don't you? You're always saying you prefer it without a condom.'

'Now you tell me!' he said.

He received a thump to the shoulder for that remark. 'There is another reason why I came around,' she said. 'Do you mind if we call off tomorrow? I've got a blister on my foot.'

'On your foot? From walking? So much for your wonderful walking boots.'

'Actually,' she said with some satisfaction,' it wasn't when I was wearing my boots. We did a walk around Watersmeet in the morning – in my boots - and after lunch we changed and went for a stroll around Lynmouth. We took the cliff train up to Lynton and walked down again. It was the walking down that put pressure on my big toe which is now inflamed. I want to rest it so that I can play tennis on Tuesday. I also need to help mum catch up on her housework.'

'It's as well that you came around tonight, then,' he said. 'I'd have been distraught not to have seen you until Tuesday. Anyway, when we go away together, I hope we're not going to have single rooms. It will be cheaper in a double.'

'You'll have to book us in as Mr and Mrs Barker,' she said. 'I like the sound of that.'

'In that case,' he said, 'I think we should have a little practice tonight. My parents won't be home for some time, yet.'

Helen was still there when Mark's mother returned from her Bingo. 'Oh!' she said as she entered the door and saw them sitting together on the settee. 'I've brought some fish and chips. I don't know if there's enough for two.'

'This is Helen,' Mark said.

Helen said 'Hello ... don't worry about me. I was just about to leave.'

This was only the second time that Mark had ever brought a girl back to his house – in fact, he hadn't actually brought her. She hadn't warned him of her visit otherwise he might have avoided it.

'I'm sure you can share mine,' Mark said.

'I had a little win,' his mother said. This explained the fish and chips. She always liked to splash out after a win at Bingo.

Mark and Helen sat together and tucked into the food, while his mother ate her own portion in the kitchen. Helen was surprised that there was no effort to fetch plates or cutlery. She had occasionally shared fish and chips with Mark when they were out together in the car, and would quite happily eat out of the newspaper with her fingers, but it seemed strange to do so in their house. It was even stranger that his mother preferred to eat in the kitchen standing up. Mark was annoyed at his mother's behaviour but said nothing. To do so would have caused unnecessary embarrassment, but he decide to tackle his mother later.

Mark and Helen finished theirs first and Helen said 'That was nice. Thank you Mrs Barker. Where did you get them?'

'From Leeman Street – on the corner,' she replied.

'How much did you win?' Mark asked, trying to move the conversation along.

'Ten pounds,' she replied.

'Did you have to share it with anyone?' Mark knew that the bingo sisters had some unwritten rules about sharing prizes but it depended on the size of the win and it often led to a falling out.

'No, but as Kate gave me a lift home, I bought them some chips as well.'

As the conversation stalled, Helen said 'I'd better make my way home. Can I just wash my hands? I don't think dad would like greasy fingers on his steering wheel.'

Mark pointed her to the washbasin and said, 'I'll walk you to your car.'

At the car, he apologised for his mother's behaviour. 'She's not used to me bringing home visitors.'

'I was the one who turned up unexpectedly,' she said. 'I should be the one to apologise. Are you going to sit in the car with me for a minute or two?'

Mark was unaccustomed to sitting in the passenger seat while Helen occupied the driver's seat. His first kiss was awkward. 'I'm not used to kissing you from this angle,' he said. 'It doesn't feel right.'

'Don't you think that women should drive?' she said, teasing him.

'No, it's not that. I'm just used to leaning over from the other direction – like I'm on top.'

'You didn't mind me being on top on your settee,' she said.

'Oh no, I liked that – and it was an easier position for both of us.'

It was another twenty minutes before the pair eventually said 'goodnight.'

'She seems like a nice girl,' his mother said as he returned to the house.

'Of course,' Mark said.

'It's about time you settled down,' she added.

'I'm not rushing into anything. I want to be able to afford a decent house before I get married. I've got time.'

Chapter Twenty-Seven

What's Going On

'I've got a bone to pick with you,' Helen said as they changed ends.

Mark was partnering Maisie and they were playing against Tom and Helen. He had no time to respond as she took her position in the opposing half of the court. He hadn't seen her since Saturday evening and had been eagerly looking forward to their next meeting especially after the week long break due to her holiday, but now he was wondering what it was that had offended her. Had he said something out of place? Or was it something he hadn't said or done? They had departed on very good terms on Saturday.

Only four people had turned up for the regular Tuesday game of tennis. Helen was partnering Tom who was always reliable as was Maisie. Mark had stopped chasing the other possible participants, feeling that as long as this four turned up each week, he could be sure of an enjoyable evening, but now he was in the doghouse and he didn't know why.

At the next change of ends, he asked her 'What's the matter?'

'I'll tell you later,' she replied abruptly.

'How's your blister?' he asked as she walked away.

'It's not too bad,' she said, but didn't thank him for his concern as she took up her position. He still didn't know what he'd done wrong.

The first set took much longer than usual as both pairs were quite evenly matched. Helen no longer needed carrying by her partner, although Mark and Maisie eventually won by eight games to six. Normally, they would now change partners, but Helen insisted that she and Tom wanted their revenge, so Mark still had no opportunity to quiz her about whatever was bothering her.

After another long set, which Mark and Maisie won again, there was no time for the usual third match, so they all agreed to call it a day.

'Where's that Steven chap who played last week?' Maisie enquired of no one in particular.

'He's getting married this weekend,' replied Mark. 'He's got a few things to organise.'

'I haven't seen a collection for him,' Helen said.

'Well, I'm not going to organise it,' said Tom. He still hadn't warmed to Steven.

'If you ask me,' said Mark, 'I wouldn't be surprised if they call it off. Apparently, they've both been arguing about where to spend their honeymoon. Steven wanted to go to Majorca or the Costa del Sol, and she wanted to go to Paris or Vienna. That's not a good start if they like different holidays. He once told me that he expected to be divorced within a few years. His parents were divorced and I don't think he treats marriage with any great reverence.'

'Apparently, he's not the only one,' said Helen, but the barbed comment was wasted on everyone except Maisie who, of course was divorced, but Helen's comment wasn't directed at her.

Maisie gave her a look but decided the comment meant nothing and asked 'Are we going for a drink? I'm thirsty.'

'Well, you know I have to duck out,' said Tom. 'I'd better be on my way. My wife's got something nice on the kitchen table.'

'Lucky old you!' said Maisie. 'What about you two lovebirds?'

'I'm a bit like Tom,' said Helen. 'I need some tea.'

'I'll buy you a packet of crisps, if you like,' said Mark. 'We can't expect Maisie to drink alone.

Reluctantly, she agreed. This was not like Helen.

As they walked towards the pub, Maisie said 'You look like you had some good weather on your holiday. That tan suits you.'

Mark realised that he hadn't complemented Helen on her tan. Was that what was troubling her? Surely not? Helen would never be that shallow.

Once in the pub with the drinks and crisps which Mark had purchased for them all, Maisie asked 'Why doesn't Tom like Steven?'

Mark answered. 'Tom doesn't like people who aren't very good at their job – and Steven messed up some of his work in his previous role, so he holds a long-standing grudge.'

After that, the conversation was rather stilted with Maisie make most of the effort. After a while, she asked 'Have you two had a row or something?'

'I don't think we've ever had a row, have we, Helen?' Mark said.

Helen hesitated, but then replied 'No, I don't think we ever had ...' Mark thought she was about to add 'yet' but she didn't.

'Well, how about one of your jokes, Mark?' Maisie asked.

Mark was still thinking about Helen's attitude, so just mumbled his old stock joke. 'What's got a bottom at the top?'

Maisie shook her head.

'A leg,' he said.

'Oh, very clever,' said Maisie.

Helen had heard it before. 'Mark knows all about bottoms, don't you?' she said.

He had often expressed great admiration for Helen's bottom, but why would she make a point of it now? He gulped his drink down and Helen followed suit. He wanted to get to the bottom of this with Helen and so he said, 'Anyone mind if we make a move?'

After bidding farewell to Maisie, Mark at last had chance to tackle Helen about her behaviour.

'Right, what's the problem?' he asked as they walked back towards Park Avenue.

'There's no problem,' she said, 'apart from Cheryl.'

'What's she been up to?' he asked.

'She told me that you made a pass at her.'

'What? Why on Earth would she say that? I told you what happened.'

'I know ... but she said she was wearing some tight trousers and you told her she had a nice bottom.'

'I never even saw her bottom. She was wearing tight trousers, but I never saw her from behind. Did she say she was also wearing a tight jumper?'

'No, she didn't mention that. She must know you prefer bottoms.'

Mark shook his head in disbelief. 'Well, you must have told her, because I didn't. I can't believe you let her upset you.'

'That's not all,' Helen said.

'Do I need to get a lawyer? What else has the stupid tart said?'

'She said that you would never want to marry me.'

Mark stopped walking and looked at his girlfriend. 'I said nothing of the sort. You know what I think her problem is. She's jealous of us because we make a great couple. Do you know if she has a boyfriend at all?'

Helen replied, 'I think she's had several boyfriends but she has trouble hanging on to them.'

'See what I mean,' said Mark. 'She's jealous ... and I think she wants some kind of retribution because I wouldn't go out with her. What she actually said was something about us naming the day. I told her that it was too early for us to think about that. That's the nearest I got to saying anything about getting married: and I certainly wouldn't go into details with the likes of her. She's a troublemaker and you shouldn't take any notice of a thing she says.'

'No, you're right,' Helen said. 'I got myself in a bit of a stew thinking about it instead of getting some sleep: but have you ever wanted to get married?'

Mark wasn't expecting that and didn't want to rush in with an answer. They were still standing on the path through the park, about fifty yards away from Park Avenue. Eventually, he said 'Of course I have. I think you're wonderful. The question is not about your suitability – it's whether I'm in a position to marry anyone. I haven't been very good at saving money. I keep spending any savings I've had on cars. I finish paying for my 1100 in a few months. That will help, but then I'd like to buy something a bit better – and newer. I'm not going to rent a house when I do get married. I want to buy my own property. It doesn't have to be anything too extravagant to start with, but I do want my own house.'

'I've got a little money saved,' she said. 'That's one benefit of not owning a car. And I know dad wants to help me when I get married.'

'We've only been going out together for a few months,' he responded. 'We both need to be sure what we're doing.'

'You've still got feelings for that other woman, haven't you - the one who hurt you?'

'No ... but it had an effect on me. For a while after, I wasn't sure I wanted anyone else, but that soon changed. However, I sometimes feel as though I've built some kind of shield to protect myself. I read a quote somewhere – someone was asked which he felt was stronger – the joy of romance or the pain of losing it. He replied, "whichever was present at the time." At the moment, I'm enjoying the joy of romance. I hope I never know the pain again.'

She put her arms around him and leaning against his shoulder, she muttered 'I just want the joy ... I don't ever want the pain.'

He kissed her hair and said 'Anyway, this is all getting a bit serious.' He had never been fond of displaying his feelings. There had been very little shows of emotion in his upbringing. He couldn't ever remember a hug or a kiss from his parents or siblings, so he was keen to change the subject. 'There's something I wanted to tell you. While you were away, I bought a book about The Peak District and in the back few pages were some adverts for Guest Houses. I thought we might explore one or two of those for a short break together.'

'That sounds nice. We can practice being Mr and Mrs Barker again.'

To use up some of his outstanding holiday entitlement, Mark took a week off work and found a temporary job working in a parts store in King's Lynn. The parts were for Skoda cars which were unloaded at the Lynn docks. The work was tedious and unrewarding, and the pay was meagre, but he felt he could use a little extra money. He decided that he wanted to make more of an effort to put his finances on a sound footing. The highlight of a boring week was when he had the chance to drive a forklift. With a minimum amount of training he moved a pallet of clutch plates from the delivery door to the appropriate stacking shelf. He was relieved when the week was over and he collected his hard earned money. He couldn't imagine ever doing that kind of work for a living, but many people did.

It might have been a good opportunity to meet new people and make friends, but he found his colleagues resentful of his presence as a form of inverted snobbery when they discovered his usual occupation. He was almost pleased to go back to work with Steven and the continually frowning Rose.

At the end of his week, he was thirty pounds better off. He decided he would save it to pay for a short break in Derbyshire. He needed to take his relationship with Helen to a new level. The incident with Cheryl had worried him. He still wondered how close he came to losing Helen. Although he had done nothing wrong, sometimes life could be cruel – or silly people could be unnecessarily vindictive. He hadn't seen Cheryl since then and that was probably a good thing because he was bound to say something he might regret.

The fact that Helen had let Cheryl bother her was disappointing, but in one way it showed how much she cared about him. If he had ever had doubts about whether Helen was the girl for him, this had made him realise how much he didn't want to face life without her.

Chapter Twenty-Eight

Let's Get Married

They arrived in Buxton late in the afternoon. It was the furthest Mark had ever driven and he was exhausted. If driving to Derbyshire was this tiring, he couldn't imagine what it would be like to drive to The Lake District or North Devon. Perhaps it was time to think about upgrading his transport. He had been thinking about his next possible motor. The 1100 had been reliable and still showed no sign of rust, but it wasn't exactly a head turner. He had been considering a Renault 15, a Ford Escort, a Hillman Avenger or possibly a Triumph 1500. The latter looked a little classier than the others. Ideally, he would have opted for a Ford Capri like Clive's, but that was probably out of his price range.

Hartington Road overlooked the Pavilion Garden, so after booking in at their reserved accommodation, they walked down to the park where there was a small lake beside the Pavilion.

'I'm not sure that lady believed we were Mr and Mrs Barker,' Helen said.

'I don't see why not,' Mark replied. 'In any case, it's none of her business. I can't say I liked the look of the place.'

'No, it wasn't very welcoming, was it?'

This was the very first time that Mark had ever booked any accommodation. In fact, the only time he had ever stayed at a hotel had been when he attended his programming course in London – an experience he didn't want to ever repeat. For this trip, he had looked at the hotels in the AA handbook, but they all seemed to be outside of his budget. He had found this particular Guest House in his Peak District Guide and now he was regretting it. In fact, he was having all kinds of bad feelings. They had temporarily gotten lost on the journey up and were both close to losing their tempers with each other.

He was now feeling exhausted. They had eaten en route at a Happy Eater, which was a recent rival to the Little Chef chain, but they'd had little to drink. At home, he usually ate about six o'clock and he was ready for his next meal, but Helen had wanted to explore this park while it was still light.

Eventually, she was ready to move on from the park, but was then eager to see the town. Mark reluctantly decided to humour her and dragged his feet beside her. At least this gave them the chance to look out for potential places to eat. A hotel on The Crescent looked promising and this was where they decided upon, but not until after a little more exploration of the town. Helen wanted to purchase some Blue John jewellery, but by now all the shops were closed, so they returned to the hotel.

'Can we have a table for two?' Mark enquired as they entered.

'We don't start serving food until seven o'clock,' was the reply,' but you can have a drink while you wait.'

Mark ordered a cider for Helen and a beer for himself. He had asked for a half pint, but he received a full pint. He was about to protest, but decided that he was very thirsty so he took a few grateful gulps. Now at last, they could sit down and relax; except that he was still at bit on edge. This break was important to him. It would be the first time that they had spent a night together and they would be inseparable for three days. It was almost like a mini trial marriage.

'I was ready for this,' he said as he replaced his glass on the small table.

'Yes, it's been a long day,' she said.

'I keep getting the feeling that people are watching us ...' he said, '...as though they know we're here for a dirty weekend ... although, of course, it's not a weekend.'

'And it's not dirty, either, 'she said. 'We're not doing anything that thousands haven't done before us. Perhaps we shouldn't sit here whispering and looking furtive. Sit back and tell me one of your jokes.'

He thought for a moment, and then said, 'Have I ever told you the one about Pinocchio?'

'I don't think so.'

'Well, he was talking with his maker. Is it Geppetto or something?'

'That sounds about right.'

'Geppetto asked how he was. Pinocchio said he was fine and he now had a girlfriend, but she kept complaining of splinters when they made love. Geppetto told him to go to Texas Homecare and buy some fine grade sandpaper. That would solve the problem he said.

A few weeks later, they met again and Geppetto asked if he had used the sandpaper. Pinocchio said he had and it had worked a treat. "So how is the girlfriend?" the old man asked.

"Girlfriend? Who needs a girlfriend?"

Helen laughed. 'He didn't need a girlfriend if he had his sandpaper.'

They both felt a little more relaxed after that.

'What are we going to do tomorrow?' she asked.

'Well, you know I've always wanted to go back to Monsal Head,' he replied. 'I've found a walk that takes us from Ashford up the hill to the top and then back through the valley – beside the river. It's just over five miles long and I'm hoping we can get refreshments when we get to the top.'

'Have you brought your new walking boots?'

'Of course! They're nestled in the boot next to yours.'

He had finally bowed to pressure from Helen to purchase some proper walking boots, although she didn't regard them as proper boots. They were actually described as fell boots, but to Mark they looked more comfortable – and cheaper! The big difference between his and those that Helen wore is that hers were made from leather, but Mark's were more of a suede finish. She wasn't sure if they were waterproof, but he didn't intend to do any walking in the rain.

They were at last ushered to their table and handed a menu each. 'Can I get you any more drinks?' the waiter asked.

Mark had finished his pint of beer, so he said 'Yes, please. I'd like another half of beer. Helen, what about you, dear?' He added the *dear* as he wanted to sound as though they were husband and wife, not that it mattered in this place.

'I think I'd like wine. Can we see the wine menu, please?'

'Of course, madam.'

The waiter returned with a separate menu and handed it Mark, who passed it on to Helen, saying 'You choose.' He had never ordered wine from a menu and didn't know what she wanted. He hoped she would only ask for a glass.

'What's the house white like?' She asked the waiter.

'It's very popular,' he replied.

'We'll have a carafe of that, please.' Once the waiter had disappeared, she said 'Don't worry, I'm paying – and I'm paying for the meal, too.'

'You are not,' he replied indignantly. 'The man pays for such things.'

'Don't be so old-fashioned! You're paying for the Guest House. It's the least I can do, so don't argue.'

He didn't argue. The waiter brought their drinks and they ordered their food. 'I hope you're going to help me with this wine,' she said. He was already feeling a little light-headed after his first pint on an empty stomach, but he finished his other half and allowed her to pour him a glass of the white wine.

By the end of the meal, he had consumed well over half of the carafe as well as his beer. Throughout the meal, he had been congratulating himself on his good fortune to be seated opposite this beautiful woman who, he now realised epitomised everything that he wanted in a wife. He would pause after almost every mouthful to gaze across to her with something more than just lust in his eyes. She returned the gazes with interest.

They both declined a dessert, pretending that the meal had filled them, when, in truth, they just wanted to clasp each other beneath the inviting sheets of their Guest House.

The room felt damp and cold when they returned. They hadn't noticed this when they had first arrived late in the afternoon when the sun was still warm, but now it felt less inviting. The bathroom was shared with other guests and was a little way down the corridor, so Mark asked Helen if she wanted to use it first. She accepted and while she was gone, he laid his pyjamas out next to the bed. He had no intention of wearing them but if he felt the need to visit the bathroom during the night, he thought it best to have them ready to wear. He also placed a packet of condoms on the bedside table.

There was nothing else he could do until she returned so he sat on the bed hoping she wouldn't be too long. The beer and the wine now had him longing for the toilet. The cold room didn't help his situation. Why was it taking her so long?

He almost ran out of the room when she returned.

A few minutes later, he was back. 'Feeling better for that?' she asked.

'Yes, thank you. I remember once talking to an old colleague who told me that in his opinion, relieving yourself can feel better than sex. After all, you can go weeks or even years without sex, but relieving yourself when you really need to can be glorious.'

'I'm not sure that I needed to know that,' she said. 'Now hurry up and get undressed. It's freezing in this bed and I need you to warm me up.'

He could see that she wasn't wearing a nightdress and he needed no urging to join her.

'And by the way.' she added, 'you won't need those condoms tonight. I'm on the pill, now.' That was a sure sign of some sort of commitment.

He almost tore off his clothes, mainly because he was eager to engulf himself in her welcoming arms, but also because he was so cold. He was used to a cold house at home, but somehow this room seemed so much worse than his own bedroom. There was a musty dampness that made it feel unhealthy. He flung his last remaining garments onto the floor and launched himself beside her. This was what he had been anticipating all day long. He'd had an erection all through their meal and even felt some stirrings at The Happy Eater. Now he could put it all to use ... except that he was no longer aroused.

He busied himself with some foreplay in the certain knowledge that he would soon rise to the occasion.

After about ten minutes, Helen realised that all was not well. 'What's the matter with Fred?'

Fred was her nickname for his appendage. 'I don't know. He's not usually this shy.'

'You don't have to tell me,' she said. 'You're probably just tired. It's been a long day.'

'I've had long days before,' he said. 'I don't believe this.'

'Don't worry about it. It happens.'

'Not to me, it doesn't. You come on top. That usually works.'

But it didn't. He heard about brewer's droop, but it had never happened to him, mainly because he seldom drank to excess. Perhaps he was trying too hard – or maybe this cold room wasn't helping.

'Just have a sleep,' Helen said. 'You'll soon be back to normal.'

He reluctantly turned over, but he knew he wasn't going to sleep whilst worrying about losing his manhood. But he did sleep. He slept right through the night and woke with an erection.

'I see Fred's back,' said Helen.

Having satisfied themselves that everything was back to normal, they were ready for a hearty breakfast, but when it was delivered, their faces fell. The fried eggs were overcooked, as were the solitary chipolata sausages. The rasher of bacon resembled the texture of cardboard and the fried bread was only half a slice each. It was all swimming in the juices of a single tinned tomato and delivered by an elderly waitress who coughed out of the side of her mouth while her lips grasped a dangling cigarette which was in danger of depositing ash over their meals. 'Tea or coffee?' she asked after she had released their plates and rescued the cigarette.

'Tea,' they both replied, but a few minutes later regretted their decision as two mugs of stewed brew were plopped on the table.

'I don't want to stay here another night,' Helen said after the waitress had left.

'I agree,' Mark responded. 'I saw loads of vacancy signs as we drove up here yesterday. We'll try one or two. They can't be any worse than this.'

The landlady was insistent that they paid for the two nights they had booked. Mark wasn't sure of his rights, but he said he would only pay for the one night after deducting his deposit and she could take his cheque or leave it. She was adamant that by booking for two nights he had entered into a contract and had to pay the full amount even if he did leave early. He stuck to his guns and she told him she would take him to court to recover the money.

He replied that he was sure the bad publicity would not be very helpful to her business.

She eventually took the cheque and they left.

After seeing dozens of places on the journey towards Buxton, there was now a distinct lack of them. They stopped at one place on the outskirts of the town, but a ferocious dog convinced them that they would carry on looking. 'Did you see all the dog hairs everywhere?' Helen asked when they returned to the car. Mark hadn't actually noticed. He was too busy avoiding the snarling animal and taking a dislike to the surly landlord who didn't seem to appreciate a pair of early callers.

They left Buxton and headed towards Ashford where they were due to start their walk. If they didn't see anything on the way, they decided that they would venture into Bakewell where there were bound to be more options. After ten minutes, Helen spotted a sign. Mark had stopped looking as they were now away from the town and he didn't expect to find anything until they met another reasonable sized place of habitation. He stopped and reversed back towards the sign. 'It's a farm,' he said. 'We don't want to stay in a farm. It will be dirty and smelly.'

'No it won't,' she said. 'I've often stayed in farms. You do sometimes get a smell, but you'll get a good breakfast.' That did it for him. After the woeful breakfast he had just endured, a good breakfast sounded ideal, but he still had misgivings. His experience of farms consisted mostly of grumpy old farmers chasing him off their pastures when he and his mates wanted to play football, but Helen was much more experienced in holiday accommodation. 'They also do afternoon teas,' she added. 'That should mean a certain level of hygiene.'

The solid stone farmhouse was situated at the end of a rough drive and Mark had misgivings about the effect on his suspension, but there was nowhere to turn around so he had to keep going. An elderly lady was feeding her chickens in the yard. 'I'll be with you in a moment,' she said in a clear authoritative voice as they got out of the car.

'That's all right,' said Helen who was gazing across the dale and enjoying the scenery. Mark was still concerned about having to return along the rough track.

'Now then,' the lady said.' Are you looking for a room for the night?'

'If you've got one,' replied Helen.

'I've only got the one. Would you like to see it?'

'Yes, please.'

Before leading the way, the lady washed her hands and well-built forearms under an outside tap and dried them with a cloth. 'I'm Mrs Clough,' she said. 'It's just this way.'

Mark remembered Margaret telling him that anyone who lived on a farm was expected to perform their share of the work. As well as feeding the chickens and doing all the housework, he wondered if Mrs Clough had to do some of the manual labour. She looked tough enough to do so, but she had a very friendly demeanour to go with her toughness. A person would need to have some resilience to face a winter in this part of the country.

As they were led up the stairs, Mrs Clough, still wearing her dirty outdoor shoes, said 'We only have the one bathroom, I'm afraid, but there's only me and my husband who uses it, so you won't be too inconvenienced, except that Matt does like his bath at the end of the working day, which is always at seven o'clock – 'cept at lambing time, when he often works 'round the clock, but we don't let the room when that happens. If you want an evening meal with us, that will be at seven when he's in the bath. The two of us eat when he's finished his bath.'

By now, they had reached the room which was a substantial size with a king-sized bed, beside which were two bedside tables with lamps. Two easy chairs stood next to the large sash window which looked out onto the fields where they could see sheep grazing.

'We'll take it,' said Helen without consulting Mark, 'and we'd like an evening meal wouldn't we, Mark?' Mark nodded. 'Would you like a deposit or anything?'

'No, of course not,' said Mrs Clough. 'You'll pay me in the morning when you leave.'

Helen hadn't even asked the price of the room – nor the meal, but he didn't feel he should raise the matter at this point, but he would tackle her later.

'Are you on holiday?' Mrs Clough asked.

'Just a short break,' Mark answered. 'We return tomorrow. We come from Norfolk,' he added just to make conversation.

'I can tell. You have a distinctive accent. How long have you been married?'

'Not long,' said Mark. He decided that any hesitation might look dishonest. 'We married in the Spring.'

'How lovely – a Spring wedding. Did you honeymoon in Paris?'

How many lies were they going to have to tell? If they told her where their fictitious honeymoon was, she might ask further awkward questions about their location, and as Mark had never been anywhere, he could easily get caught out. 'No, we skipped the honeymoon. We needed every penny for the deposit on our house.'

'So this is like your honeymoon?' Mrs Clough asked.

'You could say that,' Helen said, making gooey eyes at Mark. That bit was almost the truth.

'What are your plans for today?' Mrs Clough asked.

'We're going for a walk,' Mark replied. 'I've always wanted to have a good look at Monsal Head. I found a walk from the top that goes round to Ashford, but I thought we should start at Ashford to get the uphill section out of the way first.'

'Very sensible,' Mrs Clough said. 'It's a lovely walk. Keep a lookout for the dippers and the herons. Are you taking a packed lunch?'

'We thought we'd find somewhere to eat on the way,' Mark replied.

'I can do you both a packed lunch if you like.'

'That's a good idea, 'said Helen. 'Isn't it, Mark?'

'Yes, of course.'

'Right, come and sit in the kitchen while I make it. Would you like a pot of tea while you wait?'

The cup of tea was accompanied by a bacon sandwich. They had really landed on their feet.

Their decision to start the walk from Ashford proved to be inspired. Mark had never before tackled any proper hill walks and he was soon out of breath as they made their way up the track. He was forced to stop regularly, but Helen seemed to take it all in her stride. 'I thought you were fit with all your football and tennis,' she said.

'We don't play football and tennis up a hill,' he said with his hands on his knees as he caught his breath.

But they eventually reached the top and walked around by the hotel. At that point, it was not possible to see the view that Mark had promised. It had been several years since his previous fleeting visit and he wondered if his memory had played tricks on him. He spotted a wall in front of them where several people had gathered. He said 'I think we need to go over there.'

He was right and the view opened up before them. All those years earlier, this prospect had caused him to lose his breath and he was expecting the same response. The surprise was no longer there, but the view was every bit as he had remembered it. The disused railway viaduct that had so displeased John Ruskin when it was first proposed in the previous century, added depth of field to the magnificent landscape. It ran from a blocked up tunnel to cross the valley of the River Wye where the old track would have continued along the side of the beautiful valley.

Some of the deciduous trees were already showing signs of the autumn to come.

It was a clear dry day and it only needed the sun to come out to make the picture complete, but at least its absence had ensured their walk had not been too uncomfortably warm.

'Isn't that the most beautiful scene you've ever seen?' he asked.

'It's brilliant,' she replied, 'but you haven't seen Surprise View.'

'What's that?' he asked.

'It's in the Lake District – overlooking Derwentwater. You see the full prospect of the lake from above ... but this is lovely ... and justifies that walk up the hill.'

Mark felt a little aggrieved that she's seen something better, but at least she agreed it was beautiful.

'Let's sit on the wall and eat our packed lunch,' he suggested.

As they ate their tasty ham sandwiches, he thought to himself that this is as good as it gets. He gazed across to Helen who looked gorgeous and again down to the view, knowing that at last, he had achieved one ambition – that of sharing this magnificent prospect with the woman he loved. That was when he realised that he was in love – proper love; not just lust or unrequited loved, but real mutual love.

'I think we should get married, don't you?' he said as though it was a foregone conclusion that she would agree – and she did.

Epilogue

Now that he was retired, Mark spent a lot of time reminiscing and wondering if he had made the most of his life. How would he be remembered after he was gone? Would he be remembered? He had never achieved anything remarkable in his time on Earth. He considered his one great achievement to be that he and Helen had raised a family, put them through a good education and seen them happily married, or at least in the case of Geraldine, happy in a relationship.

He and Helen had produced three children; one of each to quote his old colleague Tom and some might say that had an element of truth; that is if one had a warped sense of humour. Their first child was Joy who had married Edward. The pair had presented their parents with two lovely granddaughters. Mark's and Helen's second offspring was Thomas who had married Belinda. They had produced three sons who had proved to be quite a handful. They had hoped for a cute little daughter like Joy's children, but after three sons, they decided not to proceed in case they ended up with a fourth unruly son.

Geraldine, who liked to be called Gerry, was living with a lady called Michelle, who preferred the name Mickey. Mark wondered why lesbians often sought a boy's name when they didn't like boys.

At first, Mark had misgivings about the relationship, but after several years together, the pair seemed so happy that he had come around to the situation and actually enjoyed their company more than that of Thomas and Belinda who always seemed to be squabbling; probably not helped by their quarrelsome three boys. Maybe the young boys quarrelled because their parents were always squabbling. Had Thomas been the one to have turned out gay, Mark might have had more of a problem accepting that, but that was down to the way he had been brought up when acts of homosexuality were seen as a criminal offence.

He often wondered what had happened to Chris and Maisie. Did they ever come out in the open about their relationship in these more enlightened times? He thought it a shame that he had failed to maintain contact with so many of his old colleagues. What tales they might all tell now. Of all those old colleagues, Ray was the only one with whom he had kept in touch and that was only through social media as he and his wife had moved to the other side of the country. He had never seen any of his old girlfriends nor the potential girlfriends that he had lusted after. How different his life would have been had Karen, Margaret or Blodwyn ever dated him. Would he have still met his true love, Helen? He viewed his failure to secure a date with Polly as a blessing.

His one great regret was that he had taken far too long to get 'off the mark.' How he would have liked to have spread more wild oats in his formative years. He had almost exited his teenage years with his virginity still intact and he considered that a huge waste of opportunity at a time when most young men would have been considered at their sexual peak. If the stories were to be believed, many of his school friends had managed it while still at school, despite attending an all boys Grammar School.

But he had no other regrets about his life to this point. During the first few years of their marriage, it had been quite a struggle financially, but by living within their means and keeping credit down to essentials, they had always managed. They had never been wealthy, but in the last few years, as their mortgage payments became ever more manageable, life had been more comfortable apart from the times when they had to find extra resources for their children's university expenses and a couple of weddings.

He had continued with a career in IT, having tackled a wide variety of roles and with various employers, but he had seen huge changes in his time. When he started out as a programmer, there had been one operator, one punch girl, one programmer and a manager. That was the sum total of the IT staff at that company. In his final role, there were dozens of programmers, dozens of analysts with fancy titles, numerous project managers, change managers and every other sort of manager. Punch girls had become redundant (as had typists) and almost every employee had a computer on their desk. Unproductive meetings now took up quite a portion of everyone's time and the office banter had altered in nature. Bawdy jokes and flirtation were taboo. It was now expected that employees could use their computers to purchase personal goods online during company time and a certain portion of an employee's work time might be taken up searching the internet for news or keeping in touch with acquaintances.

Despite the change in office banter, Mark had retained his sense of humour, even though, towards the end of his working career, he came across to younger colleagues as a grumpy old man. But if anyone meeting him for the first time regarded him as a sad old git, they would be *completely off the mark.*

Chapter Headings

As in *Further Off the Mark,* the heading of each chapter of this latest novel is the title of a sixties or seventies soul record, representing the content of that chapter. Below, I have listed these with the names of the recording artists who brought these wonderful songs to my attention.

Seven Days Is Too Long	Chuck Wood (1971) Mojo Records
(Who's) That Lady	The Isley Brothers (1964) United Artists Records
I Just Don't Know What To Do With Myself	Tommy Hunt (1962) Scepter Records
What'cha Gonna Do About It	Doris Troy (1964) Atlantic Records
Am I The Same Girl	Barbara Acklin (1968) Brunswick Record Co.
Hot Pants	James Brown (1971) Starday-King Records
Try It Baby	Marvin Gaye (1964) Tamla Records
Turn Back The Hands of Time	Tyrone Davis (1970) Dakar Records
When Love Slips Away	Dee Dee Warwick (1969) Mercury Records
Sweet Love	The Commodores (1976) Motown Records
Two Lovers	Mary Wells (1962) Motown Records
I Want You	Marvin Gaye (1976) Tamla Records

My Whole World is Falling Down	William Bell (1969) Stax Records
Ain't It a Shame	Major Lance (1965) Okeh Records
Disco Lady	Johnnie Taylor (1976) Columbia Records
The Turning Point	Jimmy Holiday (1966) Minit Records
Happiness Is Just Around The Bend	The Main Ingredient (1974) RCA Victor
It's You That I Need	The Temptations (1967) Gordy Records
Starting All Over Again	Mel & Tim (1972) Stax Records
Just One Look	Doris Troy (1963) Atlantic Records
Park Avenue	Lou Johnson (1965) Big Hill Records
Raindrops	Dee Clark (1961) Vee-Jay Records
Save the Last Dance For Me	The Drifters (1960) Atlantic Records
You Got Me Walking	Jackie Wilson (1972) Brunswick Records
Could It Be I'm Falling In Love	Detroit Spinners (1972) Atlantic Records
Hey Girl Don't Bother Me	The Tams (1964) ABC Records

What's Going On	Marvin Gaye (1971)
	Tamla Record
Let's Get Married	Al Green (1973)
	Hi Recording Group

If you've enjoyed this book you might like to try other Will Stebbings' books:

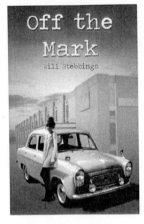

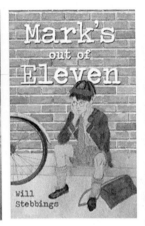

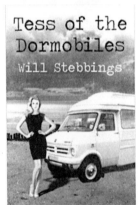

Collect the series from the bookshop at www.3ppublishing.co.uk. all at £7.99 each.